THE LAST CASEBOOK OF
DOCTOR SABABA

Lawrence
WINKLER

BOOK THREE OF THE DOCTOR SABABA SERIES

Cover Image by Mitchell Nolte Art and Illustration, Melbourne, Australia

Cover Design by First Choice Books

ISBN – 978-1-988429-58-8

בִּרְכַּת הַבָּיִת:
בְּזֶה הַשַּׁעַר לֹא יָבוֹא צַעַר.
בְּזֹאת הַדִּירָה לֹא תָבוֹא צָרָה.
בְּזֹאת הַדֶּלֶת לֹא תָבוֹא בֶּהָלָה.
בְּזֹאת הַמַּחְלָקָה לֹא תָבוֹא
מַחְלוֹקֶת.
בְּזֶה הַמָּקוֹם תְּהִי בְרָכָה
סְבָבָה   וְשָׁלוֹם.

Let no sorrow come through this gate.
Let no trouble come in this dwelling.
Let no fright come through this door.
Let no conflict come to this department.
Let there be blessing and peace in this place.

Birkat habayit

To my patients

The Last Casebook of Doctor Sababa

Prologue

The Last Casebook of Doctor Sababa

Acknowledgements

Providence has once again favored the shorn lamb and allowed me to live long enough to finish the *Doctor Sababa* series. I haven't become presumptuous here. Serendipity may fancy the faithful, but karma is a light sleeper.

This book is also of me, and my thirty years in practice as an Internal Medicine consultant on Vancouver Island. But it is not me, although it may have been who I wanted to become.

I continue to live in eternal debt to the people who made me what I am, in the quest to become as good as I can be. For those I have forgotten to pay proper homage to, minds I have been inspired by or borrowed from, I would ask your forgiveness.

These are the people I want to thank: Murray Welte, Mitchell Nolte for the plague doctor cover art, the musicians and poets, Felicity Perryman for putting it together, my faithful readers, and my patient and loving wife, Robyn, through whose tender loving care I am still alive.

Disclaimer

Prologue

Couldn't stay away, could you? The characters and drama that galvanized the Good Doctor in the first two books left you craving for more. There's a word for that. And Sababa is the cure.

It's all good. Here is more special time with the portly professor. Inside these pages live the last seven original stories of survival, suspense, and satire from the Sage of the Salish Sea. He will amuse you with his wit and wisdom, and the spontaneous combustion and thrust they generate, often mixed in unequal proportions, as he dances with the devil in the pale moonlight.

BC Bud is back on the radio, and the stocky savant is back on point. Before there was artificial intelligence, he was the real thing, working in the mysterious old ways of a masterless samurai. But now, fellow travellers, there is artificial intelligence.

Trouble, oh we got trouble... right here in Harbour City... trouble with a capital 'T'... and that rhymes with C and that stands for cool. Welcome to the winter of his Casebook and the unmaking of the man. Welcome back to Sababaland.

Winter—The Book of Water

'Now is the winter of our discontent.'
William Shakespeare, *Richard III*

Winter came in like a wraith of wrath with shattered teeth, as barren and frigid as if Pluto himself had put the world to sleep. Not so long ago in the island's brief history, people died getting there and died again the first winter they stayed.

The fourth season was a study in charcoal, pitch-black on blinding white. Sababa left his home after dawn and returned after dusk, in the same darkness. He fishtailed to work on roads so treacherous, they could have been an event in the winter Olympics. Careening down steep slopes of black ice seasoned with frost and frozen rainwater and groundwater, he slid through freezing fog and icy drizzle and rain and sleet and hail and blowing and drifting snow, against which his white dented and dimpled conveyance flew invisible. Inside the insulated walls of Harbour City Regional, the Good Doctor's short days and long nights overfilled with pneumonia and apoplexy, and pains of the ribs and loins.

The nights had grown longer than the days, breaking in an intangible pall over the face of things, the weakened eye of subtle gloom bereft of sun. Winter dawn was the colour of metal. Sababa could taste the tin of it. Bitter cold bit through everything like death, penetrating shivered skin, turning ears red and lips blue and fingers white, numbing them into a stiff paralysis.

The harbour was as grey as old newsprint. The sea had abandoned its blue, the stones their sepia, and the boats their bonhomie. Bleak reflections of dreary clouds on the open strait melted into one mood and obliterated the horizon. Fine morning mists coalesced into waves of rain before retreating into particles.

Soft snow fell from the heavens and hid the world in rolling undulations, muffling sounds, and blanketing the landmarks that once allowed navigation by ear and touch. Icicles hung like daggers, sparkling stalactites dripping from rigging and rope in the marinas and rooftops ashore. Windowpanes grew mesmerizing hexagonal prisms of frozen frosted fractals.

Sound was sharper in winter because the cold air transmitted better. It was true of snowball fights, and the slicing staccato of sharpened skates and the clacking of sticks on pucks, but not of quiet words, which floated and dissolved in frozen air saturated with sour damp leather and rubber and wet socks and mittens. Silence hung thick. Air breathed crisp and

3

frosty, and electric and heavy, visible in every exhalation. Winter blew blustery winds, whirling in frost-crisp'd frenzied spirals, howling through its desolation.

Etched in white above the silver lake, Harbour City's mountain was a pristine composition of breathless beauty. The trees had stiffened into place like burnt nerves. The firs and cedars were still green under the brilliant white, wisdom in hardship. Their branches hung low under the weight of the snow. On his rare days off, Sababa plunged in along faint trails among enormous evergreens. High up, one bough's cargo of snow would capsize, fall through the branches beneath, spread down the entire tree like a world trade tower avalanche, and descend upon the professor without warning. The deciduous trees wouldn't have done that, naked bleak twigs that they were. Winter stripped their leaves so the professor could see the distance they concealed just as old age would erase his energies to enlarge his eternity.

Winter limited Sababa's forays to the lower trails of his mountain, where he could meditate upon his frailty as a creature of temperature. Above a base of frozen mud and cedar bark, the path glistened like white quartz. Each tread was a crystalline crunchwalk, shattering the underfoot sugar of thin frosted puddles into shards of a musical mirror embedded in the hardened earth, that would last until fresh snow erased his footprints and set the trail anew once more. The need to stay upright focused his mind. Cold oxygen carried him. He stamped his feet for warmth and balance. The professor's beard was frosted solid, increasing on his chin with every moist breath. Dampness, so cold it stung, clamped icy fibres to his skin, and crept into his bones.

Springs bubbled out from the hillside and ran under the snow and on top of the ice of the creeks, frozen clear to the bottom. They were traps, hiding pools of water under a snowpack that might be three inches or three feet deep. Alternating layers of water and ice-skin let you break through until you were drenched to the waist. Other streams overflowed their banks. Ammonite and Englishman River Falls surged into deafening cataracts.

Wildlife was tenuous and durable at the same time. Most disappeared underground to sleep away the solstice. The birds were above all that. Belted Kingfishers and Steller's Jays and ravens and even Rufous Hummingbirds stuck around. Brant and Snow Geese and Trumpeter Swans and murmurations of Pine Siskins flew through in numbers.

After his hikes, Sababa arrived home to winter flowers in his back yard— snowbells and crocuses and daffodils and forsythia and hazelnut catkins and a lone optimistic loquat—and Jane's homemade soups and rib-sticking stews. Their evenings were cozy, warmed by dancing flames crackling in the stone fireplace, accompanied by a tryptophan-induced sloth, and an occasional glass of vintage port. Like the great sleeping bears hiding around them, heartbeats slowed towards zero. They dreamt deep of the coming spring, with its promises of vibrant watercolours and motion and warmth. It was in winter that Sababa pruned the dormant vineyard and planned his new garden beds.

In this most phlegmatic of seasons, the professor perfected the ephemeral lessons from Musashi's *The Book of Water*—the broad gaze of peripheral vision without moving his eyes, the calm determination and spiritual balance and flexible attitude, the having one thing to know ten thousand ways of strategy, the step by step walking the thousand-mile road, the *Flowing Water Cut* technique, and the four other attitudes of swordsmanship.

The winter subsided like grief. Stars rose until the rain fell, bringing a sweet sap run flowing back into the world of things. The fruit of the equal marriage of the sun and frost arrived as reincarnation. *O, wind, if winter comes, can spring be far behind?*

Many believed the winter to be a season of graves, but it was in the spring when sleepers failed to awake. And this was the last of what Sababa had still yet to learn, as he fell into the dark void, embraced by the vault of heaven. He wheeled with the stars and his heart broke loose on the wind.

'In the bleak midwinter, frosty wind made moan,
Earth stood hard as iron, water like a stone;
Snow had fallen, snow on snow, snow on snow,
In the bleak midwinter, long ago.'
Christina Rossetti, *In the Bleak Midwinter*

19. The Case of the Aboriginal Snowman

'They made us many promises, more than I can remember.
But they kept but one—They promised to take our land...
and they took it.'

Red Cloud

It was impossible to see across Newcastle Channel to Saysutshun Island. The swirling snowstorm had chased the first light of the day back onto a blank canvas. The only white raccoons in the world lived here, but even with more pigment and outside their dens, they would have still been invisible in the blowing bitterness. All they left was an ethereal sketch of winter branches, rustling like living things in the cold arctic wind.

The old man reminisced about his childhood visits here from across the surface of the Salish Sea. He remembered striking a hardwood stick inlaid with sharp whalebone teeth along one side into the water, catching twenty herring with every sweep to fill his father's canoe.

On the morning of the day his wife died, Wakasiah Watt opened his front door to a white wall as tall as his tenth grandson. The female phantasm which staggered out of the blizzard lifted her wood frame sinew-webbed snowshoes high enough to traverse the last of the drifts and steered her body towards the shrinking cavity she knew to be the entrance. In one last effort, she shook off the toe straps and slid her deer hide moccasins down into the lamp-lit house.

"The Great Spirit is trying to make this dirty world look clean today." He said.

"It's a white-out." Stanzy was the local home care nurse for the Coast Salish community. "Is the family still here?"

"All except for Xu'athun, He's driving up from Victoria today." Wakasiah had seven children. To save his memory from unnecessary strain, he had named them after the numbers of his Island Halkomelem dialect of Hul'q'umi'num'. Nuts'a', Yuse'lu, Lhihw, Xu'athun... *One, Two, Three, Four...* There were already twenty-six family members around Julia's sickbed, and Four Watt was coming as soon as he could.

As the hereditary chief of the Snuneymuxw First Nation, Wakasiah Watt had seen the ravages wrought on his people by the 1854 Douglas Treaty of stolen land and broken promises. In that year Chief Suquen-Es-Then made a deal with the devil. *Then the Hudson's Bay men talked to the Indians. 'This coal that is here,' they said, 'is no good to you, and we would like it; but we want to be friends, so, if you will let us come and take as much of this black rock as we want, we will be good to you.*

'The terms of the treaty are stated as follows: The condition of, or understanding of this Sale, is this, that our village sites and enclosed fields are to be kept for our

7

own use, for the use of our children, and for those after us; and the land shall be properly surveyed hereafter. It is understood, however, that the land itself, with these small exceptions, becomes the entire property of the white people for ever; it is also understood that we are at liberty to hunt over the unoccupied lands, and to carry on our fisheries as formerly.'

In return for this agreement, the Snuneymuxw received '668 blankets of varying quality, 636 white, 12 blue and 20 inferior, shirts, and rope tobacco.'

The result of the treaty is an all too familiar story. Out of a core territory that once covered four hundred square miles, they left the Snuneymuxw only one, the smallest Indian Reserve land base per capita in Canada, within a river floodplain. They had lost all their major village sites because of the Crown's failure to live up to its end of the treaty. *And now white men began to come and fix houses to live in, and they made a sawmill and cut down all our trees. Then boats called 'schooners' began to come for the coal. The Indians did a little work then; they used to carry coal out to the schooners in their canoes—not little canoes like the ones we use now, but big, big ones that could hold twelve or more men; and the white men would pay fifty cents for one canoe load of coal.* In no deliberate irony, a Snuneymuxw burial site dating back 3,500 years became Departure Bay, and the main winter village, with its longhouses that once extended the length of the beach at the head of the bay, a ferry terminal. Perhaps it was for Charon, the ferryman of Hades, who carried the souls of the deceased across the water that divided the world of the living from the world of the dead. Or perhaps it was another cruel joke. The new people destroyed and buried other sites under a 7-Eleven, a shopping mall, and the Moby Dick motel and marina.

The home and native land of the Snuneymuxw is now Reserve 1, several city blocks sandwiched between a railroad track running through its heart and the main highway that goes through Harbour City, all surrounded by the antithetical aesthetic of a hideous industrial zone—a cement plant, a steel plant, a lumber and veneer mill, and log booms to the horizon in the polluted estuary to the east.

But there was no horizon for Chief Watt today. Wakasiah's world was a Snuneymuxw snow-globe, churning in unseen currents. Almost fifty inches of snow had fallen so far that month, twenty overnight alone. It was the heaviest dump since they began keeping records in 1937. No one on the West Coast had ever seen anything like it. Environment Canada meteorologists were cataloguing it as the 'Storm of the Century.' Metro Vancouver and Vancouver Island shut down. Blowing snow buried cars, closed the highway, stranded hundreds of drivers, and paralysed transit. The premier declared a state of emergency and summoned the military. The weight of the snowpack caused a Harbour City Airport hangar to cave in and destroy several airplanes. Flights were cancelled because de-icing crews couldn't keep up—by the time they finished one side of the plane, the other was covered again. Barn roofs collapsed all over the mid-

8

island region, killing dozens of cows. The snow filled the sky and earth below. There were no footprints on this white blanket, no more patterns perfused with hidden messages.

That morning, Wakasiah's village filled with an eerie, brittle silence. Because the streets were impassable, there was no vehicle noise. The only distant sound came from a colony of California sea lions at Jack Point, their barks so constant and surreal, even the native dogs on the reserve didn't return their calls.

There was no horizon for Chief Watt today because his wife was dying. Stanzy gave her a breakthrough dose of opioid medication and held her hand. The bedroom was full of four generations of family. Her tribe adored her as their treasured matriarch. Kind and gentle and generous, Julia was a continuous one-woman potlach, giving away preserves and knitted toques and socks as gifts. She had knitted several woolen items for her favorite stocky Internal Medicine specialist.

"I thought you were knitting me a sweater, Julia?" He had asked.

"I am." She said. "But you keep getting bigger." And they both laughed until they didn't.

Julia enjoyed watching the Canucks play hockey on TV until she couldn't. Wakasiah and Julia had been married for fifty-six years when the tumour came. There was no point in being mad at cancer for being cancer. And now there was just the smell of wet deerskin and wet dog and wood smoke, and imminent death. This nursed whitemare had become his worst nightmare.

Four Watt hadn't yet arrived when the vigil ended. Just after 10 p.m., Wakesiah and his family watched Julia take her last gasps and fall as still as the world outside. Stanzy confirmed her passing and made some phone calls. Four Watt didn't answer one of them. No one could come for what remained of Julia until the next day, and maybe not even then, depending on the weather. Every other family member hugged Wakasiah on their way out of the house. Stanzy strapped her deer hide moccasins back into her snowshoes and left her tears with Wakasiah as she climbed back over the snowdrifts into the night.

The old chief sat with his wife for what seemed like an eternity. He spoke to her, in ways she would have found comforting, about all their life's experiences together. With one last kiss on her forehead, he left their memories, then their bedroom, and then their home.

Wakasiah Watt disappeared into the scenery, one with the snowflakes swirling around him. His breath warmed his face before the cold sucked it away. His chapped lips and dry throat ached from thirst and cold and the pain of his loss. He bowed his head until his chin touched his chest and kept walking. As his feet froze, his footsteps shortened, sinking in past his ankles with each stride. He put out his hand to guide his way but couldn't see through his squint and tears. The gale was a wind-chime, whipping each snowflake into a projectile, cutting through his clothes.

9

The storm crept through the collar and cuffs of his coat, and into his boots. He couldn't have felt more cold silent darkness if he had been in the bleak outer reaches of the solar system.

At the end of Shoreline Drive, Wakasiah stumbled beyond the reserve's Kltpzyxm General Store on Totem Street. *Indian Status cards accepted here. Cigarette sales. If you are in Harbour City and smoke and have Status, then this is your smoke shop. Friendly staff and yummy fries.* It was the only place he could have found a one-dollar vanilla Coke if it had been open.

The only tranquil part of the reserve, between the houses and the industrial desolation of the lumber mill, was the small *shmu°wélu* cemetery at the end of the last gravel road along the shoreline, among a few remaining firs and cedars. 'Our people used to place the deceased in trees as a burial rite.' He thought.

A few members of his tribe were interred here, some Johnnys and Goods, Whites and Browns, Sewards and Wesleys and Mansons, and 'Buffalo Knife' Thomas. And the Wyses.

Wakasiah stopped in front of the grave of Chief Joe Wyse. *Quen-Es-Then.* The biting cold had chilled his fingers and toes into a clumsy numbness and spread up into his hands and feet. It became a hungry rat, gnawing at his insides. His lips turned blue and his teeth chattered like a jackhammer. In that white wasteland, Wakasiah lost his sense of time and space. There were no sounds other than the howling and his heart beating in his chest.

He turned to see the tracks he had made, but there were none. The frigid night wrapped him in a shawl of alabaster woven wool. It chilled his blood and sank into the marrow of his bones like wet concrete.

It was here at the foot of another chief's grave that Wakasiah Watt made his snow bed. We are all bits of stellar matter that got cold by accident, bits of a star gone wrong. A snowman is the perfect man, falling from heaven unassembled, one flake at a time, before melting into oblivion.

His shivering, so violent at first, lessened, and then let go. After removing his clothes, Wakasiah burrowed into the snow. He remembered all the things that made him smile, back in that place where he first became a man. When his heart stopped, Wakasiah was smiling. Then his brain shut down, and he was gone.

'Is it nice in your snowstorm, freezing your brain?
Do you think that your face looks the same?'
David Bowie, *Sweet Thing*

'Before you cross the street,
Take my hand,
Life is what happens to you,
While you're busy making other plans.'
John Lennon, *Beautiful Boy*

At the exact moment that Stanzy slid her moccasins into the chief's house, Wakasiah's number four son was speeding up the Island Highway to what he thought was his mother's destiny.

The provincial government had put the unhappy phone call that began his day on hold. The BC Minister of Transport and Infrastructure had issued a weather warning advisory for Vancouver Island, and a strong recommendation to avoid non-essential travel. They refused any vehicle passage over the Malahat to Harbour City unless it was equipped with snow tires. Which was how Four Watt found himself delayed in a garage on the outskirts of Victoria until his brown SUV could be refitted with a new set of snowshoes. By the time they mounted and balanced his new wheels, the morning had turned into blowing snow and iced custard, obliterating any hope of safe travel.

Four Watt paid for his snow tires and steered out onto the Island Highway northbound. Both the temperature and visibility were well below zero. He squinted through his windshield to find the edge of the road and avoid any hard obstacles in his flight path. He lit the first of what would become a continuous series of Marlboros. Not the first Indian killed by these cowboys, he thought, but he sourced them cheap enough on the reserve. Four Watt chain-smoked up along the mountain chain, his tire chains in the trunk all but useless, like the shackles that still bound his people. The fourth son of a Coast Salish chief drove a Jeep Cherokee insured by Mutual of Omaha and powered by Mohawk gas.

His workmates wouldn't use his actual name, Xu'athun. They called him So Watt and Guess Watt and Now Watt and Say Watt and Nomatter Watt and What's Watt and Know Watt and Tellyou Watt and Mega Watt and Then Watt. And he would bottle up his indignation and pull a hard drag from his cigarette.

But today his mother was dying fast, and he had to make it to her bedside in time. In his mind, he could see his father and brothers and his aunties and uncles and cousins gathered around her bedside, wondering where he was. Four Watt drove through the sideways snow with as much skill as he could muster, as his Cherokee ascended towards the deceptive summit of the Malahat pass. The six inches of snow that Environment Canada had predicted to fall on the high elevations this morning was already here. It didn't stop the crazy ones from speeding past him on blind corners, but it didn't much matter. They were all driving blind now. Four Watt lit another Marlboro and switched on his radio. It tuned itself to a station he would never hear again.

11

Good Morning Harbour City... This is CNDN Coast Salish radio, 101.3 FM on your Home and Native Band. I'm your host, BC Bud...

Four Watt was an old friend of BC Bud. They grew up together, fishing and hunting and dreaming of better lives.

First, the weather... But how hard is your job if you only have to look out the window?.. Today's forecast: It's colder than the hinges of hell out there, colder than a well-diggers ass—so cold the lawyers have their hands in their own pockets, so cold their nipples can cut glass... Another snowstorm coming... There's no relief on the horizon cause there ain't no horizon...

Under the snow, an unbroken sheet of dark ice covered the road like death's welcome mat. It was black and invisible, waiting for the first contestant in a hurry.

Today is the First day of Winter on the Native Medicine Wheel—the season of the bear, cedar, air, intellect, death, elders, the stars, midnight, the north, and white people...

Four Watt was grateful for the concrete barrier that separated the two lanes, assembled the previous year after a deadly accident in these same conditions. Even with the new snow tires, His Jeep Cherokee felt as if it was slipsliding on glass. Icicles glistened on cliff face walls beyond his vision, frozen into winter's daggers.

Here's a Winter poem... Shit, it's cold... The End... Finish your corn flakes before they turn into frosted flakes, toss back that second cup of hot kapi, and get ready to greet the day...

What Four Watt couldn't see, other than everything else he couldn't see, was what was going on inside the head of the driver of the southbound 425 hp tri-axle Kenworth vacuum truck carrying 3000 gallons of human waste. The 35-year-old septic operator, Bull Sullivan, hadn't known about the small scar on his brain that was about to trip over its circuit breaker and produce his first and last grand mal seizure.

It's cabin fever season people, that time of year when four walls feel like they're going to come in here and choke the Great Spirit right out of you...

What Four Watt couldn't foresee was the set of climatic climactic coincidences that Bull Sullivan tried to deal with right before his epileptic exit from the honeywagon business. Inside of five seconds, a rockslide tumbled onto the snowfield in front of him, his truck tires discovered the treacherous black ice under it, and skidding out of control, dangerous and deadly, he collided head-on with four of the heavy concrete median dividers, pushing them into oncoming traffic in the northbound lane.

Time to lock away those firearms and hang tough. Lock and unload... No way through it except to do it...

There was only one oncoming vehicle in the northbound lane, a brown Jeep Cherokee. Stomping on his brakes, the brown driver slid between the white snow and the black ice and oblivion.

My social calendar is a total blank... Cold weather means it's big boy season... Stanzy, if you're listening... you better get you one...

The impact of the septic truck with the concrete barriers flipped it over and upside down in the northbound lane, igniting what escaped from the saddle fuel tanks and rupturing the other ones. Three thousand gallons of human sewage poured into an explosive admixture and burst into flames. Whoever coined the phrase 'raw sewage' must have realized that, like the poop oil purveyors in China, it could be cooked. Cacafuego. Hellfire. Shit's on fire, yo. Shit happens.

I don't like snow... It's white, and it's on my land...

The crash shut down the Malahat in both directions for eight hours. Hazmat crews and response officers from BC transport and environment ministries arrived on the scene. A local reporter wrote that the smell was unbearable.

Sometimes Jack Frost leads to Jack Shit...

'I never skip a class
Got my Netter cards in my pocket
I-I-I'm gunning
Don't you think I'm stunning?
Yes, you know I'm awesome.'
Harvard Medical School, *The Gunner Song*

"Excuse me." He said.

Lana, the Big Voice, looked up from her paging desk to a smart young man in a white coat. Crimson calligraphy scrolled across the top of the left breast pocket. *Harvard Medical School*. A signature in the same red thread was delicately stitched on the opposite side of his jacket. Lana guessed it might be his name. Fresh snow had speckled the young man's hair. He was wearing a bow tie decorated with little red and gold shields. Lana had never seen a bow tie.

"Can I help you?"

"Boy, it's wicked rawrout theah." He avoided any eye contact. "I'm looking for Doctah Sababer." Lana couldn't quite place the accent.

"His week to report cardiograms." Lana said. "It's early enough. You might catch him in the electrodiagnostic reading room. I can't page him for you because that space is impermeable to radio waves."

"Would you be so kind as to direct me to that paht of the hospital?" Lana drew the young man a map.

"It's down this hallway." She made a mark on the map. "It's not very obvious. No sign on the locked door. You may have to knock."

Down the hallway, at the mark shown on the map, the young man knocked. There was no answer. He put his ear to the door. There was the sound of dictation on the other side. He knocked again. The door flew inward, although the stout man leaning back in his reclining chair should have been too far away to have opened it.

"Who are you and what do you want?"

"Hahwahyha." The young man offered. "I'm looking for Doctah Sababer."

"What for?" The stout man was observing and analyzing his intruder.

"I'm Alex Hahding, his new resident." The young man said. "From Hahvud."

"You come in on a crimson tide?"

"That's Alabama." He said. "I'm from M.G.H. in Boston."

"Massachusetts General." The stout man said. "I trained there."

"Man's Greatest Hospital." Alex said.

"What are you doing in this backwater?" Asked the stout man.

"I want to be an Internist." Alex said. "My faculty advisor, Doctah Gerald Winklah, told me I should sign up for an elective with the great

14

Doctah Sababer, the Sage of the Salish Sea. He's supposed to be wicked smaht."

"You're a long way from Mecca, Bahney." Said the stout man. "You sure you want to do this."

"I already set up my rotation." Alex said. "Approved by Hahvud and UBC. And the Good Doctah, too."

"You want to see a patient in the ER?"

"Shouldn't I wait for Doctah Sababer?" The stout man handed him a piece of paper. *Sylvie Denis...*

"You've already done that.' Sababa said. "And if your Harvard powers of observation are as Brahmin brilliant as they appear to be, we're both in for an interesting ride."

"But..."

"Welcome to Sababaland." The professor said. "Page me when you've seen the patient. And Alex."

"Yeah?"

"Lose the bow tie."

'Science is an attempt, largely successful, to understand the world, to get a grip on things, to get hold of ourselves, to steer a safe course. Microbiology and meteorology now explain what only a few centuries ago was considered sufficient cause to burn women to death.'

Carl Sagan

Of all the emergency physicians that Alex Harding could have encountered in his first elective experience at Harbour City Regional, the karma vending machine dispensed him the least civil and the most combat-hardened medic of the department. Cliffy Carlton had referred the new resident's first patient. He tried to welcome the Bostonian as warmly as he knew how, but he didn't know how.

"What's the bow tie for?"

"At Hahvud we don't end our sentences with prepositions." Alex said.

"My apologies." Cliffy said. "What's the bow tie for, dickhead?"

"It's an act of defiance." Alex hadn't made eye contact. "Worn by the enlightened cognoscenti. I'm thinking of giants like Thomas Edison and Le Corbusier and Walter Gropius and Vladimir Horowitz and Abraham Lincoln and Winston Churchill and Theodore and Franklin Roosevelt."

"Funny." Cliffy said. "I'm thinking of midgets like Pee-wee Herman and Jerry Lewis and Groucho Marx and Dagwood Bumstead and Louis Farrakhan and Orville Redenbacher and Colonel Sanders and Boo-Boo Bear and Porky Pig and Huckleberry Hound and Mickey Mouse and Donald Duck. Real doctors ride bareback"

"You're not from Massachusetts." Alex said.

"Your referral is in Bed 2, Masshole." Cliff called over his shoulder.

An hour later, Alex asked Cheri Sundae to page his preceptor. Sababa bounced into the ER three minutes later. Cliffy waved to him from across the room.

"Hey, Sab." He said. "How do you get a Harvard medical resident out of your emergency room?"

"How?"

"Tip him for the pizza." Sababa turned to his new protégé.

"Off to a good start, Alex." He said. "Making new friends with the locals, I see."

"This fuckin' guy is a philistine." Alex said.

"Maybe." Sababa said. "But he's our philistine. And you'll find that, here in the land of Canaan, we get skittish about trumpets blaring at walls we spent so much time and labour to construct. You may want to reign in the Yankee Doodle Dandy."

"Should I tell you about our patient?" Alex asked.

"Please."

"Pissah." Alex said. "Sylvie Denis is a 32-year old physical therapist who presents today with a 5-year-history of cold intolerance, hives, leg pain and swelling, bruising, patchy ulcers, skin pigmentation, all progressive despite steroids and anticoagulants for presumed vasculitis."

"Exam?"

"As mentioned." He said. "And Raynaud's phenomenon, palpable purpura, and livedo reticularis."

"Lab?"

"Normal complete blood count and metabolic panel, sedimentation rate, C-reactive protein, rheumatoid factor, antinuclear antibodies, antineutrophil cytoplasmic antibodies, anti–double-stranded DNA, anticentromere antibodies, cryoglobulins, and Coombs tests. Coagulation tests all normal except for elevated fibrinogen and D-dimer."

"Imaging?"

"Ultrasound of her legs shows chronic venous clots of both great saphenous veins.

"So what you got?"

"Excuse me?"

"Internal Medicine is a Confucian discipline, Alex. Numerological, in big strokes. First to know are the three steps to proper fact acquisition for meaningful clinical intervention: (1) What you got, you got, (2) What you

16

don't got, you don't got, and (3) What you do with what you got and what you don't got depends on context."

"Yah huh."

"So then, what have you got?" Alex recounted his findings.

"A young woman with some kind of clotting disorder resulting in leg ulcers." He said.

"Occurring when?"

"Excuse me?"

"What season is it?"

"Winter."

"Hmmm. Let's go see her." Sababa and Alex knocked on the curtain of bed 2.

"Sylvie, this is Doctor Sababa." Alex said. "He fills the vacuum that Nature abhors."

"Dr. Harding has told me some of your story, Sylvie." Sababa said. "Is there a specific time when your symptoms get worse?"

"When it's cold outside. She said. "This time of year is horrible." After Sababa confirmed Alex's examination findings, he interrogated his new apprentice.

"What kind of fibrinogen do you think is causing Sylvie's problem, Alex."

"Must be some kind of cryofibrinogen." Alex said. "A protein that precipitates out in the cold and causes tiny clots in the circulation."

"And what conditions produce this protein?"

"Two kinds." He said. "Essential or primary cryofibrinogenemia, which has no obvious causes, and secondary cryofibrinogenemia, which does."

"Like what?"

"Infections, malignant or premalignant disorders, vasculitis, autoimmune diseases, and certain drugs." Alex said. "But Sylvie has no evidence of such an association."

"So far." Sababa said. "I suspect you are right, but we need to look. So what do want to do?"

"Serum cryofibrinogen assay, blood cultures, HIV, Epstein–Barr virus, cytomegalovirus, varicella zoster, herpes simplex, and hepatitis C virus, immunoglobulins, and a skin biopsy looking for small-vessel microthrombi, fibrinoid damage, and vessel wall fibrin. I'll confirm the presence or absence of obligatory and additional criteria and add stanozolol 2 mg twice a day to her other therapies."

"Well done." Sababa smiled. "Anything else?"

"Not that I can think of." The good doctor turned to their patient.

"Sylvie." Sababa said. "You need to come in from the cold."

"Oh yeah." Alex said. "Killah." Dr. Gung Ho approached on an obtuse trajectory.

"Need you to see a patient, Sab." He said. "Who's the bow tie guy."

"Alex Harding." Sababa said. "He's my new resident."

"I went to Hahvud." Alex said.

17

"Were you visiting your sister?"

"Whatevah." Alex said. "You have a referral?"

"Jean-Baptiste Lully." Gung said. "32-year-old ski instructor at Mount Washington with a one-week history of fever and malaise. Three days ago, he developed a non-itchy rash over his chest and abdomen, and blackish discoloration of the tips of all his digits, mostly his toes. In six hours from onset, the discoloration progressed up to his wrists and above his knees. Came in this morning with respiratory failure, pregangrenous changes, and bruising up to his navel. I've just intubated him. He's on a ventilator in the acute room. His blood pressure is a little soft."

"Let's go see." Sababa said. Across the hallway, the three physicians found the disaster that was Jean-Baptiste Lully. His legs were misshapen and mottled in green and purple.

"Time heals all wounds." Alex said.

"Not this time." Sababa said. "His skiing days are over. What do you have back from the lab and imaging, Gung?"

"Hemoglobin and platelets half of what they should be, white blood cell numbers, and LDH are elevated, and he has evidence of liver and kidney dysfunction. D-dimer is positive and Doppler ultrasound of his legs shows reduced flow in all vessels."

"Did you order serum cryoglobulins?" Alex asked.

"Bingo, Bow tie." Gung said. "Positivo."

"So what you got, Bahney?" Sababa asked.

"Symmetric peripheral gangrene with multi-organ failure secondary to catastrophic Type II or III mixed cryoglobulinemic vasculitis."

"From?"

"Hepatitis C infection." Alex said. "Most likely."

"And what are you going to do for Mr. Lully."

"Start him on broad-spectrum antibiotics, pulse methylprednisolone, rituximab, pegylated INFα and ribavirin, heparin and dobutamine infusions, and arrange for plasma exchange."

"And admit him to the Death Star."

"Yah huh." Alex said.

"Welcome to Sababaland, Alex." Gung said, before returning to the less acute patients on the other side of the hallway as Cliffy Carlton flew another pass and foreclosed on the conversation.

"Hey Sab." He said. "How do you know someone went to Harvard?"

"Dunno." Sababa said. "How?"

"They tell you." Cliffy said. "You and Krusty want to see another referral?"

"This fuckin' guy..." Alex said.

"Paulina Strübing." Cliffy began. "24-year-old meteorologist came out of the cold today with a weird rash, acute abdominal and flank pain, nausea and vomiting, dark red urine, and fevers and chills. She's in lucky bed number 7."

18

"Exam?" Sababa asked.

"Pale with mild jaundice." Cliffy said. "Generalized lymph node enlargement, violaceous circular papulosquamous rash. Nothing else."

"Lab?" Alex asked.

"Anemic with elevated reticulocyte count, LDH, and bilirubin, and reduced haptoglobin. Peripheral blood smear showed spherocytes, polychromasia, nucleated red blood cells, anisocytosis, poikilocytosis, and neutrophilic erythrophagocytosis. Direct antiglobulin test was positive for anti-C3d and negative for IgG. Cold agglutinin titre was negative. Urine was positive for 3+ blood but negative for red blood cells."

"Alex?"

"Rapid onset of immune hemolytic anemia and rash." He said. "Pretty wide differential. I'd like to see the patient."

"Right answer." Sababa said. "'Let's go do that." Inside the curtain of bed 7, Cliffy made introductions.

"Paulina, this is Doctor Sababa, the Sage of the Salish Sea." He said. "And this is his resident just off the boat, Dr. Hahahahding. He's from Hahahavard."

"Like in *Love Story*?" Paulina asked.

"No." Cliffy said. "The other one."

"May we repeat some of Dr. Carlton's exam, Paulina?" Alex asked.

"OK." She said. "I hope you can find out what's wrong with me. This is the third time in two months my urine has been red. It's getting scary."

"We'll do our best." Alex examined her rash with a magnifying glass. "Hold up your hands, Paulina." He said. Paulina held up her hands.

"The rash is affecting her palms and soles, Cliffy."

"So?"

"So this narrows the etiological possibilities."

"To what, Alex?" Sababa asked.

"Pityriasis rosea, drug eruptions, psoriasis, lichen planus, eczema, erythema multiforme, mycosis fungoides, and acute febrile exanthems."

"Like from what."

"Coxsackievirus, scabies, and tinea, and Rocky Mountain spotted fever." Alex said. "Also, the tip of her nose has a reddish-blue coloration, there is acrocyanosis of her left index and ring fingers, and her left big toe is almost black."

"Oh. yeah." Cliffy said. "I forgot to mention that." Alex failed to make eye contact.

"So now what, gentlemen?" Sababa asked.

"Probable viral-induced rash and autoimmune hemolytic anemia." Alex offered. Cheri Sundae held up two fingers from behind her polycarbonate protection.

"Dr. Leyblanca, Sab." Sababa picked up line 2.

19

"¿What hab ju got up there, Cabrón?" Asked the pathologist. "Thees patient, Paulina Strübing."

"Why, what have you found, Juan?"

"She has a positive Donath-Landsteiner antibody test." He said.

"Thanks, Juan." Sababa said.

"I call ju." *Click.* Sababa motioned for Alex and Cliffy to leave the cubicle and follow him to the consultant's desk, out of range of Paulina's hearing.

"She has Donath-Lansteiner antibodies." He said.

"Meaning what?" Cliffy asked.

"She has paroxysmal cold hemoglobinuria... PCH." Alex said. "First condition recognized as an autoimmune disease. Associated with infections and neoplasms. When you add in the rash, I'd bet she has a Coxsackie A9 infection."

"I might agree with you, Alex." Sababa said. "But I'll take that bet."

"What do you mean?"

"Way back when it was first recognized in the 1850s, PCH was connected with another infection, one which caused peripheral gangrene, first described by Goetz in 1885."

"I don't know." Alex said.

"There's a first time for everyone, Krusty." Cliffy said.

"He who knows syphilis knows medicine." Sababa's pager buzzed on his belt buckle.

"Dr. William Osler." Alex said. "She has syphilis?"

"It's the cause of her paroxysmal cold hemoglobinuria." Sababa said. "Alex, you're going to admit Paulina to our general medical ward on the fifth floor. Tell me what else you're going to do for her."

"She'll need to be kept warm, rehydration, urine alkalinization, antihistamines, transfusion with four warmed, washed, packed RBC units based on her hemoglobin, screening and confirmatory test for syphilis, lumbar puncture to look for neurosyphilis, penicillin 2.4 M IU IM weekly for three weeks, and Ceftriaxone 2 g daily for 10 days."

"Anything else?"

"Not that I can think of." Alex said.

"You'll need to tell her."

"Oh, right." He said.

"Gently."

"Got it."

"I have to see a patient in the operating room, Alex." Sababa said. "But you have three patients to finish working up and admit, so that should keep you out of trouble for a while. Not a terrible morning for your first day in Sababaland."

"Wicked pissah." Alex said.

"Perfect winter trifecta of cryofibrinogenemia, mixed cryoglobulinemia, and paroxysmal cold hemoglobinuria." Sababa said. "You wouldn't see all that on a good day at Man's Greatest Hospital."

"Thanks, Doctah Sababer." Alex said.

"Page me when you're done." The portly professor's thick curly hair bounced through the automatic sliding frosted glass doors, on their way to his next adventure.

'My fever broke
Fever broke
My fever broke as you watched over me.'
Todd Rundgren, *Fever Broke*

The bright operating room lights glared over the table in the centre of the room, eliminating shadows, interrogating the subject of their focus. In a cold capsule of sea green and silver, they glistered off the flawless sterile instruments arranged on the stainless steel table below.

The smear of menthol petroleum jelly above every lip around the table helped deaden the acrid arc-welded ash-flavored tang of burning human flesh rising in a last puff of gray-white secondhand smoke from the surgical field. A din of unscored discord murmured above the Bovie buzz of the cautery instrument, and the sounds of all the other machinery in the room.

"Who is that masked man?" Asked the surgeon. Buddy Benway looked up from closing the wound he had made an hour earlier.

"It's the Prone Ranger." Said the anesthetist from behind his sterile lichen green curtain that separated the patient's head from Buddy's disembodiment.

"Who called him?"

"I did."

"What for?"

"You might not have noticed at your end of the universe, Buddy, but up here where the science lives, your latest victim is floundering in deep kaka." The anesthetist waved the newly masked intruder around the rest of the operating table to his hypnotic headquarters behind the drapes.

Banjo Paterson was a crackerjack gaswallah. He had dedicated his entire life to meticulous redundancy. Banjo began every OR slate by running through his checklists and cockpit-drills like a pilot circling his plane, ensuring that every piece of hardware was safe to fly, although you might not guess that from the casual custom graffiti on the anesthesia cart containing his medications and equipment next to his gas machine.

Succinylcholine is red... Etomidate is blue...When your day goes to shit...Then I'll breathe for you. You might not guess that from the crossword puzzle in his lap. And you might not guess that from the fact that in the OR at least, Dr. Banjo Paterson wore nothing below his waist. Knowing is better than guessing, but not always.

Harbour City Regional's resident biomedical technology geek, Murray 'Leatherman' MacGyver, the guru guardian of all things electromechanical, had customized and turbocharged the Dräger anesthetic machine that delivered Banjo's milk of amnesia. Murray considered 'supernatural' as just another null word. *One man's magic is another man's engineering.*

He had converted Banjo's basic Ford F-150 gas machine into a Ferrari 812 GTS, capable of delivering any concentration of any mixture of oxygen, medical air, nitrous oxide, or volatile anesthetic. He had equipped it with state-of-the-art rotameters, pressure gauges, adjustable pressure-limiting pop-off valves, regulators, vaporisers, high-flow flushers, and an integrated mechanical ventilator and manual reservoir bag. There were safety electronic sensor failure warning devices—all the bells and whistles—ventilator alerts comprised by oxygen failure alarms and a chain-linked ratio-controlled slave nitrous-oxide regulator hypoxic-mixture alarm, a cylinder Pin Index Safety System with non-interchangeable NIST and DISS pipeline gas hose Schrader valve connectors, and physiological monitor interlock distress signals for abnormal ECGs blood pressure, oxygen saturation, end-tidal carbon dioxide, heart rate, and temperature. As Sababa approached, the last three alarms began screaming in pain.

"How's the patient, Banjo?" Sababa asked.

"Coming apart like a hooker's panties on a Saturday night." Banjo moaned in a falling fifth and a two-toned sigh.

"Hey, Sab." Buddy interrupted. "What's the definition of an anesthetist?"

"What?"

"Someone half-awake keeping someone else half-asleep." He said. "What do you call an anesthetist in a suit?"

"Dunno."

"The defendant."

"We're kind of busy here right now, Buddy." Banjo said. "Trying to keep you out of your own suit."

"What you got?" Sababa asked.

"Nathanael Greene." He said. "40-year-old heating contractor came into the ER in the wee hours with a low-grade fever, right lower quadrant abdominal pain and tenderness, a high white count with a left shift, and a CT scan showing swelling of his appendix, all of which made for a diagnosis of acute appendicitis. Buddy cut into him an hour ago, after I put him under with 200mg of propofol and sevoflurane, followed by 70 mg of rocuronium bromide for endotracheal intubation. While Buddy was turning his colon into a semi-colon, I dosed him with droperidol, sugammadex, lidocaine, and flurbiprofen. Ten minutes ago, he became sweaty and rigid, his masseters muscles became the jaws of steel, his heart rate shot up to 160 beats/minute, his end-tidal carbon dioxide level went into the sky, and his temperature soared to 41.5°C."

"You gave him sevoflurane?" Sababa asked.

"Use it all the time." Banjo said. "I've never seen this before."

"And you consider yourself a proficient sandman, Banjo?"

"I put the pro in propofol, Sab." Banjo said. "Sleep with the best."

"So, you understand that the sevoflurane you gave Mr. Greene triggered an uncontrolled flood of intracellular calcium from his skeletal muscle sarcoplasmic reticulum into his bloodstream." Sababa said. "Thus causing a massive hypermetabolic increase of muscle contraction activation, oxygen consumption, carbon dioxide production, ATP breakdown, and heat."

"Now why would he do something like that?"

"Because he has a defective calcium channel ryanodine-1 receptor gene mutation in his sarcoplasmic reticulum membranes." Sababa said. "Although there are at least six others."

"Whew... What a relief." Banjo said. "For a moment there, I thought he had malignant hyperthermia."

"He does."

"Why didn't you say so?"

"I did."

"Did you have to be such an Internal Medicine flea about it?"

"Flea?" Buddy asked.

"Fucking little esoteric asshole." Sababa said. "For my edification, Banjo, what made you decide to pass gas for a living?"

"Being a unicorn was too hard." He said. "This is the closest thing I could find to breaking the law. Anesthesia... knocking people out since 1856."

"You're supposed to knock them out, not knock them off."

"Thanks for reminding me," Banjo said. "You going to help me save Nathanael's nutmeg here, or what?"

"Today's cure is brought to you by the letter 'D.'" Sababa said. "You do have dantrolene in that tool kit of yours, don't you Banjo?"

"Yeah."

"Give him 2.5 mg/kg IV now." Sababa said. "It inhibits the calcium release cascade. Repeat as needed. I'll admit him to the Death Star and write up his orders." Banjo's first dose of dantrolene restored Nathanael's vital signs to normal.

"You know that pigs also get malignant hyperthermia, don't you Banjo?" Sababa said. "Farmers use halothane cones in swine yards to expose piglets to the anesthetic. Those that die are MH-susceptible and save the expense of raising an animal whose meat can't be marketed."

"Didn't know that." Banjo admitted. "On account of the fact that I don't put pigs to sleep."

"You can do that without anesthesia, Banjo." Buddy said. "Hey, Sab. Where do you hide a $100 bill from an anesthetist?"

"Dunno."

"In the cabinet with the sterile gloves." Said the surgeon. "If you can cure this guy's malignant hyperthermia, maybe you can cure Banjo's boredom?"

"The cure for boredom is curiosity." Sababa said.

"What's the cure for curiosity?" Banjo asked.

"Becoming a surgeon."

'I think I've got a touch of island fever
I do believe I feel a bit sautéed...
Jimmy Buffett, *Island Fever*

'Everybody's got the fever
That is somethin' you all know
Fever isn't such a new thing
Fever started long time ago.'
Peggy Lee, *Fever*

Sababa's pager went off in his pocket as he finished the last line of Nathanael Greene's orders in the Death Star. It was Alex. He was excited.

"I've just seen this wicked frickin' pissah patient on the fifth-floor medical ward." He said.

"You've met the charming Team Leader and Care Coordinator head nurse, Samara Morgan?" Sababa asked.

"Lesbian witch hardo." Alex had met Samara. "Personality of a dead clam."

"Coming now." Sababa said. A few minutes later, a large blur bounced through the stairwell doors like a wallaby in a bushfire. His Colombian leather briefcase flew an Immelmann turn over the nursing station before landing on the chart rack Samara was guarding with her hundred-dollar clipboard. She would have jumped out of her pantsuit if the Valentino

Garavani silk scarf hadn't blocked the exit. Her tongue made clicking noises.

"Use your words, Samara." Sababa said. "Use your words."

"I'm going down to see Big Nurse." She said. "I'll have you arrested for attempted murder."

"Don't be silly. Samara." Sababa said. "Who would believe that? Everyone knows that if I wanted to kill you, I would have injected an undetectable lethal dose of insulin between your toes."

"And making threats." She stammered. "I'll have you arrested for making threats."

"And they might believe you." Alex said. "Unless I tell them it never happened."

"I expected more refinement in an Internal Medicine resident from your Ivy League pedigree." Samara said.

"Look who wants the moon." Alex said. Samara made for the stairwell. Sababa called after her.

"It's faster on your broom." The professor turned his attention to his protégé.

"OK, Bahney." He said. "Tell me a story"

"Armen Tamzarian." Alex said. "42-year-old school principal admitted yesterday by Dr. James Ruben Andrews with a month-long history of intermittent fever and chills, drenching night sweats, muscle pain, and a 20-pound weight loss."

"Exam?"

"Febrile, with bilateral leg tenderness to palpation and a blanching maculopapular rash, and nontender lymph nodes in his groin."

"Lab?"

"High sedimentation rate and C-reactive protein."

"Imaging?"

"Total-body PET/CT scan showed diffuse hypermetabolic enlarged lymph nodes."

"So what you got?" Sababa asked.

"Fever of unknown origin." He said.

"Not for another two weeks."

"Oh, yeah."

"Let's go to the bedside." Sababa and his apprentice found their patient in the room at the very end of the hall.

"This is the Doctor Sababa I told you about, Mr. Tamzarian." Alex said. "He's wicked smaht."

"Որտեղից եք, Արմեն?" Sababa asked. *Where are you from, Armen.*

"Երևան." He said. *Yerevan.*

"Սրճարանների քաղաք." *City of Cafés.*

"Դուք այնտեղ եք եղել?" *Have you been there.*

25

"Երկար ժամանակ առաջ. Ես այցելեցի եղասպանության հուշահամալիր և Լևոնի Աստվածային ստորգետնյա քարանձավ." Sababa said. *I visited the Genocide Memorial and Levon's Divine Underground Cave.*

"Մեր ժողովուրդը ողբերգական և քմահաճ պատմություն ունի." *Our people have a tragic and whimsical history.*

"Չկա չարիք՝ առանց բարիք." *There is no evil without goodness.*

"Mr. Tamzarian speaks English, Doctah Sababer." Alex said.

"I know." He said. "Armen, how many times have you had this problem?"

"At least four other episodes over the last ten years." Sababa looked at his resident.

"I heard nothing about a past medical history." Alex protested. "He didn't tell me."

"You didn't think to inquire?" Sababa asked. "You remember William Faulkner's famous axiom?"

"He went to Yale."

"And Oxford."

"Oxford, Mississippi."

"Faulkner claimed the past is never dead. It's not even past." Sababa said. "So how does this little historical nugget change the diagnosis?"

"It becomes a periodic fever syndrome." Alex said.

"What kind?"

"An autoinflammatory condition."

"From what?"

"OK, then." Alex said. "Important to remember that these are not autoimmune diseases like lupus and rheumatoid arthritis and similar conditions caused by antibodies to innate healthy tissue antigens."

"I'm looking for a differential diagnosis."

"Genetic mutations in molecules involved in regulating the innate 'hard-wired' immune defense system responses against infectious agents and other danger signals." Alex said. "But we usually diagnose these diseases in infancy or childhood."

"I'm still waiting."

"OK, then." Alex said. "Adult-onset Still's disease, Schnitzler syndrome, and chronic recurrent multifocal osteomyelitis."

"What else?"

"There are case reports of PFAPA in Japanese adults using cimetidine." Alex said.

"But Armen isn't Japanese." Sababa said. "Nor was he taking cimetidine." There was a blank screen where Alex's face should have been.

"What's the most common autoinflammatory disorder, presenting with recurrent fever, abdominal pain, and serositis, affecting people of Mediterranean descent, including Turks, Sephardic Jews, Arabs, and Armenians?" Sababa said. "Caused by mutations in the MEFV gene on chromosome 16, which codes for the protein pyrin resulting in the inappropriate activation of the inflammasome and release of the pro-inflammatory cytokine IL-1β?"

"Familial Mediterranean Fever?" Alex asked. "But Mr. Tamzarian is foddy-two-years-old."

"When you have eliminated the impossible, whatever remains, however improbable, must be the truth." Sababa said. "Late-onset FMF is defined as diagnosis above 40 years of age, which while still a rare occurrence, still accounts for 0.5% of patients with the condition."

"Can you treat this, Doctor Sababa?" Armen asked.

"Absolutely." He said. "Dr. Harding here will draw some more blood for genetic testing and send you home today on an oral medication called colchicine. Slam dunk." The portly professor's pager buzzed a welcome on his belt.

"I'll be right back." He said. "Alex, explain all this one more time to our principal." A few minutes later, Sababa returned with a new referral.

"Dr. La Capuche wants us to see a patient on the psych ward." He handed Armen a card. "Call Mercy at my office and tell her I want to review you in a week."

"Do you like Armenian cognac, Doctor Sababa?" He asked.

"Of course."

"I will bring you a bottle of Ararat." He said. "Maxim Gorky said it transfers the strength of the sun into the spirit."

"As soon as we transfer the strength of your spirit back out into the sun." Sababa shook Armen's hand. He signalled for his protégé to follow him down the hallway and stairwell, deep into the depths of Harbour City Regional.

"Where are we going?" Alex asked.

"Away from the sun." Sababa said. "To where the lunacy lives."

'There is no dark side of the moon really.
Matter of fact it's all dark.'
Pink Freud, *Eclipse*

Dr. Robert La Capuche was waiting for our mediconauts at the security door to the psychiatric ward. He pressed the button that buzzed them into the asylum.

"This is my new resident, Bob." Sababa said.

"I'm Dr. Hahding." Alex said. "From Hahvud."

"That's what it says on your bow tie." La Capuche said. "That doesn't prove you're from Harvard, but the fact that you are even wearing a bow tie speaks strongly in favour."

"You don't wear ties here?" Alex asked.

"Nothing that our patients could weaponize against us." The psychiatrist said. "Think about that."

"What you got, Bob?" Sababa asked.

"Harold Peridol." He said. "35-year-old disc jockey with paranoid schizophrenia managed with clozapine and diabetes treated with insulin. Came in last night with acute restlessness, muteness, profuse sweating, and confusion. He was trying to climb the wall, crawling over the floor, making gestures of eating, smoking, and picking up things from the carpet. He broke a mirror and a wardrobe door. The psychiatric nurse who visited him at home thought it was a hypoglycemic episode and called an ambulance. Blood glucose was normal. Because of his agitation, we admitted him here with the help of the police. Physical examination was impossible, as he required restraining. The hospitalist on call gave him an intramuscular injection of butyrophenone for his acute psychosis."

"And?"

"Harold's mental state had improved by this morning, but his temperature had spiked to 40°C, his heart rate was fast, blood pressure all over the place, and his muscles were rigid. We did a white count and a muscle enzyme level."

"And?"

"White count was high, but his creatine phosphokinase level was on another planet, up at 10,844 I.U./liter."

"Alex?"

"He may have had a partial complex seizure from his clozapine last night, but today he has classic neuroleptic malignant syndrome." He said. "Ten percent mortality. We need to bring him to the ICU for a cooling blanket, aggressive rehydration to protect his kidneys, and treatment with dantrolene and bromocriptine and diazepam."

"First described in France in 1956 as *syndrome malin des neuroleptiques*." Sababa said. "What do you mean 'we,' Alex?"

"Ya suh!" Alex said. "I mean I'll examine and work up Mr. Periodol and admit him to the unit."

"And then grab a bite to eat and meet me at Manzanita at one o'clock."

"Manzanita?"

"My office." Sababa said. "We have a full afternoon clinic. You have wheels?"

"I take the Rattlah."

28

"There's no subway in Harbour City." Sababa said. "Although we have our share of forgotten coal mine shafts and tunnels."
"Oh."
"I'll pick you up outside the ER in an hour." Sababa said. "Wear something colourful. Environment Canada is forecasting a blizzard."
"Pissah." Alex said.

'
> I once loved a lass from Zeballos
> Whose comportment was totally callous
> When she grows old and stout,
> Wracked with chilblains and gout,
> She'll embrace me without so much malice.'
> Ion Zwitter, *Avant News* (with apologies)

Dr. Alex Harding walked backwards into the wind to reach the horn he heard in the whiteout. He couldn't see Sababa's dimpled and dented white Honda in the snowstorm. When the professor reached over and opened the passenger door, Alex dove into the black interior. The vents of the front and rear defrosters screamed at both windshields.
"Wicked winters here in Canada." He said.
"Your nor'easters are worse in Boston." Sababa pulled out of the hospital parking lot into a channel of white tire tracks. "This almost never happens on Vancouver Island."
"Almost never?'
"Hardly ever." Sababa tap-danced his accelerator and brakes to manoeuvre around vehicles polishing the ice beneath them with spinning tires. They passed other casualties half-buried in snowbanks. Sababa fishtailed around corners and slid through all the traffic signs into a final glide down the steep slope to his downtown clinic.
"You've done this before." Alex said.
"I grew up in Northern Ontario." Sababa said. "My driving test would have killed most earthlings."
The stocky savant pulled up beside the Italian prune plum tree that served as his seasonal almanac. Its springtime white blossoms exploded into a popcorn riot. Summer produced buckets of large dark purple fruit with rich sweet and lemon tart, amber flesh. In autumn, Sababa would slice chicken-of-the-woods ribbons from the bright yellow outer edge of an immense sulfur shelf bracket fungus that emerged from its trunk. And

in winter, its bare limbs produced a humble serenity that reminded the professor of his mortal fragility.

Sababa and Alex climbed the back stairs to a doorway, inlaid with stained glass, and marked by a sign. *Manzanita Medical.*

They kicked the snow off their shoes and entered a foyer, suffused in winter light. A redheaded middle-aged woman with cat-eyed frame glasses sat typing behind a counter and a big-screen Power Mac G4, under a photo of a bowl of multicoloured cereal with a diagonal red line through it. *No fruit loops.*

"Hi, Mercy." Sababa said.

"It's hot and cold running crazy week, Boss."

"Mercy makes the world less cold and more just." He said. "Mercy, this is Dr. Harding, our new resident."

"What's doin'?" Alex said.

"He must be from Harvard." Her eyes never left her transcription.

"How did you know?"

"It is my business to know what other people don't know." One of Sababa's eyebrows rose high on his forehead. "Your greeting was from Boston and your bow tie is from across the Charles River. It's not rocket science." Sababa handed Alex the first chart from the top of the pile.

"The resident's room is that way." He pointed down the hallway.

"Benjamin Aaron." Alex called into the gathered multitude. A sudorific young man rose from one of the waiting room chairs and followed him down the corridor.

"Before you see the next patient, Boss, the Good sisters are here to speak to you about their aunt and uncle."

"OK." Sababa turned to look at three middle-aged native ladies hoping for a chance to speak to him.

"Are there any good women here?" He asked. The waiting room filled with boisterous laughter as the ladies followed him into his sanctum sanctorum. Sababa motioned for them to take a seat. There were only two chairs on the other side of his desk. The two oldest sisters, Bee Good, and Dew Good, sat down first.

"I'll stand." Said the youngest, Pretty Good.

"How's Julia?" He asked.

"We don't think that auntie will last out the day." Bee said. "Stanzy comes over this morning to increase her comfort medication."

"Julia's waiting for her son, Four Watt, to come up from Victoria." Dew added.

"Rough day for that." Sababa said.

"He'll try his best." Pretty said. "We've been giving her green slug slime water and wild cherry bark tea for her breathing." No one spoke for a while after that.

"But that's not why you're here, is it?" Sababa said.

"We're here about our uncle, Wakasiah." Bee said.

30

"What about him?"

"We're worried about what he'll do when auntie dies." Dew said.

"What do you mean?"

"Wakasiah is a Coast Salish chief, Doctor Sababa." Pretty said. "He and auntie have been together for sixty years. He won't want to continue living after she's gone."

"But the extended family, as many as there are, can look after him."

"He's a strong man." Bee said. "He will make his own path."

"What can I do?" The professor asked.

"Uncle respects you, Doctor Sababa." Dew said. "Speak to him about taking care of himself." No one spoke for a while after that.

"I'll find a way to see him tomorrow." He said. The Good women nodded and thanked him. They passed Alex hovering in the doorway, as they left.

"Are those real Indians?" He asked.

"They prefer First Nations."

"Are they different from our American natives?"

"We didn't exterminate ours." Sababa said. "Although we also took their land in trade for smallpox, bubonic plague, chickenpox, cholera, the common cold, diphtheria, influenza, malaria, measles, scarlet fever, sexually-transmitted diseases, typhoid, typhus, tuberculosis, and pertussis."

"You seem to get along well."

"Don't scratch them too deep." Sababa said. "What you got?"

"Benjamin Aaron." Alex began. "34-year-old BC Hydro power line technician referred by Dr. Tictac Tarmac for a two-month history of lethargy, confusion, episodic chills, and profuse sweating, associated with a twenty-pound weight loss."

"Exam?"

"Mild delirium, significant diaphoresis, and signs of dehydration. All of Dr. Tarmac's lab results were normal."

"Temperature?"

"Temperature?"

"I asked you first." Sababa said. "You know, temperature—how cold or hot a thing is."

"I had nothing to measure that." Alex protested. Sababa reached into his Columbian leather bag and pulled out a non-contact digital infrared forehead thermometer. "Let's go see him."

Down the hallway, in the resident's room, Alex introduced his mentor.

"Mr. Aaron, this is Doctah Sababer." He said. "No man lives or has ever lived who has brought the same amount of study and natural talent to the detection of disease."

"That's a ringing endorsement." Ben said. "So what's wrong with me, Doc?" Sababa held up his forehead gun and pulled the trigger. *32.1°C.* Alex's eyeballs strained to leave their orbits.

31

"He sure doesn't have a temperature." He said.

"Au contraire, Bahney." Sababa said. "He has a temperature. It's just five degrees centigrade below normal. That calls for an explanation."

"There is a wicked blizzard blowing sideways outside." Alex said.

"Perhaps you have forgotten the concept of mammalian thermoregulation." Sababa logged into the resident's room computer and brought up the patient's imaging history.

"Aha." He said. "Ben, do you remember having an MRI of your brain last year?"

"Uh-huh." He said. "I was having some headaches."

"What did they tell you?"

"They said it was tension." He said. "And they went away."

"Did they tell you about missing a corpus callosum, the part of your brain that connects your two cerebral hemispheres?"

"Nope."

"Unreported in 5-10% of cases." Sababa said.

"So what does that mean?" Ben asked.

"It means you have a rare condition called Shapiro's syndrome." Sababa said. "Only fifty cases reported in the world."

"Fifty-one." Alex said. "Wicked pissah."

"Can you fix it?" Ben asked. Sababa scribbled on a prescription pad and handed him the finished scrawl.

"What's this?" Ben asked.

"Clonidine." Sababa said. "100 micrograms every 8 hours. Reboots the hypothalamic thermoregulatory set-point. Tell Mercy I'll see you in three weeks."

"I may still be here if this snowstorm doesn't lift." He shook the hands of the two physicians and left to speak with Sababa's assistant.

"Let's see this next one together." Sababa went to grab a chart off the top of the pile before he realized there was no pile.

"Where is everybody?" He asked.

"I rebooked the ones that were here so they wouldn't get caught in the storm on their way home." Mercy said. "The ones that weren't here said they weren't coming and rebooked for the same reason." Sababa looked out at the one remaining patient in his waiting room.

"No one else here but us penguins." He said. "You may as well come in, Sarah." A young woman followed them into Sababa's office. The stocky savant perused the chart.

"Sarah Medhurst Troughton." He said. "26-year-old figure skating coach referred by Dr. Nicholas Rivera for a recurrent history of purple blisters on both thumbs over the interphalangeal joints." Sarah held up her blistered thumbs.

"The pain gets in the way of my coaching." She said. "Sometimes it involves my middle fingers as well."

"Any special time they occur?" Alex asked.

"Every winter for the last three years." She said. "Especially in the morning."

"Hmmm." Sababa scrolled through her lab results. "Normal complete blood count, cold agglutinins, cryoglobulins, cryofibrinogen, and serum protein electrophoresis. No serological evidence of autoimmunity. I see Dr. Rivera did a skin biopsy that showed only nonspecific changes of necrotic keratinocytes, dermal edema, deep lymphohystiocytic infiltrate with periecrine accentuatio, and lymphocytic infiltration and extravasated erythrocytes around dermal vessels, without vasculitis. Why didn't Dr. Rivera send you to a dermatologist?"

"I saw Dr. Sitsofsky last year."

"And?"

"He lost interest when he couldn't talk me into buying his cosmetic products."

"Good old Dr. Commodus Skin Laser." Sababa said. "His interest is only skin deep."

"Do you know what this is, Doctor Sababa."

"Perniosis."

"Huh?"

"We also call them chilblains."

"Is it frostbite?"

"No."

"What then?"

"It's a localized abnormal inflammatory response in susceptible individuals to nonfreezing cold ambient. We don't know the cause."

"Is there anything that can make it go away?"

"There are some general measures you can try." He said. "Keep your hands warm and dry in cold weather by wearing gloves, take nicotinic acid and soak your hands in Epsom salts. If that doesn't work, you can try this calcium channel blocker." He handed her a prescription for nifedipine.

"That's it?" She asked.

"In medieval times, Bald's Leechbook recommended a mixture of eggs, wine, and fennel root." He said. "But my recipe works better."

After Sarah left, Sababa looked through the blinds of his windows. The world was filling up white fast.

"We're on call, Alex, and I've already had three referrals come through on my pager." He said. "I'll give you a lift back to the hospital and you can be the point man tonight. But I'll also spend the night on a cot in Harbour City Regional. It's too dangerous to drive my poor Honda up and down to and from the lake in this weather."

"OK." Alex said.

"You also went to Harvard as an undergrad?"

"Four H-er." He said.

"I went to M.I.T. for my first two degrees."

"I heard that." Alex said.

"In my sophomore year, I used to walk to the Harvard football field every summer afternoon wearing a black-and-white striped shirt. I'd go up and down the field for ten minutes throwing birdseed all over the grass and blowing a whistle, before leaving."

"And?"

"At the end of the summer, in the first Harvard home football game, a referee walked onto the field and blew his whistle. It delayed the game for an hour, waiting for all the birds to leave the field."

"Wicked."

"Yeah." Sababa said. "Never mess with a man from Tech."

'Yeah, we rum-bum-bum-bum
Feeling hot, hot, hot.'
Buster Poindexter, *Hot Hot Hot*

It was already dark when Sababa and Alex made it back to the hospital through the raging blizzard. They had to take a long alternate route to avoid the crushed carnage on Harbour City's treacherous hills. Streetlamps receded as blurred halos into the night. The two physicians kicked white clotted clumps of snow from their shoes on their way into the emergency department.

"Why don't you see the first referral while I catch up on some discharge summaries." Sababa said. "Call me when you're done."

"Yah huh." Alex said.

Sababa's pager buzzed on his belt loops a half-hour later. He returned to the ER to find Drs. Capitaine and Harding engaged in animated conversation.

"How are you, Myles?" Sababa asked.

"Living the dream."

"Sometimes dreams are wiser than waking." He said. "I see you've met my new resident."

"Nice guy." Myles said. "Although he seems wound a little tight."

"He's from Harvard."

"So he mentioned." Myles said. Sababa turned to his student.

"Sup?"

"Paulo Aegineta." Alex began. "38-year-old Brazilian tourist, here on holiday to ski Mount Washington despite a long-standing problem with

34

asthma. Presents with a year-long history of intermittent red plaques on his legs that improved with the use of oral corticosteroids for the asthma attacks. In the previous month, his skin lesions became diffuse and associated with fever, muscle pains, and nausea and vomiting."

"Exam?"

"Febrile at 39.1°C." Alex said. "He has these tender papules and erythematous edematous plaques all over his body, sparing mucosa, palms, and soles. Blood count showed 11,000 white cells with 90% neutrophils, everything else normal."

"So what you got?"

"Young man with recurrent fever, an elevated white blood cell count, and tender, red, well-demarcated papules and plaques that improve with steroids.' Alex said. "Classic presentation of acute febrile neutrophilic dermatosis. Sweet's syndrome."

"First described in 1964 by Robert Douglas Sweet." Sababa said. "Also known as Gomm-Button disease in honour of the first two patients Sweet diagnosed. Good guess."

"Guess?"

"Conjecture." Sababa said. "Good conjecture. Good, but not great."

"Why not great?"

"Because it's wrong." Sababa said. "He doesn't have Sweet's syndrome. He has a Type 2 Sweet's syndrome-like reaction mediated by immune-complexes first described in 1987 by Kuo and Chan."

"To what?"

"Yeah, to what?" Myles added.

"Where does he live in Brazil?" Sababa asked.

"Why is that important?" Alex asked back.

"Let's go see him." On the other side of his cubicle curtain, Alex made introductions.

"Paulo, this is Doctah Sababer." He said. "He's wicked mad killah." A look of terror crossed the tourist's face.

"Boa tarde." *Good evening.* Sababa said. "Prazer em conhecer você." *Pleased to meet you.*

"O prazer é meu." He said. *My pleasure.*

"Onde você mora no Brasil, Paula?" *Where do you live in Brazil.*

"Santarém." He said. "No estado do Pará. Onde o rio Tapajós encontra a Amazônia." *Santarém. In Pará state. Where the Tapajós River meets the Amazon.*

"Uma vez eu possuía uma ação chamada Tapajós gold." *I once owned a stock called Tapajós gold.*

"Você teria perdido todo o seu dinheiro." *You would have lost all your money.*

"Eu fiz." *I did.* He said. "Você gosta de tatu-galinha?" *Do you like tatu-galinha.*

"É ilegal caçar animais selvagens no Brasil." *It's illegal to hunt wildlife in Brazil.* He paused for a breath. "Tem gosto de frango." *It tastes like chicken.*

"Qual é a sua receita favorita?" *What's your favorite recipe.*

"Ceviche de fígado cru. Com cebolas." *Raw liver ceviche. With onions.*
"Bingo." Sababa. said.
"Bingo?" Paulo and Alex and Myles asked together.
"Which disease affected Baldwin IV of Jerusalem, King Henry IV of England, Vietnamese poet Hàn Mặc Tử, and Japanese daimyō Ōtani Yoshitsugu? What afflicted sufferer did Jesus cleanse as one of his miracles?" Sababa asked. "What European strain 3 ailment spread along the migration, colonisation, and slave trade routes from West Africa to the New World and then infected the native *Dasypus novemcinctus* of Latin America?"
"Dasypus novemcinctus?" Paulo and Alex and Myles asked together.
"The species that migrated north from Central and South America crossing the Rio Grande into the United States from Mexico in the late 19th century?" He asked. "The animal hunted for its meat in East Texas during the Great Depression, where they referred to it as poor man's pork, the 'Hoover hog' that German settlers called Panzerschwein?" *Armored pig.*
"Dasypus novemcinctus?" Alex offered.
"Exactly." Sababa said. "The wild nine-banded armadillo is a carrier because of its low body temperature. In Portuguese, it's called 'tatu-galinha.' Paulo loves to eat its raw liver as ceviche with onions."
"I'm afraid we're not getting all the connections here, Sab." Alex spoke for all the assembled. Sababa pointed to a needle sticking out of Paulo's leg. No one saw him put it there. Paulo hadn't felt it go in. Alex and Myles let their eyes grow wide.
"Whoa." They both said.
"You both know Anthony Fauci, one of the world's leading experts on infectious diseases?" Alex and Myles nodded.
"He said what you should have known." *It's extremely likely that the people who have never been exposed to a human who has leprosy, it's very likely they got leprosy from exposure to an armadillo.*
"How did you know it wasn't Sweet's syndrome?" Alex asked.
"No truncal or mucosal involvement." Sababa said. "And the real estate."
"Real estate?" Myles asked.
"Location. Location. Location."
"I have leprosy?" Paulo asked. Sababa nodded.
"From the armadillo liver ceviche?" The professor nodded again.
"We gave it to them." He said. "They're just giving it back."
"What happens now?" He asked.
"Now, Dr. Harding here will do a punch biopsy of the edge of your skin lesions to look for acid-fast staining organisms and request our resident neurologist Dr. Oliver Lax to see you for nerve conduction studies."
"Perhaps this is why my skiing is not so good anymore?" Paulo asked.
"Perhaps." Sababa said.

"Is there a cure?"

"You have the multibacillary form of Mycobacterium leprae." He said. "You'll need 12 months of multidrug therapy with rifampicin, dapsone, and clofazimine. Your relatives will need vaccination with Bacillus Calmette–Guérin."

"In Brazil, we believe that Hansen's disease is transmitted by dogs, associated with sexual promiscuity, and thought to be punishment for sins or moral transgressions." Paulo said. "It is still stigmatised."

"You're lucky you didn't live in Venezuela during the iron rod reign of dictator Juan Vincente Gomez at the beginning of the last century." Sababa said. "Among his accomplishments, he became the richest man in South America, fathered 84 illegitimate crotch goblins, and eradicated leprosy from his country."

"Why am I lucky not to have lived there and then?" Paolo asked.

"Gomez reasoned that most lepers in his country were beggars and heretics." Sababa said. "He killed them all."

"I still have my faith." Paulo said. "It will sustain me."

"When nations are to perish in their sins, 'tis in the Church the leprosy begins." Sababa said.

"Obrigado, Dr. Sababa." Paulo said. *Thank you.*

"De nada, Paulo." *You're welcome.* He said. "Oh, and Paulo?"

"Si?"

"Lay off the armadillo."

Dr. Trace Pangloss punched his cuboid head and crooked teeth through the curtain crease, like a Pulcinella in a puppet show.

"Another one for you in bed 3, Sab." He said. Alex and his preceptor followed him to the consultant's desk.

"This is Alex Harding." Sababa said. "My new resident."

"What's with the bow tie?" Trace asked. "Where are you from?"

"Ovah heah, ovah theah." Alex said. "What's doin'?"

"Eric Bywaters." Trace began. "47-year-old optometrist with a two-week history of swelling around both eyes. Three days ago, he saw our faceless oculist guru, Dr. T.J. Eckleburg, who made a diagnosis of preseptal cellulitis and prescribed an antibiotic. It didn't work. Blood cultures have been negative. Yesterday, he developed joint and muscle pains, feverishness, sore throat, multiple erythematous patches and hives over his entire body, and swelling of the left parotid gland. He saw a walk-in clinic quacksalver who thought his new symptoms were an allergic reaction to T.J.'s prescription and changed them to another class of antibiotic."

"Did this ever happen before?" Alex channelled the patient's past medical history.

"A year ago, Eric presented with an episode of high fever associated with arthritis and a rash on his trunk and limbs." Trace said. "Another doc-in-the-box didn't know what it was but pulled the steroid trigger and it all went away."

"Exam?" Alex had taken the reins.

"Temperature of 39°C." Trace said. "Tenderness in both eyes and around the left parotid gland. Nil else."

"Lab?"

"High white count with a left shift, low platelets, aggravated liver function, and elevated ferritin level."

"Imaging?"

"CT scan of his head and neck tonight shows periorbital soft tissue swelling with heterogeneous enhancement around both eye sockets and diffuse swelling of the left parotid gland with periglandular infiltration."

"Let's see what's behind curtain number 3, Alex." Sababa said. Trace introduced his two colleagues to the optometrist.

"I'm getting pretty desperate for an answer here, Doctor Sababa." Eric said. "This has been a distraction to my refraction."

"Permit me to focus for a moment on my pupils, Eric." He said. "Alex, what colour is Mr. Bywaters' maculopapular rash?"

"Pink." Alex said. "It's pink."

"What shade of pink?"

"I don't know." He said. "Pink pink."

"Trace?"

"Salmon pink."

"You agree, Alex?" Sababa asked.

"We don't have salmon in Boston." He said. "We have scrod."

"What's a scrod?" Trace asked.

"It's the cheapest young cod or a haddock or whatever other white fish is on the menu." Sababa said.

"Doesn't sound like I'm missing much." Trace said.

"What's the differential diagnosis of Eric's periorbital swelling?" Sababa asked.

"Angioedema, lymphoma, and connective tissue diseases such as dermatomyositis and lupus." Alex said.

"And what condition is characterized by the triad of persistent high spiking fevers, joint pains, and a distinctive salmon-colored bumpy rash?" Sababa looked into three pairs of unaccommodating pupils.

"Adult-onset Still's disease." He said. "You've heard of the Yamaguchi criteria?"

"Diagnosis requires at least five features, with at least two of these being major diagnostic criteria." Alex said. "Eric has a high fever, arthritis, skin rash, left-shifted white count, sore throat, and no apparent infection. But what about his swollen eyes?"

"Atypical cutaneous manifestation." Sababa said. "And his serum ferritin is forty times higher than normal."

"What is this thing you say I've got, Doctor Sababa?" Eric asked.

"It's a rare inflammatory disorder."

"Is there a remedy?" Before he could reply, Dr. Capitaine signalled his wish to confer outside the curtain. After a brief absence, the professor returned to answer Eric's question.

"Dr. Harding here will order some more investigations, load an initial dose of intravenous corticosteroid, and send you home with a prescription for and some information about prednisone." Sababa said. "I'll see you in my clinic in three weeks." He handed his pager to his apprentice.

"I'll see this next patient, Alex." He said. "She's the spouse of a radiologist and her husband is touchy about coeducational exercises involving his family."

"In return, you can field the overnight referrals." Sababa said.

"No problem." Alex said. "Is that a quid pro quo?"

"You're a resident, Alex." He said. "You get to work from can't see morning to can't see night. We'll catch up after my Department of Medicine sunrise meeting."

"If the sun ever comes up in this storm." Alex said.

"At sunrise, everything is luminous but not clear." He said. "Internists worship the night. That's where the revelations live."

> 'Young man rhythm's got a hold of me too
> I got the rocking pneumonia
> And the boogie woogie flu.'
> Johnny Rivers, *Rockin' Pneumonia and The Boogie Woogie Flu*

"Hi, Diana." Sababa found her in the special treatment room, where Myles said she'd be. By the time she returned the greeting, he'd already sleuthed out several important facts: (1) She was breathing faster than normal, (2) Her ears and the tip of her nose and her fingers were blue, with black discoloration at the end of her left fourth finger, and (3) Her husband was agitated. Sababa knew Dr. Alan Statham as a capable Harbour City radiologist whose usual demeanor was cucumber cool.

"What do you think is going on here, Sab?" He asked.

"Don't get ahead of the healing, Alan." Sababa said. "I just got here. What's been going on, Diana?"

"Two weeks ago, while teaching my elementary school class, I developed a dry cough and a fever." She said. "I saw my GP, Dr. de Meath, and she put me on this antibiotic." Diana handed an empty pill bottle to the portly professor. *Amoxicillin-clavulanate.*

39

"β-lactam." He said. "Then what."

"It didn't seem to make any difference." She said. "I got more and more short of breath and whenever I went outside, my fingers turned red and then blue."

"Keep going."

"A week ago, I saw Petronilla's locum, who sent me for some blood tests and gave me this." She handed over another plastic container. *Clarithromycin.*

"A macrolide." Sababa said. "Better."

"I thought I was improving." Diana said. "And then, three days ago, I got worse. Much worse. It's more difficult to catch my breath and my nose and ears and fingers stay blue. The tip of my left fourth finger looks like it has gangrene."

"It does." Sababa said. "Dry gangrene."

"From what, Sab?" There was distress in Alan's voice.

"Something changed the playing field four days ago." Sababa said. "What did you take that I don't know about yet?"

"Nothing." Alan said.

"Alan gave me ibuprofen." Diana said.

"You did?" Sababa was asking her husband.

"I thought it would decrease the inflammation." He said. "It's a non-steroidal anti-inflammatory agent."

"I know what it is, Alan." Sababa said. "I also know that it's the reason that Diana's condition is worse."

"What do you mean?" Alan asked. Sababa threw a chest x-ray up on the treatment room viewer. The radiologist let out a sigh.

"Right middle lobe infiltrate." He said.

"What kind?"

"Pneumonia." Alan said. "What do you mean?"

"What kind of pneumonia?"

"Isn't there only one kind?"

"Nope." Sababa said. "You ever heard of a guy named Koch? Nineteenth-century microbiologist who came up with four flawed postulates: (1) The microorganism must be found in abundance in all organisms suffering from the disease but should not be found in healthy organisms. (2) The microorganism must be isolated from a diseased organism and grown in pure culture. (3) The cultured microorganism should cause disease when introduced into a healthy organism. (4) The microorganism must be re-isolated from the inoculated, diseased experimental host and identified as being identical to the original specific causative agent."

"I don't understand." Alan admitted.

"Of more relevance, there are four players in this game, if it's an infection." Sababa said. "The host, the organism, the milieu, and the treatment. The host can be immunocompetent or immunocompromised in various forms. The organism can be viral, bacterial, fungal, or, in this case, other. The milieu can be aspiration, structural, community-acquired, or hospital-acquired. And the treatment can be 'static' or 'cidal.'"

"What does that have to do with Diana?"

"You're a shadow puppet." Sababa said. "But in my more illuminated universe, that doesn't make you a doctor, that makes you a tourist. Never bring a knife to a gunfight."

"I don't understand." He said.

"No, you don't." Sababa said. "But not only you. Dr. de Meath chose a β-lactam antibiotic to kill an organism that has no cell wall. Her locum prescribed an antimicrobial agent that would stop it from growing but wouldn't kill it. You gave your wife a medication that inhibits neutrophil chemotaxis."

"What's that?"

"Non-steroidal anti-inflammatories paralyse white blood cells in their tracks." Sababa said. "No white cell mobility, no immunity. No justice, no peace."

"Are you saying that I made Diana's infection worse?"

"Absolutely." He said. "Diana has an atypical community-acquired 'walking' pneumonia she got from one of her students. It's early, but still the season for mycoplasma."

"What's causing my blue fingers?" She asked.

"Dr. de Meath's locum had the insight to order a direct Coombs antiglobulin test and cold agglutinins." He said. "Your titres came back high at 1:16000."

"How does that work?" Alan asked.

"At lower temperatures, IgM antibodies to mycoplasma activate the complement cascade causing red cells to burst and clog up her distal capillaries. Blue fingers and toes and the tip of her nose."

"And ears." Diana said.

"And ears." Sababa wrote out a prescription.

"Stay warm inside, no cold drinks, and take this tetracycline prescription." He said. "All of it. Call my office and tell Mercy I'll see you in a week."

"Can I bring my husband?" Diana asked.

"Of course." Sababa smiled. "He should have recovered from the humiliation."

Shadows ran from themselves on the blank canvas behind the eyelids of Sababa's slumber. They danced to a symphony in white major, white noise nights in white satin, blinded by the white before Christmas. Scents of lily-white jasmine, the almonds of white heliotrope, and the apricots of white oleander perfumed the white room white sheets.

The professor tasted white peppered white meat with white wine and white rice and white bread, and a white chocolate mousse of egg white and white sugar. His white matter and white blood cells, asleep in his white coat, watched a white-knuckled whitemare of white fang and white rhinos and white elephants and great white sharks running White Nile whitewater over white cliffs into white light. An old man with a white cane waved a white feather and a white flag. White was his colour of mourning. He asked Sababa about the great white way and the great white hope, white magic and white lies, the white man's burden and white privilege, white knights and white power, and white trash and white-collar crime. *White in the moon the long road lies that leads me from my love.*

The winter sun was missing from the polar horizon. Sababa rose from his hospital cot early for the mandatory monthly Department of Medicine meeting. He found most of his colleagues trying to grab a quick java in the main lobby at Code Brew, bunched up like a handful of fat fingers on a touchscreen phone.

Marquis Shu Ying had ordered his piccolo latte, Ernie 'The Big Easy' Hacker his flat white, Dasco Boet his straight black, Ed Hyde his anemic decaf, and Sid Shalimar his cappuccino.

"Quadruple expresso, Professor?" Asked the barista.

"Espresso doppio doppio." Sababa confirmed. "By whatever beans necessary."

All the men walked together down a side hallway, on their journey to the Forbidden Zone. Inside the Administration Board Room, the big bear patriarch of the department, Peter Zaias, Chief Defender of the Faith, seer of the Sacred Scrolls, waited for them to find their favorite fabric Mayline chairs. Their landings agitated powerful earthy union odours of dust and must and rotting corpses from the particulate debris of past deliberations, lurking under the table in the claret pile carpet. For here was the morgue of ambition.

The final department member strolled into the midst of his peers after they had all taken their seats. Dr. Wayward Woods, still missing an internal clock, arrived clutching his Tim Hortons Double Double, like a monk late for a monastery mass.

The scorn of previous hospital administrators, their picture frames lining the fuzzy light green-yellow padded walls in full black and white mediocrity, scowled down at the reluctant assembly.

The white stippled acoustic tile ceiling, constructed to absorb the screams of the defeated, bored out with pot lights and grooved in a railway yard of track lighting, was controlled by a far wall bank of knobs and switches to focus photons and heat.

A long teak conference table, halfway between a boat and a racetrack, polished with oil and buffed with a soft towel, filled the centre, racing the waist-high wooden wall sideboard cabinet next to it down the length of the room. The only two items on the table were an open box of tissues, and a multifunction business-class conference digital phone console. Dr. Zaias picked up a handset and dialed zero.

"Lana, can you announce the start of the Department of Medicine meeting?" The hospital switchboard operator's Big Voice broadcast the assembly overhead.

At the far end of the room, a wall-mounted HDTV screen hung next to a melamine whiteboard on an easel with a rainbow tray of desiccated felt markers. Whoever had written this message on the whiteboard would have had to have picked the lock to the Board Room.

'An Island Health administrator was driving past a farm one day when he noticed a pig with a wooden leg. He thought little of it until a week later, driving by the same farm, the pig now had two wooden legs. The third week, the pig had three wooden legs, and after seeing the pig in the fourth week with four wooden legs, he had to inquire.

The bureaucrat tracked down the farmer and asked him about the strange sight. "Well, that there is the greatest pig alive." The farmer said. "A month ago, he saved my wife and kids and me from our burning house by waking us up in the middle of the night just in time for us to escape without any harm."

The manager continued to prod the farmer about the pig's wooden legs.

"Well." The farmer replied. "This pig is one of the family. A couple of weeks ago, our youngest boy fell in the creek, and this wonderful pig fished him out in time to save him from drowning. He is one special pig."

The official, losing his patience, inquired again about the wooden legs.

"Last week, I fell off my horse and my foot got caught up in the stirrup." The farmer said. "This great pig ran alongside the horse and me and untangled me and saved my life. He's the greatest pig in the world."

Caving in under the suspense, the medical mandarin shouted. "All right already, enough. He's a great pig. But what about the wooden legs?"

"Well now, a pig like that." The farmer said. "You don't eat him all at once."'

Dr. Zaias called the council to order and requested approval of the previous meeting's minutes. A cacophony of grunts echoed around the table. They dealt with the more mundane aspects of their otherwise exciting existences, leaving a paper trail of 'ayes' and 'nays' and tabled motions until the next time. Halfway through the proceedings they were joined by the man in the thousand-dollar suit, held together with impeccable cuffs and collars, silk ties and linen handkerchiefs, and new silver cuff links to secure his Cardin shirtsleeves. In his manicured fingers he held a recently purchased platinum pen, poised to doodle on monogrammed paper holding the timeless, the ageless, reports. Both his old cufflinks and writing paraphernalia had been professionally purloined by Maxey Road, an American Hell's Angel patient of Sababa's, during what Malcolm thought had been a heartfelt hug for the excellent medical care he had received during his stay at Harbour City Regional.

Malcolm Canmore was the Chief Hospital Administrator of Harbour City Regional, the CHA, the CEO, the COO, the COG, the CAD, the CON, the CUR, the grand omnipotent stomper of supermen. In a universe that used chaos as fuel, Malcolm represented order. Every day, he cleaned his navel with a cotton bud soaked in witch hazel.

Sababa muttered under his breath. He and Malcolm were natural foes, and the Good Doctor preferred it that way. And Malcolm disliked men like Sababa because, whereas men made the rules for Malcolm, Sababa knew that only Mother Nature made the rules for him, and Sababa scorned the ones made for and by Malcolm.

"You think I'm the devil, don't you, Sababa?" Malcolm once asked.

"You're not the devil, Malcolm." He said. "You're practice."

But the manicured monogrammed man had a devilish special agenda item he wanted to add at the last minute, the way he always did.

"As you know, gentlemen, Island Health, like its predecessor the Vancouver Island Health Authority, and the Central Vancouver Island Health Authority before that, is no more."

"What have they entitled this entitled evasive entity now?" Sababa asked.

"To answer that, I've invited the latest managementship of the health region to speak to us this morning. It is my great pleasure to introduce an old friend and colleague, our new chief executive, Foster Care." A tanned muscular older clone of the last managementshipwreck strode into the Boardroom accompanied by a full crop of wavy white hair above a wide grin full of perfect white teeth, and eight of his minions. They were from the Underworld.

"Thank you for that glowing introduction, Malcolm." Foster began. "Our health region authority has been renamed to better reflect the new values of our reorganization. Henceforth, we shall be known as iHealth." He took a bite out of a shiny apple and placed what was left on the board room table.

"To complement the new digital database debacle?" Sababa asked. Malcolm glared.

"This is Doctor Sababa, Foster." He said. "His specialty is street medicine."

"Perhaps that's where he should practise?" Said Der Weisse Engel. "I understand you have an issue with our new Electronic Health Record initiative?"

"I have a billion." Sababa said. "That's what it's cost us in American dollars so far, money that could have been better spent on a dialysis unit, gastroenterology and interventional cardiology recruitment, and a new ICU."

"Growing pains." Foster protested.

"Why do you think we have so many medication and treatment errors?" Sababa asked. "Why do you think that Dasco Boet and the rest of us that do critical care have gone back to paper?"

"Sometimes you have to break a few eggs to make an omelet." Foster said.

"You can't polish a turd." Sababa said. "Gentlemen, I give you the Dunning–Kruger effect, another low ability bureaucrat overestimating his aptitude. If you're incompetent, Foster, how can you know you're incompetent? The skills you need to produce a right answer are the skills you need to recognize what a right answer is. Gentlemen, I give you a full metal administralian afflicted with the cognitive bias of illusory superiority, an ultracrepidarian excusing his ignorance with the law of triviality, sliding down Hanlon's razor."

"Hanlon's razor?" Foster asked.

"Never attribute to malice that which is adequately explained by stupidity." Sababa said. "The ratio of supporters to critics rises and then falls to oblivion. Anything you worship will eat you alive."

"Our iHealth rebranding and launch will make us a Centre of Excellence."

"All the name changes are bureaucratic bloat." Sababa said. "The only thing all you serial Bananas Fosters have done is downgrade us from a real Centre of Excellence to a Centre of Effort and now, a Centre of Eh. Throw physic to the dogs; I'll none of it."

"We will run this health care system, Doctor Sababa." Foster said. "With or without your support."

"You couldn't run a bath."

Big Voice went critical in the boardroom's overhead speakers. *Code Blue. Emergency acute room... Code Blue. Emergency acute room... Code Blue. Emergency acute room...*

A few wisps of smoke, the only remnants of Sababa ever having attended the meeting, rose from the seat of his Mayline chair.

> 'When you know who you are; when your mission is clear and you burn with the inner fire of unbreakable will; no cold can touch your heart; no deluge can dampen your purpose. You know that you are alive.'
>
> Chief Seattle, *Duwamish*

Pandemonium played for keeps in the Harbour City Regional emergency acute room. Sababa entered a maelstrom of physicians and ER and ICU nurses and ECG and laboratory portable x-ray technicians and respiratory therapists swirling around an unconscious native elder. The EMT ambulance attendants and paramedics that had delivered him to this promised land took turns administering CPR and counting chest compressions.

In the middle of the mêlée, Dr. Alex Harding was the sultan of swing.

"I'm in charge." He shouted. "Stop CPR." The paramedic performing compressions was grateful for the break.

"No pulse!" Angie yelled.

"Flatline!" Regina roared after hooking up her monitor leads.

"Pupils fixed and dilated!" Dr. Gung Ho called out.

"Continue CPR." Alex instructed. Another paramedic restarted the compressions. "Do not jostle the patient."

Dr. Ho fired an endotracheal tube into the old man's airway and handed off the Ambu bag he had attached to one of the blue uniforms. Dr. Carlton dropped an esophageal probe into the bottom third of the old man's esophagus.

"We need a story here, boys." He said.

"76-year-old local Snuneymuxw chief." Said the senior paramedic. "Found by one of his daughters at the cemetery in the reservation. More like a reservation in the cemetery. No comorbid diseases. She didn't know how long he'd been exposed."

"A long time." Cliffy said. "His core temperature is only 19 °C." There came a flurry of fists and fingers.

"We can't get venous access." Michaela shouted.

"You won't." Alex said. "He's too shut down. Can we get an extracorporeal membrane oxygenation machine?"

"Only if you fly back to Boston and bring us one." Cliffy said. Alex fired two spring-loaded B.I.G. bone injection guns into both the old man's tibias, connected two pressurized litre bags of warmed saline, and ran both wide open into the old man's marrow.

"I have a femoral central line." Gung said. He hooked up a third bag of warmed isotonic crystalloid as Alex placed two peritoneal catheters into the chief's abdominal cavity and infused two more warmed litres.

"Epinephrine 1 mg IV now." He said. "And begin low-dose IV dopamine 2.5 mcg/min."

"Finger-stick glucose normal." Dina said. Michaela placed an indwelling Foley catheter in the old man's bladder.

"You got a name?" Alex asked.

"Watt." Cliffy said.

"A name."

"Watt."

"What?"

"No, Watt." Cliff said. "Wakasiah Watt."

"You need anything more than a complete blood count, electrolytes, and BUN and creatinine?" Asked the lab tech with the blood sample Dr. Ho had retrieved from his central venous line.

"Add a serum lactate, fibrinogen, creatine kinase, and lipase." Alex ordered. "RT, I need an initial blood gas, uncorrected for temperature."

"On it." Said one of the blue uniforms.

"Temperature now 21 °C." Cliffy said. "Should we also warm him externally?"

"No suh." Alex said. "Onna-conna the afterdrop in core temperature and pH you'll produce from his frozen periphery."

"Well look at Herschel Shmoikel Pinchas Yerucham Krustofsky here." Cliffy said. "Where did you get so smart?"

"Light dawns ovah Mahblehead." Alex said.

"Huh?"

"It's an expression of affection, Cliffy." Sababa said. "Run with it."

Twenty minutes into the resuscitation, Alex drained the peritoneal fluid he had instilled and ran in another two litres of warm saline. Sweat drenched those who had taken turns performing chest compressions.

"Temperature now 25 °C." Cliffy said.

"Stop CPR." Alex ordered. The EMT doing compressions collapsed off the patient's chest.

"No pulse!" Angie yelled.

"Flatline!" Regina roared.

"Pupils fixed and dilated!" Dr. Gung Ho called out.

"Continue CPR." Alex instructed. Another paramedic restarted the compressions.

"Epinephrine 1 mg IV now." He said. "And start a norepi IV infusion at 1 mcg/minute."

Dr. Ho read out the arterial blood gas and other lab results to the assembled multitude. Every number was as ugly as it could be.

"Dead of winter." Cliffy said.

"He's not dead until I say he's dead." Alex said. "And that won't happen until he's warm and dead."

"You've been eating the yellow snow, Krusty."

"Pissah." Alex said.

"Too bad he's a Coast Salish native and not a Greenlandic Inuit." Sababa mused.

"Why is that?"

"Fifteen percent of them have a trehalase enzyme deficiency."

"Meaning what?"

"Trehalose is a sugar composed of two glucose molecules." He said. "It's the major carbohydrate energy storage molecule used by dragonflies and grasshoppers and locusts and butterflies and bees for rapid flight, but it also reduces the freezing point of fluids. Tardigrades, also called water bears, are microscopic multicellular organisms that can survive freezing at low temperatures by replacing most of their internal water with the trehalose, preventing the crystallization that otherwise damages cell membranes. Both the resurrection plant and New Zealand wetas also use it to survive being frozen solid."

"So if Wakasiah Watt here was an Eskimo pie, he'd have a better chance of surviving this severe hypothermia."

"We don't use the term 'Eskimo' anymore." Sababa said. "It means 'eater of raw meat.'"

"It may still be an accurate description of what this exposure will have done to him."

Twenty more minutes into the resuscitation, Angie's voice exploded across the acute room.

"He's shivering!" She shouted. "He's shivering!"

"Temperature now 30 °C." Cliffy said. "What's the temperature of the room?"

"It's always room temperature." Alex said. "You know about the Hahvud Law?"

"The school?"

"No, the rule." Alex said. "Under controlled conditions of light, temperature, humidity, and nutrition, the organism will do as it damn well pleases. Stop CPR." The RT performing chest compressions crawled off the table.

"I can feel a pulse." Angie yelled.

"He has a rhythm." Regina pointed to the monitor waveform. "But it's slow. And weird."

"Get me a 12-lead." Alex ordered. The ECG technician who had waited an hour for this moment ran off a cardiogram.

"Wow." Cliffy grabbed it off the machine. "Profound junctional bradycardia, prolongation of all ECG intervals, and an acute ST-elevation global myocardial infarction."

"Nope." Sababa said. "Those are just Osborn J waves. Give me a rhythm I can dance to." Cliffy thumped the old man's breastbone. Ventricular tachycardia danced across the monitor screen.

"Well, that helped a lot." Sababa pulled the paddles from the defibrillator. "360 watt-sec Regina." The ER nurse dialed in the joules and pressed the charge button. A rising whine filled the room.

48

"Clear!" Sababa roared, and everyone watched Wakasiah Watt's chest jump into the air before he thumped back into normal sinus rhythm and onto the table.

"Pupils still fixed and dilated." Dr. Ho called out.

"I have a pressure of 70 mmHg systolic." Angie let the arm cuff down.

"This guy is some Brownie." Alex said. Stanzy, who had joined the festivities after she arrived with the family out in the waiting room's underwater light, the sigh who came in from the cold, flashed him a disapproving glare.

"That's not what you think." Alex said. "In Boston, it's somebody with a high tolerance for cold temperatures, from the L Street Brownies, who were famous for swimming in frigid ocean waters in the winter."

"Not acceptable." Stanzy said.

"OK." Alex said. "I'll have a portable chest x-ray now please."

"You're watching history here." Sababa said. "Hypothermia was the ultimate weapon of war in many military campaigns, from Hannibal's loss of half his men in the Second Punic War in 218 B.C. to the destruction of Napoleon's armies in Russia in 1812, to the annihilation of the German 5th army in the Battle of Stalingrad. Hypothermia killed the passengers of the RMS Titanic and RMS Lusitania and MS Estonia. Exposure exterminated Polar explorers Franklin and Scott and their men. Much of our knowledge has come from horrendous human experimentation during World War II. The Nazis threw some of their victims into boiling water for rewarming."

"You always provide a perspective designed to please, Sab." Cliffy said.

"Pupils react to light!" Dr. Ho called out.

"Hey, Cliffy." Alex said. "Differential diagnosis for resurrection. Go."

"You're confusing resuscitation with resurrection, Krusty."

"Are you kidding me?" Alex said. "This guy is better than Lazarus. This guy could be Frickin' Jesus Christ himself."

"You sure he's alive?"

"Life is water at the right temperature in the right atmosphere in the right light for a long enough period of time." Wakasiah moved his arms and legs with purpose. "He's alive."

As the effort spent on the successful resuscitation sank into the muscles and sinew and bones of the participants, everyone went about their designated responsibilities. They prepared Wakasiah for his journey to Tranquility Base. As Sababa watched them wheel the chief out of the acute room, he sat at the consultant's desk to dictate his consultation and debrief his young apprentice on his performance.

"How did I do?" Alex asked.

"Fine." Sababa said. "You did fine."

"Almost everyone seems friendly enough."

"Don't look for friends here, Alex." Sababa said. "You won't find them. None of these people understand you. They never will. Mediocre

49

internists will see you and feel themselves wilting in your shadow. Do not shrink to console them. If you're lucky, one day when you're old and wizened like me, you'll find a young doctor with little regard for anything but their craft, and you'll train them as I train you. Until then, step by step, walk the thousand-mile road. You have greatness in you, Alex. Don't you dare disappoint me."

"Does that ever happen?" Alex asked.

"You're the fourth resident I've had this year." He said. "Of the three who came before you on my watch, one switched to law school, one got pregnant, and one died. You're my last hope, Alex. You'd better not do anything funny."

Sababa punched his computer keyboard and selected a tune from his music library on a secret drive hidden deep inside the hospital computer network. Rock 'n roll filled the empty room.

'I've seen it before
It happens all the time
Closing the door
You leave the world behind...
You know that you are
As cold as ice to me.
Foreigner, *Cold as Ice*

'Snowflakes are one of nature's most fragile things, but just look what they can do when they stick together.'
Vesta Kelly

The casual reader might be interested in Wakasiah Watt's journey to the underworld from the end of Shoreline Road. What he or she might not know is the four elements that formed the Snuneymuxw chief's spirit—his *snenç* corpse, his inner and outer *s-hulí* soul, his *shxweli* life force, and his *st'leluqum* ghost. He believed that the day he made his snow bed on the grave of Chief Joe Wyse, his body would die and his soul would walk the two-day forest trail around a mountain lake to reach the netherland river valley where it would live with his ancestors in the afterlife, pulling canoes, hunting and fishing, shapeshifting into guardian animals, ceremonial winter spirit singing and storytelling and dancing on the longhouse floor, embarking on vision quests, and hosting potlatches. Here were fir tips for nutrients, maple wood for smoking meat, the leaves for regalia, and the bark for soaking wool. Here were medicines for healing—pitch to cure TB, salal to coagulate a wound, seafoam for warts, deer fat for eczema, and moss to soften hair.

But Wakasiah was conflicted about leaving his living family. He hoped his *shne'um* shaman might still save him by recovering his soul as he travelled between the two worlds. The old man found himself gazing down into the valley of the shadow when he had completed the first day of his trek. It was cold. He shivered for a second time. He felt warm water in his marrow and belly, his heartbeat return to his chest, and the cacophony of seagulls and frantic noises, before the first light rose on the spume-spangled surface of the Salish Sea, the reflected mirrors of flashing lighthouses, dense star trails in the heavens, and then the golden glow of resurrection.

Wakasiah Watt's eyes opened to find the Good sisters and the rest of his living family and Stanzy gathered around him.

"I didn't know you were coming." He said.

"It would have been rude to tell you." Pretty Good said. No one mentioned his son, Four Watt. Wakasiah squinted at another familiar face at the end of his bed.

"Takta Sababa." He said.

"Hulítun." Dew Good said. *Healer.*

"And I'm your critical care nurse, Mary." Said the unfamiliar face. "Is there anything you need?"

"I'm hungry." The elder said. "Is there a restaurant nearby to eat lunch when I'm better?"

"There's the White Spot." It was out of Mary's mouth before she realized how bad it had sounded. "And Montana's is just down the street."

"That's a cowboy place." He said. "We're Indians."

> 'Grief does not expire like a candle or the beacon on a lighthouse. It simply changes temperature.'
>
> Anthony Rapp

There are three leading concepts in thermodynamics: energy, entropy, and absolute temperature.

It might first appear that Sababa's energy was infinite. He seemed to be a perpetual motion machine. But there are no 'hottest' parts of hell because that implies a temperature difference, and any competent physicist could use this to run a heat engine and make some other part of hell cool. This is impossible and contravenes the basic laws of chemistry. Entropy embodies the concept of falling apart. Every inanimate object is eventually room temperature.

And temperature variation must obey the ideal gas law. No matter how much pressure was applied to the portly professor, Sababa's ability to absorb and apply new knowledge, occupying that constant space between hot-blooded and cold-blooded, maintained the temperature necessary for sustaining life.

The first patient that Dr. Alex Harding saw at Harbour City Regional, Sylvie Denis, did have primary cryofibrinogenemia as the cause of her leg ulcers. She had a relapse the following winter but has stabilised on more aggressive immunosuppressive therapy and has returned to her job as a physical therapist.

To ski or not to ski was never the question. Instructor Jean-Baptiste Lully always maintained that his was the only sport where you spent an arm and a leg to break an arm and a leg. Despite Sababa's best efforts to treat his mixed cryoglobulinemia, the wet gangrene worsened in all four limbs. After Dr. Piggy Muldoon amputated both legs above the knee, Jean-Baptiste went into septic shock and it was downhill from there.

Meteorologist Paulina Strübing was not as pure as the driven snow. A forecast of six inches was received on her back with her legs in the air. The bad blood of syphilis had put her under the weather. Her secondary paroxysmal cold hemoglobinuria went away with Sababa's antibiotic treatment, but not before she required amputation of the front half of her left foot, and her right index and ring fingers from dry gangrene. Paulina was lost to follow-up.

Dr. Sababa's administration of dantrolene in the operating room saved heating contractor Nathanael Greene from the malignant hyperthermia that Dr. Banjo Paterson had induced with his sevoflurane anesthetic. His surgeon discharged him a few days later. Nathaneal's genetic testing returned positive for a ryanodine 1 receptor mutation on the long arm of chromosome 19. His family tree lit up like Christmas.

Armen Tamzarian's familial Mediterranean fever responded better to Sababa's colchicine prescription than Sababa responded to the school principal's sunny Ararat Armenian cognac. Jane Sababa threatened to spirit away Sababa's free spirit into a disembodied spirit in the spirit world if the holy spirit ever moved him in that spirit again.

Harold Peridol spent three days in the Death Star with his neuroleptic malignant syndrome before he was stable enough to transfer to the fifth-floor medical ward. Dr. Robert La Capuche discharged him on less noxious medications for his paranoid schizophrenia. He continues to see Doctor Sababa in his Manzanita clinic for diabetic management. In his job as a disc jockey on CNDN radio, Harold often plays Jimmy Buffett's *Island Fever* or Todd Rundgren's *Fever Broke*, dedicated to the professor who saved him.

Because of her chilblains, Sarah Medhurst Troughton had to give up teaching figure skating to become the flat-track roller derby coach of the Harbour City Hydras. She has since changed her name to Buzzsaw.

Benjamin Aaron, the BC Hydro power line technician, had his hypothalamic thermoregulatory set-point rebooted with Sababa's prescription for clonidine. His body temperature is now normal. The portly professor published his case in the medical literature as the 51st Shapiro's syndrome on the planet.

Paulo Aegineta's PseudoSweet's Syndrome vanished with Sababa's multibacillary multidrug treatment of his leprosy. Back in his home city of Santarém, Brazil, Paolo often yearns for raw armadillo liver ceviche. With onions.

The adult-onset Still's disease that blinded the far-sighted plans of optometrist Eric Bywaters is now in remission with Sababa's administration of steroid and methotrexate therapy." And Alex Harding can now identify the colour of a salmon.

Dr. Alan Statham's wife, Diana, is the picture of wellness again since Sababa stopped the radiologist from dabbling in the white art that belonged to the stocky savant. Every spring the radiologist supplies the Good Doctor with rare heirloom tomato starters, in exchange for his latest fictionalized book of memoirs.

Wakesiah Watt, the revered hereditary chief of the Snuneymuxw First Nation, was in hospital for the funerals of his wife, Julia, and his son, Four Watt. But he abandoned any further attempts to join them in their afterlife underworld, grateful as he was to realize how much the Good sisters and the rest of his family and tribe loved him that much to want him to stay until it was his turn. His time to walk the two-day trail came three years later. No one knows for sure, but some have dreams of him happy in the netherworld river valley, singing and storytelling and dancing on the longhouse floor.

And what of the oxymoronic health authority and its new managementshipwreck, Foster Care? Sababa didn't trust a man who could blow hot and cold with the same breath. He knew that the hot heads and cold hearts of these dark suits would bring an evil malevolence to Harbour City Regional, but he didn't yet know what it was, or its name. They would call her *VICTORIA*.

In the meantime, Sababa remained in that constant space halfway between hot-blooded and cold-blooded, maintained the temperature necessary for sustaining life, that of the outside condensation on a glass of ice-cold whiskey on a hot day.

20. The Case of the Cedar Shakes and Shingles

'When this old world starts getting me down
And people are just too much for me to face
I climb way up to the top of the stairs
And all my cares just drift right into space.'
The Drifters, *Up on the Roof*

He wasn't the same young roofing stud muffin he had been when he started. It seemed like only yesterday. Today his knees crackled like breaking branches, his skin was old leather, and the same white crawled through his beard as the flakes that fell on his job site.

The winters came around fast now, but his youth was all used up, and the bills kept piling up like drifts of snow. For thirty years he had earned a living with these hands and those tools, and it was too late to change course now. He hoped to make fifty before they put him underground.

But with the way he'd been feeling all week, that wouldn't happen. He had developed a headache and feverishness, pain in his right ear, and a case of the whirlies, which his wife suggested should keep him away from high places.

The call had come from Jack Nash, the owner of the tavern in Cedar, who had discovered the leak and needed it fixed. Jack had built the Crow and Gate back in 1972 before the ink was dry on the new provincial liquor laws that would allow neighbourhood pubs. The South Saxon had taken it on as a labour of love. He imported timber and furnishings and windows and memorabilia as the raw material of his dream. Construction entailed great attention to detail—pegged exposed beam and plaster, massive stonework open fireplaces, heavy wood trestle tables, low ceilings, dark wood, bar service only—all clad with authentic pub memorabilia from the U.K.—to create the perfect ambiance of a southern Tudor-style English country pub. Jack had created ten acres of Sussex in the middle of nowhere, complete with an English garden and a pond with a resident family of frolicking black swans.

The Crow was the first public house in British Columbia and a template of what a neighbourhood drinking hole should be—a parallel universe where an independent publican was free to operate outside the brawny arm of the beer oligarchy's distribution channels. The Crow served imported bitters and other beers and made their food from scratch. It wasn't a destination restaurant so much as it was a destination. Beef dip sandwiches and crab cakes and oyster stews and steak & kidney pies and Melton Mowbrays and Scotch eggs—The plain fare was as authentic as the cursive on the blackboard. And the leak in the roof.

"How much do you think this will cost me?" Jack had asked.

"Sky's the limit." The roofer smiled.

Holden Corso strapped on his back brace and cracked his fingers to make them work. He hoisted the composition bundles and shouldered their dead weight up his extension ladder. He climbed up again with a rusty coffee can full of galvanized nails, the whittled stub of a pencil, a chalk line, a spirit level, his tool belt, and his radio.

Up on the roof, Holden Corso had a view of surrounding hayfields, the Douglas fir forest around Quennell lake, and the ice caps of the coastal mountain range. The silence was as deafening as the air was rarified.

If Holden on been on this roof in the summer, overlooking the adjacent grassy field of the Cedar Sunday market, he would have enjoyed a feast for all his senses. He let that wash over him before he set to work.

In his mind's eye were plain clad country folk at their clatter of stands and tables and tents, trading with rough gnarled hands and sun-wrinkled faces and the smell of sweat and earth. Amid the squeals of children and sips of coffee, he recognized each of the vendors from their hippy hair and the same clothes they wore to the market every week.

There were homemade breads and savouries and sweets from the Red Bird and Well Bred bakeries and MagPies and the Bite Me Cookie Company and Beaver House fudge, jams and jellies from Sue's Preserves and I be Jammin, Russian garlic from the handlebar moustache at one end of the fair, exotic spices and Carolina reaper hot pepper sauce from the Iranian at the other, grass fed beef from Henry and Jones and other meats from Depot Dawgs and Cedar Valley Poultry, cheese from the Happy Goat Cheese Company, fish and shellfish from Driftwood Seafood and Captain Jack, pasta and sauces and salsas and soup mixes from Seafire Soups, eggs and vegetables and fruit and honey from farms with names like Fat Chili and Dancing Frog and YellowPoint and Greenfire and Omega Blue, coffee and tea from Misty Ridge, nursery plants from Island Passions, fresh flowers from State of Grace, faery birdhouses from Westholme Wonder Works, incense sticks and candles from Twilight Aromas, handmade soaps from Sarah's Garden and Seatree Body and Home, and leather and pottery and artisanal clothes and jewelry and similar craftwork from two dozen other skilled artists.

But that was then, and this was now and now was the time for the roofer to refocus his mind and energy on the task at hand. He turned on his radio for company.

Rise and Shine Harbour City... This is your woke up call on CNDN Coast Salish radio, 101.3 FM on your Home and Native Band. I'm your host, BC Bud...

Holden brushed off the snow to track down the source of the leak. He found broken shakes, gaps in the flashing, and signs of local wear and tear. He split the damaged shakes with a hammer and chisel, removed the pieces with a set of pliers, and used a hacksaw to cut off the nails that secured the broken shakes. Holden's confidence in his ability to wield sharp and heavy tools on a pitched surface was shaky. But he still got by with the notion that sweat dries, blood clots, and bones heal.

If you're working outside today trying to perfect your ice tan, remember that 150 people die every year from being hit by falling coconuts... Don't worry, Twinkies, drug makers are developing a vaccine...

He pushed a roll of tarpaper across the slope, running the dark edge down his chalk line like he'd been bending over a star chart unrolled forever. He set his shakes in courses, climbing from drip edge to roof beam, each as secure as the nails could make them.

All dreams spin out from the same web close to the Great Spirit... Everyone who is successful must have dreamt of something... Here's a little number from our snowflake friends, The Drifters...

Holden used his utility knife to trim the new shakes to fit the gaps made by the old ones, allowing room for expansion. He slid the new shakes into position and secured them each with two galvanized nails at an upward angle below the edge of the shake above it.
After placing a wooden block against a new shake, he struck it with his hammer to tap it into place and used a putty knife to seal any exposed nail heads with roofing cement.
He sat in the vault of heaven, swinging his hammer hand along the peak of the roof, snow patching, metal flashing.

On the roof, it's peaceful as can be... and there the world below can't bother me...

Down on the ground, it was hard for him to measure how well he was doing, but up on the roof he was sustained by the clear consensus of the ghosts of the great roofers of yesteryear, nodding their approval at work well done. And then he smelled the burning tires and rotten fish and sewage and déjà vu and fear.
"Allahu Akbar!" He cried. "I see you, Mohammed!"

On the roof, the only place I know... where you just have to wish to make it so...

Holden Corso felt nausea churning in his stomach and saliva rising in his throat. His sweat dripped like mud. All the fetid fetors forced him to hold his breath. His right forehead went into spasm. Holden tore off his pants and underwear, almost tumbling off the roof before regaining his balance. He uttered profane curses as blue as the air. His hips gyrated as he rubbed his groin into a frenzy. The twitching of his forehead migrated to the other side and down his neck into his left arm which then fell useless at his side. In a fraction of a split second, at the speed of an electric discharge, like the second coming, the roofer experienced ecstasy and ejaculation and epilepsy in less than the time it took him to slide off into oblivion.

We are made from Mother Earth and we go back to Mother Earth... Ground zero...

And like the vendors of the Cedar Sunday Market, Holden Corso went back to the land.

You can't wake someone who is not asleep...

'I see you rushing now
Tell me how to reach you
I see you rushing now
What did Harvard teach you?'
The National, *Sea of Love*

The day before Holden Corso performed his swan dive off the sloped roof of the Crow and Gate Pub, Alex Harding waited in line at Code Brew to buy an early morning cup of coffee.
"Next." The barista was a sculpture of transdermal metal and subdermal ink. "What can I get you?"
"Truth serum." Alex said. "Something to allow me to hear the hiss of daybreak extinguished."
"Can you be a little more specific?"
"I'll have a regulah."
"What's that?"
"Cream and two sugahs."
"Anything else?"
"One of those dunkies." He pointed to a donut on a shelf in the glass display case.
"You mean a beavertail?"
"Yah huh, whatevah." Alex counted out the strange new coins and made for the nearest stairwell to the Harbour City Regional basement. Sababa had told him about the 'bunker,' that sterile subterranean windowless doctor's lounge, where he might meet other medical staff to share in conversation and commiseration. In the deepest bowels of the hospital,

Alex found a numbered door and used his key card to enter. Inside were a few staff photographs and paintings on bone-white walls, a bank of printers that spat out corrugated patient lists, shelves of medical texts and clinical journals, and bulletin boards which advertised lectures and concerts and rental properties and second-hand sales and the latest creative pursuits of professional spouses. Odours of ozone and cleaning fluids and old coffee and pastry butter, and insomnia permeated the space. He hovered in front of a framed formula.

A Statistical Method for Resolving Clinical Disputes in Medical Practice

$$CW = a + b/(c + 1)K_1 + d/3 + e + f/25 - 4(g) - 2(K_2) + h/44,000 \text{ where}$$

CW = clinical wisdom
a = years of postgraduate training
b = years in practice
c = number of failing attempts to pass specialty boards
K_1 = prestige constant (derived from source of MD degree)
   1 = Harvard or John Hopkins
   2 = other East Coast medical school
   3 = other US medical school
   4 = foreign medical school
d = journal articles published, excluding single case reports
e = journals subscribed to
f = total accumulated Category I CME credits
g = malpractice suits lost or settled
K_2 = diminished capacity constant:
   1 = specialized in dermatology, OB/GYN, or psychiatry
   2 = employed in VA hospital
   3 = over 50% annual gross income derived from weight reduction clinics
   4 = addicted to alcohol, sedative-hypnotics or narcotics
   5 = currently taking phenothiazines for major psychiatric disorder
h = annual gross income

An odd number of spartan uneasy chairs circled a coffee table in the middle of the room, three of which were occupied. An obstetrician, Dr. Olaf Octagon, was waiting to deliver a baby, the orthopedic surgeon Dr. Piggy Muldoon was waiting to replace a hip, and Dr. Banjo Paterson was waiting for a call from whichever operating room called him next.
"You the new guy?" Banjo asked.
"Alex Hahding." The new guy said. "I'm from Hahvud."
"Well, that would explain the bow tie." Olaf said. "What would explain your exile?"
"I'm doing an Internal Medicine elective with Doctah Sababer." Alex took the lid off his coffee regulah.

"What did you have to do to win that prize?" Piggy asked.

"I requested it." He took a bite of his beavertail. "What can you tell me about him?"

"Sababa?" It was Banjo's turn. "When he was a kid, he wanted to be an astronaut. Went to M.I.T. and got degrees in aerospace engineering and biology and worked for NASA until he got into med school. Talked the dean into giving him $300 so he could present a paper in Las Vegas during his third-year finals. Lost the lot on a roulette wheel within five minutes of arriving at his hotel. He could talk you into eating your own shit and tell you it was nice. Even then, he was establishing a reputation as a hawk-eyed, fearless seer who would never give up and do whatever it took until he found that needle in a haystack. He once saw a patient complaining of a buzzing in his right ear that would wake him at night. Three ENT docs had examined the man and found nothing. Sababa brought him into the ER after midnight and found the wasp that was living on his eardrum. Anomalies bugged him. As a clinical clerk, the surgeons kicked him off their service because he kept finding reasons they didn't need to operate."

"What happened to the astronaut thing?"

"Sababa had the right stuff but decided he liked Internal Medicine more." Banjo said. "Went to Rio before his Royal College qualifying exams to lie in a hammock overlooking Ipanema beach." *My Harrison's, Miguel. The urge is strong today.*

"My faculty advisor, Doctah Gerald Winklah, said something about Sababer hitchhiking around the world for five years before his residency." Alex said. "Is that true?"

"He refers to it as his residency in street medicine." Olaf said. "He worked as a casualty officer in Cape Town, a pathologist and anesthesia registrar in Denmark, and a family doc in Australia and New Zealand while he lived and travelled through where the wild things were."

"Which brings us to who and what he is now." Alex ate his last beavertail morsel.

"Sababa is a genius, but he's a sonofabitch, Alex." Piggy said. "He's the guy to teach you medicine alright, and the one you want looking after you when the shit hits the fan. What he does, he does for the greater good, with a deep generosity of spirit. He is whatever Harbour City needs him to be, both healer and philosopher-king. But I'm not sure he should be your role model. Exposure to his mindset and values comes with a low therapeutic ratio. His is a thin margin between treatment and toxicity. Compared to Sababa, Occam used a safety razor. He's sarcastic and, as you'll see, intolerant of bureaucracy and other obstacles to getting at the truth."

"But you will learn about yourself under his tutelage." Olaf said.

"How's that?" Alex asked. "What would I learn that I don't already know?"

60

Banjo grinned at the new guy.
"Can you dance with the devil in the pale moonlight?'

'Good, good, good, good vibrations (oom bop bop)
She's giving me excitations (excitations)
Ah, ah, my my, what elation.'
Beach Boys, *Good Vibrations*

The overhead page extracted Alex from his collegial tutorial and patched him through to the professor.
"There are two referrals on the general medical ward." He said. "Call me when you're done."
A brown middle-aged matron with an old-fashioned starched white nursing uniform and cap greeted the young resident emerging from the fifth-floor elevator doors.
"Merry crease muss.' She said. "Hostess."
"I'm Alex Hahding." He began. "Doctah Sababer's resident."
"You are his aso shit?" She asked. Alex nodded.
"He is my payborit ductor." She said. "I yum Sophia, de head nurse of flor fibe."
"Where's Samara Morgan?" Alex asked.
"She hus lept to continue her edu-kay-shun." Sophia pointed at the stairwell with her lips. "I yum de berry huppy bunny-fish-yaree."
"Well, Sophia, I'm here to see two of your patients." Alex handed her a piece of paper inscribed with the names. *Brian Wilson... William Werbeniuk...*
"As a mutter of puck, I cun help wheat dat." She said. "Palo me." They walked into a double room down the hallway.
"Dey are penis dere brick-pus." Sophia said. "I will open delight." Two young men looked up. One was listening to an audiobook. The other was watching snooker on his television.
"Ay-bree-buddy, dis is Ductor Hardine." Sophia said. "He is a novo shit of my payborit ductor." Both patients stared at Alex's bow tie.
"I weel leeb you in piss." Sophia said as she headed back to the nursing station.
Ninety minutes later, Alex retraced his steps to page his mentor. He wasn't prepared for the exhilaration that accompanied Sababa's arrival.
"Sophia!" He shouted. "You're back."

"Dey hab gibbon me my job again!"

"Where's Samara?" He asked.

"In life, der are weiners and loosers." She said. "Samara dot she was a weiner."

"She was a weiner." Sababa said. "Let's be frank." And they laughed together in the joy of the reunion.

"I see you've met my new resident, Dr. Harding."

"I hab, but his English is excru shitting lee difficult to understand."

"I'm going to take him to see our two referrals." Sababa said. "We'll catch up later."

Down the hallway, Alex introduced the portly professor to his patients.

"Who's on first?" Sababa asked.

"Brian Wilson." He began. "22-year-old Harbor City works department worker who presented with a three-month history of recurrent attacks of prolonged hand swelling."

"Why is he in hospital?"

"I'm not sure, but I think Dr. Poldy Bloom admitted him because he knew you were on call today."

"Sometimes that happens." Sababa looked at the man's hands. They were swollen shut.

"I couldn't feed myself or go to the toilet." Brian said.

"In the past, Mr. Wilson's hands would swell a little while riding his motorcycle or mowing the lawn." Alex continued. "But yesterday he used a jackhammer for the first time at work, and his hands and forearms went full-on Popeye. No other problems, no family history of anything, and negatory review of systems."

"Exam?"

"Otherwise normal now." Alex said. "No dermatographism."

"Labs?"

"All unremarkable or negative." Alex said. "CBC, sed rate, immunoglobulins and IgE, complement levels, ANA, VDRL, cryoglobulins, skin prick testing, nada." He watched Sababa remove a tuning fork from his Columbian leather bag.

"Are you going to test his hearing?" He asked.

"Nope."

"Are you going to test his dorsal column sensation?"

"Nope." Sababa said. "I'm going to do something provocative for a change." The stocky savant struck the tuning fork tines against one of his kneecaps and placed the stem footplate on one of the Brian's. In less than a minute, the patient's knee was as big as a blowfish. Sababa repeated the manoeuvre on Brian's right forearm with the same inflated result.

"Whoa." Alex said.

"Vibratory angioedema." Sababa said. "We could have done localized histamine determinations at the time of stimulation but it doesn't matter."

"What is it?" Brian asked.

"You have an unusual swelling to vibration." Sababa said. "It's what we call a nonimmunological immediate-type hypersensitivity reaction."

"Does this mean I can't work?" He asked.

"Not with pneumatic drills, at least for a while." Sababa said. "We can desensitize you to this reaction with longer and longer periods of exposure until you don't respond to the stimulus at all."

"What now?"

"Now you go home with a note that Dr. Harding will provide for your employer, and an appointment to begin the desensitization program he'll set up with our outpatient physiotherapy department. I'll see you in my office in three weeks."

"Thanks, Doc." Brian said.

"Pleasure." Sababa refocused his attention on Alex.

"Tell me about Brian's roommate." The massive man in the next cubicle unplugged his earphones and sat up on the side of his bed.

"Big Bill Werbeniuk." Alex said. "43-year-old professional pool player. Patient of Dr. James Ruben Andrews. Admitted last night in heart failure."

"Misspent youth, Bill?"

"Choose a job you love, and you will never have to work a day in your life." The big man said. "You here to break my balls, Doc?"

"Nope." Sababa said. "I'm here to sort out your heart failure."

"No so, Sab." Alex said. "It's strange. Dr. Andrews asked us to sort out his tremor."

"What's so strange about that?" Sababa asked.

"He doesn't have one."

"Hmmm." Sababa said. "Like Sherlock Holmes in *The Adventure of Silver Blaze*."

"What do you mean?"

"The curious incident of the dog in the night-time." Sababa said. "But the dog did nothing in the night-time."

"And?"

"That was the curious incident." Sababa said. "So what are the plausible explanations for the absence of tremor?"

"One, there may not have ever been a tremor." Alex said. "The man is a professional pool player after all, and a tremor would be a major handicap."

"Continue."

"Two, the tremor may be intermittent."

"And?"

"Three, the patient may have taken something that suppressed the tremor."

"How did they treat Big Bill's heart failure on his admission last night?" Sababa asked.

"With all the medication he had been taking for his heart failure until now." Alex said. "And a new beta-blocker, propranolol. Strange."

"What's strange now?" Sababa asked.

"My faculty advisor, Doctah Gerald Winklah, was the neurologist who discovered that beta-blockers could improve familial, senile, or essential tremor. The *New England Journal of Medicine* published his work in 1974."

"Which brings us to the question of why Big Bill has heart failure." Sababa said. "At the tender age of 43."

"Dunno."

"What would be available in any pool hall or billiards parlour that could suppress a tremor for a professional pool player?" Sababa looked into blank eyes. "Where you look is where the ball will go. How much alcohol do you drink before every match, Bill?"

"At least six pints of lager before a match and one pint for each frame." Bill said. "Somewhere between 40 and 50 pints a day. I deduct it as a business expense on my tax returns."

"Hence the heart failure." Sababa said. "Alcohol-induced dilated cardiomyopathy. There's always a shot... you just have to find it."

"Maybe his tremor is from alcohol withdrawal." Alex said. Sababa turned to their patient.

"Bill?"

"I had the tremor long before I started drinking." He said. "Since I was a kid. It goes away when I'm asleep. And I don't go without a drink long enough to go through any withdrawal."

"So, no." Sababa said. "You have what we call an essential tremor, Bill. You're in good historical company—Oliver Cromwell, King Louis XV, John Adams, John Quincy Adams, Samuel Adams, Robert C. Byrd, General Douglas MacArthur, Joseph McCarthy, Eugene O'Neill, John Diefenbaker, and Katharine Hepburn—they all had the same shakes as you."

"What causes it?" Bill asked.

"We don't know." Sababa said. "But it has to do with alterations in the LINGO1 gene and GABA receptors in the cerebellum."

"If you can't find the one being hustled in the pool room, it's you." The big man said.

"Not at all." Sababa said. "The good news is that the propranolol that Dr. Andrews started you on for your heart failure will treat your tremor as well. You don't have to drink alcohol to play your sport well anymore."

"That's a suggestion, right?" Bill asked.

"It's a professional recommendation." Sababa said. "It will also help you lose weight."

"Show me a good loser and I'll show you a loser." He said. "What happens now?"

"You're out of heart failure." Sababa said. "Dr. Harding here will organize some outpatient tests and an office appointment and prescribe your discharge medication."

"That's great, Doctor Sababa." Bill said. "I'm playing in a tournament tomorrow."

Outside the room, Alex posed a question to his spiritual leader.

"I'm not sure he'll take the beta blocker." Alex said. "In some sports, it's considered a performance-enhancing drug."

"You miss 100% of the shots you don't take." Sababa said. "After you're done here, grab some lunch. I'll pick you up outside the ER at 12:30."

Alex sat at the nursing station to write up his consultation notes. He had learned how to hack the portly professor's secret M drive, the one hidden deep inside the hospital computer network. With a couple of mouse clicks, he selected a tune from Sababa's music library.

'Friends, can you feel me vibrate?
Essential tremors is such a strange way
I'm entertained till I'm numb
You gotta take it as it comes.'
    J. Roddy Walston and The Business, *Take It as It Comes*

'Do it nice and easy now don't lose control
A little bit of rhythm and a lot of soul
So come on, come on, do the locomotion with me.'
    Kylie Minogue, *The Loco-Motion*

"How's my favorite medical office assistant today?" Sababa trailed Alex into the second-floor think tank that was Manzanita Medical.

"It's loco-motion week, Boss."

"I will show Mercy to whoever she will show mercy." He pulled the first chart from the large stack on the counter and handed it to Alex.

"See one, do one, teach one." He said. "It's 'do one' time." Alex looked out on a sea of furrowed faces. His tongue tripped over a name.

"Bento de Góis." A dark middle-aged woman pushed a much older man in a wheelchair down the hallway to the resident's room.

"Joe Lee." It was the portly professor's turn to spin the wheel of fate. A young Chinese man followed him into his sanctum sanctorum. Once seated, Sababa read the patient's accompanying letter. *Dear Doctor Sababa, Please see this 31-year-old market gardener with a history of epilepsy. Is it safe for me to perform some dental work?*

"Dr. John Holliday referred you?" He asked.

"My dentist." Joe said. "He told me he wouldn't fix my teeth unless I was cleared by a medical specialist."

"Tell me about your epilepsy." Sababa said.

"I had a lot of seizures as an infant." Joe said. "They came back a couple of years ago, but none since Dr. Oliver Lax put me on an anticonvulsant."

"Which side of your body did they begin on?"

"The left side." Joe said.

"Which explains your right-sided buphthalmos."

"What's that?"

"Your right eye bulges a bit." Sababa said.

"It's also sore." Joe added. Sababa took a penlight from his Colombian leather bag and shone it on the gardener's right eye.

"Leukocoria." He said.

"Which is?

"White pupillary reflex." Sababa said. "What happened to your naevus flammeus?"

"I'm having some trouble with all these big words, Doctor Sababa." Joe said.

"The port-wine stain that used to be on the right side of your face in the distribution of your trigeminal nerve." Sababa said. "Where did it go?"

"I don't know." He said. "It faded, gone by my eighteenth birthday."

"Why did you become a market gardener, Joe?" Sababa asked.

"I wasn't much good in school." He said. "I enjoyed working in the soil better." Sababa's fingers and mouse navigated to the Harbour City Regional diagnostic imaging department. He typed in his username and password, and then Joe's name and search criteria.

"Oliver Lax ordered a CT scan of your brain when he was investigating your seizures." Sababa said. "Did he ever tell you what it showed?"

"Some of your big words." Joe said.

"Intracranial leptomeningeal angiomatosis?"

"That was it." He said. "And something about a train."

"Tram track calcifications." Sababa took a microscope slide from his Colombian leather briefcase.

"Open your mouth, please." He said. Joe opened his mouth. Sababa pressed the slide on the vermilion border of his lower lip and watched it blanch white. "Positive vitropression."

"What's that?" He asked.

"Joe, you have what we call a hemangioma, extra blood vessels, in your lower lip, in the retromolar trigone, and in the lower surface of your tongue. Your right-sided facial port-wine stain and brain and eye involvement are all related. Doc Holliday was wise to suspect that you had something that might make for dangerous dentistry."

"You have a name?" Joe asked.

"Type I Sturge-Weber syndrome." Sababa said. "Named after two of Queen Victoria's physicians. Also called encephalotrigeminal angiomatosis."

"What causes it?"

"A random somatic activating mutation in the GNAQ gene."

"Whatever." Joe said. "What now?"

"Now I write to Doc Holliday and tell him to leave well enough alone unless his work will be in an area without hypervascularization. An oral surgeon with in-hospital hemostasis expertise will have to deal with any anatomy fraught with extra blood vessels. Now I get you to see our faceless oculist guru, Dr. T.J. Eckleburg, about your right-sided glaucoma. Questions?"

"How do you know all this stuff?"

"A little science. A little magic. A little chicken soup." Sababa saw Alex hovering in his doorway. "I'll send a consultation letter to Doc Holliday with a copy to your family physician." After the two men shook hands, Sababa turned his attention to his young resident.

"What you got, Bahney?"

"Bento de Góis." Alex's pronunciation was better the second time. "71-year-old retired funeral director. Patient of Tictac Tarmac. Presents with a chronic history of progressive asymmetric proximal weakness and sensory disturbances. Nothing fascinating." Sababa raised an eyebrow.

"What's he here for?"

"A diagnosis." Alex said.

"He doesn't already have one?"

"He does." Alex said. "But his daughter has never been happy with it."

"Tell me more."

"Mr. de Góis was well until about the age of 50 when he developed difficulty walking because of buckling of his left knee. Over the next two decades, the weakness spread to his left arm, right leg, and right arm, and he experienced pins and needles with numbness of the left arm and altered temperature sensation of the lower limbs with periods of burning feet."

"And?"

"Our local neurologist, Dr. Oliver Lax, performed several investigations." Alex said. "Brain MRI showed atrophy of the cerebellum, cerebrum, and cervical spinal cord. EMG showed denervation and reinnervation, consistent with axonal motor-sensory neuropathy. Electrophysiological studies, quadriceps and sural nerve

67

biopsies, and bloodwork added nothing more. Lax told them it was a hereditary sensory and motor neuropathy. Mr. de Góis has been wheelchair-bound for the last year. There is a family history of two brothers, one of whom has some kind of cerebellar ataxia and the other who has a neurological illness comprising pyramidal features. His daughter is frustrated and wants more information."

"Exam?"

"Missing the index and middle finger of his left hand." Alex said. "His legs are cold, bluish, and swollen. He has saccadic eye movements on pursuit, asymmetric muscle atrophy, and weakness and fasciculations of his proximal muscles with absent reflexes. Sensory deficit consisted of reduced sensation to all modalities in all four limbs."

"Where's he from?"

"Australia, I think."

"You think?" Sababa asked. "Let's go see him." Inside the door of the room at the end of the hallway, the resident introduced his adviser.

"This is Doctah Sababer." Alex said. "He works in the area under the curve."

"Pleased to meet you, Bento." Sababa said. "You're from Australia?"

"Bloody oath." Everyone watched Alex's smile light up the room.

"Tell me, how did you lose those two fingers?"

"Pet crocodile."

"You had a pet crocodile?"

"They make great pets." Bento said. "Everybody had one. They're all over the island. You have to watch them, even when they're little buggers. They bite and spin and can strip your fingers in a second flat."

"Why didn't you have any other normal kind of pet?" Alex asked. "Like a dog or a cat."

"Crocodiles." Bento said.

"You're from Groote Eylandt in the Gulf of Carpenteria." Sababa mused. "Home of the Anindilyakwa People."

"How did you know that?" Bento asked.

"It is my business to know what other people don't know." He said. "Only place in Aussie where it's legal to own a saltie as a pet."

"Do you think you can find out what's wrong with my dad, Doctor Sababa?" Bento's daughter asked.

"Already working on it." He said. "Alex, what do you think of Mr. de Góis's eyes?"

"Not a lot." Alex admitted. "There may be a little lid retraction, a bit of pseudoexophthalmos perhaps."

"Perhaps." Sababa said. "This seems to be a day of bulging eyes."

"They say I'm a birdman." Bento said.

"You know about the Bird People of Groote Eylandt, Alex?" Sababa asked. The resident shook his head.

68

"About five percent of island inhabitants have a hereditary degenerative spinocerebellar disease, but we only determined its provenance in the 1990s." Sababa said. "It turned out that this condition originated in Yemeni Sephardic Jews from north-eastern-central Portugal during the Middle Ages and passed to patriarch's William Machado and Antone Joseph in the Azores. The Josephian strain migrated through Holland and Japan and India and Taiwan to Macassar traders from Sulawesi, who spent half of every year for three centuries harvesting *trepang* sea cucumbers in the Blue Mud Bay area on the eastern coast of Arnhem Land. They were the warp and woof of this story of migration and trade and sex and gene interchange—all the lasting features of the human tale—an awful lot of travel for the interchange of the tiny amine blocks which caused so much trouble."

"Do you have a name?" Bento asked.

"It has several." Sababa said. "It's called Azorean Disease or Machado-Joseph Disease or spinocerebellar ataxia type 3. We suspect an environmental factor superimposed on a genetic flaw."

"What's the genetic factor?" Alex asked.

"A mutation in the ATXN3 gene on chromosome 14q containing lengthy irregular repetitions of the code 'CAG', which produces an abnormal chaperone protein called ataxin-3, which causes degeneration of cells in the hindbrain."

"And the environmental factor?" Asked Bento's daughter.

"An abnormal high ratio of manganese to magnesium which inactivates the Mn/Mg catalyzed endonuclease 1 enzyme which protects against these excess trinucleotide genetic sequences."

"Groote Eylandt produces a quarter of the world's manganese at the BHP mine on Blue Mud Bay." Bento said. "I used to work there before I lost my fingers."

"It comes as no surprise." Sababa said.

"So, there is no cure." His daughter asked.

"No cure." Sababa said. "Just physical and occupational therapy with an optimal diet and lifestyle and exercise regimen. We'll get some genetic studies done on you and the family."

"OK, thanks Doctor Sababa." Bento said. Outside the resident's room, the professor made his point.

"You see how fascinating your birdman turned out to be?" He asked.

"Wicked pissah." Alex said.

"Batter up." Sababa took the chart on top and handed it to his apprentice.

"Susan Rodriguez." Alex called.

"Here." Came almost a whisper. She followed him down the hallway.

"Sarah Bellum." Sababa called. A middle-aged woman rose from the oxblood Childersburg traditional lounge chair in the far corner of the waiting room. She wobbled on a wide, unsteady stance and gait.

Supporting an arm, the professor escorted her into his sanctuary. He read the referral note from Dr. James Ruben Andrews. *Dear Sababa, Please see this 44-year-old jam maker for a two-week history of ataxia. Only other medical problem is bacterial vaginosis which has been difficult to eradicate. Many thanks, JRA*

"How can I help, Sarah?" He began.

"I stagg-er every-where I go." Her speech was clumsy. "Peo-ple treat me like I've been drin-king but I haven't."

"How long have you had your vaginal infection?"

"Months and months, Doc-tor." Sarah said. "It seems like for-ever. I'm tired of sme-lling like a three-day-old fish."

"Have you any idea why Dr. Andrews is having so much trouble getting rid of it for you?"

"None." She said. "I have-n't had any in-tim-ate rel-a-tions-hips for almost a year now. And I'm ta-king the-rapy to reb-al-ance my horm-ones and rev-it-al-ise my yo-ni to bec-ome more go-ddess-like."

"Your yoni?"

"It's Sans-krit." She said. "It means 'sacr-ed space,' or vag-ina."

"And how are you revitalising your yoni?"

"With va-gi-nal stea-ming and smo-king." She said. "You know of this treat-ment, of course."

"I've never smoked a vagina." Sababa admitted. "How does that work?"

"By squa-tting over ei-ther boi-ling wa-ter or a wood fire to which I add mug-wort, rose-ma-ry, worm-wood, and ba-sil." Sarah said. "V-stea-ming is an an-cient art, prac-ticed in As-ia and Af-rica for thou-sands of years."

"I would think it could be dangerous." Sababa said.

"I have scal-ded and burnt my-self a few times." Sarah said. "But it does-n't seem to be hel-ping my res-is-tant in-fec-tion."

"Because it's the cause." Sababa said. "Tell me, Sarah, what antibiotic has Dr. Andrews been giving you for your bacterial vaginosis?" She handed him a half-empty medicine bottle from her purse. Sababa looked up her medication record on the Pharmacare website.

"You've been taking metronidazole for three months now." He said. "I need to perform an examination." Sababa handed her a gown, motioned towards the changing booth, and explained what needed to come off and stay on. He performed only enough elaborate manoeuvres to find the cause of her problem, wasting no time. He tested her finger-to-nose coordination and for other manifestations of dysdiadochokinesia. When he asked her to stand straight and close her eyes, she almost fell over.

"What's go-ing on with me?" Sarah asked, back in her clothes.

"The metronidazole has affected your cerebellum." Sababa said.

"Can you fix it?"

"It should be reversible." Sababa said. "First, stop taking it. No more exposure of your tender parts to boiling water or open flame."

"But..." Sarah protested.

70

"If you were meant to grill your gonads, you would have been born with a box of matches." He said. "Here are requisitions for some bloodwork and a CT scan of your posterior fossa, and a prescription for clindamycin, to restore your holy mackerel to its natural freshness. Tell my medical office assistant I'll see you in three weeks."

Sarah thanked the professor and staggered off to seek Mercy. Alex entered as she left.

"Something fascinating, I hope, Bahney?"

"Not sure." He said. "Susan Rodriguez is a 53-year-old paging operator at Harbour City Regional referred by Dr. Poldy Bloom for a two-month history of spasmodic dysphonia."

"Not good to have a hoarse voice in that kind of occupation." Sababa said.

"No suh." Alex said. "She was originally referred to our neurologist Dr. Oliver Lax, who diagnosed multiple system atrophy and sent her to the ENT surgeon, Dr. Theodor Billroth for consideration of botox injections, or surgery as a selective laryngeal adductor denervation-reinnervation procedure or thyroplasty."

"What did Ted do?"

"Sent her to Regala, the hospital speech pathologist who figured there was a whole 'notha going on and referred her to us."

"And what did you find, my clever padawan?" Sababa asked.

"Her affect is off." Alex said. "She laughs and cries, sometimes at the same time. Her voice varies between a whisper and a honk. Cranial nerves and the rest of her exam are normal, except for an exaggerated jaw jerk reflex and intermittent dry cough."

"Let's go see her." Sababa and his apprentice marched in step down the hallway where the young resident introduced the professor.

"Susan, this is Doctah Sababer." Alex said. "He's the ultimate extinction rebel."

"How's Lana?" Sababa asked.

"She's doing extra shifts on switchboard for me so I can see you." Sue said. "This is all very confusing to me, Doctor Sababa. You're the fourth physician I've seen about this, and I'm no better. I can't go back to work until my voice recovers."

"I understand." Sababa said. "Are you having any trouble swallowing?"

"A bit." She said. "Sometimes I choke if I eat too fast."

"Can you repeat this after me, Susan?" He asked. "Buy Bobby a puppy."

"Bpuy Bpobpbpy a bpubpbpy." She said. Sababa took a penlight from his breast pocket.

"Can you open your mouth for us, Susan?" Susan opened her mouth.

"Watch carefully, Alex." Sababa said. "We don't take as much time as we need to observe anymore."

Susan's tongue writhed like a garter snake mating ball. The involuntary twitching migrated down her neck.

"Fasciculations." Alex said.

"Fasciculations." Sababa agreed.

"What is it?" Susan looked into the faces of her two doctors. "It's not good, is it?"

"It's not good, Susan." Sababa said. "You have a condition we call motor neurone disease."

"I've never heard of that one." She said.

"Most people know it as ALS." Sababa said. "You have what we call the bulbar variant."

Susan laughed and cried at the same time.

"It's going to kill me, isn't it?" She asked.

"Not for a while, Susan." Sababa said. "And we'll be there for you, all the way through this. We need a few more investigations—EMG, blood tests, MRI, and a modified barium swallow exam. And Regala will be very important to support your speech and swallowing function, so you'll be seeing her. Alex and I have to go back to the hospital now, but I'll explain more about what happens next when I see you in a week." He turned his attention to his student.

"There's a general staff meeting in the bunker." Sababa said. "We'll go there before we see the patients in emergency. Should be what you call fascinating."

'Took a class Big fun Modern Ethics 101
First day learn why Ethics really don't apply.'
Steve Taylor, *Since I Gave Up Hope I Feel a Lot Better*

Just after sunset, Sababa and Alex drove back to Harbour City Regional in time for the extraordinary general staff meeting. Camouflaged to the point of invisibility, the white dimpled and dented Honda Civic ploughed rapid and relentless through all the graded snowbanks on the way.

Down in the dungeon, the special plenary session was about to begin. There was standing room only for physician latecomers to the meeting. The professor and his protégé took gunfighter positions against the back wall of the voluminous room, now filled with a hundred accredited doctors, a congregation far beyond what any fire marshal would have approved. Three generations of hospital bureaucrats earlier, those who survived Sababa's scourge had exacted their revenge by dropping the medical staff lounge into a sterile windowless room in the hospital basement and ensured that all their meetings and hopes would forever remain equally subterranean.

72

At the front of the bunker, on a raised dais erected for this one assembly, sat a pious nucleus of academic and administrative apparatchiks, their demeanor and disposition determined to judge and bludgeon any independent outsider who dared threaten their authority.

The hospital switchboard operator's Big Voice broadcast the conclave commencement overhead. The Chief of Staff, the most prepotent master of control, a diminutive general practitioner named Dr. Petronilla de Meath, a Napoleanna bone apart, a harpy hag of a harridan henpecking harassment, attempted to call the meeting to order before the noisy hubbub settled into a chaotic commotion.

"Who's the chairperson?" Alex asked.

"Our Chief of Staff." Sababa said. "She's a doctor."

"Oh? Which kind?"

"Witch."

"Which which?"

"Which what?"

"Which doctah?"

"Right." Sababa said.

"Order! Order, please." Petronilla shouted. There came a semblance of lesser disarray among reluctant mutterings. "I would like to begin by welcoming Artie Shafer, the chairman of VIU's Research Ethics Board, Foster Care, the chief executive officer of our new regional health authority, and their executive assistants. This restructured managementship has partnered with a local university committee of experts to devise guidelines for improved ethical decision-making." A systolic murmur of discontent reverberated through the crowded underground chamber.

"It is my great pleasure to introduce an old friend and colleague, our new chief executive, Foster Care." A tanned muscular man with a full crop of wavy white hair above a wide grin full of perfect white teeth took the podium.

"Thank you for that glowing introduction, Petronilla." Foster began. "As you may or may not be aware, we have renamed our health authority to better reflect the new values of our reorganization. Henceforth, we shall be known as iHealth." He took a bite out of a shiny apple and placed what was left on the raised edge of the lectern.

Instead of applause, a faint voice sang at the back of the crowded room. *I'll wait in this place where the sun never shines... Wait in this place where the shadows run from themselves...*

Petronilla glared. Foster continued.

"Artie, you've been the driving force behind our new collaborative venture in establishing robust and rigid rules of medical moral conduct." Foster said. "Perhaps you'd like to present the latest revision of our prescribed principles for ethical decision-making."

"Thank you, Foster." But for a small mutation in his DNA, Shafer could have been a weasel. "As you all know, VIU's Research Ethics Board has established local control of all proposed and ongoing research and clinical investigations."

"Congratulations." Came a voice from the back of the room. "You've eliminated them."

"Doctor Sababa!" Petronilla detonated her gavel on the wooden table.

"To build on that positive outcome, we have decided, in collaboration with the new health authority, to expand our influence to include the day-to-day ethical concerns that arise in your clinical practice."

"Hallelujah!" Rebounded off a bunker wall.

"We are saved!" Echoed off another.

"Order!" Petronilla's ears belched smoke.

"I'm sure that, once you've reviewed the vast amount of work we've woven into these recommendations, you will embrace the opportunity to implement them. Think of them as commandments." Artie said. "First slide, please." The room darkened, dragging all hope into a black hole.

Ethical Decision-Making

is a process, best done in a caring and compassionate environment. It will take time, and may require more than one meeting with the patient, the family, and team members.

1. Identify the Problem
2. Identify Stakeholders
3. Identify Alternatives
4. Identify Factors
5. Propose and Test
6. Make the Decision

"You see." Artie said. "Logical, intuitive, concise, and user friendly. And this is the user menu in the iHealth Ethicsware 1.0 workbooks we'll be passing around. Next slide, please."

A Framework for Ethical Decision-Making

1. Collect information and identify the problem.
    1.1. Be alert and sensitive to morally charged situations
    1.2. Identify what you know and don't know
    1.3. State the case with as many of the relevant facts and circumstances as you can gather
    • What decisions have to be made?
    • Who are the decision-makers?
    • Be alert to actual or potential conflict of interest situations.
    1.4. Consider the context of decision-making i.e. Clinical Issues
    • What is the patient's medical history/ diagnosis/ prognosis?
    • Is the problem acute? chronic? critical? emergent? reversible?
    • What are the goals of treatment?
    • What are the probabilities of success?

- What are the plans in case of therapeutic failure?
- In sum, how can the patient be benefited by medical, nursing, or other care, and harm avoided?

Preferences
- What has the patient expressed about preferences for treatment?
- Has the patient been informed of benefits and risks; understood, and given consent?
- Is the patient mentally capable and legally competent? What is evidence of incapacity?
- Has the patient expressed prior preferences, e.g., Advanced Directives?
- If incapacitated, who is the appropriate surrogate? Is the surrogate using appropriate standards?
- Is the patient unwilling or unable to cooperate with treatment? If so, why?
- In sum, is the patient's right to choose being respected to the extent possible in ethics and law?

Quality of Life/Death
- What are the prospects, with or without treatment, for a return to the patient's normal life?
- Are there biases that might prejudice the provider's evaluation of the patient's quality of life?
- What physical, mental, and social deficits is the patient likely to experience if treatment succeeds?
- Is the patient's present or future condition such that continued life might be judged undesirable by him/her?
- Are there any plans and rationale to forego treatment?
- What are the plans for comfort and palliative care?

Contextual Features
- What chapter is this in the patient's life?
- Are there family/cultural issues that might influence treatment decisions?
- Are there provider (e.g. physicians and nurses) issues that might influence treatment decisions?
- Are there religious, cultural factors?
- Is there any justification to breach confidentiality?
- Are there problems of allocation of resources?
- What are the legal implications of treatment decisions?
- Is there an influence of clinical research or teaching Involved?

2. Specify feasible alternatives.
3. Use your ethical resources to identify morally significant factors in each alternative.

3.1. Principles
- Autonomy: Would we be exploiting others, treating them paternalistically, or otherwise affecting them without their free and informed consent? Have promises been made?
- Non-maleficence: Will this harm patients, caregivers, or members of the general public?
- Beneficence: Is this an occasion to do good to others? Remember that we can do good by preventing or removing harms.
- Justice: Are we treating others fairly? Do we have fair procedures? Are we producing just outcomes? Are we respecting morally significant rights and entitlements?
- Fidelity: Are we being faithful to institutional and professional roles? Are we living up to the trust relationships that we have with others.

3.2. Moral models
3.3. Use ethically informed sources
3.4. Context
3.5. Personal judgements

3.6 Organized procedures for ethical consultation
4. Propose and test possible resolutions.
    4.1. Find the best consequences overall
    4.2. Perform a sensitivity analysis
    4.3. Consider the impact on the ethical performance of others
    4.4. Would a good person do this?
    4.5. What if everyone in these circumstances did this?
    4.6. Will this maintain trust relationships with others?
    4.7. Does it still seem right?
5. Make your choice.
    5.1. Live with it
    5.2. Learn from it

Instead of applause, a faint voice sang in the back of the room. *Write it, cut it, paste it, save it… Load it, check it, quick, rewrite it…*

"Lights, please." Artie said. Light returned to the room. "Our team will be available to you for consultation on any ethical concern which requires our advanced level of sophistication. And, so we're clear—DNR means 'Do Not Resuscitate.' It does not mean 'Do Not Treat.' Questions?" A hand went up at the back of the room.

"Yes, Doctor Sababa."

"I would like to take this occasion to express my thanks to you and the new managementshipwreck for simplifying the moral dilemmas and ethical burdens we face in caring for sick patients and their families. I commend your approach for its comprehensiveness and attention to detail. I'm not sure what we ever did before you gave us access to this algorithm and its 52 simple iterations. Because sometimes we doctors of impure hearts and simple minds, faced with confusing options, can suffer from analysis paralysis. But being an authority on paper does not grant you authority over a group until you earn it and they give it to you."

"Do you have a question, Doctor Sababa?" Petronilla fumed.

"Just one." Sababa said. "If I encounter a complex ethical concern, can I count on you to be there to help make the hard decisions easy?"

"Absolutely." Artie said.

"How about during a cardiac arrest at four in the morning?" Sababa asked. "Can you dance with the devil in the pale moonlight?"

Everyone heard the pin drop.

"I'm sure you are all very nice people." Sababa said. "But you just got mugged by reality. The adults in the room will continue to handle the tough existential questions. Stay low, lawyer up. Now go the fuck home."

'Moving in a series of convulsive spasms, like someone
with an epileptic fit, with his face distorted
and his eyes wild like a lassoed horse bracing his legs.'
Tom Waits, *Crossroads*

Dr. Cliffy Carlton was having a bad shift. He had been swimming in a sea of millennial snowflakes and cupcakes and drug-seekers for almost eight hours.

"You smoke a pack a day and drink like a fish, but you haven't taken your three-dollar medication for two months because you can't afford it?" He asked one victim.

"I'm waiting for a test."

"I'm the test." Cliffy said. "The test is negative. The test thinks you're a penis wrinkle."

"You don't care?"

"So little, I nearly lost consciousness."

"I find your attitude offensive."

"I find it funny." Cliffy said. "I guess that's why I'm happier. It says here on your wambulance sheet that your chief complaint is that you need Dilaudid, a turkey sandwich, and a cab voucher to get home."

"I think that's what it's called." He said. "The only thing that works for the pain starts with a 'D.'"

"A likely story—and probably true." Cliffy wrote a prescription and handed it to the patient. "This should help, and it's cheap." Cliffy said. "We call it cost-effectiveness."

"It says 'Discharge.'"

"Starts with a 'D.'" Cliffy saw Sababa and his bow-tied Brahmin come through the automatic sliding frosted glass doors of the emergency entrance. "Gotta go."

"How's your wonderful world of woe tonight, Cliffy?" Sababa asked.

"Just attending to the kindness of strangers in the bear market of ideas." Cliffy said. "Sometimes verbal ingenuity is not enough. I see you've brought along Boo-Boo Bear."

"What exactly is your problem, Chowdahead?" Alex asked.

"You can live in any world you want, but I have to work in this one." Cliffy said. "Let me phrase this so I don't hurt your feelings. You annoy the ever-living fuck out of me."

"I'm sorry if I caused you any offense."

"Don't be humble, Masshole. You're not that great." Cliffy said. "Hell, I don't even think you're that smart."

"I was a Rhodes Scholar."

"All Rhodes Scholars had a glorious future in their past." Cliffy said. "And now you're Sababa's scut monkey."

"Which I consider a great privilege." Alex said. "What about you? You seem to lack precision."

"A little inaccuracy saves tons of explanation." Cliffy said. "We live in a world in which courage is in less supply than genius."

"And authenticity."

"The secret of life is honesty and fair dealing." He said. "If you can fake that, you've got it made."

"Gentlemen, please." Sababa said. "We have work to do. What you got, Cliffy."

"Sorry, Sab." Cliffy said. "Desiree Bourneville, 28-year-old art gallery owner presenting with an acute episode of sudden loss of consciousness preceded by numbness and tingling of the index and middle fingers of her left hand."

"Exam?"

"Not the sharpest knife in the drawer." Cliffy said. "She has a ragged laceration of her tongue, some kind of weird raised acne on her face, and an area of leathery roughness on her lower back."

"Hmmm." Sababa mused. "Lab?"

"Bloodwork showed a mild microcytic hypochromic anemia and eosinophilia."

"Let's go see." Sababa said. Inside Desiree Bourneville's curtain, Cliffy made introductions.

"This is Doctor Sababa, Desiree." Cliffy said. "And this is his resident, Krusty the Clown." Alex smiled at the patient and then scowled at the ER doc.

"Dr. Carlton has told us some of your story, Desiree." Sababa said. "You have no recollection of what happened tonight?"

"None." She said. "It's never happened before."

"How long have you had the skin problem on your face?"

"As long as I can remember." She said. "I saw a local dermatologist about it several years ago. He told me it was a strange medical condition and said he could fix it with what he called a copper vapour laser."

"Commodus Sitsofsky?"

"Yeah, that's him." Desiree said. "I told him I didn't want him using something that sounded like some death ray from outer space." Sababa removed a thick flashlight from his Colombian leather briefcase.

"May we have a look at your back, Desiree?" The art gallery owner turned to reveal the open side of her gown.

"Turn off the lights, Alex." Sababa clicked on the button at the end of his electric torch. A thick beam of purple light lit up the darkened room like a combat lightsaber. "In a dark place we find ourselves, and knowledge lights our way."

"What's that?" Desiree asked.

"Wood's lamp." Sababa said.

"What's that?"

"Ultraviolet light source." He said. "Now watch, gentlemen. Your focus determines your reality." Sababa shone the beam where she couldn't see it. An entire grove of foliage lit up across her back."

"Hypopigmented ash leaf macules." He said. "Cliffy, your area of leathery roughness is called a Shagreen patch and your weird acne is called adenoma sebaceum."

"That's right." Desiree said. "That's what Dr. Sitsofsky called it."

"Which brings us to the name of your condition, Desiree." Sababa said. "Bahney?"

"Tuberous sclerosis." Alex said.

"How does all that connect to why she presented the way she did tonight?" Cliffy asked.

"Desiree, you had a seizure tonight." Sababa said. "Related to your condition."

"Is that why I bit my tongue?" She asked. Alex and Sababa nodded at the same time.

"It's a rare multisystem genetic disorder of mutations on two genetic loci, TSC1 and TSC2." Sababa said. "They code an abnormal hamartin-tuberin complex which results in a loss of control of cell growth and cell division, and a predisposition to benign tumors in the brain, kidneys, heart, liver, eyes, lungs, and skin."

"Will I be OK?" Desiree asked.

"You'll need some more bloodwork and diagnostic imaging and, depending on what we find, periodic surveillance testing." Sababa said. "We rarely start people on antiepileptic drugs for a single seizure, but you will have an underlying structural reason for your episode, so medication is a good idea. Dr. Harding here will organize this and arrange for you to return to my office when the test results become available."

"Can I drive?" Desiree asked.

"I don't know." Sababa said. "I've never seen you behind the wheel of a car." He watched her jaw slacken.

"You can drive." He said. "Don't make me look bad."

In his peripheral vision, Sababa intercepted the movements of Dr. Gung Ho, closing on his air space.

"What?" He asked.

"How's your Swahili, Sab?" Gung asked.

"I manage." He said. "You have a native speaker?"

"Happygod Msuvan." Gung said. "Very native. 22-year-old farmer from Tanzania, just off the boat."

"How so?"

"He was heading to Tsawwassen on the mainland, but his cab driver dropped him off at the BC ferry terminal there and he kept on going. Had a seizure on the Queen of Alberni."

"Why was he going to Tsawwassen?"

"To find a doctor that had once worked in his village." Gung said. "She found a cure for some condition that was killing off his friends and family."

"Dr. Louise Jilek-Aall." Sababa said. "Albert Schweitzer's Angel."

"How would you know something like that?"

"It is my..."

"Yeah, yeah, OK." Gung sighed. "It is your business to know what other people don't know. So, who is she?"

"All in good time." Sababa said. "Let's go see your Mr. Happygod."

Gung Ho pulled back a curtain to reveal a hospital bed which contained a big black man, nodding like he was praying at the holy Western Wall and, in some arcane way, he was.

"Habari, Happygod." Sababa said. "Unaendeleaje?" *How are you doing.*

"Si nzuri sana." *Not so good.* The farmer said. "Kichwa changu kinauma." *My head hurts.*

"Kwa nini umekuja Canada?" Sababa asked. *Why have you come to Canada.*

"Kuona Daktari wa Mama." He said. *To see Mama Doctor.*

"Je! Kwanini hukuona tu muuguzi katika Kliniki ya Ujumbe ya Kwiro huko Mahenge?" Sababa asked. *Why didn't you just see the nurse at the Kwiro Mission Clinic in Mahenge.*

"Kwa sababu yeye ni mchawi wa Ngindo." He said. *Because she's a Ngindo witch.*

An animated soup of vowels and consonants filled the entire space of the cubicle until Sababa and Happygod stopped talking.

"I have to hear this." Alex said.

"What's the story?" Gung asked.

"Our Wapogoro farmer here has a rare condition of involuntary head movement called nodding syndrome, or 'amesinzia kichwa' in Swahili. It's associated with a generalized seizure disorder called Kifafa, which means 'little dying' or 'half-dead and rigid.' Louise Jilek-Aall established an epilepsy clinic in the Mahenge mountains in the 1960s with a small box of phenobarb and a big dose of goodwill and determination. She became a UBC professor and retired in Tsawwassen years ago."

"And Happygod came all this way to see her?" Gung asked.

"He didn't trust the nurse of the clinic because she was from a different tribe." Sababa said. "His village believes that witchcraft causes Kifafa. Or it's punishment for the misdeeds of the victim or his family. They fear the same spirit might jump from the epileptic to anyone nearby through contact with the saliva or the excrement of the affected. It's a disgrace to the entire family. The Wapogoro are superstitious about developing epilepsy—no spinning so you won't become dizzy, hit no one on the head in a fight, no hunting the fish-eagle because of how it drops on its prey like an epileptic falling to the ground in an attack, no killing a chicken by cutting its neck nor watching anybody else doing so, because a decapitated bird jerks like it's having a seizure, and never eat a bird killed

80

in this way unless a medicine man has provided a special root to cook it with. Everyone runs away instead of protecting and helping the convulsing person who, unconscious during an attack, can hurt himself."

"So, is this his first seizure?" Alex asked.

"I doubt it." Sababa said. "He has burn marks all over his body, likely from falling into cooking fires."

"Fungua mdomo wako, Happygod." He said. *Open your mouth.* The farmer opened his mouth.

"Several scars on his tongue." Sababa said. "Not his first rodeo."

"If he's a poor farmer, how did he afford the fare to travel here?" Gung asked. Sababa put the question to Happygod, who reached over into an old, frayed sports jacket and removed a package wrapped in brown paper. He opened it to a dozen stones, sparkling blue and violet. The vowels and consonants flew barrel rolls.

"He's been in the Mererani hills mining tanzanite." Sababa said. "That would pay him more than enough."

"Unaweza kunisaidia, Mganga?" Happygod asked. *Can you help me, Medicine Man.*

Sababa explained he would get him a supply of the medication he needed and send a letter to the Mahenge clinic to continue his prescription. It would only work if Happygod took the vitamin B supplement he also prescribed, to counteract any intentional witchcraft he might be subject to, on his return home.

"Asante sana, Doktor." He said. *Thank you.*

"Karibu, Happygod." Sababa said. *You're welcome.*

Sababa handed his pager to Alex, taking point for the nocturnal referrals to come.

"Where did you learn your Swahili, Doctah Sababer?" He asked.

"Climbed Kilimanjaro in the 1980s. I couldn't speak a word on the way up." Sababa said. "But it's amazing what you can pick up on the way down. Made a lot of money playing the black market in Arusha. And that was the end of the beginning of that."

'We ain't fakin'
Whole lotta shakin' goin' on.'
Jerry Lee Lewis, *Whole Lotta Shakin' Going On*

Just before noon the next day, Alex paged his mentor from the Harbour City Regional emergency room.

"What you got, Bahney?" Sababa asked.

"Dr. Capitaine wants us to see a guy that EMS brought in." Alec said. "Fell off a roof into a snowbank in Cedar. He's not waking up."

"What did his brain CT scan show?"

"Non-hemorrhagic coup-contrecoup traumatic contusions of both temporal lobes."

"On my way." Sababa found Drs. Harding and Capitaine waiting at the consultant's desk in the acute room.

"How are you, Myles?" Sababa asked.

"Living the dream." He said.

"I have a dream in a dream in a dream." Sababa looked over at an intubated and ventilated unconscious man on a bed covered with a warming blanket. He made quick mental notes from the patient's appearance, the data flashing across his monitor, and the concerned expression of his nurse, Michaela.

"Diga me." He said. *Tell me.*

"Holden Corso." Alex began. "46-year-old roofer who fell off the Crow and Gate roof this morning while fixing a leak. This is his wife, Barbara, and Jack Nash here is the owner of the pub whose roof Holden was working on this morning before his nosedive.

"This is Doctah Sababer." Alex said. "He's the last man at the end of history."

"What's wrong with my husband, Doctor?" Barbara asked. "Why doesn't he wake up?"

"A good question indeed." Sababa said. "To be in a coma, you need to have a problem with either the brainstem or both hemispheres. I'm told that Holden has sustained bruises on both temporal lobes, but that still shouldn't be enough to cause him to remain unconscious. Drs. Capitaine and Harding and I are going to review Holden's CT scan next door. We'll be back in a minute."

In an adjacent room, Myles pulled up the roofer's brain CT scan.

"Look here, Sab." He said. "Small non-hemorrhagic contusion of the left temporal lobe with a contrecoup injury on the opposite side."

"That's not a rebound injury affecting his right hemisphere." Sababa said. "There's a more subtle low-density process within the anterior and medial parts of the temporal lobe and the island of Reil."

"What from?" Myles asked.

"What's blue and doesn't fit?"

"Dunno."

"A dead epileptic." Sababa said. "Holden may have had a generalized grand mal convulsion that launched him off the Crow and Gate roof, but I'll bet it began with a focal seizure from whatever is affecting his right temporal lobe. Let's examine him in more detail."

Back in the acute room, Sababa first spoke to the ER nurse.

"Michaela, please give our friend here a milligram of IV lorazepam."

"Sab, he's comatose." Myles said. "What is that going to do?"

"Watch." Sababa said, and Holden Corso woke up and spat out his endotracheal tube.

"Where am I?" He asked. "Who are you people?"

"Michaela, hang the first 400 mg of a diphenylhydantoin loading dose." Sababa said. His nurse mixed and piggybacked the anticonvulsant into Holden's IV. Everyone looked at the professor.

"Non-convulsive status epilepticus." Sababa turned to the patient's partner. "Barbara, has your husband complained of any recent symptoms?"

"He's had a headache and feverishness, ringing in his ears, hearing loss, and vertigo for the last week." She said. "I tried to tell him he shouldn't be up on a roof in the middle of winter if he was feeling woozy, but he wanted the work."

"Have you noticed anything strange about his behavior?"

"He's been hyperactive and agitated, rambling on at length about trivial things, writing quotes and drawing roof plans, and praying on his knees five times a day. Strange."

"Why strange?"

"Holden was born into an Anglican family but practised no religion." She said. "It was like he was someone else."

"Like he was Vincent Van Gogh?" Sababa asked. "There's a part of the human brain, the temporal lobe, that is associated with religious experiences and epilepsy."

"What do you mean?" Jack asked.

"Van Gogh suffered from temporal lobe epilepsy but, between seizures, his illness had other components in common with Holden's presentation."

"Like what?" Myles asked.

"A formal set of behavioural phenomena." Sababa said. "Van Gogh had a compulsion to draw and write. Every night, after 16 hours of painting in tertiary colours, he wrote long letters, the shortest of them six pages in length. His torrential 37-year lifetime correspondence of 200 letters filled 1,700 pages."

"What else?" Alex asked.

"Van Gogh had intense spiritual interests and experiences." Sababa said. "He was the son of a clergyman, and a theology student and lay preacher before turning to art."

"And?" Barbara asked.

"An unstable sexual drive." Sababa continued. "He went through periods of hypersexuality, hyposexuality, bisexuality, and homosexuality, including a stormy affair with Paul Gauguin which prompted him to cut off his own ear."

"Holden would never do any of those things." Barbara protested.

"Not normally." Sababa said. "But we're here because your husband is not himself. You said that Holden was rambling and belligerent which, together with his temporal lobe epilepsy, completes the five trait requirements for diagnosis."

"Of what?" Myles asked.

"Hypergraphia, hyper-religiosity, altered sexuality, circumstantiality, and intense non-linear mental viscosity." Sababa said. "Holden has Geschwind syndrome, named after one of my Boston professors, Norm Geschwind."

"I thought Van Gogh had Ménière's disease." Alex said.

"Or bipolar disorder, chronic sunstroke, acute intermittent porphyria, digitalis toxicity, chronic lead poisoning from pica ingestion of his paints, green fairy absinthe intoxication, or syphilitic general paresis of the insane." Sababa said. "But no. Geschwind syndrome."

"Just Van Gogh and Holden?" Myles asked.

"And Abraham, Moses, Jesus, Mohammed, Saint Paul, Joseph Smith, Pope Pius IX, Joan of Arc, and God himself."

Holden ate the tissues from a box on his tray table. Other inanimate objects found their way into his mouth and he rolled his tongue around them.

"Try not to do that, Holden." Barbara said.

"What about his Bell's palsy?" Myles asked.

"It's not a Bell's palsy." Sababa took an otoscope off the wall. "Although involves the geniculate ganglion and cries out for an explanation." He went to look in Holden's right ear and stopped.

"What's this, Myles?" Sababa pointed to a vesicular eruption in the entry to his ear canal.

"No shakes, all shingles."

"I swear it wasn't there when he came in." Myles protested.

"Possible." Sababa said.

"What is it?" Barbara asked.

"Type II Ramsey-Hunt Syndrome." Sababa said. "Also known as shingles oticus. It's a reactivation of the same virus that gave Holden his childhood chickenpox. Your husband has herpes zoster encephalitis as the cause of his temporal lobe seizure and cranial nerve abnormalites."

Holden Corso lay back on his hospital bed. His face had no expression, but his eyes darted towards every visual stimulation.

"What's this, Holden?" Sababa pointed to his watch. Holden didn't recognize it.

"How about this?" Sababa took a pen from his breast pocket. Holden stared into space.

"He's more passive than he has been all this past week." Barbara said.

"A lamb by comparison." Holden played with his penis.

"Hmmm." Sababa mused. "So that's it."

"That's what?" Jack asked.

"Holden doesn't have Geschwind syndrome anymore." Sababa said. "That can only occur in single hemisphere temporal lobe epilepsy. But since he contused his left temporal lobe in the fall this morning, he has damage to both temporal lobes."

"Meaning what?" Myles asked.

"Holden has another neurological disorder characterized by docility, compulsive oral tendencies, visual agnosia and distractibility, and memory dysfunction and hypersexuality."

"Does it have a name?" Barbara asked.

"Klüver-Bucy syndrome." Sababa said. "It's quite rare."

"Let me see if I understand this, Doctah Sababer." Alex said. "You're saying that Holden here developed an HVZ encephalitis from a Type II Ramsey-Hunt syndrome which caused a complex partial seizure and Geschwind syndrome which converted into Klüver-Bucy syndrome when he fell and contused his left temporal lobe when his right-sided temporal lobe fit generalized into non-convulsive status epilepticus."

"Yep." Sababa said. "Went to sleep with Geschwind and woke up with Klüver-Bucy."

"You ever heard of Occam's Razor?" Alex asked.

"We must talk about the wonderful world of medical logic, Bahney." Sababa said. "Nobody knows how many universes there are. Theory places no limit—all possibilities in an unlimited number of combinations of 'natural' laws, each sheaf appropriate to its own universe. But this is just theory and Occam's Razor is much too dull."

"Is there anything you can do for him, Doctor Sababa?" Barbara asked.

"You bet." Said the portly professor. "Dr. Harding here will admit him, order some additional laboratory investigations, perform a diagnostic lumbar puncture, consult our neurologist, Dr. Oliver Lax, start him on a course of intravenous acyclovir and corticosteroids, and continue his anticonvulsant therapy."

"Will he ever be himself again?"

"Just like Van Gogh said."

"What's that?" Barbara asked.

"Only when I fall do I get up again."

'The extent of your consciousness is limited only by your ability to love and to embrace with your love the space around you, and all it contains.'
Napoleon Bonaparte

The casual reader may be granted amnesty for forgetting the spectral continuum of consciousness, memory, dreams, and coma, for amnesty is a communal form of forgetting.

Sababa's higher consciousness derived from his continual self-conscious attempts to raise and expand his consciousness to create a quantum consciousness that could produce the stream of consciousness to solve any problem at hand. He knew that no problem could be solved from the same level of consciousness that created it, that there was no birth of consciousness without pain, and that, although consciousness did not always solve the problem, the suffering might be more meaningful. Consciousness was usually upon him before he could get out of the way; it was only possible through change, and change was only possible through movement.

Memory is a corrupt and treacherous, false consciousness. You don't remember what happened. What you remember becomes what happened. Some things you remember never happened. The brain recalls what the muscles grope for. Sababa's photographic memory was embedded in his read-only random-access long-term virtual core memory, a programmable working memory cache he could jog when he needed to achieve some laudable goal at hand. It was the lash with which his yesterday flogged his today and tomorrow.

The portly professor knew that memory could never recapture reality. Memory could only attempt to reconstruct it backwards. And for Sababa, reality was so much more important and interesting than living happily ever after. And it was still the only place to get a decent meal.

Dreams are an altered state of consciousness. Holden Corso had a whiff and a dream, a bad dream, a fever dream, a daydream, a wet dream, in a dream sequence that would almost kill him. Sababa would become his dream big dream catcher sweet dream come true.

And finally, coma is a loss of consciousness. Whether on any coma scale, in a diabetic coma, Kussmaul's coma, insulin coma, hepatic coma, uremic coma, metabolic coma, hyperosmolar coma, myxedema coma, vegetative coma, or coma vigil, the lights are on but nobody is home.

Most people hate hospitals. But not the internists and their residents. For them, a hospital is a magical place. It's poetry, the rhythm of the machines, the crackle of the paper gowns, a place full of promise and excitement and surprises. It's a consciousness lifter, a memory-maker, where coma awakens and dreams come true.

'Men think epilepsy divine, merely because they do not understand it. But if they called everything divine which they do not understand, why, there would be no end to divine things.'

Hippocrates

Life is a fracas on unmapped terrain, and the universe a geometry stricken with epilepsy.

Brian Wilson, the young works department worker, underwent several months of desensitization therapy for his vibratory angioedema, but he continued to swell up at even the sight of a jackhammer. He now plants flowers and trees along the Harbour City waterfront.

Big Bill Werbeniuk's essential tremor disappeared with Sababa's prescription for propranolol, but the World Professional Billiards and Snooker Association deemed it a performance-enhancing drug. Bill continued to drink at least six pints of lager before each billiards match and one pint for each frame. He died of intractable heart failure and penury in Vancouver, six days after his 56th birthday.

Doc Holliday backed off all the dental work he had planned to perform on Joe Lee, the market gardener he had referred to the Sage of the Salish Sea. After the faceless oculist guru, Dr. T.J. Eckleburg, fixed his glaucoma, Joe coexisted with his Sturge-Weber syndrome for the rest of his natural life. When asked about his secret to longevity, he always quoted his internal medicine specialist. *A little science. A little magic. A little chicken soup.*

Bento de Góis, the elderly eight-fingered funeral director, died in his sleep of Machado–Joseph disease ten months after Sababa gave him his diagnosis. It is the wisdom of the crocodiles that shed tears when they would devour.

The motor neurone disease that killed Lou Gehrig's fastball and Stephen Hawking's slow expansion of the universe swept Susan Rodriguez's big voice and small muscles away faster than Sababa's 'not for a while' reassurance. It may have been his business to know what other people don't know, but it didn't require him to inflict brutality on the last remnants of fragile hope.

Sarah Bellum's metronidazole-induced cerebellar dysfunction reversed itself within weeks of her discontinuing the antibiotic. Her bacterial vaginosis also cleared up once she stopped smoking and steaming her tender parts. Sarah returned to jam-making and named a new peach, patchouli, and passion fruit spread for the portly professor. *Sababa's Slippery Slope.*

Art gallery owner Desiree Bourneville's brain CT showed multiple bilateral calcified subependymal nodules consistent with the stocky savant's diagnosis of tuberous sclerosis. Her EEG demonstrated focal epileptiform discharges. She has had no further seizures since after starting Sababa's anticonvulsant medication regimen and is scheduled for routine surveillance tumor imaging. She presented the professor with a print of Zur Lehre der Talgdrüsengeschwülste, a portrait of a man with her disease painted in Munich in 1903.

Sababa started Happygod Msuvan on an anticonvulsant for his Kifafa seizure disorder. Happy took the ferry back to Tsawwassen to visit Mama Doctor, before boarding a succession of airlines on his return to Tanzania. Since he gave up farming for full-time fossicking, Happygod has found two million dollars-worth of Tanzanite, proceeds from which he donated to expand the Kwiro Mission Clinic in his Mahenge mountain home, except for the large stone he sent to Jane Sababa.

Foster Care and his VIU iHealth Ethicsware collaborators continued to sleep while the front-end loaded, front-line internists made all the important life and death decisions.

And Holden Corso, the roofer with the HVZ encephalitis from a Type II Ramsey-Hunt syndrome which caused a complex partial seizure, and Geschwind syndrome which converted into Klüver-Bucy syndrome when he fell and contused his left temporal lobe when his right-sided temporal lobe fit generalized into non-convulsive status epilepticus? Alex confirmed all his diagnoses with imaging and tests of blood and cerebrospinal and vesicle fluid analysis but, despite receiving the right antiviral and anticonvulsant medication, Holden continued to have relapses for which Doctor Sababa gave him yet another eponym.

"You also now appear to have Mollaret's meningitis." He said. Holden gave up roofing to become an artist. He paints in tertiary colours. Some have compared his technique to that of a one-eared Dutchman.

One evening, after one of Jane's brilliant dinners at their lakeside refuge, Sababa and his protégé retired to discuss their Case of the Cedar Shakes and Shingles, over vintage port and Cuban cigars.

"For centuries, epilepsy was the exact expectation of someone possessed by the Devil." Sababa said. "There was no better explanation, and it allowed you to admit his existence. If there was a Devil, that meant there was a God."

"No God?"

"Epicurean paradox." Sababa said. "If God exists, then God is omnipotent, omniscient, and morally perfect. If God is omnipotent, then God has the power to eliminate all evil. If God is omniscient, then God knows when evil exists. If God is morally perfect, then God has the desire to eliminate all evil. Evil exists. If evil exists and God exists, then either God doesn't have the power to eliminate all evil, or doesn't know when evil exists, or doesn't have the desire to eliminate all evil. Therefore, no God."

"But you still dance with the Devil in the pale moonlight." Alex said.

"I said there was no God." Sababa said. "I didn't say there was no Devil."

'Men think epilepsy divine, merely because they do not understand it. We will one day understand what causes it, and then cease to call it divine. And so it is with everything in the universe.'

Hippocrates

21. The Case of the Ruptured Rosary

'The next person that tells me I'm not religious,
I'm going to shove my rosary beads up their ass.'
Joe Biden

The Uplands Petro-Canada gas station was open twenty-four hours a day, seven days a week. Outside was a sign in large letters, channeling the smoke-free environment that the national air carrier is so proud to provide. *Free air...* Inside were always two things you would never find—fresh food and courtesy.

Expiration dates on rows of off-brand junk food chips and cookies and pickled curiosities had gone missing, erased years before in some misguided attempt to control inventory turnover. Lottery tickets, the surtax on desperation, a tariff on people who were bad at math, smiled up from the glass case beside the till. An adjacent pantry pack of Slim Jims held a thirtieth of the lethal dose of sodium nitrite.

Lou Rothman was not the world's most ill-mannered attendant, but he was in the running. Lou was always running—swiping credit cards, answering the phone, restocking the shelves and the walk-in cooler, rotating the frozen drink machines, mopping the floors, scraping the mould off the ice bucket bottoms, emptying the rat traps, and filling the dumpster, every aspect of which accounted for his hostile disposition.

Perhaps it was the smell that made him surly, that lingering pungent chemical cocktail of cigarettes and coffee and high-fructose corn syrup and ammonia and gastric acid and insect corpses. It was strongest right after the rain when it seemed to come from deep underground, wafting up through thin fissures in the asphalt.

For all we know, it was the steady mechanical hum of the flickering fluorescent lights or the random pockets of cold and warm air following him around inside the convenience store that infected his mood. Or the deleted security tapes or the strange noises that came through the walls in the middle of the night. Or maybe it was because the days were getting shorter, the nights coming earlier and staying later, and the winter weather turning colder. It mattered little. Every commuter needed gas and free air and water. Nobody ever complained about the aesthetics.

Rothman's temperament could have come from his consistent consumption of beef jerky and peanuts and Red Bull and Colts cigars. He used to sneak off to the restroom for a quick smoke but, because he was always running, and because he kept the toilets locked and the cash register open, Lou left his small cigar tips lit and planted in his face. He tried to ignore the constant warnings from his boss and the Harbour City fire marshal that, in his proximity to the gas pumps, he had become his own improvised explosive device. And he tried to ignore the customers.

On the day in question, Lou tried to ignore an irritating cough from a financial advisor named Rudolf Jaksch von Wartenhorst, the gulping noises from a Home Hardware employee, Ben Watt, a dizzy notary public, Benedict Adamantiades, and the yellow eyes and red rash of a Central American teak farm owner, Phil LeBoit. He found it more difficult to disregard the attentions of librarian June Cleaver, restaurant supervisor Caroline Savage, motel chambermaid Erna Petri, legal secretary Janet Leigh, cinema concessionaire Paulette Ehrlich, bridal gallery owner Maria Callas, practical nurse Margaret Houlihan, and BC lottery commission ticket vendor Bente Affleck.

Petro-Canada is an acronym for Pierre Elliott Trudeau Rips Off Canada. Its most famous employee before Lou Rothman was Dick Assman, a Regina attendant who had been a guest on David Letterman. Petro-Canada's principal business activity involved digging up vast amounts of solar energy buried beneath the pristine Alberta landscape, to suffocate humanity to death with toxic fumes. In their proactivity, catering to autonomous self-driving vehicles, the company executive planned to inscribe braille on all the pumps.

Petro-Canada had 1500 service stations across this great nation. Lou had hired himself from the one with the two signs in the front window. *Help wanted* and *Self-service.*

He had seen almost everything in his five years as a gas station attendant. He had seen unleaded gasoline come in and the lead go away. But he didn't see it coming back, the day that an estranged husband gunned down his wife and the mother of his five children from behind, as she was refueling her minivan at pump number two. All he saw was her 13-year-old daughter in the passenger seat, screaming.

His testimony to the RCMP was polite and soft-spoken.

"Son of a bitch never even got out of his car." Lou said.

'How I wish I could forget
Those happy yesteryears
That have left a rosary of tears.'
Mel Torme, *Memories of You*

One week later, on the other side of the Island Highway from where
Louis Rothman had seen the murder at pump number two, a Dutch
beekeeper, aging like milk in a sauna, slogged along a muddy forest trail
that ran behind the houses between Arnhem Terrace and Tulip Place.

Amsterdam Park was so small that Harbour City didn't list it on their
website. The path was nothing more than a crooked track of moss and
dirt and random rocks under a tall canopy of fir and cedar. The winter
rains had melted the leaves underfoot to icy slush, coarse with grit. But
for Bergen Opzoom, it was still a delightful piece of earth, a walk in the
park. He loved the absolute stillness of the place. Ollie had wept in
uncontrollable spasms when he buried his ragged dog under these trees
a decade earlier. Almost no one would find either of them here.

The beekeeper was a gregarious old man. His friends, and he had many,
called him Ollie, although no one knew why. Ollie Opzoom kept the
beehives behind his house on Amsterdam Crescent, next to the park.
That eliminated any trekking traffic in the first three seasons and the cold
weather was why Ollie had it to himself in the winter. His hair had
whitened over the years like the snow that now covered the ground. His
were the only footprints.

Ollie plugged the sides of his head with wireless earphones and tuned his
phone to a local radio station as he walked through Amsterdam Park in
the fading light of the late afternoon.

*'Uy' skweyul, Harbour City... This is the afternoon show on CNDN Coast Salish
radio, 101.3 FM on your Home and Native Band... I'm your host, Silas Seaweed...*

Ollie left his beehives alone in the winter, except for the sugar syrup and
probiotics he provided. With any luck, they would survive to the first
cleansing flight of spring, something he was no longer sure he would be
here to witness.

*A good chief gives, he does not take... Take only what you need and leave the land as
you found it...*

In recent weeks, Ollie began having fevers. He felt ill and fatigued, his
appetite had vanished, and he had lost too much weight. His muscles and
joints and abdomen ached, and his skin had erupted in tender nodules
and ulcers. He was shorter and shorter of breath on minimal exertion.

His legs and feet were numb and painful at the same time. He took a granola bar from his coat pocket with aching fingertips that had turned from blue to black.

Before eating, always take time to thank the food...

Ollie thanked his food.

Remember what Chief Maquinna said, back in the late 1700s... Once I was in Victoria, and I saw a very large house... They told me it was a bank and that the white men place their money there to be taken care of, and that by and by they got it back with interest... We are Indians and we have no such bank, but when we have plenty of money or blankets, we give them away to other chiefs and people, and by and by they return them with interest, and our hearts feel good... Our way of giving is our bank...

And then today, for the first time in his life, Bergen Opzoom saw claret-coloured carnage in his morning ablutions. He was halfway along the Amsterdam Park trail, when the rest of his blood volume burst into the space behind his abdominal cavity, between Arnhem Terrace and Tulip Place.

Coyote is always out there waiting, and Coyote is always hungry...

'More! More! is the cry of a mistaken soul.'
William Blake

A week and a day after the Petro-Canada shooting and a day before Ollie Opzoom's circulating blood volume exploded into his retroperitoneal space, Alex Harding lined up for his early morning regulah at Code Brew behind a thin spectre of a man, as angular and hollow-cheeked and spindle-shanked as his mentor was not. The eye contact was fleeting but hooked by thorns.
"Alex Hahding." The young resident said. "I'm from Hahvud."
"Well, lah-de-dah." The stick man stared at the bow tie. "They loaded up the clown cars today... Erg Hebberig. I'm the new internist at Harbour City Regional."
"Killah." Alex said. "I'm working with Doctah Sababer."
"Ah, yes." Erg said. "The supposed Sage of the Salish Sea."
"He's wicked frickin' pissah."

"I'm sure." Erg said. The Code Brew barista with the subdermal ink and transdermal metal showed her readiness to take his order.

"How much for a cup of coffee?" He asked.

"Two dollars." She said. "And refills are free."

"I'll have a refill." Erg said. There followed a short discussion.

"Where's your office?" Alex asked.

"Here." Erg pulled a thumb drive from his left pocket.

"But where are you going to see your patients in follow-up?" Alex asked.

"Won't be doing that." Erg said. "There's no area under the curve."

"So how will patients and physicians contact you?"

"Here." Erg pulled a mobile phone from his right pocket. "Now, if you'll excuse me, Doogie, I have some trail-blazing to do. Life is short and time is money."

Alex called the portly professor to the emergency room an hour later. He turned to watch a Colombian leather briefcase fly an aerobatic hammerhead stall turn, before landing upright beside the consultant's desk computer.

"What you got?" Sababa asked.

"Heebie-jeebies." Alex said.

"What from?"

"I just met a skinny Morlock in the Code Brew line pretending to be a samurai." Alex said. "He said he was the new internist."

"Meneer Dokter Hebberig." Sababa said. "He promised to do a locum for me a couple of years ago. Reneged on the locum and came anyway. Then he left for what he thought were greener pastures."

"What happened?"

"He must have tired of all the skiing and kite surfing in Vancouver." Sababa said. "Money for nothing and your chicks for free."

"Why did you invite him back into your department?"

"We didn't." Sababa said. "He was the only applicant for an Internal Medicine Island Health job posting. We had already lost control of our recruitment process to The Oxymoron."

"Oxymoron?"

"They refer to themselves the Health Authority but they have neither." Sababa said. "Erg wouldn't have been my first choice. The love for material things grows like a fungus in his soul and destroys the loveliness of his heart utterly—insider trading, outside the law, underarm bowling, overhead avoidance—he knows the price of everything and the value of nothing."

"When I asked him where his clinic was, he pulled a thumb drive from his pocket."

"That's also where he keeps his conscience, his ethics manual, and his generosity of spirit." Sababa said. "They'll make his burial shroud with pockets."

"Don't throw a frisbee into his yard, Sab." Alex said. "You'll never see it again."

"Erg has a wonderful head for money." Sababa said. "There's this long slit on the top. I wouldn't give him too much thought. Some people are so poor all they have are precious metals. Your gold is inside you, Alex. Some men pursue pleasure with such breathless haste that they hurry past it. Now, what you got besides the heebie-jeebies?"

"Janet Leigh." Alex began. "46-year-old legal secretary with a two-day history of nausea, abdominal discomfort, joint pains, and hand and ankle weakness on her right side. Claims to have had a flu-like illness a week before that. Came in this morning after several bouts of vomiting, one with a cup of bright red blood in it. Her kidney function was off, but Dr. Pangloss thought it was just dehydration. John Falstaff scoped her and found swollen clusters of purple spots at the bottom of her stomach and first part of the duodenum. He said it looked peculiar."

"What else did he say?"

"He said to call you."

"We do peculiar." Sababa said. "Exam?"

"Normal vital signs." Alex said. "Some mild epigastric tenderness. Neuro exam showed weakness of wrist flexion, thumb abduction, and ankle dorsiflexion, and decreased sensation of her right fingertips and foot."

"You have a name for that?"

"Mononeuritis multiplex." Alex said.

"What was it about her abnormal kidney function that suggested it was just dehydration?"

"Nothing." Alex said. "Her fractional excretion of sodium was greater than two percent, renal failure index greater than one, urine sodium greater than 40 mEq/L, specific gravity less than 1.010, and urine to plasma osmo ratio less than 1.3."

"Meaning?"

"The actual problem is her kidneys." Alex said. "Urinalysis also positive for protein and microscopic blood."

"Then what, my young fledgling, is the problem?" Sababa asked. "What you got?"

"Middle-aged woman with a viral-like prodrome who presents with gut and joint and kidney problems and mononeuritis multiplex."

"Differential diagnosis?"

"Infections such as Lyme disease, HIV, or parvovirus B19, immune-mediated conditions like rheumatoid arthritis or lupus, sarcoid, cryoglobulinemia, vasculitides like polyarteritis nodosa and eosinophilic granulomatosis with polyangiitis, and the sting of the Pacific sea nettle jellyfish, *Chrysaora fuscescens.*"

"Don't get fancy, Bahney." Sababa said. "You'll hurt yourself and kill my patient. It's the middle of winter and Janet Leigh hasn't likely been swimming the Strait of Georgia."

"Sorry." He said. "You bring out the worst in me."

"That's all the possible causes you can think of?" Sababa asked. "You didn't tell me about her rash."

"She doesn't have a rash." Alex shrugged.

"She will." Sababa said. "Let's go see her."

Behind the curtain of cubicle 7, the resident introduced his mentor.

"This is the medical specialist I told you about, Janet." Alex said. "He's a purveyor of instant karma."

"You were an expert witness in one of our trials last year, Doctor Sababa." She said.

"I'm afraid I don't recall the details." Sababa said. "I've always had a terrible memory, as far back as I can remember."

"My boss said you were like trying to nail Jell-O to the wall."

"Only because he was so busy shoveling smoke." Sababa laughed. "Dr. Harding here has told me of your recent problems."

"Do you know what's causing this?" Janet asked.

"I do." Sababa said. "You have Henoch–Schönlein purpura, a condition named after the two German physicians that first described it in the 1860s. It's an inflammation of small blood vessels from deposits of immunoglobulin A and complement 3 complexes, a type of leukocytoclastic vasculitis. It causes a rash of small areas of bleeding under the skin we refer to as palpable purpura."

"But I don't have a rash." Janet protested. Sababa pointed to her legs on which the portly professor's description was surfacing before her eyes.

"My right hand and foot don't work anymore." She said. "Is that also from your long-dead German doctors' disease?" Sababa nodded.

"What happens now?" Janet asked.

"Now we admit you to our medical unit, Dr. Harding orders some more bloodwork and performs skin and kidney biopsies, we consult our neurologist, Dr. Oliver Lax, to do some nerve conduction studies, and you win a 5-day course of methylprednisolone pulse therapy."

"And then I can go home?" She asked.

"You might leave hospital sooner, Janet, if we can set up your infusions as an outpatient." Alex turned to his mentor. "Wasn't a breakthrough in our understanding of this condition supplied by Regius Professor of Medicine at Oxford, Sir William Osler, in his 1914 British Medical Journal article, *The Visceral Lesions of Purpura and Allied Conditions*?"

Sababa smiled a Sababa smile and grunted.

'Look wise, say nothing, and grunt. Speech was given to conceal thought.'
Dr. William Osler

'And what's this rash that comes and goes
Can you tell me what it means?'
Redgum, *A Walk in the Light Green*

Dr. Myles Capitaine navigated through the ER to intercept the trajectories of the portly professor and his protégé.

"How are you, Myles?" Sababa asked.

"Living the dream."

"The forest is blanketed by the greenest ferns and moss and bonsai-like trees, a wild majesty that beckons dreamers." Sababa said. "What you got?"

"Paulette Ehrlich." Myles began. "37-year-old cinema concessionaire who presented last evening with an acute exacerbation of chronic obstructive pulmonary disease. She had smoked half a pack of cigarettes per day for 20 years, before quitting two years ago."

"A little young for COPD, isn't she?" Alex asked.

"That's what I thought." Myles said. "There was no history of intravenous methylphenidate use but she has a problem with arthritis and recurrent hives, reviewed in consultation by a rheumatologist in Vancouver and by our own Dr. Skin Laser, Commodus Sitsofsky."

"And what did that dynamic duo come up with?" Sababa asked.

"The skin guy wondered if she had alpha-1 antitrypsin deficiency because of the emphysema and arthritis." Myles said. "And the joint guy wondered if she had granulomatosis with polyangiitis because of the hives."

"Eosinophilic granulomatosis with polyangiitis can cause hives." Sababa said. "But granulomatosis with polyangiitis cause all kinds of skin lesions except hives. Alpha-1 antitrypsin deficiency can cause emphysema and arthritis but again, no hives. So what's the question, Bahney?"

"What can cause her obstructive lung disease and arthritis and urticarial skin lesions?" Alex asked. "Did these two consultants do any bloodwork?"

"Yep." Myles said. "Alpha-1 antitrypsin levels were normal but both C3 and C4 complement levels were low."

"Hmmm." Sababa brought up Janet's imaging studies on the consultant's computer. "Chest x-ray shows relative hyperlucency of her lung bases. So does her thoracic CT scan. Let's go see her."

Inside the curtain of her cubicle, Myles introduced the savants.

"Janet, this is Doctor Sababa." He said. "He's the reason the universe goes to all the trouble of existing. And this is his resident, Dr. Harding."

"Charmed." She said. "What's going on?"

"You have an emphysematous condition that has damaged the bottom half of your lungs, associated with low levels of immune system complement proteins, arthritis, and an inflammatory process affecting your skin."

"You have a name?" She asked.

98

"HUVS." Sababa said. "Hypocomplementemic urticarial vasculitis syndrome."

"What causes it?"

"We don't know."

"Why just the bottom of my lungs?"

"Not sure." He said. "But there is greater blood flow per unit volume in the lung bases, resulting in a greater elastase burden from the inflammation, and more unopposed elastolysis at the bottom."

"This is dissolving the blood vessels in my lungs?"

"Something like that."

"Can you stop it?"

"We've been having some success with a medication called dapsone." Sababa said.

"What else do you use that for?"

"Leprosy." He said.

"Sweet."

"Water can quench your thirst or put out a fire." Sababa said. "It doesn't mean its uses are related in any other way. You'll be fine. Dr. Harding will be back later to explain how this will all go down." He and Alex left her cubicle to find Trace Pangloss waiting outside.

"Free movie passes and popcorn." Janet called after them. "If you're right."

"You've met Dr. Pangloss, Alex." Sababa said. "Our metaphysico-theologo-cosmologo-noodleologist. What you got, Trace?"

"Phil LeBoit." Trace said. "37-year-old Harbour City sawmill owner who presents with a two-day history of a reddish-purple, papular rash on both arms and elbows. Three weeks ago, public health vaccinated him for Hepatitis A to prepare him for a visit to the teak plantation he bought in Nicaragua this autumn."

"Why didn't he get a Twinrix combination A and B immunization?" Alex asked.

"He's been an inactive carrier of Hepatitis B for eight years already." Trace said.

"Rest of exam?" Alex asked.

"Nada."

"Lab?" Sababa's turn.

"Equally nada."

"Let's go see." Sababa followed Trace and Alex into the sawmill owner's cubicle.

"Phil, these are our Internal Medicine consultants, Doctors Sababa and Harding." Trace said. "Cognitive dissonance is the psychological stress experienced by an individual who holds two or more contradictory beliefs, ideas, or values at the same time."

"And?"

"They don't have any."

Sababa removed a magnifying glass from the depths of his Colombian leather briefcase and squinted hard at LeBoit's rash.

"So what is this, Alex?" He asked.

"Leukocytoclastic vascultits."

"I could not fail to disagree with you less." Sababa said. "Ooga Chaka principle."

"What's that?"

"We choose the disease that gets us hooked on a feeling and high on believing." Sababa put away his hand lens. "This is a lymphocytic vasculitis."

"But that's not even an actual condition." Alex protested. "Most clinicians consider it a mere epiphenomenon, a happenstance secondary to a pathologic process, never a pathologic process itself. What could it have come from? And how do you know without a biopsy?"

"I know. I see, I remember. I do, I understand." Sababa said. "Phil has an aberrant hypersensitivity reaction to the Hepatitis A vaccination he received 20 days ago. You'll do the skin biopsy. Set him up for eight weeks of low molecular weight heparin injections. No steroid or immunosuppressive therapy because of his Hep B carrier state."

"Is that it?" Alex asked.

"I solved the case. My work is done." Sababa said. "But you, grasshopper, never finish. Call me when you've seen the consults on the medical ward. Sababa handed Alex a piece of paper inscribed with two names. *Maria Callas... Bente Affleck...*

"I'll be in the stress lab, pushing my fellow citizens towards near-death experiences."

> 'To the elements it came from Everything will return.
> Our bodies to earth, Our blood to water,
> Heat to fire, Breath to air.'
>
> Empedocles

The last victim had rolled off the treadmill when the portly professor's pager hummed in his pocket.

"Be there in ten." Sababa blew through the fifth-floor stairwell doors three minutes later.

"Magandang umaga, Sophia." He said. "Kumusta ang arow mo?" *Good morning, Sophia. How's your day.*

"Berry pine, Ductor Sababa." She said. "Your Harbard grud-wait is penis and eggs-pekting you."

"Thanks, Sophia." Sababa watched Alex make his way back down the hallway to the nursing station.

"OK, Hotshot, what you got?"

"Maria Callas." Alex began. "69-year-old bridal gallery owner admitted last evening by Dr. Tarmac. Severe dehydration, renal dysfunction, and electrolyte abnormalities on a 4-year history of chronic persistent large volume diarrhea. In the last month, she's lost ten pounds and developed muscle pain and a rash."

"Why did she come in last night?" Sababa asked.

"Rectal prolapse accompanied by bright red blood." Alex said.

"Exam?"

"As described." He said.

"Lab?"

"High white count and creatinine and muscle enzymes, low sodium and chloride and potassium." Alex pulled up Maria's medical imaging results on Sophia's nursing station computer.

"CT chest and abdomen showed a large exophytic enhancing mass in the rectosigmoid colon extending inferiorly into the anus along the mucosal lining with well-delineated lobular contour and central feeding arterial branches suggestive of villous adenoma."

"Let's go see her." Sababa said. In a far-flung room down the fifth-floor hallway, Alex made introductions.

"Maria, this is Doctah Sababer." He said. "His is the warrior's twofold way of pen and sword, and he has a taste for both."

"Good to know." Maria said. "Do you know what's wrong with me, Doctor?"

"I do." Sababa said. "What's causing her heliotropic rash and muscle inflammation, Alex?"

Alex shrugged. Sababa held up her hands.

"What are these violaceous plaques over her metacarpophalangeal joints?"

"Gottron's papules?" Alex equivocated.

"And, therefore, the cause of her rash and inflamed muscles?"

"Dermatomyositis." He said.

"And its associated incidence with malignancy?"

"Ten percent." Alex said.

"So, the cause of her rectal prolapse?"

"Tubulovillous adenoma or adenocarcinoma."

"You have the name for a rare disease characterized by a large hypersecretory rectosigmoid villous adenoma causing persistent large-volume secretory diarrhea, electrolyte abnormalities, and renal dysfunction?" Sababa asked.

"Uh..."

"Nope." Sababa said. "Try McKittrick–Wheelock syndrome, named after Leland S. McKittrick and Frank C. Wheelock. You should know them. They were Harvard Medical School boys."

"Before me." Alex said.

"Let every man be master of his time." Sababa said.

"I have cancer?" Maria asked.

"Close." Sababa said. "But not quite."

"Is it causing my rash and muscle pain?" She asked.

"It's causing the condition that's causing your rash and muscle pain." Sababa said.

"What Dr. Harding just mentioned?"

"Dermatomyositis." Sababa said. "It's a rare autoimmune disease."

"So, both problems I have are rare?" Sababa nodded.

"We do rare."

"Are they treatable?" She asked.

"Of course." Sababa said. "Dr. Harding here will organize some more investigations, fix your salt and water imbalance, request a consult from one of our esteemed general surgeons to remove the culprit polyp, and start you on a corticosteroid medication until we determine if your dermatomyositis goes away by removing the tumour."

"And if it doesn't?"

"Then I have more magic tricks in here." Sababa patted his Columbian leather bag. He and Alex excused themselves to review their next referral. Along the corridor, even farther from Sophia's nursing station, Alex paused outside a room.

"Bente Affleck." He began. "34-year-old lottery ticket vendor admitted last evening by Dr. James Ruben Andrews with altered mental status, irritability, high-grade fever and a Glasgow Coma Score of 8/15, on a 12-month history of low-grade intermittent fevers, joint pain and swelling, and shortness of breath. Dr. Andrews had been seeing her for what he thought was rheumatoid arthritis for which he had prescribed non-steroidal anti-inflammatory medication. Three months before this admission, Bente experienced worsening esophageal dysmotility and Raynaud's symptoms."

"How did she get onto a general medical ward, instead of a more acute care unit?" Sababa asked.

"The ER doc referred her to Ernie Hacker." Alex said. "He thought she had lupus cerebritis, started her on high-dose intravenous methylprednisolone along with fluid and electrolyte correction, and admitted her here."

"Without neurovitals monitoring, brain imaging, lumbar puncture, or septic workup?"

"Uh-huh."

"And where is The Big Easy today?" Sababa asked.

"Uktoowally, I cun help wheat dat." Sophia rejoined the dynamic duo. "Ductor Hacker is playing wack wack. Dis is why Ductor Andrews asked you to see her. Eat snot pear."

"Thank you. Sophia." Sababa said. "What else you got, Bahney?"

"On exam, her vital signs are now normal." Alex continued. "She still has some mild photophobia with optic disc hyperemia and blurred margins, and splinter hemorrhages and cotton-wool spots on fundoscopy. Still not the sharpest knife in the drawer but she is now almost back to normal, so I guess that Dr. Hacker was right."

"About what?"

"About her encephalopathy being from lupus."

"Not so fast, Grasshopper." Sababa said. "It's never lupus. What else on exam?"

"She has reddish plaques on her cheeks, poikiloderma of Civatte on her neck, swollen hands and lips, sclerodactyly, subungual hyperkeratosis, synovial thickening in joints of hand and feet, and an enlarged non-tender liver."

"Lab?"

"Hemoglobin was low, ESR and muscle enzymes were high." Alex said.

"That's it?" Sababa watched his resident's head nod up and down. "Let's go see her."

Sophia introduced the portly professor to his new patient.

"Bente, dis is Ductor Sababa." She said. "Ay-bree-buddy apree shits his noh lej and injenwiti."

"Pleased to meet you." She said. "Have I ever sold you a lottery ticket?"

"I don't think so, Bente." Sababa said. "I've done the calculations, and the chances of winning are identical whether or not you play. They're a surtax on desperation."

"Somebody has to win." She said.

"The certainty of something happening doesn't increase the chances that it will happen to you." Sababa said. "Miserable stays miserable. Happy doesn't buy lottery tickets. And you appear to be involved in a different game of chance."

"Lupus?" Bente asked.

"It's never lupus." He said. "In your case, Bente, it's more than that. Whatever this is also has features of other autoimmune conditions—scleroderma, polymyositis, and rheumatoid arthritis."

"You have a name?" She asked.

"It's an overlap syndrome called mixed connective tissue disease."

"Is it fatal?"

"In some individuals with certain manifestations."

"What are my chances?"

"Better than my winning the lottery." Sababa said. "Dr. Harding here will order some more tests and change your medication so we can reduce the dose of your steroid therapy." The professor's pager vibrated in his warm nether regions.

"We'll write some notes in your chart so Dr. Hacker can pick up where he left off."

"But why can't you look after me?" Bente asked.

"Perhaps Sophia can talk to Dr. Andrews about speaking to Dr. Hacker..."

"I yam your uhd vo kut, Bente." Sophia said. "We need to be care-pull about the medical pull it ticks but I will call Ductor Andrews to arrange it." Sababa heard a whisper as they left down the hallway. *Wack wack Ee jut.*

"Where are we going now, Doctah Sababer?" Alex asked.

"First-floor Step-down unit." He said. "Patient of Poldy Bloom."

"Problem?"

"He's not inviting us for tea and scones."

Outside the telemetered Step-down Unit doors on floor one, boxes of rubber gloves in assorted sizes sat on an aluminum trolley, next to a laundry bin for scrubs and linens, and a garbage bin for disposable masks and shoe covers and bouffant caps. A battery of wall-mounted sanitizers and infection control notices flanked the entrance.

"Waste of good alcohol." Sababa and his accomplice rubbed their hands and entered.

Inside, the walls were just cream, and the floor just gray. There was no decoration at all, save the limp sun-bleached curtains that separated and encircled the beds. They may have once been a revitalizing colour of green that could have awakened memories of springtime and hope, but that had all faded away. The frosted windows were frozen in their frames. Monitors hung behind the pillows of every bay, above the clinical chrome clutter of medical gas outlets and aspirators that penetrated the walls, and the aneroid gauges and dials and meters and valves, and rubber and plastic tubing, that measured and regulated their flow. It was here, Sababa had observed, was where you could suck and blow at the same time. The hissibilation of this activity, and that of the infusion alarms, alerts and prompts, and automatic blood pressure devices reverberated off the chrome and were swallowed by the sombreness.

Patient prognosis was an inverse function of the number of CADD pumps on the IV poles surrounding the bed. The contract for every gas and liquid and solid had gone to the lowest bidder. Each patient was on a diet and every amenity was on a budget.

No flowers or scents or other forms of natural beauty were permitted entry to the healing process. In their efforts not to offend or inspire, the bureaucrats had sunk the spirit.

The charge nurse, Serafina, was hovering over her applesauce and medication administration record MAR chart, dispensing the ten o'clock drugs. A nursing school mantra of dispensation echoed in her head. *Right dose, right route, right patient... three checks...*

Poldy Bloom, waiting at the nursing station, pulled a chart from the racks and acknowledged his colleagues.

"Sababa..." Poldy looked worried. "Alex..."

"What you got?" Asked the professor.

"Benedict Adamantiades." He began. "43-year-old right-handed notary public who arrived after midnight with acute onset right-sided weakness, fever, headache, and difficulty with gait and speech."

"Carry on."

"On admission, he was alert and oriented. His temperature was 38°C, pulse was a little fast but regular, and blood pressure was 150/80 mm Hg. He had oral aphthous ulcers and dark red tender lesions on both anterior aspects of his legs. Genitourinary exam showed scrotal ulcers and bilateral epididymitis. He slurred his speech but he could name, repeat, read, and follow instructions. His cranial nerves and fundoscopic examination were normal but his gait was wide-based and unsteady. There was mild weakness of all limbs, more prominent on the right. Muscle stretch reflexes were normal, but plantars were extensor in both legs. His coordination was impaired in proportion to weakness in all four extremities. He had mild neck rigidity with a positive Brudzinski's sign."

"Lab?"

"High erythrocyte sedimentation rate and C-reactive protein. Rest of his bloodwork and cerebrospinal fluid results from a lumbar puncture all returned normal."

"Imaging?"

"Chest x-ray, ECG, echocardiogram, and abdominal ultrasound were all normal." Poldy said. "Brain MRI showed diffuse cerebral atrophy and chronic ischemic lesions in both cerebral hemispheres. Digital subtraction angiography showed complete blockage of flow in both internal carotid arteries just above their bifurcations."

"What you got, Bahney?" Sababa asked.

"Classic stroke syndrome in a young adult." Alex said.

"From what?"

"Well, that's the question then, isn't it?"

"I know the question." Sababa said. "What I'm after is the answer."

"I use a mnemonic." Alex said. "T-H-E M-I-S-S-E-D C-V-A."

"Which stands for?"

"Tumor-Hysteria-Encephalitis + Migraine-Idiopathic-Seizure-Syphilis-Disseminated sclerosis + Cardiac (arrhythmia, endocarditis)-Vascular (hypertension, hypercoagulability, vasculitis)-Aneurysm (or arterio-venous malformation)."

"What a wasteful shamanic ritual you've created for nothing." Sababa said. "If you can't reason from effect to cause, you will lose the ability to reason from cause to effect. So, which one of your memory aides has affected our notary public here?"

"Some form of vasculitis, I'd say."

"Would you now?" Sababa asked. "And which form might that be?"

"He has oral ulcers with skin and genital involvement." Alex said. "If Benedict had any eye symptoms or signs, but he doesn't. His ophthalmologic exam is normal..."

"And?" Sababa asked.

"I would have bet it all on Behçet's disease." Alex said.

"Named after the great Turkish dermatologist, Hulusi Behçet, who first described it in 1937. Smoked like a chimney." Sababa said. "Also called Silk Road disease because of its increased prevalence in the areas surrounding the old silk trading routes in the Middle East and Central Asia. Hippocrates may have also described it in his 5th century BC *Epidemion*. Let's go see him."

Behind a faded curtain, Poldy Bloom made introductions.

"Benedict, this is Doctor Sababa." He said. "He's a philomath polyglot polymath, and this is his resident, Doctor Harding."

"Howdy do." Benedict slurred, or something close to it.

"Have you had these ulcers in your mouth before, Ben?" Sababa asked. The notary nodded.

Sababa took the ophthalmoscope off the wall behind Ben's bed and asked if he could look into his eyes. The notary nodded again. When Sababa finished peering, he replaced the instrument and raised an eyebrow.

"Nothing, right?" Alex asked. Sababa pointed to the patient's vital sign monitor, the most vivid animation in the cubicle, dancing across the screen.

"What colour is this?" He aimed his index finger at the red waveform of Ben's blood pressure tracing.

"Dunno." The notary noted.

"How about this one?" Sababa pointed to the lime green ECG tracing. "Dunno."

"And this one?" He drew his finger across an undulating yellow roller coaster of oxygen saturation.

"Nope." Ben said.

"Lost his colour vision." Sababa said. "Subtle, but proof that there is inflammatory optic nerve involvement. He's got vasculo-neuro-Behçet's."

"What's that?" Benedict slurred, or something close to it.

"You have an inflammatory disorder which has blocked off both major arteries that supply blood and oxygen to your brain, Ben." Sababa said. "You've had an unusual stroke."

"Can you cure me?"

"No, but we can make you better." Sababa said. "Dr. Harding here will order some more tests, provide you with some lidocaine mouthwash and ointment for your mucosal ulcerations, start you on some oral analgesics and antibiotics, and speak to you about taking aspirin, pentoxifylline, prednisolone, and pulse cyclophosphamide. We'll organize some physiotherapy and home care until you are well enough to look after yourself."

"Can I go back to work?" Ben asked.

"You charge people for your signature." Sababa said. "I'm sure you can handle it."

'An acquaintance of mine, a notary by profession, who, by perpetual writing, began first to complain of an excessive wariness of his whole right arm which could be removed by no medicines, and which was at last succeeded by a perfect palsy of the whole arm... He learned to write with his left hand, which was soon thereafter seized with the same disorder.'

Bernardino Ramazzini (1633-1714)

'It's getting dark too dark to see
Feels like I'm knockin' on heaven's door.'
Bob Dylan, *Knockin' On Heaven's Door*

The blizzard had buried the steps up to his private entrance under two feet of fresh snow. Sababa and Alex stumbled to the top and kicked their shoes against the doorframe on their way into the Manzanita Medical back hallway. Mercy was typing, as Mercy always was.

"It's vasculitis week, Boss." She didn't look up from her iMac screen.

"He that has no charity deserves no Mercy." Sababa dealt Alex a chart from the top of the patient pile.

"Make me proud." He said. Alex called out into the crowded waiting room.

"Rudolf Jaksch von Wartenhorst." A thin, well-dressed middle-aged man rose from the leather chair in the farthest corner and followed him down the hall and into the resident's room. Sababa picked up the next folder.

"June Cleaver." A pale elderly woman stood and accompanied the portly professor into his sanctum sanctorum.

Sababa perused the letter from the referring physician. It surprised him to see it was from the office of Harbour City's own faceless oculist guru,

107

Dr. T.J. Eckleburg. *78-year-old librarian with Fever of Unknown Origin. I told her you would find it.*

One of the stocky savant's eyebrows rose towards his mop of curly black hair, before subsiding to the level of the other one.

"How can I help, June?" He looked at and through her.

"Dr. Eckleburg says I have an infection, but he doesn't know where." She said. "That's why he sent me to see you."

"Why does he think that?"

"I haven't had any energy for over a month and a half." She said. "And I've been getting these fevers almost every day. My family doctor has done all kinds of blood tests and cultures and x-rays, but he hasn't found the problem."

"Why did he send you to Dr. Eckleburg?" Sababa asked.

"Yesterday I had some blurring of the vision in my left eye, but the ophthalmologist said he couldn't find anything abnormal."

"Does your jaw hurt when you chew your food?"

"My tongue does as well." She said. "How did you know?"

"It is my business to know what other people don't know." Sababa handed her a cloth gown and asked her to change in the adjacent examining room. When June was draped and comfortable on his cabernet-coloured examining table, the professor performed a brief but esoteric examination, taking her blood pressure in both arms, palpating several pulse points, and peering into her eyes with his ophthalmoscope. When he pressed on her temples, June Cleaver groaned in agony.

"I'll be back in a few minutes." Back in his office, Sababa pushed on his intercom button.

"Yes, Boss."

"Mercy, please get T.J. Eckleburg for me."

"On it." She buzzed him back a minute later.

"T.J. on one, Sab." Sababa picked up line one.

"So, what is it?" The faceless oculist guru asked.

"She has cranial arteritis."

"Impossible." T.J. said. "Her eye exam was normal."

"I don't care." Sababa said.

"Her ESR was normal." He protested.

"She's an old lady with iron deficiency anemia and rouleaux formation, a high white count, hypogammaglobulinemia and I don't even know if her blood sample was clotted, vibrated too long in a short tube, inadequately mixed, overdiluted, or reported wrong. Her CRP is in the sky, so her sed rate is falsely normal. She has jaw claudication, different blood pressures in each arm, temporal artery tenderness, and decreased pulses everywhere. Arteries are the rivers of our consciousness. She has cranial arteritis."

"A stab in the dark." T.J. said.

"Au contraire, mon ami oculiste." Sababa said. "This is a medical emergency. If I don't start her on prednisone today, she's the one who'll be in the dark. You of all people know how giant cell arteritis can cause sudden blindness. Delay is dangerous."

"She'll need a temporal artery biopsy."

"When do you want to do it?" Sababa asked.

"Aren't you going to do it?" T.J. asked.

"You're the eye surgeon."

"It doesn't pay me for the time it takes."

"Play stupid games, win stupid prizes." Sababa said. "Look, T.J. We've both been in this rodeo before. The official powers of evil have ruled that the temporal artery biopsy is the responsibility of the ophthalmologist."

"But you're going to start her on steroids, and I won't be able to get to this for a few days at least." T.J. said. "And your treatment will ruin any chance to make a tissue diagnosis."

"You have a week after I start therapy before the biopsy turns to shit." Sababa said. "Tell your medical office assistant to coordinate with Mercy. And make sure you get me a long enough arterial segment, so we don't miss it."

"There's one thing I don't understand."

"What's that?"

"Why hasn't anyone killed you yet."

"Charm, T.J." Sababa said. "The quality in others that makes us more satisfied with ourselves. I'm the dead green bug on the golden leaf of occasion."

"Hmphh." T.J. harrumphed. "Charm strikes your sight, but merit wins your soul. And some would maintain that your soul belongs to Jesus."

"Which brings me to my last question." Sababa said.

"Which is?"

"If Jesus could heal any blind person he met, then why not heal blindness?"

"I guess I'd be out of job." T.J. said. "I'll get back to you with the biopsy results. Ciao." *Click.*

Sababa went back into his examining room to explain her condition and his proposed tests and treatment. He wrote out several requisitions and prescriptions and asked her to make another appointment with Mercy two weeks after Dr. Eckleburg's biopsy. Alex found him in the hall on his way back into his office.

"Diga me." He said.

"Rudolf Jaksch von Wartenhorst." Alex began. "54-year-old financial advisor referred by Dr. Nick Rivera for a two-year history of chronic cough. That's his only symptom. Dr. Hyde, our local respirologist, saw him first, followed by several other pulmonary specialists in Victoria and Vancouver."

"And?"

"Nada." Alex said. 'Some thought he had cough variant asthma, atopic cough, or gastroesophageal reflux cough, but these theories remain unsubstantiated. He's never smoked and has no occupational history. Empiric treatment with half a dozen antibiotics made no difference to his symptoms. Nor does he appear to have any unusual causes of chronic cough, such as cervical spondylosis or a heterotopic salivary gland at the base of his tongue."

"I once had a patient who had a severe chronic cough from a tiny hair touching his left eardrum." Sababa said. "His symptoms vanished the second I removed it. Exam?"

"Not much." Alex said. "Bit of conjunctivitis. Low-grade decrescendo early diastolic blowing murmur audible on the left lower sternal border at 3rd and 4th intercostal spaces consistent with the leaky aortic valve found on echo. Nil else."

"Lab and imaging?"

"Zero, and I mean zero." Alex continued. "Normal hematology and chemistry and autoimmune bloodwork, sputum studies, pulmonary function and diffusing capacity, negative bronchoscopy and methacholine provocative testing and esophageal pH monitoring, and normal chest and paranasal sinus x-rays. High-resolution CT chest showed some mild tracheal calcification." He watched Sababa's left eyebrow defy the underestimated gravity of his statement.

"Let's go see him." Mercy pointed to a specific chart in the diminishing pile and pantomimed an aerial hand-slap as Sababa and Alex passed her on their way down the hall towards the resident's room."

"What was that?" Alex asked.

"High five." Sababa said.

"What for?"

"HiV." He whispered. "It's code."

"Oh." On the other side of the resident room's door, Alex introduced his mentor. "Rudolph, this is Doctah Sababer. He hears his inner voice with great clarity and lives by what he hears."

"Such people become crazy." Said Herr Jaksch von Wartenhorst. "Or they become legend."

"I'm working on legend." Sababa said. "But crazy is catching up fast." He turned to his protégé.

"Tell me about Rudolph's nose, Alex."

"It's not particularly oh-so-bright."

"What about its saddle shape?" Sababa said. "Combined with his leaky aortic valve and conjunctivitis."

"Of course." A Zen slap smacked Alex. "The Great Pretender. Why didn't I think of syphilis sooner?

"Because you would have been wrong." Sababa said. "Saddle-nose deformity is a characteristic of congenital syphilis, conjunctivitis of secondary syphilis, and aortitis occurs only in the tertiary form. Very unusual to be everywhere at once."

"So, what is it then?"

Sababa cupped his palms over Rudolph's ears and then asked his resident to do the same.

"His left external ear is warmer than his right." Alex said. Sababa squeezed Rudolph's left pinna and watched the man grimace in pain. He elicited the same response by pressing on each side of his breastbone.

"So what you got?"

"Chronic cough and costochondritis and inflamed ear cartilage and a leaky aortic valve and conjunctival injection and..."

"And calcification of his trachea." Sababa smiled at Alex's epiphany. "Light dawns ovah Mahblehead."

"What is it?" The patient asked.

"Rudoph, you have a rare condition called relapsing polychondritis. Your immune system is making antibodies against your own type II collagen, attacking your cartilage and causing your cough."

"What can you do?"

"What should we do, Alex?" Sababa asked.

"We could send him to Vancouver for an 18F-fluorodeoxyglucose positron emission/CT scan and biopsy the cartilage of his left external ear."

"Or?" Sababa asked.

"Or because airway involvement is a major cause of morbidity and mortality in patients with relapsing polychondritis, we should start him on prednisone now and order anti-cartilage antibodies later."

"Congratulations, Alex." Sababa said. "Today you are a man."

After the two physicians explained the clinical situation in more detail, provided lab requisitions and a prescription, and asked Rudolph to make a return appointment, they left the resident's room to find a single chart remaining.

"What happened to the high-fiver, Mercy?" Sababa asked.

"Told me he was worried about getting home in the storm and he was feeling a lot better." She said. "He thought it was just a virus."

"It is." Sababa said. "Call his family doc to get him back here."

"On it."

"Let's see this last one together, Alex." Sababa picked up the chart and looked around.

"No one here but us chickens." He said. "Carolyn Savage?" A middle-aged woman struggled to her feet and staggered behind the two physicians into Sababa's sanctum sanctorum. She sat down across from the portly professor's desk. Alex took the chair beside her and watched his instructor peruse the referral documents. *58-year-old Ideal Café waitress with new lung and kidney problem on a background of peripheral neuropathy secondary to thiamine deficiency. Over to you... Dr. Dunsmuir, Campbell River.*

111

"Ideal Café." Sababa said. "I always stop for their liver and onions on my way up to fish at Dr. Tarmac's cabin in Port Neville on Johnstone Strait. How can we help, Carolyn?"

"I don't feel well, Doctor Sababa." She began. "I haven't been able to work for six months now. My hands and feet are numb, my arms and legs are weak and heavy, and I've lost my balance. They told me I had a thiamine deficiency, but I've only been getting worse taking these vitamins."

"What else?"

"I've been short of breath." She said. "I have blood in my urine and my ankles swell."

"Does the swelling go down overnight?"

"No."

"Which organ system dysfunction is it not, Alex?"

"It's not cardiac." He said.

"Correct." Sababa said. "It's renal."

"What does that mean?" She asked.

"Your kidneys aren't working very well, Carolyn." Sababa flung the chest x-ray Dr. Dunsmuir had sent with her up on his view box. "Alex?"

"Diffuse bilateral perihilar opacities." He said. "Some kind of chronic interstitial disease." Sababa logged into the radiology site on his desk computer.

"Her chest CT scan this morning at Harbour City Regional shows alveolar ground-glass opacities and air bronchograms."

"What does that mean?" She asked.

"Whatever this is has also affected your lungs." Sababa clicked on a laboratory link.

"You asked Dr. Dunsmuir to get some more blood tests this week." She said. "Is that what you're looking at now?"

"Uh-huh."

"Do they tell us anything?"

"Uh-huh."

"What?"

"You have high titres of anti-myeloperoxidase anti-neutrophilic cytoplasmic antibodies."

"What does that even mean?" She asked. Sababa looked up at his resident.

"What does that mean, Alex?"

"It means you have microscopic polyangiitis, Carolyn." He said. "It's a rare form of systemic, pauci-immune, necrotizing, small-vessel vasculitis caused by some inflammatory trigger which upregulates p-ANCA antibodies that bind neutrophils, resulting in their degranulation and release of toxins that produce endothelial injury."

"Whoa." She said.

"Whoa." Alex agreed. Sababa handed him the page of other lab results he retrieved from the printer.

"And?" She asked.

"And we need to bring you into hospital for some additional investigations, including a kidney biopsy and bronchoscopy, triage for therapeutic plasmapheresis and dialysis, induction corticosteroids plus or minus cyclophosphamide or rituximab, and maybe other stuff."

"Maybe other stuff?" She asked.

"It's a technical medical term, Carolyn. Dr. Harding will explain it and arrange for your admission." Sababa turned to his apprentice.

"We're on call tonight, Alex." He handed him a piece of paper inscribed with names. *Erna Petri... Ben Watt...* "When you finish here, Mercy has agreed to plough her way back through the snowbanks and drop you at the hospital. Page me after you see these two patients in the ER."

"What will you be doing?' Alex asked.

"Exploring the philosophical interdependency of scholasticism and pragmatism on behaviorism and voluntarism."

"Huh?"

"I'll be explaining the concept of the wolf pack to a lone wolf." Sababa said. "Good will hunting."

"You're meeting with Erg Hebberig?" Alex asked.

"We're having a coffee at Code Brew." Sababa said. "I'm talking to him. I'm not listening to him. It's not social."

"Listen, Sab, I know this Dr. Affluenza type. Selfish gene hardwired to self-enrichment, regardless of any harm he might do to others. Cheats at solitaire. What do you hope to achieve?"

"I want him to discover some magnanimity."

"And what if he rejects your appeal?"

"There will be an existential slap." Sababa said. "So hard, even Google won't be able to find him."

It should have been that twilight hour between the day and night shift at Harbour City Regional, but this was winter, and the darkness had already arrived.

Dr. Erg Hebberig sat alone at a Code Brew table in the hospital central court. Decked out in designer labels, Northface taupe green man purse slung across one shoulder, in any other clothes he would have appeared too young for his new appointment as an Internal Medicine staff specialist—in board shorts and an old T-shirt in another season, he could have been mistaken for a surf-bum. Holding out his dominant hand, Erg doomscrolled his smartphone screen in supplication to the fading signal of the last generation of clinical savants, soon to be extinguished forever on the new frontier cult of managed care.

The coffee shop was almost deserted save for a few relatives locked in limbo until closing time and inmates in transition, pushing their IV poles toward a tobacco fix outside in the snow. A lone barista, ornamented in subdermal ink and transdermal metal, presided over aromas of cloying muffins and marijuana, stale dishwater, and old garbage juice. The last offerings in the café display case held together with so much sugar, they should have come with their own insulin syringe and a ball-peen hammer. *In case of emergency, break glass.*

A bouncing medusa of black curly hair came out of nowhere, roaring down the main hallway in black gumboots and clutching a Colombian leather bag. He motioned to Erg to join him at the concession counter.

"Coffee first." Sababa said. "Save the world later."

"Nothing for me."

"My treat."

"In that case, I'll have a caffè vanilla frappuccino."

"One espresso dopio dopio and one..."

"Caffè vanilla frappuccino." Erg said.

"We don't have that." The barista said.

"You have Kopi Luwak?"

"What's that?"

"Indonesian coffee berries, eaten and fermented and partially digested and defecated by the Asian palm civet." Sababa said. "*Paradoxurus hermaphroditus.*"

"We don't have that." The barista said.

"Doesn't matter." Erg said. "What's the most expensive?"

"That would be our pumpkin spice latte."

"Fine."

"Fair trade?"

"Doesn't matter." Erg said. The barista's arms worked the machinery.

"One espresso dopio dopio and one unfair trade pumpkin spice latte." Sababa paid as Erg took the drinks back to his table.

"I'm pretty busy trying to build my practice here, Sababa." Erg took a sip of pumpkin spice. "What did you want to talk to me about?"

"Nash equilibrium." Sababa said.

"What's that?"

"A collection of individual behaviours in social game theory, where there is no benefit for any player to switch strategies. Everyone is satisfied with their choices at the same time, so the game remains in equilibrium."

"Give me an example."

"A pride of lions does better hunting in a pack." Sababa said. "Individual specialists in a Department of Medicine do better with consensual, mutual support in both innovation and defense."

"Zounds. An ambush." Erg said. "A real lion does not concern himself with the opinion of a sheep. You mean 'consensual' as in sex?"

"As opposed to rape, yes." Sababa said. "We all maintain our own offices for patient access and continuity and to support local skilled paramedical employment. By giving of our time and energy to lecture colleagues and patient groups, we give back to the community. Everyone serves on various hospital committees without payment. And we step up to cover each other's call whenever someone is on leave or incapacitated by personal or family illness or bereavement. Over many years we have created a mycorrhizal superspecialist superorganism. Together we do better when we support each other."

"You give this musketeer speech to all the new recruits?"

"Nope." Sababa took a sip of his espresso.

"Why me?"

"Erg, you haven't been here a week yet and you've already declared your intention to put remuneration ahead of responsibility." Sababa said. "You've advised our electrodiagnostic clinic staff you will invade their space to host your clinics and that you'll be cherry-picking referrals that allow you to perform consultations and stress tests at the same time. You've made it clear that you won't see patients in follow-up because it doesn't pay enough, and you don't want to have your own office because of the overhead cost."

"Not quite true." Erg protested. "I asked Dr. Martino if I could hold my clinics in his office when he wasn't using it."

"And he turned you down because you didn't want to pay him anything towards the lights and heat and the privilege."

"Your generation is stupid." Erg said. "The only thing alive in here is that ticking clock. The rest of you died a long time ago."

"Go ahead." Sababa said. "Call me old-fashioned."

"Dinosaurs." Erg raised his voice. "You're all fools for wasting your money on maintaining your own offices. The provincial government should find us clinic space inside the hospital and provide staff, transcription services, and medical equipment. And all at no cost. Why don't you see that?"

"You eat the Tsar's bread, you are the Tsar's man." Sababa said. "It's the difference between an autonomous professional and a voiceless civil servant. True independent wizards are always looking for opportunities to help others. Houseboys are always asking *What's in it for me?*"

"What's wrong in asking?" Erg said. "Life is a shit sandwich. But if you have enough bread, you don't taste the shit."

"Before you came back to Harbour City, I spoke to a few of our colleagues who worked with you on the mainland."

"And?"

"They found little humour in your misplaced priorities." Sababa said. "They said that you always had the best sporting equipment because you complained to the manufacturers at the end of every year of use so they would replace it for free, you only attended the blood donor clinics because you thought they were giving it away, you avoided unhealthy looking people at the mall in case you had to perform CPR on your day off, and that you have two legs but pretend one is amputated—for the parking space. They think that you only became a doctor for the money."

"Is that what you think?" Erg rolled his eyes. "Well, gosh darn, Sababa, I became a doctor because ever since I was a little boy, I wanted to help people. You know, I don't tell this story often, but I remember when I was seven years old, one time I found a bird that had fallen out of its nest, so I picked him up and I brought him home and I made him a house out of an empty shoebox and..." Erg's laughter was macabre.

"I became a doctor for the same three reasons everybody does: Marx, Nietzsche, and Freud—money, power, and sex. There are only so many caffè vanilla frappuccinos out there, and I mean to get me some. Why did you become a doctor?"

"To dance with the devil in the pale moonlight." Sababa said.

"There won't be any pale moonlight for me." Erg said. "I'm specializing in 'Heart Health.'"

"If they have it, they don't need you." Sababa said. "Money for nothing and your chicks for free."

"Money for almost nothing." Erg said.

"That money will buy a bed but not sleep; books but not brains; food but not appetite; finery but not beauty; a house but not a home; medicine but not health; luxuries but not culture; amusements but not happiness; religion but not salvation—a passport to everywhere but not heaven." Sababa said. "Money doesn't change men, it unmasks them. If a man is greedy, the money brings that out, that's all. And to be clever enough to get all that money, you have to be stupid enough to want it."

"Do you know the difference between this coffee and your opinion?" Erg asked.

"What?"

"I asked for this coffee."

"Think about what I've said." Sababa left as fast as he had arrived. Erg looked through the contrails at the barista.

"You hear all that?" He asked.

"Uh-huh."

"And?"

"You know the worst thing that you could do with Sababa?" He asked.

"What?"

116

"Underestimate him." The barista smiled. "That'll be fun."

'The principle of my school is quite different. In the other schools, techniques are displayed like merchandise adorned with colors and flowers, so they can be turned into a way of making a living, which is not the true way.'
Miyamoto Musashi

⚕ ⚕ ⚕

'All women are lips, nothing but lips.'
Yevgeny Zamyatin, *We*

"How did it go with our Dr. Van Helsing?" Alex asked.
"As you might have guessed." Sababa said. "Wooden shoes, wooden head, wooden listen."
"I doubt if he'd give you the steam off his piss."
"He's a cockroach." Sababa said. "Refuses to evolve, and yet he'll survive us all. Our cozy little bushido world is being undermined from outside and within, Bahney. What you got?"
"Erna Petri." Alex began. "42-year-old Long Lake motel chambermaid referred by Dr. Chowdahead Carlton here." Cliffy's ears blew smoke rings.
"Yankee Doodle keep it up..."
"You two need to bury the hatchet." Sababa pressed his hands together.
"I get to pick the anatomy." Cliffy said.
"The story, lads." Sababa said. "Let's hear the story."
"Followed by her dentist for a month-long history of loosening teeth, bleeding gums, and nosebleeds." Alex continued. "Saw her GP a week ago for left-sided facial pain and swelling. He prescribed a course of antibiotics for what he thought was sinusitis."
"And?"
"She presents tonight with low-grade fever, blocked nose with bilateral bloody nasal discharge, gum swelling, ulcers of her palatal mucosa, severe lower gum pain when she drinks, and left ear discomfort when she swallows." Cliffy added. "She also has new shortness of breath and aching behind her left eye which keeps her from sleeping at night. Exam consistent with her history."
"I'm not sure what that means." Sababa said. "Lab?"

117

"High ESR." Cliffy said. "Rest normal."

"Imaging?"

"Normal chest x-ray." Alex said. "A cone beam CT scan today showed buccal and palatal bone destruction near her posterior upper teeth."

"Let's go see, shall we?" Sababa asked.

Behind the curtain of cubicle 7, Alex introduced his instructor.

"I don't trust doctors." Erna said.

"We have that much in common." Sababa said. "Show us your teeth, Erna." Her lips and cheeks pulled back to reveal fat scarlet gums studded with tiny flecks of blood, like a thick jam of overripe fruit.

"Hmmm." Sababa mused. "This has a name, gentlemen."

"Looks like strawberries." Cliffy said.

"Strawberry gingivitis." Alex added.

"Pathognomonic for what?" Sababa asked.

"Wegener's granulomatosis." Alex said.

"We don't call it that anymore."

"Why not?" Alex asked.

"Because that son of a bitch was a Nazi."

"Really?"

"Uh-huh." Sababa said. "Wegener was a member of Hitler's *Sturmabteilung* brownshirts before he joined the genocide machinery performing medical experiments on victims of the Łódź ghetto in Poland."

"So what do we call it now?" Cliffy asked.

"Granulomatosis with polyangiitis." Sababa said.

"Which is?" Erna asked.

"A rare but serious inflammation of blood vessels in many organs."

"How serious?" She asked. "I don't want any of your poisons."

"Without my poisons, the average survival is five months." Sababa said.

"And with your poisons?" Erna asked.

"Some patients lead normal lives and can remain in remission for 20 years or longer."

"I'll take the poisons." She said. The most exquisite pleasure in the practice of medicine comes from nudging a layman toward terror, then bringing him back to safety again.

"I thought you would." Sababa said. "Dr. Harding will return later to admit you to the medical clinical teaching unit. He'll explain why you need a biopsy of your strawberry gums and a blood test called myeloperoxidase c-ANCA/anti-PR-3 antibodies, and he'll get you started on your poisons."

"Which ones?" She asked.

"Prednisolone and methotrexate, for now." He watched Erna text them into the Google search engine on her cell phone.

"Careful you don't hurt yourself, Erna." He said.

Alex took his mentor over to the consultant's desk, where Dr. Ho was waiting.

"Is this second referral your case, Gung?" Sababa asked.

"Ben Watt." He began. "64-year-old hardware store employee who presents with a one-year history of recurrent aspiration pneumonia and difficulty swallowing. He has a five-year history of asthma and allergic rhinitis complicated by recurrent sinusitis and nasal polyps. For the last two months, Ben has experienced feverishness and night sweats, dry cough, diffuse abdominal discomfort, and a ten-pound weight loss. In the last two weeks, he's developed insidious hearing loss and recurrent episodes of gastrointestinal bleeding."

"Exam?" Sababa asked.

"Uveitis of his left eye." Gung said. "Sensorineural hearing deficiency, absent gag reflex, impaired phonation, poor laryngeal elevation, impaired tongue movement, and flaccid dysarthria."

"Multiple lower cranial nerve involvement." Alex confirmed.

"Lab?"

"Mild anemia, raised eosinophil count, ANCA-negative." Gung said. "Buddy Benway scoped him last week and found numerous bleeding esophageal ulcers. Started him on a proton pump inhibitor, but there's been no improvement in his symptoms."

"CT of his chest and paranasal sinuses showed focal aspiration pneumonia in his right lower lobe, small nodules in his right upper lobe, multifocal bronchiolitis in bilateral upper and lower lobes, and bilateral chronic maxillary sinusitis." Alex added.

"And so, my gallant guardians of the galaxy, what you got?"

"Dunno."

"You've just described the prodromal allergic stage, the second eosinophilic stage, and the final vasculitic stage of a rare systemic eosinophilic necrotizing disease." Sababa said. "You should have a name?"

"Churg-Strauss syndrome." Alex said.

"We don't call it that anymore."

"Why not?" Alex asked. 'Were they Nazis as well?"

"No." Sababa said. "They were Jews."

"So why can't we call it after them?"

"Multiculturalism." Sababa said. "Based on the lie that all cultures are equal."

"So, what do we call it now?" Gung asked.

"Eosinophilic granulomatosis with polyangiitis." Sababa said. "Let's go meet the lucky contestant." Alex did the honours behind the cubicle 2 curtain.

"Ben, this is my boss." He said. "Doctor Sababa is the embodiment of weaponized logic."

"OK." Ben said. "What's going on, Doc?"

"You have an unusual autoimmune condition playing havoc with your small and medium-sized blood vessels." He said. "It's called eosinophilic granulomatosis with polyangiitis."

"Sounds serious."

"Can be." Sababa said. "In your case, according to the five-factor risk stratification score of the French Vasculitis Study Group, you have a 26% five-year mortality probability."

"Are those good odds?" Ben asked.

"If you're not in the 26% cohort."

"Is there anything you can do to improve my chances?"

"Oh, yeah." Sababa said. "Dr. Harding here will admit you to hospital, arrange some further investigations, including brainstem auditory evoked potentials and a biopsy of your nasal cavity, and start you on a course of methylprednisolone and mepolizumab. if we can pry it from the hands of the bureaucrats in Ottawa, or cyclophosphamide, if we can't."

"What about my work?"

"What about it?"

"Well, alright then." Alex told Ben he would be back to see him, as Cliffy Carlton made another pass.

"Hey, Brahmin." He said. "Another one for you and the Sage."

"Take a numbah, Bozo."

"You're the one with the bow tie, Masshole."

"Boys. Boys. Boys." Sababa said. "What you got, Cliffy?"

"Margaret Houlihan." He began. "35-year-old practical nurse with a 15-year history of non-pitting, non-pruritic, recurrent swelling of both her lips, worse on the upper one. Some flyby lightweight told her she had angioedema. Treatment with oral anti-allergy medications and systemic steroids didn't work. Attacks had ranged from days to years between, but within the last month the swelling has persisted and increased, and now seems permanent. Her lips have become hard, cracked, and fissured with a reddish-brown discoloration."

"Why did she come in tonight?"

"Painless peripheral left-sided facial weakness." Cliffy said. "Bell's palsy."

"Not so fast, Criscojack." Sababa said. "What else did you find on physical exam?"

"Nothing." Cliffy said. "Apart from severe swelling of both lips. They feel firm and rubbery, like a squash ball or hockey puck."

"Lab?"

"All normal." He said. "Except..."

"Except?"

"She saw our plastics boy, 'Pretty Boy' Troy, three weeks ago."

"And?"

"He did an incisional biopsy of her upper lip."

"And?"

"I haven't seen the results." Sababa began hammering the keyboard of the computer on the consultant's desk.

"Hmmm." He said. "As I thought."

"What?" Came out of Cliffy and Alex at the same time.

"Our pathologist, Dr. Juan Leyblanca, signed off the histology as showing dilated lymphatic vessels and an inflammatory infiltrate of lymphocytes and non-caseating granulomas in the subepithelial connective tissue, consistent with a diagnosis of Miescher's cheilitis."

"Well, that's it then." Cliffy said.

"What?"

"Whatever he said it was."

"Miescher's cheilitis doesn't cause facial paralysis." Sababa said.

"Oh."

"Take us to the bedside." Cliffy took Sababa and Alex behind a curtain and made introductions.

"I know Doctor Sababa." Margaret said. "He doesn't seem to adhere to any rules." Her lips were like large crimson polyps.

"The only sensible way to live in this world is without them." Sababa said. "Are you able to stick out your tongue?" Margaret snuck what she could manage out from between her massive lips, crevassed with deep, long fissures.

"Internal Medicine is a Confucian discipline, gentlemen. Numerological, in big strokes." Sababa said. "Here we have the classical triad of a condition with only 400 reported cases in the world—fissured tongue, facial paralysis, and lip swelling."

"You should have a name." Alex said.

"Melkersson–Rosenthal syndrome." Sababa said.

"Nazis or Jews?" Alex asked.

"Swedes." Sababa said. "But no one has come up with an alternative to the eponym. I should prefer that you do not mention my name at all in connection with this case, as I choose to be only associated with those crimes which present some difficulty in their solution."

"My lips are sealed." Margaret said. "What causes it?"

"You have witchcraft in your lips." Sababa smiled. "We don't know, although the hallmark of non-caseating granulomas and its increased incidence with Crohn's disease, sarcoidosis, leprosy, and other similar conditions offer tantalizing possibilities."

"Anything you can do?" She asked.

"Helping hands are better than praying lips." Sababa said. "We'll start with off-label anti-TNF-alfa therapy, infliximab every 8 weeks, until we can stabilize the disease process."

"And then?"

"We'll get Dr. Troy to provide some lip service—Conway's reduction cheiloplasty repair with local flaps to get you back below Mick Jagger range."

"How long do I need to wait before I can get the surgery, Doctor Sababa?" She asked.

"As long as a year, Margaret." He said. "Stiff upper lip."

"I wish." She said. Sababa turned his attention to Alex.

"After you finish up with these three cases, Alex, the night will still be young, and pregnant with possibility." He said. "If we get through all our work by noon tomorrow, you might get the rest of the afternoon off."

"In Boston, we call that DOMA."

"DOMA?"

"Day off, my ass."

"Education never ends, Watson." Sababa said. "It is a series of lessons with the greatest for the last."

'Who'll walk me down to church when I'm sixty years of age
When the ragged dog they gave me has been ten years in the grave
And senorita play guitar, play it just for you
My rosary has broken, and my beads have all slipped through.'
Elton John, *Sixty Years On*

His pager found Sababa lost in a daydream rêverie. He was reading electrocardiograms but, in his exhaustion, all the tracings had run over each other in their rush to evade interpretation. This summons was more insistent and noisier than normal, whatever that was. He dialed the number displayed on the screen. It was Alex. He was excited.

"What?"

"You need to come." He said. "Now."

"On my way." *Click.*

Sababa made his way down the hallway to the ground floor CT scanner room. A technician in a white coat sat in front of the computer workstation that processed the imaging information inside the radiation-shielded walls of the console area control room. Alex flanked her on one side and Mako Brisk, the on-call radiologist, stood on the other.

Through the large thick lead-equivalent x-ray glass control window was an unrestricted view of the patient on the narrow examination table sliding in and out of the short central tunnel inside the large donut-shaped gantry. Based on rigorous mechanical engineering principles of thermodynamics, fluid mechanics, and heat transfer, the HVAC system ensured a stable temperature, ventilation, relative humidity, and dust-free environment for the premium 128-slice million-dollar machine. Alex had found Sababa's music library on the secret M drive hidden deep inside the hospital computer network. Johnny Cash moaned in the background. *I fell into a burning ring of fire... I went down down down... and the flames went higher.*

A red warning light above the shielded automatic main door began flashing.

"Take a deep breath and hold it." She said into her microphone. The patient took a deep breath and held it. The x-ray tube and electronic x-ray detectors inside the scanning frame buzzed and clicked and whirred and rotated around the patient at 200 revolutions a minute.

"Breathe." She said. The patient took a claustrophobic breath.

"Hey Boss." Alex said.

"Sababa." Mako nodded.

Everyone watched the slices of abdomen peel onto the control room computer screen. Sababa's eyes went back and forth in rapid saccades from the vital signs displayed on the patient monitor. One of his eyebrows rose towards the white stippled acoustic tile ceiling.

"You want to tell me what the hell is going on here, Bahney?"

"Yah huh." Alex began. "Bergen 'Ollie' Opzoom, 60-year-old beekeeper found semi-conscious, hypotensive, and hypothermic in Amsterdam Pahk early this morning. Four-week history of fever, 35-pound weight loss, and a painful bluish discoloration of his fingertips, which later turned black with worsening discomfort. History of childhood rickets, chronic hepatitis B infection, and late-onset hypertension. Brought in by EMS in severe abdominal pain associated with left-sided distension."

"So I see." Sababa said. "What happened in the ER?"

"I can help with that, Sab." Dr. Myles Capitaine was in the house.

"How are you, Myles?" Sababa asked.

"Living the dream."

"The most pitiful among men is he who turns his dreams into silver and gold." Sababa said, "But that's another fly-in Dutchman. You were saying?"

"We treated his hypovolemic shock with four litres of crystalloid until he stabilized and became lucid enough for us to get a history and proceed with investigation." Myles said. "He had an elevated white cell count and sed rate. I called Buddy Benway, the on-call surgeon, but he said he would need an abdominal CT scan before he would come in for an acute abdomen. And here we are."

"Mako?" Sababa asked.

"As you can see, gentleman." He pointed to the CT images of Ollie's belly. "Mr. Opzoom here has sustained a massive retroperitoneal bleed."

"From what?" Alex asked.

"Not my department." Mako said.

"Oh, but it is, my special shadow puppet." Sababa said.

"How do you figure that?"

"Mako, you need to crack open the angio suite."

"We don't start before nine."

"You do today."

"I'll need a better reason than 'because I said so,' Sababa." Mako protested. "What are you looking for?"

"A rosary."

"He's got a rosary." Mako said. "A rachitic rosary from expansion of the anterior rib ends at his costochondral junctions, secondary to his childhood vitamin D deficiency."

"That's not the rosary I'm looking for."

"What other kinds of rosary are there?" Asked the radiologist.

"Hmmm. Let me see." Sababa said. "There are four mysteries of the rosary in Catholicism—joyful mysteries, sorrowful mysteries, glorious mysteries, and luminous mysteries. I have a 60-year-old with a history of chronic hepatitis B and mysterious late-onset hypertension who presents with ischemic gangrene and unexplained retroperitoneal bleeding. What could he have?"

"A string of visceral artery aneurysms." Mako said. "The 'rosary sign' on mesenteric angiography that will confirm your suspicion of polyarteritis nodosa."

"Well done, Mako." Sababa said.

"But if you're already sure that Ollie has PAN, why do you need the angiogram to make the diagnosis?"

"I don't." Sababa said.

"Non capisco."

"I don't need the angiogram for you to confirm the diagnosis." Sababa said. "I need you to embolize the ruptured aneurysmal bleeding source with gelatin sponge particles and micro coils, so I don't have to listen to Buddy Benway bitch and moan about having to open up a patient." He looked deep into the defeated face of Mako Brisk. Some of us, transitioning from medical providers to recipients, still hold a warm nostalgia for a time when medical care made eye contact.

"You're going to write about this someday, aren't you?" Mako asked.

"It's not that there are no certainties, it's an absolute certainty there are no certainties." Dr. Brisk called through to the angiography suite to expedite Ollie's next procedure. Sababa turned his focus onto his resident.

"Lots to do here, Alex." He said. "Mr. Opzoom will need three units of packed red blood cells if my differential hematocrit calculations are accurate. His hepatitis B requires treatment, and we'll use a four-dose infusion of rituximab before beginning leflunomide for his polyarteritis. He'll need an amputation referral to a hand surgeon in Vancouver for his fingertip gangrene. You know what else to do for his ICU admission orders. I'll call the Death Star to let them know he's coming."

But Sababa didn't have to do that. He turned again to find two of his best Tranquility Base critical care nurses, Vanessa and Jan, arms folded.

"We already heard." Jan said. "We'll need a Zen pizza." Sababa handed over his credit card.

"Order the Buddhist special." He said.

"Buddhist special?" Vanessa asked.

"The most humble pie." He said. "Make me one with everything."

'Life is laughter amid a rosary of death.'
Federico Garcia Lorca

'The point is, ladies and gentlemen, that greed—for lack of a better word—is good. Greed is right. Greed works. Greed clarifies, cuts through, and captures the essence of the evolutionary spirit. Greed, in all of its forms—greed for life, for money, for love, knowledge—has marked the upward surge of mankind.'
Gordon Gekko, *Wall Street*

The casual reader should recognize that extreme acquisitiveness may be a marker of the upward surge of mankind, but it is not its cause. Erg Hebberig's addition to the Department of Medicine at Harbour City Regional was a mixed and conflicted blessing. He was an extra pair of hands, but they were always in someone else's pockets. There is a great deal to see in the tilt of a hat on a man.

The nature of our motivation determines the character of our work. And with the few physicians who have jumped on the Avarice Express, as rare as they are, there is a very fine line between listening and stalking.

Unscrupulous doctors receive kickbacks from laboratories or entities selling medical devices. Some perform unnecessary procedures. Others deliver one level of service but bill at a much higher level. 'Unbundling' is where the doctor invoices for several items charged as one global service. Some physicians so over-schedule themselves they miss abnormal lab results or fall into other lapses in good medical practice. Still others charge exorbitant fees for illegitimate narcotic prescriptions or lend their licenses to unscrupulous Internet drug sales sites to cash in on dysfunction, rather than cure disease.

The mixture of greed with vanity has resulted in the paramedical cosmetic, bariatric and Lasik surgery booms. Plastic surgeons and hair transplant physicians hire 'counselors' or 'assistants' to screen prospective patients with strong-arm used car salesman pressure tactics.

The mix of greed with envy begets intense competition as deceitful advertising to generate 'business.' Despite the earnest efforts of medical governing bodies, such activity has gained acceptability and legality.

Sometimes greed doesn't clarify.

The blend of greed with sloth and a dash of insanity explains the motivation for doctors prosecuted because they substituted saline for flu vaccinations or used non-pharmaceutical grade Botox to save a buck or two, or disposed of hazardous waste in conventional trash bins, or fabricated clinical study records in pharmaceutical trials, or threw away patients' records because proper disposal costs money.

The combination of greed with dishonesty produces physician expert witnesses who will say whatever the hiring attorney wants if the price is right.

The fusion of greed with naivete or financial desperation entices newly licensed or elderly physicians to 'front' clinics owned and operated by laypeople or sophisticated organized crime rings, who use the puppet physician's license to commit fraud—such can be the pressures of overwhelming student debt or inadequate retirement savings. Or, with our American cousins, HMOs penalise physicians for not seeing enough patients fast enough to maximize corporate profit.

Greed, for lack of a better word, is dangerous.

No one is greedy except from vanity, the notion that you're better than people if you can display more superfluous property than they can. He who is greedy is always in want. He who is not contented with what he has would not be contented with what he would like to have. Poverty wants much; but avarice, everything. Greed's worst point is its ingratitude. Luck brings bitter friends. To want too much sometimes drives the luck away. You must want just enough, and you must be courteous with the gods.

The character of Sababa's dog Shiva, when she was alive, overflowed with effortless qualities—loyalty, devotion, selflessness, unflagging optimism, unqualified love—that would forever elude the character of Erg Hebberig.

You succeed in life when all you want is what you need. Blessed is he who expects nothing, for he shall never be disappointed. Sababa's creative self-interest, the precise basis of the categorical imperative, motivated a desire to achieve, not a desire to beat others.

We make a living by what we get. We make a life by what we give. There are only good and bad things and black and white things and no in-between anywhere.

'The greatest achievement is selflessness.
The greatest worth is self-mastery.
The greatest quality is seeking to serve others.
The greatest precept is continual awareness.
The greatest medicine is the emptiness of everything.
The greatest action is not conforming with the world's ways.
The greatest magic is transmuting the passions.
The greatest generosity is non-attachment.
The greatest goodness is a peaceful mind.
The greatest patience is humility.
The greatest effort is not concerned with results.
The greatest meditation is a mind that lets go.
The greatest wisdom is seeing through appearances.'

Atiśa Dīpankara Śrījñāna (982–1054)

'Habits are to the soul what the veins and arteries are to the blood,
the courses in which it moves.'

Horace Bushnell

There is something evil about a class of diseases that turns your immune system into a blind butcher of your bloodstream.

Janet Leigh's skin biopsy confirmed Sababa's diagnosis of Henoch–Schönlein purpura. Her kidney biopsy showed IgA nephropathy with only a few crescentic glomeruli. Nerve conduction studies demonstrated multifocal sensorimotor axonal neuropathy. All her manifestations responded well to methylprednisolone pulse therapy and maintenance on low-dose oral steroid. She is back working as a legal secretary where she reminds her employers never to call Doctor Sababa as a hostile witness.

The cinema concessionaire, Paulette Ehrlich, improved with dapsone therapy. Her hypocomplementemic urticarial vasculitis is a distant memory, although she still has some minor residual lung damage. On their rare date nights out, Jane and the portly professor sometimes avail themselves of Paulette's offer of 'free movie passes and popcorn.'

Phil LeBoit's skin biopsy confirmed Sababa's suspicion of lymphocytic vasculitis caused by a Hepatitis A vaccination. The professor stopped the low molecular-weight heparin treatment when the rash resolved four weeks later. Phil returned to his Nicaragua teak farm to find new landowners growing money on trees that he thought belonged to him. There was no one there to complain to.

Sababa would have to reach deep into his Colombian bag of magic tricks to help Maria Callas out of her predicament. Dr. Jules Martino had the easier task of resecting the large hypersecretory rectosigmoid villous adenoma that was causing the secretory diarrhea, electrolyte abnormalities, and kidney dysfunction of her McKittrick–Wheelock syndrome. But when Maria's dermatomyositis failed to dissolve after her surgery, Sababa suspected she might have another primary tumor as the cause. He found it in the hoarseness of her vocal cords. Harbour City's ENT surgeon, Dr. Theodor Billroth, performed the biopsy that confirmed invasive cancer and scheduled Maria for a laryngectomy. She left a note beside where they found her in the bridal gallery. *No one will silence my voice.*

Sophia spoke with Dr. James Ruben Andrews about speaking to Dr. Hacker about Bente Affleck's request to switch her attending physician to Doctor Sababa. Ernie was cognizant of the unwritten rule that, if a patient wanted to change doctors, it was not only a bad idea to refuse, it was an invitation to disaster. When 'The Big Easy' met the portly professor in a hallway a few days later, Sababa gave him an update on the lottery ticket vendor's medical status.

"The anti-double-stranded DNA and anti-ribonuclear protein antibody titres I ordered returned high, confirming your diagnosis of mixed connective tissue disease." He said.

"Mixed connective tissue disease?" Ernie asked. "Is that what she had?'

"You didn't know?" Sababa asked. "But you gave her a cosmic dose of steroid."

"How is she now?' He asked.

"Much better." Sababa said.

"So what's the problem?" Ernie watched one of Sababa's eyebrows head north. "Look, Sab, you know the one about the time the medical staff went hunting. A flock of birds flew overhead. The medical student jumped up first, pointed his shotgun at the sky, admitted he wasn't sure if they were ducks or not, and didn't pull the trigger. The psychiatrist aimed next but then considered how he might feel about shooting the ducks and let them fly away. The internist looked at the ducks, identified the genus, species, markings, migration pattern, and geographical distribution, and also didn't fire a shot.

The surgeon unloaded all his shells into the air. Several of the birds fell. He then turned to the pathologist and asked him to check if they were ducks?"

"And your point?" Sababa asked.

"If it walks like a duck, and quacks like a duck, it's a duck." He said.

"You're not a surgeon." Sababa said. "You're supposed to be an internist."

"Close enough." Ernie called over his shoulder.

Two months after Sababa began treating Benedict Adamantiades, for his vasculo-neuro-Behçet's disease, the notary public had almost recovered. For the colchicine prescription that maintains his remission, Benedict awarded the stocky savant a notorious seal of approval.

T.J. Eckleburg's biopsy of June Cleaver's temporal artery corroborated Sababa's diagnosis of giant cell arteritis as the cause of the librarian's mysterious fever. Thanks to the professor's low-dose prednisone regimen, June's circulation is back at work and her work is back in circulation.

Financial advisor Rudolf Jaksch von Wartenhorst's chronic cough, together with all the other manifestations of relapsing polychondritis, disappeared on Sababa's corticosteroid treatment. In gratitude, he offered to review the Good Doctor's investment portfolio and provide an hour of free financial advice. It didn't last anywhere that long. *You're not doing this for the money.*

After the acute treatment of her microscopic polyangiitis with systemic corticosteroids and rituximab, Caroline Savage entered a more stable azathioprine maintenance phase of her illness. Her peripheral neuropathy persisted despite treatment. She remained dialysis-dependent despite two weaning attempts and is awaiting renal transplantation. Sababa still meets her for coffee over his liver and onions at the Ideal Café, on his way up to fish at Dr. Tarmac's cabin in Port Neville on Johnstone Strait.

Erna Petri was eager to begin the portly professor's poisons after she finished her Google search and the oral surgeon's strawberry gums biopsy confirmed her diagnosis of granulomatosis with polyangiitis. She continues on maintenance doses of prednisone and methotrexate, following a successful remission with induction therapy. Erna received a disability allowance from her former employer for her work as a chambermaid. She was fitted for a full set of dentures. Her upper left second premolar edentulous ridge showed exposed buccal and palatal bone. No one, not even the Sage of the Salish Sea, saw the *Pneumocystis jirovecii* pneumonia coming.

The biopsy of Ben Watt's nasal cavity returned a verdict of eosinophilic granulomatosis with polyangiitis. The bureaucrats in Ottawa declined Sababa's application for mepolizumab but Ben responded well to second-line glucocorticoid and cyclophosphamide therapy. He retired from his hardware store job and can once again swallow with confidence.

The witchcraft in Margaret Houlihan's lips took nine months for Sababa's infliximab therapy to stabilize her Melkersson-Rosenthal syndrome enough for surgery. Dr. Christian 'Pretty Boy' Troy performed a Conway reduction cheiloplasty repair and smile transplant. Back in the clinical teaching units of Harbour City Regional as a practical nurse, she asked Sababa about his indifference and lack of adherence to the rules.

"Rules are for children, Margaret." He said. "This is war, and in war, the only crime is to lose. Integrity doesn't need rules. If you can't solve a problem, it's because you're playing by them. Hell, there are no rules here—we're trying to accomplish something." Or something like that.

Ollie Opzoom's mesenteric angiogram showed a rosary of multiple visceral arterial swellings and a culprit ruptured inferior pancreaticoduodenal artery aneurysm as the cause of his retroperitoneal hemorrhage. Mako Brisk performed a successful embolization and transferred Ollie to the Death Star for further investigation and treatment of his polyarteritis nodosa and chronic Hepatitis B infection, and amputation of his gangrenous fingertips. His critical care nurses, Jan and Vanessa, observed the new internist, Dr. Erg Hebberig, visiting Ollie's bedside, and *gesprekken met* the *hkhkkh-shhhurp-mar-flurpa-durpa* sounds of the Dutch language. Flies enter an open mouth. When the gregarious beekeeper was stable enough to transfer out of the Death Star, he requested a change of his attending physician to Dr. Hebberig.

This didn't disturb Sababa at all. The professor was cognizant of the unwritten rule that, if a patient wanted to change doctors, it was not only a bad idea to refuse, but an invitation to disaster. Erg Hebberig was as unfeeling as Ollie Opzoom's fingertips. Content to play the long game, Sababa knew that although the karma bus might sometimes be delayed, it was still coming. Make yourself honey and the flies will devour you.

> 'Where there are humans,
> You'll find flies,
> And Buddhas.'
> Kobayashi Issa

22. The Case of Ondine's Curse

'Beware the night, child.
All cats are black in the dark.'
Jean Genet

It was his parent's fault he was born blind, with his eyes closed. When he opened them two weeks later, his irises were as bright blue as the sky. Over the next year, they would become eerie: chartreuse glinted windows into the fires of Hell, or so thought the witch hunters of the Middle Ages. Most of his 250 pounds were muscle and sinew; his legs were long and muscular. Wounds he had received from aggressive encounters with others like him had scarred his tan complexion. He was the ultimate loner, a wild renegade remote from the rest of us. The lord of the stealthy murder, he had committed acts of infanticide and cannibalism, and faced his inevitable doom with a craven and cruel heart.

Like the Canadian arctic Inuit, East African Masai warriors, steppe nomads of Mongolia, South Dakota Sioux, and Professor Jordan Peterson, he ate nothing but meat. His ancestors had roamed the Americas when humans crossed the Bering land bridge from Asia 40,000 years ago. Chartreuse glinted windows watched the Spaniards conquer the Aztecs and the Pilgrims land at Plymouth Rock. They bore witness to the first Mormons arriving in Utah, prospectors invading the California gold fields, and Argentine gauchos herding cattle in the pampas. Their meanderings prowled the banks of the Mississippi, Colorado, and Amazon rivers, and crossed the high, windy passes of the Sierra Nevada, the Rocky Mountains, and the Andes. From the Yukon to the Straits of Magellan—over 110 degrees of latitude—and from the Atlantic to the Pacific, they once laid claim to the most extensive range of any other warm-blooded creature in the Western Hemisphere. The ancient Incas laid out their capital city of Cuzco in his image.

It was Piper Slagoon who spotted him first, just after midnight, lurking on the slips of the Harbour City Yacht Club. Piper was a retired wine merchant, and he and his wife had spent the day preparing their Hunter Legend 40, *Liquidity*, for the five-day winter regatta scheduled to begin the following morning. Venus Slagoon was down below decks, asleep in the V-berth while Piper sat at the navigator station in the cockpit, pouring over charts and sipping one last glass of Napa Cabernet from an exceptional vintage.

Movement caught the corner of Piper's vision. Thirty-five million years of evolution had created a flexible backbone to accommodate extended strides, strong leaps that could reach 45 horizontal and 15 vertical feet, and short running bursts of 45 miles an hour. His long, heavy tail, two-thirds of his ten-foot length, provided balance on quick turns and uneven ground. Webbed skin and fur between his toes muffled any sound as he walked. His hind tracks overlapped his front ones, covering them up.

When he was hungry, he roamed in a zigzag, skirting open areas and taking advantage of cover. He focused his keen senses to pick up the slightest movement, odour, or sound. He had night vision six times better than Piper Slagoon. He was the epitome of speed and precision, a fascinating embodiment of the spirit and aura of vast, rugged, and uninhabited places.

Without a hyoid bone in his throat, he couldn't roar like the greater members of his tribe, but he could purr like they couldn't. He could growl and hiss and snarl and chirp and whistle and bleat like a lamb. He purred as he pussyfooted past Piper's portholes.

"What's that, Honey?" Venus called from the V-berth.

"Cat." Piper said.

"Sounds like a pretty big cat."

"Could be." Piper picked up his cell phone and speed-dialed a number.

"911, what's your emergency?" Asked the dispatcher.

"There's a cat on the C Dock boat shed pier at the yacht club."

"You need the fire department?"

"It's bigger than that." Piper said. "We need firepower."

"On their way." She said. *Click.*

"Who was that, Honey?" Venus asked.

"Wrong number." In ancient times they worshipped cats as gods; felines had not forgotten. The beast who had crept past *Liquidity*'s cockpit held the Guinness record for the number of common names—panther, catamount, painter, American lion, Mountain lion, Mexican lion, Florida panther, silver lion, red lion, red panther, red tiger, brown tiger, deer tiger, ghost cat, mountain screamer, Indian devil, sneak cat, king cat, painted cat—and what they called him around Harbour City. *Cougar.* Here was a colossal cat, a cosmic cat, a living example of Bergmann's ecogeographical rule—populations and species of larger size inhabit colder environments, while populations and species of smaller size live in warmer regions.

Piper was one of those rare individuals who had seen a cougar ambush in the wild, five years earlier on the ridges above the city. The Roosevelt elk grazing in a glade had been unaware that a stalking predator that had fixed its gaze, lowered itself in a crouch, stretched its head forward with whiskers spread wide and ears erect, and turned to the front. It held its position until the elk had approached within 50 feet of him.

Flattened against the ground, the cougar shot forward in three bounds, in an angle of attack from the rear, its weight on its hind legs so that it could adjust its position to maintain control, landing on the ground just short of his victim. It grasped the elk's neck and shoulders with the front

132

paws, claws extended, with enough force to knock it over. The nerve density in its four two-inch long canines allowed the cat to 'feel' its way between the vertebrae in a fraction of a second, wedging the backbone apart and breaking the spinal cord at the base of the skull. The force generated by the cougar's jaw muscles could crush a man's head. Piper watched the cat drag the elk under a tree.

Using its teeth, it plucked the fur from the point of incision, then opened the flank behind the ribs with its claws. It pulled out the stomach and intestines and dragged them away from the carcass.

With the four carnassial teeth at the rear of its mouth, adapted for cutting meat, tendons, and sinews, it ate the heart, lungs, and liver first because these organs contained more protein, fat, and vitamins than muscle tissue. The liver held a high proportion of amino acids, and glycogen, the primary source of metabolic energy. The mountain lion then consumed ten more pounds of muscle. The story of cats is a story of meat.

After this first fast-and-gorge feed, Piper watched the cougar hide the carcass by using its front claws as rakes to drag in pine needles, tree limbs, and small twigs to cover his kill, protecting it from scavengers and keeping the meat cool and fresh. Piper knew it would come back for the rear quarters and then the muscle on the inside of the legs. All that the cat left uneaten was the head, large bones, hide, and digestive tract.

The night sky erupted in the flames of kaleidoscopic strobes and flashlight beams from five RCMP Ford Interceptor cruisers swirling on the wood and water of the piers and boatsheds. Piper came up from below but the cougar had disappeared. He stood in the middle of G Dock and stared up at the onshore illuminated police presence. A female officer motioned to him from behind the chicken wire entrance at the top of the gangplank.

"Open the gate." Four other Mounties joined her at the marina entrance.

"Not until you train your gun on me." He said.

"Why?" She asked.

"I'd rather take the chance of you shooting me than this mountain lion doing worse." Veronica Marsden drew her sidearm and aimed at the yachtsman. Piper made it to the top of the ramp and opened the entryway.

"Where is it?" Veronica asked.

"Headed towards the fish cleaning station at the end of my dock." He said. "It was climbing through sheds and creeping around boats. Some still have people on them."

"Same cat spotted around Newcastle Island the past couple of weeks." She said. "It's only a hundred yards away. Let's go." The five officers left Piper in a hurry, but the yachtie followed them until he had an unobstructed view of his pier. The cougar flexed tense under the hazy halo at the end of it, showing no fear of the approaching police. Piper watched it jump into Newcastle channel and swim towards the condo units on a nearby seawall.

The two shots that Veronica Marsden fired from her Smith & Wesson pistol sounded like the roaring fires of Hell. It was 1:30 am. The big cat rolled over slow. The first, or maybe it was the last of its lives, sunk into the waterline. Cats come and go without ever leaving.

No one said anything, but they were all thinking it.

Can you dance with the devil in the pale moonlight?

'He rich ate and drank freely, accepting gout and apoplexy as things that ran mysteriously in respectable families ...'
George Eliot, *Silas Marner*

A week after Veronica Marsden shot the cougar, Piper Slagoon had become a local marine celebrity. Not only were the yacht club members talking about his bravery in opening the gate at the top of the ramp while the wildcat was still at large, but *Liquidity* had beaten the other nine sailboat entrants in every race of the five-day winter regatta.

Venus had prepared Piper an evening feast fit for such a victory. They dined on brie and bacon soufflé, pan-seared foie gras, steak smothered in Roquefort butter sauce with sautéed palm hearts and prawns, and a whipped cream-covered chocolate mousse, each course accompanied by its appropriate wine match. After dinner, Piper rugged up in his Patagonia down jacket and went up top with a snifter of brandy and a Cuban Montecristo No. 2 while Venus took care of the dishes in the sloop galley. Under the custom canvas stern canopy, he sat back in his Baja bucket seat, put his feet up into the spokes of his commodore wheel, lit his stogie, and turned on the radio. Waves of smoke and sound filled his space with satisfaction.

Good evening, Harbour City... This is Silas Seaweed, the Snuneymuxw seer of squaw candy, sweat lodges, and slave labour... coming at you from CNDN Coast Salish radio, 101.3 FM on your Home and Native Band...

Piper could see his breath in the frozen night air, even between puffs of his cigar. He looked out at the night sky and the sheds and slips that surrounded him and wondered why some of his dock mates had vanished. All three of the boat shed occupants on his starboard side had gone missing—yacht charters owner George Wallace, tugboat captain Hank Moody, sailmaker Jack McKay, and all three of his friends on the adjacent finger slips of G Dock—locksmith Noirtier de Villefort (who they had taken away early that morning), marine mechanic John Ruskin, and sailing instructor Wilhelmina Mozart. He wished they could have been there to help him celebrate his victory.

First, a few words from Billy Mills, the Oglala Lakota brother who won a gold medal in the 10,000 metres run at the 1964 Tokyo Olympics...

The final drag of his Cuban torpedo made Piper feel light-headed and off-balance. He felt the left side of his face droop and the right side go numb. His vocal cords snapped shut as his diaphragm contracted into rhythmic, involuntary spasms.

In my youth I respected the world and life, I needed not anything but peace of heart...

He tried to call for Venus between hiccups, but his voice was hoarse, his speech garbled, and he couldn't recognize the sound that emerged from where his cigar had fallen. *Mneeeee-mnachchchch!*

I asked for power, that I might achieve... I was given weakness, that I might learn to obey...

His wife rushed up from the galley to find her Count of Monte Cristo asleep and slumped back in his commodore chair, his eyes dancing. In the dim lighting along C Dock, Piper was blue, and his chest was still.
"Breathe!" She howled. "Breathe!" Piper took a breath, but only once before falling back to sleep. His colour returned and left again.
"Breathe!" She screamed. "Breathe!" Piper took another breath before falling back to sleep. But again, only one.

I asked for health, that I might lead a long life... I was given infirmity, that I might appreciate each minute...

Venus scrambled down the companionway to grab her cell phone, punctuating every second step with her desperate mantra. *Breathe!... Breathe!... Breathe!...*
She speed-dialed the same number that Piper had phoned a week earlier.
"911, what's your emergency?" Asked the same dispatcher, Josepha Moondyne.
"My husband's having a stroke." Venus said. "Wake up! Breathe!" Piper and Josepha took a breath.
"Where are you?" Asked the operator.

"Harbour City Yacht Club." Venus said. "C Dock. Breathe!" Piper and Josepha took a breath.

I asked Mother Earth for strength, that I might have my way... I was given weakness, that I might feel the need for Her...

"Ambulance on the way." Josepha said. The sound of sirens shattered the frozen night, coming fast.

I asked to live happily, that I might enjoy life... I was given life, that I might live happily...

It's easy to live happily. The trick is to keep breathing.

'Castaways on the shores of loneliness.'
Jean-Dominique Bauby, *The Bell Jar and the Butterfly*

"You rang?"
"Sorry to wake you, Sab."
"But?"
"Cliffy Chowderhead tried to fire a brain-dead patient past my Bruins goalie stick into the Death Star."
"He can't do that." Sababa said. "It's a closed unit, and Cliffy isn't on the guest list."
"He said it was a harvest festival, and I could have my pick of organs." Alex said. "He's already called the BC Transplant on-call pager."
"Get him to meet us in the ER in twenty." The professor said. "Call Oliver Lax to bring the EEG machine and technician to the bedside. I'll be in." Sababa washed and dressed in the same efficient hurry he had mastered over the previous thirty years of practice.
"One of the usual calamities?" Jane asked as he was heading out the door.
"This one might be more unusual." Sababa fired up his dimpled and dented white Honda Civic and careened down his long driveway on the lake and into the Doppler-distorted distance. Less than six minutes later, rounding the last iconic intersection corner of Dufferin Crescent at Dufferin Crescent on two wheels, he lurched to a stop in the slot reserved for the on-call internist. Sababa bounced through the automatic frosted glass sliding doors of the Harbour City Regional ER. *Whoosh.*
Cliffy Carlton met him with two cups of coffee.

"Departure lounge special." He held one out to Sababa.

"Funny." Sababa took the coffee. "Where's Alex?"

"Making it a true daily double behind curtain number 3." Sababa followed him inside the cubicle. The ventilator hissed its disapproval.

"What you got?" He asked.

"Noirtier de Villefort." Alex began. "54-year-old locksmith just returned from having his yacht, *Bolt from the Blue*, decked out with teak in Indonesia. According to a neighbour on his dock, it took him two months to make the seven thousand-nautical mile trip from Madura Island near Surabaya on Java."

"And how did he get here?"

"Same neighbour called 911 when he found him barely conscious a couple of hours ago." Alex said. "He'd been vomiting and frothing at the mouth and complaining of abdominal pain and dizziness. EMS had to intubate him at the scene after he became comatose."

"And now?"

"LOBNH." Cliffy said.

"What the hell is that?" Alex asked.

"Lights on but nobody home, Masshole." He said. "Hemodynamically intact but Glasgow coma scale of E1VTM1, quadriplegic and atonic and areflexic, pupils fixed and dilated, absent doll's eyes, no brainstem reflexes, no respiratory effort, and no withdrawal from pain. Either this man is brain dead or my watch has stopped."

"Not so fast, Sherlock." Sababa said. "Lab?"

"All normal except slight respiratory acidosis, which improved with continuous mechanical ventilation." Cliffy said.

"Imaging?"

"CT brain was normal, Sab." Cliffy said. "But it could still be normal with a big brainstem stroke this early in the game."

"He's right, Sab." A fresh voice joined the conclave. "Permit me to confirm." Oliver Lax switched off the ventilator and attached a T-piece to Noirtier's endotracheal tube. They watched his carbon dioxide meter jump off its scale.

"Positive apnea test." Said the neurologist. "Celestial discharge and organ donation pending. The brain is the most important organ in the body."

"According to the brain." Sababa said. "It's not that I don't value your professional opinion, Oliver, but I only invited you here because you were bringing your tool kit."

"You think he has non-convulsive status epilepticus?" Oliver asked.

"Nope." Sababa said. They all watched the EEG technician attach the last of his 25 electrodes to the locksmith's scalp. A ballet of normal alpha and beta waves danced across the writer unit.

"He's not brain dead." Sababa said. "He's not even comatose. First named by Fred Plum and Jerry Posner in 1966."

"What do you mean?" Cliffy asked.

"Unlike persistent vegetative states, in which the upper portions of the brain are damaged, and the lower portions are spared, locked-in syndrome is caused by damage to specific portions of the lower brain and brainstem, with no damage to the cerebral hemispheres." Oliver said. "Our locksmith here appears to be locked-in."

"No organ harvest?"

"No organ harvest." Sababa asked Cheri Sundae to page the transplant team. "In India, where this is more common, children presenting with undiagnosed locked-in syndrome are piled onto funeral pyres or buried alive." No one spoke until that had sunk in.

"So he knows what we're saying?" Cliffy asked.

"Every word." Sababa said. "Think of how horrible that feels, from shock to anger to frustration, knowing that someone could harvest your organs or put you in a grave still alive—your existence reduced to that of a jellyfish or a hermit crab dug into a rock."

"Why haven't we heard more about this?" Cliffy asked.

"We should have." Sababa said. "There are some famous victims. Jean-Dominique Bauby was a French journalist for Elle magazine who suffered a massive stroke in December 1995 and awoke 20 days later, locked-in and paralyzed except for his left eyelid. By blinking, he dictated one alphabetic character over a great length of time to write his memoir, *The Diving Bell and the Butterfly*. He died from pneumonia three days after they published his book in 1997. Before his stroke, he had a contract to write a book based on *The Count of Monte Cristo*. In the past, one died from a massive stroke. But improved resuscitation techniques have now prolonged and refined the agony."

"Who else?" Alex asked.

"Steven Hawking and Rabbi Ronnie Cahana come to mind." Sababa said. "In his 1844 novel, *The Count of Monte Cristo*, Alexandre Dumas even created a fictional locked-in 'soul trapped in a body that no longer obeys its commands.' *He was a corpse with living eyes, and at times, nothing could be more terrifying than this marble face out of which no anger burned or joy shone.*"

"So, what are the causes of locked-in syndrome?" Cliffy asked. "Alex?"

"Sure." He said. "Brainstem cerebrovascular accidents like basilar artery stroke or hemorrhage or other circulatory system disease, myelin sheath destruction from disease or osmotic demyelination syndromes like central pontine myelinolysis, traumatic brain injury, other brain-stem lesions, medication overdose, and curare poisoning."

"One more." Sababa pulled a magnifying glass from his Colombian leather bag and examined Noirtier's skin.

"Dunno." Alex admitted.

"Look here." Sababa pointed to an area on the back of Noirtier's left hand. "Very unusual to find flange marks. The encounter is painless."

138

"Two small spots." Oliver said.

"Miniscule punctures." Sababa agreed.

"From what?" Alex asked.

"Permit me to reintroduce you to Sababa's Three Rules of Medical Analysis, Bahney." Sababa said. "Number one: What you got, you got."

"Huh?"

"What you got?"

"A locksmith with a locked-in syndrome and a normal EEG."

"Number two." Sababa said. "What you don't got, you don't got."

"Any abnormal brain imaging." Alex said. "Or any of the causes I mentioned for his locked-in syndrome."

"Number three." Sababa said. "Context is everything."

"I don't get any of this." Alex said.

"Let's start over." Sababa said. "What you got is a man with EMNP."

"EMNP?" Cliffy asked.

"Early morning neuroparalysis." Sababa said. "With absent brainstem reflexes mimicking brain death with a history of colicky abdominal pain and vomiting."

"OK."

"And two tiny puncture marks on the back of his hand." Sababa said. "In a man who sailed home from Java, after getting his yacht decked out in teak."

"Still don't get it."

"Whatever neurotoxins have cause this complete total locked-in state cannot cross the blood-brain barrier and are operating on both presynaptic and postsynaptic motor endplate membranes." He said. "Correct?" Alex and Cliffy and Oliver and the EEG technician shook their heads in the affirmative.

"Alpha- and beta-bungarotoxins." He pivoted towards the ER ward clerk. "Cheri Sundae, get me the Harbour City Animal Control on call please."

"On it, Sab." Cheri began punching buttons.

"If this was a bite from a common cobra, we would expect to see local swelling, blistering and necrosis, and incomplete postsynaptic neural blockade." Sababa said. "What we have here is 15 times more toxic than a cobra. In Vietnam, American soldiers used to call them the 'five-step snake,' meaning that if you got bitten by a krait, you would take five steps and then die."

"Animal Control on line 1 for you, Sab." Cheri held her handset high.

"Hello, this is Doctor Sababa in the hospital emergency department." He said. "Get the police to go with you to the Harbour City Yacht Club. Berthed at a finger slip on G Dock is a yacht called *Bolt from the Blue*. On it you will find a live venomous Malayan Krait, also called a Blue Krait. It's four feet long and crossbanded with a bluish-black pattern separated by broad yellowish-white interspaces."

"How will we recognize it?" Asked the disembodied voice.

"It won't be wearing a vest." Sababa rolled his eyes.

"Why not?"

"It has no arms."

"Oh." Said the disembodied voice. "What do you want us to do with it?"

"Kill it." Sababa rolled his eyes back the other way. "And bring me its head." *Click.*

"Really?" Cliffy asked. "You expect us to believe that a poisonous snake that stowed away on his boat two months ago in Indonesia bit this guy in his sleep?"

"When you have eliminated the impossible, whatever remains, however improbable, must be the truth." Sababa said. "Elapidae kraits bite at night."

"What now?" Alex asked.

"You'll write up his eternal care unit orders and I'll arrange for an expedited courier of antivenom."

"Malayan krait antivenom?" Cliffy asked.

"Nope." Sababa said. "The only place to get that is from the Queen Saovabha Memorial Institute in Bangkok and we don't have the time to source what we need from that far away."

"What do you mean?" Alex asked.

"The San Diego Zoo Reptile Department has Australian Tiger Snake antivenin." He said. "Good enough and should be here in a few hours."

"Is there any way for him to communicate with us until he makes enough new neuromuscular junctions?" Alex asked.

"Funny thing about krait bungarotoxins." Sababa said. "The diaphragm appears to be most resistant. Sometimes locked-in patients can still snort their way into a conversation, isn't that right, Sailor? One for yes, two for no." The locksmith, Noirtier de Villefort, sniffed once between ventilations.

"You don't want us to stop trying, do you Noirtier?" Sababa asked. The locksmith sniffed twice. Sababa explained he would be on the ventilator for a few days, but that he would recover neurological function and make a full recovery.

"You should be back on your boat in no time." He said. "Although you may want to change its name."

Dr. Lepage: We want you to take it easy for a few days.
Jean-Dominique Bauby: What do you think I'm doing now?

140

'Many strokes, though with a little axe,
hew down and fell the hardest-timber'd oak.'
William Shakespeare, *King Henry VI*

Across the expanse of the ER, Alex and his preceptor observed Dr. Myles
Capitaine feign a random walk in their direction.

"How are you, Myles?" Sababa asked.

"Living the dream."

"Like all dreamers, I mistook disenchantment for truth." Sababa said.

"You need something?"

"Piggy Muldoon just did a right-sided scaphoid fracture open reduction
and internal fixation on a young woman in the cast clinic."

"That would be orthopedics."

"They performed the procedure with an intravenous regional block."

"That would anesthesia."

"She's now paralyzed on her left side."

"That would be neurology."

"Piggy's freaking out" Myles said. "He's having a meltdown."

"That would be psychiatry."

"I tried to get Oliver Lax to come back, but he said to get you to see her."

"That would be Oliver." Sababa said. "Tell us the rest of the story."

"Sure." Myles looked relieved. "Loretta Lynn is a 36-year-old clinical
audiologist who fell on her right wrist and broke her scaphoid bone while
snowboarding four weeks ago. Right after Piggy's procedure this
morning, she developed a left-sided headache with tearing of her left eye,
droopy left eyelid, and a stuffy left nostril, followed by paralysis of her left
arm and then her left leg. Only other medical problem is fibromyalgia."

"Exam?"

"Physical confirms upper motor neuron left hemiplegia." Myles said.
"Hypersensitivity of the left side of her face."

"Lab and imaging?"

"Bloodwork and ECG within normal limits." Myles said. "Coagulopathy
workup results and echo and CT brain still pending. Will you see her?"

"Let's go." He and Alex visited cubicle 6, where Myles introduced them
to Piggy's patient.

"This is Dr. Harding, Loretta, visiting us from Boston." He said. "And
this is Doctor Sababa. He puts the hiss in histology, the path in pathology,
the fizz in physiology, the gas in gastroenterology, the room in
rheumatology, the pull in pulmonology, the sigh in psychiatry, and the
oomph in oomphectious disease."

"Can he put the nirvana back in neurology?" She asked.

"I can try." Sababa said. "This is not your first rodeo, is it, Loretta?
You've had this problem before."

"Once." She said. "After I had my appendix out at Surrey Memorial Hospital six years ago. Before I moved to Harbour City."

"And what did they say was the cause?" Sababa asked.

"They didn't." She said. "At first, they said I had a stroke. Then, when I got better, they said I had a transient ischemic attack. They did all kinds of investigations as an outpatient but found nothing."

"And the migraines?" Sababa asked.

"I used to suffer from them as a young girl." She said. "But I don't get them much anymore."

"Nobody in the family experience this?"

"Not that I know of." Sababa asked if he could examine her with her consent.

"Of course." She said. When he tested her muscle strength. Loretta produced normal tension against each manoeuvre, but then gave way and provided no further resistance. Sababa looked up to find Piggy Muldoon slipping through a curtain of concern.

"What is it, Sab?" He asked. "Has she had a stroke?" Sababa smiled a Sababa smile.

"Wanna play a joke on your chiropractor, Piggy?" He asked. "The next time he works on your neck, go limp and soil yourself."

"Quit messing around." Piggy said. "Has she had a stroke or not?"

"There are six subtypes of hemiplegic migraine, according to the ICHD classification system of nomenclature." Sababa said. "Some are autosomal dominant familial and some are sporadic, and some can cause permanent neuro deficits."

"C'mon, Sab."

"What I showed you is called 'give-away weakness.'" He said. "Unlike classical spasticity, it is not 'clasp-knife' in nature, not velocity dependent but attention dependent."

"So?"

"So if you add that to her history of classical migraine, a previous similar episode of transient hemiplegia after an anesthesia trigger, her allodynia and ancillary unilateral cluster-like symptoms, and the rostrocaudal march of motor symptoms on the same side of the body as her headache." Sababa took a breath. "That Loretta is a white female younger than a typical stroke patient with not-quite-normal adjustment disorder score on her Beck Depression Inventory would answer your burning question... It's not a stroke."

"What the hell is it then?"

"MUMS."

"MUMS?" Piggy asked.

"MUMS." Sababa said. "Migraine with unilateral motor symptoms."

"Will it go away, Doctor Sababa?" Loretta asked.

"Did you hear the one about the woman whose whole left side wouldn't work?" Sababa smiled. "She's all right now."

"So, what do we do?" Piggy asked.

"We admit her to your service overnight for surveillance, get the rest of the investigations done, and wait for her neurologic deficits to resolve without intervention, and send her home on zinc."

"Zinc?" Myles asked.

"Synaptic zinc is a potent modulator of neurotransmission." Sababa said. "It may prevent future episodes."

"Do I have to admit her to my service, Sab?" Piggy asked. "She's not my problem."

"That is debatable."

"OK, but don't let this get out anywhere." Piggy said. "What should I record as the reason for her admission."

"MUMS the word." Sababa said.

It was now midmorning, and Trace Pangloss motioned to Sababa and his protégé from an adjacent cubicle.

"Need you guys in here." He said. Alex went full Michael Corleone.

"Just when I thought I was out..." He said. "They pull me back in..."

"It's that old curse of knowledge thing." Sababa said.

"Curse of knowledge?" Trace asked.

"The cognitive bias of assuming that others have the same background to understand." Sababa said. "What you got."

"See for yourself." Trace pointed to his semiconscious patient. "John Ruskin, 43-year-old marine mechanic brought in by EMS three hours ago, disoriented to time and place with a left hemiparesis, increased tone on his left side, and bilateral Babinski extensor plantar responses."

"Family?" Sababa asked.

"His wife, Julia, is in the waiting room."

"We are the boat, we are the sea, I sail in you, you sail in me. Go get her." Sababa performed a focused neuro exam while Trace was away.

Julia Ruskin sailed in on a sea of sorrow.

"This keeps happening to John and no one can tell us why." She said.

"What is it that keeps happening?" Sababa asked.

"Every few weeks we end up in emergency with these episodes." She said. "Last time he had a seizure. John has had two MRIs, we've seen neurologists in Harbour City and Victoria, and no one can tell us why."

"He has a history of migraines with aura, no?" Sababa asked.

"Since childhood." Julia said.

"And a progressive mood disorder?"

"Uh-huh."

"And urinary incontinence and problems with memory and reasoning?"

"In the last few months." She said.

"But he doesn't have high blood pressure or high cholesterol or diabetes or a history of smoking?"

"None of those."

"But there are similar cases in his family." Sababa said.

"John's mother and grandfather suffered from headaches and strokes." Julia said. "They both died of dementia."

"Drs. Pangloss and Harding and I are going to look at John's MRIs." Sababa said. "We'll be right back." Julia's eyes welled up. *Tears lift your boat off the rocks, off dry ground, carrying it downriver...*

At the consultant's desk, Alex pulled up the imaging studies on the computer.

"Hmmm." He said. "Progressive pattern of various-sized multiple confluent white matter lesions around the anterior temporal lobes, external capsule, basal ganglia, periventricular white matter, and the pons."

"Which are?" Sababa asked.

"Subcortical lacunar infarcts." Alex said.

"From what?"

"What do you mean?"

"Knock, knock."

"Who's there?"

"Ve vill ask ze questions." Sababa said. "Middle-aged man with a history of migraine with aura since childhood, no traditional cardiovascular risk factors, recurrent lacunar strokes, and early dementia and family history of same, who presents today with acute encephalopathy. What you got?"

"Dunno."

"Trace?"

"No idea."

"You know the diagnosis, Alex." Sababa said. "Come on, take a shot. I'm won't fire you every time you get it wrong."

"Familial hemiplegic migraine?" Alex guessed.

"You're fired." Sababa smiled. "I know you know this, Bahney. Marie-Germaine Bousser and Élisabeth Tournier-Lasserve published their original observations in a 1993 edition of Nature Genetics—a condition that afflicted Friedrich Nietzsche and composer Felix Mendelssohn."

"Some kind of hereditary stroke syndrome." Alex said. "All I can come up with. What is it?"

"CADASIL." Sababa said.

"CADASIL?"

"CADASIL." Sababa said. "Cerebral autosomal dominant arteriopathy with subcortical infarcts and leukoencephalopathy. Most common form of hereditary stroke disorder. Caused by mutations in the Notch 3 gene on the long arm of chromosome 19 which results in loss of its protein beta sheet structure and abnormal accumulation at the cytoplasmic membrane leading to the progressive deterioration of vascular smooth muscle cells."

"Right." Trace said.

"Let's go tell Julia." Sababa said. The three men returned to the bedside "Do you know?" She asked. The stocky savant nodded.

144

"John is in a CADASIL coma, Julia." Sababa explained the condition.
"Is it bad?" She already knew the answer.
"We can prove the diagnosis with a skin biopsy." Sababa said. "There is no specific treatment. But we will provide John with all the supportive care we can and aim for some improvement and quality time."
"That's what he used to say."
"What?"
"If the boat is suspect and not solid from the start, it will spring a leak and fall apart." She said.
"Julia, Dr. Harding will explain things in more detail and arrange for John's admission." Sababa handed a piece of paper to his apprentice. "Call me when you've seen these two patients on the fifth floor." Alex glanced at the names. *George Wallace... Hank Moody...*
He watched the portly professor stop to speak with his internist friend and colleague, Dr. Dasco Boet. He didn't hear their conversation, but he would hear about it later.
"What a country." Dasco said.
"What do you mean, Boet?" Sababa asked.
"I just saw a young guy with a right middle cerebral artery thrombotic stroke." He said. "His wife phoned for an ambulance they rushed him to the ER. I got a stat CT brain scan which showed he was the perfect candidate for a clot-buster. Everything happened in less than the golden hour."
"And?"
"He refused treatment." Dasco said.
"What?"
"Yep." He said. "Total left-sided paralysis, his wife begging him to get the cure, and he turned it down."
"Why?" Sababa asked.
"He told me he could get a bigger disability benefit and still hold a cold beer with his left hand." Dasco screwed up his face. "What a country."

'I don't wanna stay at your party...
I just wanna be your tugboat captain.'
Galaxie 500, *Tugboat*

"Good Morning, Sophia." Alex said as he emerged from the fifth-floor elevator.

"Huppy Pri-day, Ductor Harding." She said. "Who will you see today?"

Alex handed her the two names. *George Wallace... Hank Moody...*

"Mister Wallis is in pibe por-teen." She said. "Mister Moody is in pibe twain-tee but I yam berry wor-eed por him beecaws he tries to make seks with all my nurses. It is a nooy-sahns. Palo me." Sophia grabbed the two charts off the rack at her nursing station and led Alex down to the first room.

"George, are you penis yor brick-pus?" She asked, as they entered.

"All done." George said. "Who's this?"

"Dis is Ductor Harding." She said. "He is a medicule grad-waite prom Harbard. He will see you bee-pore Ductor Sababa ah-ribes."

"Doctor Sababa?" George asked.

"My payborit." Sophia turned to Alex. "Ductor Oliber Lax udmeetted George lust ebening. Plis be care-pull, Alex. He is para-lised and excru-shitting porn to pauls."

An hour later, the same stairwell door opened for a stocky middle-aged man. Below a bouncing medusa of black curls, a Littman Master Cardiology black and brass stethoscope draped over his shoulders. He carried a well-used Colombian leather briefcase, the inside of which held secrets of survival. He found Alex writing notes at the nursing station.

"What you got, Bahney?" He asked.

"First is George Wallace." He began. "63-year-old yacht charters owner admitted last night by Dr. Lax with sudden paraplegia."

"From what?"

"That's what Dr. Lax wants to know."

"Oliver is a very practical neurologist." Sababa said. "Why, he's practically a neurologist. What was George doing when it happened?"

"Nothing." Alex said. "Sitting on his boat."

"And two hours earlier?"

"Does it matter?"

"Nothing matters very much, and few things matter at all." Sababa said. "But this does. Let's go see him. Tell me the rest of the story on the way down the hallway."

"Otherwise fit and healthy." Alex said. "Exam shows paraparesthesia with no sensory level, paraparesis, and an indwelling catheter. Labs normal except for an elevated CSF protein on a lumbar puncture. Had an MRI yesterday, but I haven't seen it yet."

"Differential diagnosis?"

"Primary or secondary vascular disorders like anterior spinal artery syndrome or aortic dissection or saddle embolism, inflammatory disorders like acute transverse myelitis, toxic or allergic disorders, non-inflammatory spinal space-occupying disorders, and non-spinal disorders like Guillain-Barré."

"And which one does George have?"

"Not sure." Alex said.

"In the Four Stages of Competence theory, you appear to still be in the second conscious incompetence part."

"How do I improve that?"

"Concentration." Sababa said. "And the acquisition of new skills."

"And where do I get those?"

"From failure, Grasshopper." He said. "You get competence from concentration and recurrent failure. We know ourselves only as far as we've been tested. Let's go see your Mr. Wallace."

Inside room 514, Alex introduced the professor.

"This is Doctah Sababer, George." He said. "Here to do an analysis of your paralysis."

"Can you fix this, Doctor?" George asked.

"First things first, but not necessarily in that order." Sababa said. "What were you doing two hours before you lost control of your legs?"

"Working out at Harbour City Fitness." He said. "Weight training."

"Doing what?"

"Lifting weights."

"How?" Sababa asked.

"I'm getting back into my winter 5-day split workout schedule." George said. "Life has its ups and downs. Yesterday I began with a routine of full barbell back squats."

"How did it go?"

"I may have overdone it a bit." George said. "Sweat is your fat crying."

"Did you hear or feel a pop?" Sababa asked.

"Uh... yeah." He said. "I had to stop because of the agony. My personal trainer told me 'no pain, no gain' and that pain is just weakness leaving the body."

"Or entering it." Sababa said. "Dr. Harding and I will be back in a minute, George. We're going to look at your scan."

Alex led the way to a nursing station monitor and opened a series of windows on the screen.

"Hmmm." He said. "Major signal abnormalities in the anterior two thirds of his superior thoracic spinal cord between T2 and T9, with hyperintensity at T2. Sagittal views show hyperintense signal compatible with cytotoxic myeloedema and spinal cord ischemia, and multiple acute intrasomatic Schmorl herniations through the superior and middle thoracic vertebral plateaus."

"Ergo?"

"I'd say Mr. Wallace has sustained a fibrocartilaginous embolism of his spinal cord." Alex said. "From his weight-lifting."

"You're well on your way to the ultimate level of the Four Stages of Competence theory, Alex."

"Which is?"

"Unconscious competence." Sababa said.

"I'm not sure how you become competent if you're unconscious."

"Funny." Sababa smiled. "How about through a few hundred more nights on call."

"Not funny." Alex said. "Let's go tell him."

Back at George's bedside, Sababa posed a riddle.

"George, are you familiar with aphorism number 8 from the 'Maxims and Arrows' section of Friedrich Nietzsche's *Twilight of the Idols* or *How to Philosophize with a Hammer*?"

"Can't say I am." He said.

"What does not kill me makes me stronger."

"Oh, yeah." George said. "I've heard that."

"How about Sababa's counter-aphorism number 8?"

"Don't know that one."

"What was supposed to make me stronger tried to kill me." Sababa said. "Your overloaded back squats caused low-energy traumatic rupture of the annulus fibrosus with intervertebral disc nucleus pulposus emboli, which flew into blood vessels that supply oxygen to your spine, causing arterial occlusion and cord ischemia. In your case, you've picked off branches of the anterior and both posterior spinal arteries, and the arteria radicularis magna of Adamkiewicz which handles the blood supply to nerves that regulate your bowel and bladder function."

"Will it get better?" George asked.

"We're hopeful." Sababa said. "We diagnose most cases post-mortem, so you're ahead of the pack."

"I need my legs back." George's voice crackled into a choke and a cough. "Socrates said that it's a disgrace for a man to grow old without ever seeing the beauty and strength of which his body is capable. I need to get back to the weights."

"Socrates drank poison hemlock." Sababa said. "You're lapping up the purple Kool-Aid. Weightlifting is not a sport. Picking up a heavy thing and putting it down again is indecision. Think you can find another hobby?" George nodded without enthusiasm.

"I may be paralysed from the waist down, but not from the neck up."

"You'll have another scan tomorrow morning." Sababa said. "I'll come back and tell you what it showed in the afternoon."

Alex and his mentor crossed the Wallace line for the patient in room 520.

"Who lives here?" Sababa asked.

"You've seen him before." Alex said. "Hank Moody is a 31-year-old tugboat captain admitted six weeks ago with fever and status epilepticus. His family doc, Nicholas Rivera, got you to see him in the ER. You stopped his seizures with phenytoin loading and levetiracetam, topiramate, and midazolam-coma therapy, did an LP which came back PCR-positive for type 1 herpes simplex virus, and treated him with intravenous acyclovir."

"I remember him well." Sababa said. "Herpes encephalitis. Nice guy."

"Not anymore."

"What do you mean?" Sababa asked.

"He came in again three days ago with what Nick thought was a stroke." Alex said. "He'd been eating a half dozen big meals a day, putting all kinds of other inedible things in his mouth, reacting to every movement or inanimate object in his room, but not recognizing anything or anyone he should know, and trying to have sex with all the nurses on the floor. Between these episodes of extreme behavior, he's placid and apathetic, fearless even, and he can't remember a thing. When he says anything, his language is foul and profane."

"Hmmm." Sababa mused. "Almost like the first experiments."

"Experiments?"

"The ones they performed back in the 1930s." Sababa said. "Chasing the brain localization of mescaline effects, they removed both temporal lobes of rhesus monkeys and found visual agnosia, hyperorality, hypermetamorphosis, altered sexual expression, differences in diet, and psychic blindness, and an inability to recognize the emotional importance of events."

"Who were these guys?"

"The German psychologist and Iowan neurosurgeon for who the syndrome was named." Sababa said. "Heinrich Klüver and Paul Bucy. You've already seen this with Holden Corso."

"Oh, yeah." Alex tried to introduce his teacher to his patient, but it went nowhere. Hank Moody didn't recognize Sababa from their first encounter and was so absorbed in filling his mouth and tracking everything else, it would have made no difference if he had. Sababa held out his wrist and pointed to his watch. Hank stared at the moving minute hand in puzzlement, then turned the air blue around them."

"Has he had any more imaging since admission?" Sababa asked.

"MRI yesterday."

"Let's see." They made their way back down to a nursing station monitor and the stocky savant opened a series of windows on the screen.

"Here's the first MRI six weeks ago when he presented in status epilepticus." Sababa said. "Isolated bilateral hippocampus T2 hyperintensity and swelling." He clicked on the most recent imaging.

149

"MRI yesterday now shows isolated bilateral hippocampal atrophy."
Alex said. "We live in the golden age of localization. He's lost that part
of his brain."
"You know there are many causes of Klüver-Bucy Syndrome, Alex."
Sababa said. "But herpes simplex encephalitis and status epilepticus are
two of them."
"What now?" Alex asked.
"Now we stop all his other medication, start him on carbamazepine and
come back tomorrow."
"Maybe the change in therapy will stop him cursing."
"He's a tugboat captain, Alex." Sababa said. "Nothing can change that."

Little strokes fell great oaks.'
Benjamin Franklin

From his home base on floor 6, Piggy Muldoon launched a drone onto
Sababa's pocket pager. The professor called him back.
"Your loyalty program has run out of coupons for today." Sababa said.
"Gotta see this one, Sab." Piggy protested. "It's an emergency."
"You told me there was no such thing as an orthopedic emergency."
"It's not orthopedic."
"Coming now." Sababa and Alex climbed a floor into the rarefied air of
the combined orthopedic and urology ward.
"Nothing like the smell of rubbing alcohol and ammonia to revive the
flagging spirit." Sababa said. "The smelling salts of surgical slumber.
What you got, Piggy?"
"Josepha Moondyne." He began. "55-year-old patient of Tictac Tarmac,
admitted last night with a history of recurrent falls and a broken left hip
I fixed in the OR after midnight."
"Tell us why we're here, Pig." Sababa said. Alex pulled the chart from
the rack and scanned the ER admission notes and the copy of Dr.
Tarmac's office record.
"She's off her face." Piggy said. "Doesn't know where or even who she
is, slurs her words, and just sits there drawing circles."
"Hmmm." Sababa said. "Hyperkinetic perseveration errors, unlike in
Alzheimer patients who make semantic perseveration errors. What have
you found, Bahney?"

"Longstanding history of diabetes and hypertension and high cholesterol." Alex said. "Dr. Tarmac's notes detail a three-year history of mental deterioration, language and movement disorder, muscle ataxia, multiple falls, fainting episodes, and urinary incontinence. She has flow processing retardation and impaired concentration with reduced ability to perform everyday tasks like managing finances, preparing meals, eating, bathing, and driving. Her husband is having trouble coping."

"There is a difference between cortical and subcortical dementia." Sababa said. "Cortical dementia affecting the gray matter causes loss of 'higher' functions like memory, language, and semantic knowledge whereas white matter subcortical dementia affects executive functions, brain processes responsible for planning, cognitive flexibility, abstract thinking, rule acquisition, initiating appropriate actions and inhibiting inappropriate actions, and selecting relevant sensory information. It causes derangements in mental manipulation, attention, personality, and emotional stability."

"Her high blood pressure has been uncontrolled despite serial increases in number and doses of antihypertensive medication." Alex said.

"She's not taking her pills." Sababa said. "I once heard a joke about amnesia, but I forgot how it goes. Let's go see her."

"If it's alright with you eggheads, I've got a full house here." Piggy said. "I'd like to continue my rounds for now. Can you come and get me once you've solved the problem?"

"Of course, Piggy." Sababa said. "Wouldn't think of interrupting Ezekiel 37:1-14."

"Huh?"

"You know. The valley of dry bones and the resurrection of the dead." Sababa pulled a tune from his music library on a secret drive hidden deep inside the hospital computer network. He and Alex danced down the hallway. *Knee bone connected to the thigh bone... Thigh bone connected to the hip bone... Dem bones, dem bones gonna rise again... Now hear the word of the Lord.*

Twenty minutes later, Alex and Sababa emerged from Josepha Moondyne's room. The portly professor curled an index finger at Piggy's procession and pulled him back to the nursing station.

"Well?"

"Some luminaries from the School of Medicine at the National Yang-Ming University in Taiwan reported the results of a modified Mini-Mental Status Test in the *Journal of Clinical Neuroscience* in March of last year." Sababa said.

"So?"

"It teases out the various kinds of vascular dementia."

"So?"

"There was one vascular dementia that scored the lowest."

"So?"

"Josepha Moondyne also scored the lowest."

151

"So Josepha Moondyne has this kind of vascular dementia?"

"More than likely."

"Sab, I didn't consult you for 'more than likely.'" Piggy said. "I consulted you for more."

"She was also off the charts on the Hachinski Ischemic Scale."

"Jesus Christ." Piggy exploded. "Do you have a diagnosis, or what?"

"I'm not Jesus, Piggy." Sababa said. "Josepha had an MRI early this morning. It will show Binswanger's Disease."

"Who the hell is that?"

"Otto Ludwig Binswanger." Sababa pulled up the images on one of the nursing station computers. "Nineteenth-century Swiss psychiatrist and neurologist. Friedrich Nietzsche was one of his patients. Don't they teach you anything in bone school?"

"What does the MRI show?" Piggy asked.

"Alex?"

"Very cool. They did a susceptibility-weighted imaging study." He said. "Extensive chronic ischemic leukoaraiotic white matter lesions with multiple microhemorrhages in both cerebellar and cerebral hemispheres, brainstem, and deep nuclei, and a new hemorrhagic infarct in the right thalamus."

"And the cause of her most recent fall and mental deterioration." Sababa said. "Binswanger's subcortical leukoencephalopathy."

"Can you fix it?" Piggy asked.

"It's not a bone, Pig." Sababa said. "She will improve to some extent as her thalamic hemorrhage resolves, but there is no cure for her subcortical vascular dementia. We'll finesse her hypertension and other vascular risk factors, start her on donepezil to increase her cerebral acetylcholine, an SSRI to increase her brain serotonin, and get the occupational and physiotherapists involved to mitigate future falls. Questions?" Piggy shook his head.

"I have one." Sababa said.

"What?"

"How was this an emergency?"

"Any internal medicine problem is an orthopedic emergency." Piggy said.

"Which is what you'd expect from a specialty in which sticks and stones cause everything."

152

Mercy's eyes never left her big iMac screen as the two medicos entered through Manzanita's back door.

"It's apocalyptic apoplexy week, Boss." She said.

"I will show Mercy to whoever I will show mercy." Sababa smiled. He handed the top file folder off the clinic stack to Alex.

"Consider yourself lightly; consider the world deeply." Alex called into the assembled multitude in the waiting room.

"Yūko Gotō." A young Asian woman with rosy cheeks followed Alex down the hallway to the resident's room. Sababa detected an asymmetry in her gait that his apprentice failed to see.

"Clint Norcross." He called. Sababa deduced it was his mother who accompanied the adolescent boy to his sanctum sanctorum.

"How can I help, Mrs. Norcross?"

"Clint is only seventeen, Doctor Sababa, but I asked for this referral from Dr. James Ruben Andrews because the pediatricians and neurologists and immunologists and psychiatrists and psychologists and sports medicine specialists couldn't find anything wrong." She said. "He had been an honour roll student in his high school and star hockey defenseman with the Junior 'A' Harbour City Clippers, but in the last three years his episodes have affected his participation and performance at school and in sports."

"Episodes?" Sababa asked.

"They start with a high fever and a sore throat." His mother said. "A few days later, Clint goes weak, can't concentrate, and sleeps for 20 hours a day for a week at a time. These spells occur every couple of months and between them, he's normal."

"Can you wake him during these episodes?" Sababa asked.

"Uh-huh." She said. "But his behaviour is immature and antisocial and moody, he speaks in slurred phrases, and he eats anything with sugar he can get his hands on. His pupils are dilated, he neglects his grooming and, on the last day of each episode, he develops an intense body odour and profuse armpit sweating. And then, for no reason, he snaps out of it and is good for another couple of months."

"Can you remember your dreams, Clint?"

"They're pretty intense." The boy said. "Snakes and sharks and sex with my wife."

"Your wife?"

"He doesn't have a wife." His mother said.

"I do in my dreams." Clint insisted.

"According to his records, Dr. Andrews has investigated Clint's problem." Sababa said. "Hematology, chemistry, toxicology, hormonal pituitary axis, lumbar puncture, brain CT and MRI and nuclear scans, EEG and polysomnography, muscle biopsy test for mitochondrial myopathy, extensive psychiatric evaluations..."

"All normal." The mother said. "What are the odds that you know what's wrong with Clint?"

"About one in a million." Sababa said.

"Sorry?"

"That's the prevalence of this condition." He said. "Only fifty-eight cases recorded in the medical literature. Clint makes it fifty-nine."

"You have a name?" She asked.

"Kleine–Levin syndrome." He said. "Also known as Sleeping Beauty syndrome."

"What causes it?" Clint asked.

"We don't know." Sababa said. "Although it's linked to the LMOD3 gene on chromosome 3."

"Can you prove he has it?" Asked the mother.

"It's a clinical diagnosis." Sababa said. "But I would like to get a single-photon emission CT of his brain in Vancouver the next time he goes into one of his episodes. It should show low perfusion of his thalamus."

"Will it ever go away?" Clint asked.

"Absolutely." Sababa said. "Median duration is eight years. All gone by age thirty."

"But horrendous to live through in the meantime." Clint's mother said. "Is there nothing we can do?"

"We can trial a course of lithium carbonate after we get the SPECT scan." Sababa said. "It works about half the time, although we'll have to measure blood levels and watch his kidney and thyroid function."

"Shake off this downy sleep, death's counterfeit." He handed a requisition to Clint's mother. "Tell Mercy I'll see you both after the scan."

Sababa found Alex waiting outside his office.

"Come in." He said. "What you got, Bahney?"

"Yūko Gotō." Alex began. "22-year-old right-handed fish hatchery technician referred by Dr. Poldy Bloom for a right middle cerebral artery-distribution stroke and connective tissue disease."

"Connected?"

"No." Alex said. "Connective."

"Go on."

"A month ago, Ms. Gotō presented to the Harbour City Regional ER with left-sided weakness and slurred speech worsening over 5 days. She had been unwell for 3 weeks with fever and fatigue and had developed a rash over both cheeks ten days before presentation."

"Initial exam?"

"Fever of 39°C, malar rash, pharyngeal erythema, and diffuse cervical lymph node enlargement. Neuro examination showed dysarthria and left-sided hemiparesis and hemianesthesia."

"Lab?"

"Low white blood cell count, high sedimentation rate, elevated liver enzymes, and red blood cell casts and protein in her urine." Alex said. "Autoimmune panel was positive for rheumatoid factor, an antinuclear antibody titre of 1:1,600 in a homogeneous pattern, and anti-double-stranded DNA antibodies. Serum C3 and C4 complement levels were low and extensive infectious workup was negative."

"Imaging?"

"Brain MRI revealed acute ischemic infarction in the right middle cerebral artery territory." He said. "Digital subtraction MR angiography showed narrowing of the distal internal carotid and proximal anterior and middle cerebral arteries, with rich basal collaterals from the bilateral posterior cerebral arteries."

"Like a puff of smoke?" Sababa asked.

"Puff of smoke."

"Moyamoya in Japanese." Sababa said.

"Moyamoya syndrome."

"And what, Grasshopper, is the difference between moyamoya disease and moyamoya syndrome?"

"Moyamoya disease is an inherited disorder of bilateral cerebral artery constrictions and tiny, weak collateral vessel tangles prone to bleeding, aneurysm, and thrombosis." Alex said. "Moyamoya syndrome can be unilateral and secondary to fibromuscular dysplasia, sickle cell disease, atherosclerosis, inflammatory diseases, and vasculitis."

"And the cause of Yūko Gotō's moyamoya syndrome?" Sababa asked.

"Oliver Lax and Ed Hyde thought her ischemic stroke was secondary to lupus." Alex said. "No evidence of Libman-Sacks endocarditis or antiphospholipid syndrome. She responded well to a three-day course of pulse methylprednisolone, followed by oral prednisone and aspirin. Her symptoms improved."

"So why is she here?"

"Dr. Hyde." Alex said. "She told me she'd rather have Dr. Pepper. Once was enough."

"Let's go see her." Down the hallway past Mercy's reception area, Alex made introductions.

"Yūko, this is Doctah Sababer." He said. "One well-trained physician of the highest type will do better work for a thousand people than ten specialists."

"Pleased to meet you." She said.

"Likewise." Sababa asked if he could examine her and corroborated Alex's findings of a resolved large vessel stroke.

"What should we do now, Professor Sababa." Yūko asked.

155

"Now we need to speak to a neurosurgeon friend of mine in Victoria." Sababa pressed the intercom and Mercy's mellifluousness melted into the room.

"Yes, Boss?" She asked.

"Mercy, try and raise Tecumseh Sun at Victoria General for me, please and thank you."

"On it." She was back in less than a minute later. "Line 2 for Dr. Sun, Sab."

"Hey Tecumseh." He said. "Where do you hide a hundred-dollar bill from a neurosurgeon?"

"Dunno, Sab." Tecumseh admitted. "Where?"

"Stick it to his kid's forehead." Something approximating laughter gurgled on the other end of the line.

"How can I help?"

"Right-handed young woman who presented with SLE and a right MCA stroke." Sababa said. "MRA shows moyamoya syndrome. She'll need one of your ECIC superficial temporal artery to middle cerebral artery bypasses, encephalomyosynangiosis, encephaloduroarteriosynangiosis, or whatever other alphabet soup procedure you think appropriate."

"OK."

"And one other thing." Sababa said.

"What's that?"

"I need a brain biopsy."

"Don't be silly."

"You'll be right there, Tecumseh."

"Oh, I thought it was for you."

"And?"

"To do a brain biopsy, you would need a brain." Something approximating laughter gurgled on the other end of the line. "I'll organize a SPECT to show us the details of her new blood supply. Put me back to Mercy. We'll be in touch." *Click.*

Sababa explained the relationship of Yūko's connective tissue disease to her moyamoya syndrome and outlined the various available medical therapies. He asked her to make another appointment with him after she had seen Dr. Sun. Alex waited until after she left.

"I'm a bit confused here." He admitted.

"About what?"

"You always say it's never lupus."

"No, I sometimes say it's never Lupus."

"But this is lupus."

"Yes, but not always."

'Didn't feel any pressure...
Fading in an admission
Guess we shared an open mind.'
Pet Shop Boys, *An Open Mind*

Dr. Cliffy Carlton was waiting behind the big automatic frosted glass sliding doors of the Harbour City Regional ER. *Whoosh.*

"You on call tonight, Sab?" He asked.

"Both of us." Alex said.

"I was talking to the professor, Bow tie."

"We're both on call, Cliffy." Sababa said. "What you got?"

"Alice Walker." He began. "30-year-old alpaca rancher who came in this afternoon with right orbital pain, double vision, and unable to look to the left. I figure she must have some kind of sixth nerve paralysis."

"Doesn't sound like a single cranial nerve abnormality." Alex said.

"Like I said, Pee Wee." Cliffy said. "I was talking to the professor."

"Alex is right, Cliffy." Sababa said. "That's not an isolated cranial nerve problem. Let's go see her."

"I figure she had some sort of stroke." Cliffy said. "But all her lab results and brain CT were normal." He introduced both physicians to his patient.

"This is Doctor Sababa, Alice." He said. "You've heard of the butterfly effect, that small things can have non-linear impacts on a complex system?"

"You mean like a butterfly flapping his wings can cause a typhoon?" Alice nodded.

"He's the butterfly." Cliffy said. "His sidekick here, Dr. Harding, is standing on the shoulders of a giant butterfly." Sababa held up his index finger. Alex almost held up his middle one.

"Follow." Sababa said. Alice's eyes tracked the finger to the left with no problem, but when the professor moved in the other direction, her left eye stopped in the midline, and her right eye danced at the endpoint of her gaze.

"Not a sixth nerve palsy?" Cliffy asked.

"She has a left-sided unilateral internuclear ophthalmoplegia." Alex said.

"She's picked off that side of her medial longitudinal fasciculus, resulting in a palsy of the medial rectus and a dissociated gaze-evoked nystagmus in the abducting eye." Sababa pulled his finger towards Alice's forehead and watched both her eyes bounce.

"Upbeat nystagmus." Alex said. As the stocky savant brought his finger in towards Alice's nose, her eyes crossed to focus.

"Convergence is preserved." Alex noted.

"Stroke, right?" Cliffy said.

"One possibility." Alex said.

157

"What are the others, Bahney?" Sababa asked.

"Unilateral INO?" Alex said. "Inflammatory causes like multiple sclerosis and Behcet's and SLE."

"It's never lupus." Sababa said.

"So you keep reminding me." Alex continued. "And infectious causes like cryptococcosis and others."

"Which one do I have?" Alice asked.

"Well, that's the special question of the day." Sababa said. "No conventional risk factors, Cliffy?"

"None."

"Hmmm." He mused. "Then you are in the 'and others' category, Alice. Have you had problems with any of your alpacas this year?"

"This last autumn, one of my Huancayo yearlings lost control of her hind legs and then her forelegs. He was paralysed for about a month before he recovered. For a while there, we thought he was a goner."

"You find something in his ear canal?"

"Our vet pulled it out with forceps." Alice said. "He said it was a female."

"They always are." Sababa said.

"What?" Cliffy and Alex asked together.

"Ixodes pacificus." Sababa said. "Western black-legged tick. You find more of them?"

"They were slow-feeding on almost a quarter of the herd." Alice said. "Some were engorged to almost a centimetre long. The vet removed them, injected all our alpacas with ivermectin, and sprayed their ears with *Frontline* fipronil. He assured us he got them all."

"I don't think so." Sababa said.

"What do you mean?"

"When did you get your rash?"

"How did you know I had a rash?" She asked.

"It is my business to know what other people don't know." Alice scrolled her phone and opened a thumbnail. A photo of a large red and white abdominal target-shaped rash filled her screen.

"Bulls-eye." Sababa said. "Stage one."

"I had joint pains as well. My family doctor said it was an allergy and would go away." Alice said. "And it did. What was it?"

"Erythema chronicum migrans." Alex said.

"Big words." She said.

"It was a big rash." Sababa said. "But now you present in the second stage of the disease, with neuroborreliosis."

"Neuro..."

"Lyme disease."

"I have Lyme disease?"

"Uh-huh." Sababa said.

"That's what my naturopath said." Alice spluttered. "How did he know?"

158

"He didn't." Sababa said. "He tells everyone they have Lyme disease. But even a broken clock is right twice a day."

"And it's caused by the ticks, Doctor Sababa?"

"By the spirochete bacteria they carry." He said. "Called *Borrelia burgdoferi*, after Willy Burgdorfer, the Swiss-American medical entomologist who first found it in 1981, six years after the first cluster of cases mistaken for juvenile rheumatoid arthritis was described in Old Lyme, Connecticut."

"You can fix it, right?" She asked.

"Right." Sababa said. "Dr. Harding will arrange your admission tonight. He'll do some more bloodwork and a lumbar puncture to look for specific antibodies with ELISA and Western blot serological testing, request an orthoptic consultation with our own faceless oculist guru, Dr. T.J. Eckleburg, and start you on intravenous ceftriaxone for three days, followed by doxycycline for two weeks at discharge."

Dr. Gung Ho slipped into the cubicle and mumbled in Sababa's ear.

"We'll be there in five." He said. After some further advice to the alpaca rancher about herd immunity, the professor and his acolyte found the next emergency physician and patient behind the curtain of cubicle 8.

"Wilhelmina Mozart." Gung began. "61-year-old right-handed sailing instructor brought in tonight with confusion. Two weeks ago, she developed some mild right arm and leg weakness, which is all I can find on examination. Oriented in all three spheres. Just back from CT."

"Hello, Wilhelmina." Sababa said. "I'm Doctor Sababa and this is my colleague, Dr. Harding. Dr. Ho has asked us to see you."

"About what?"

"About why he has asked us to see you."

"I see." She said.

"Did you have a recent fall?"

"About a month ago." Wilhelmina said. "On my dock at the yacht club."

"Did you hurt your head?"

"Uh-huh."

"Which side did you fall on?"

"This side." She rubbed her left temple.

"Can you show me your left hand?" Wilhelmina held up her right hand.

"Is that port or starboard?"

"Port." She said.

"Show me your right index finger?" Wilhelmina fiddled with the fingers of her left hand." Sababa held up his left ring finger.

"What's the name of this finger?" Wilhelmina grew frustrated.

"Can you tell me what the sum of four plus seven is?" Wilhelmina couldn't tell him the answer. Sababa went to the consultant's desk and returned with a pen and a piece of paper.

"Write your name and address for us." Wilhelmina looked at the pen before she put it down.

"Gung?" Sababa asked. "Alex? You know the name for this?"

"Some kind of stroke." Gung said. "But I'm not sure which kind."

"A stroke can cause it." Sababa said. "But Wilhelmina has a more specific problem. Do either of you know the name attached to these findings of right-left disorientation, finger agnosia, agraphia, and acalculia?"

"Gerstmann's syndrome!" Alex blurted.

"Light dawns ovah Mahblehead." Sababa said. "In 1924, the Austrian neurologist Josef Gerstmann reported the case of a woman much like our Wilhemina here. She had suffered a left-sided stroke. He was correct about the anatomical localization of the damage to the inferior parietal lobule of the dominant hemisphere, at the angular and supramarginal gyri, Brodmann area 39 and 40, near the temporal and parietal lobe junction. But he may have been wrong about a common functional denominator causing the damage."

"What do you mean?" Alex asked.

"Gerstmann thought he had discovered a *grundstörung*, a basic disorder of the single neural substrate underpinning those cognitive abilities that fail in his syndrome." Sababa said. "Other neurologists who came later didn't buy the unified entity theory. MacDonald Critchley called it an enigma of 'silent areas' involving 'ineloquent' associative cortex. Arthur Lester Benton, another neurogeek from Iowa, pushed 'the latent aphasia hypothesis.' Nobody knows what is going to happen, but afterwards everyone can explain it. Gerstmann's syndrome is the result of disconnection of 'crossroads' fibre tracts in the dominant parietal white matter."

"And how does this little digression help Wilhelmina here?" Gung asked.

"It doesn't." Sababa said. "But to know ten thousand things, know one well."

"Why that one?" Gung pulled up her CT scan on the consultant's desk computer.

"It's a gateway into the human brain." He said. "And the mind is a gateway to the sublime." They all stared at the images.

"From the sublime to the ridiculous." Alex said.

"Massive left frontoparietal subdural hematoma." Gung said. "From her fall."

"Cheri Sundae." Sababa turned his attention to the ER ward clerk. "Please raise the on-call neurosurgeon in Victoria for me."

"On it." She was back in less than a minute later. "Line 3 for Dr. Sun, Sab."

"Hey Tecumseh." He said. "You the head honcho tonight?"

"Twice in one day?"

"I have a middle-aged woman with Gerstmann's syndrome and a big subdural who needs a brain drain."

"Send her down." Tecumseh said. "I'll muster the troops." *Click.*

Back at Wilhelmina's bedside, Sababa explained his plan.

"You're messing with my head, Doctor." She said.

"No, Wilhelmina. that's Dr. Sun's specialty."

"How does he do that?"

"You'll need to have an open mind."

'Infected minds to their deaf pillows will discharge their secrets.'
William Shakespeare, *Macbeth*

Alex thought his night was almost over when he got the call. Sababa had left him with the pager and driven home through a snowstorm for a few well-earned hours of sleep before their perpetual Groundhog Day began all over again.

"Dr. Adams?" It was Cliffy Carlton.

"Adams?" Alex asked. "You mean like Raymond Adams, the Father of Neurology?"

"No, I mean like Patch Adams, the clown doctor with the bow tie."

"What is it you want, Chowderhead?" Alex asked.

"I got called up here to Floor 5 from the ER to see some old gomer who walked into a wall and fell on the floor." Cliffy said. "They thought it was a cardiac arrest, but it wasn't. I tried to call your maharishi master but the Big Voice said to talk to you first."

"I'll be right up." Alex took the stairs two at a time. The faster he dealt with this uninvited intrusion, the sooner he could get some sleep himself. Cliffy met him at the top of the stairwell.

"What you got?" Alex asked.

"Who are you now, the Sage of the Salish Sea?"

"You called me." Alex said. "I'm all ears."

"Another one of Nature's cruel jokes." Cliffy said. "Jack McKay, 54-year-old sailmaker, admitted yesterday afternoon with a four-day history of progressive headache, blurred vision, and mild confusion. Forty pack-year smoker and a background of chronic alcohol use disorder."

"Exam?" Alex took no small pleasure in watching Cliffy's eyes roll around in his head.

"On admission, Jack's vital signs and general physical were normal, but he appeared malnourished and disheveled. Smell of alcohol on his breath. He was inattentive, disoriented to time and place, and couldn't read the eye chart despite insisting he could see it. Except for continual

161

roving eye movements, the rest of his ophthalmologic and neuro exam was normal."

"Lab?"

"Complete blood count showed hemoconcentration and elevated white count with a left shift."

"Imaging?"

"Brain MRI demonstrated subacute infarcts in the territories of posterior cerebral, anteroinferior cerebellar, superior cerebellar, and thalamic arteries. Transesophageal echocardiogram was normal."

"And?"

"And the nurse looking after him said he walked straight into a wall as if it wasn't there." Cliffy said. "Jumpin' Jack Flash had a DNR order because of the strokes on his MRI so she called a 'slow code.' His c-spine x-ray and ECG were normal, so we got him back into bed and I called you."

"Why?"

"Because of this." Cliffy threw Jack's portable chest x-ray up on the nursing station view box. Alex let out a slow whistle.

"Snowstorm." Cliffy said. "Like outside."

"It's called miliary because the fine nodular interstitial pattern looks like pearl millet seed buckshot." Alex said. "Wide differential including infections like viruses, fungi, nocardia, salmonella, and healed varicella pneumonia, miliary metastases from all kinds of cancers, sarcoidosis, pneumoconioses and hypersensitivity pneumonitis, hemosiderosis, proteinosis, and histiocytosis."

"But it's not any of those, is it?"

"In a malnourished alcoholic smoker, this is only going to be one thing." Alex reached for an outside line. "I'm going to call in my boss. He'll want to be here."

Twenty minutes later, a medusa of black curls bounced out of the fifth-floor stairwell.

"Where is he?" Sababa asked. Cliffy introduced both of the other physicians to the sick sailmaker.

"What's your poison, Jack?"

"Jack, of course."

"Jack London? Jack Kerouac?" Sababa asked. "Two of my favorite alcoholic writers."

"Jack Daniels." Jack said. "It's a wild man's drink. Should come with bail money because you don't know where you're going to end up, but you know when you get there, you won't be wearing any pants."

"How much Jack do you drink, Jack?" Sababa asked.

"Jack doesn't ask silly questions. Jack understands." Jack said. "Until the demons stop calling my name."

"How's your vision?"

"Perfect." He said. "20/20." Sababa turned off the room lights.

"Are the lights on or off, Jack?" He asked.

"On." Jack said.

"And now?" Sababa did nothing.

"Off." Sababa turned the room lights back on, reached into his Colombian leather bag, and pulled out a tape measure.

"Can you see the numbers on this ribbon, Jack?" Sababa asked.

"Of course."

"Tell me when we reach the number 22." Sababa pulled the tape through one hand with the other.

"Now." Jack said. Sababa had already finished.

"Watch his eyes." He said. "Let's try this again, Jack. Tell me when we reach the number 34."

"Now."

"Notice how Jack's eyes don't follow the tape." Sababa said. "There is no optokinetic nystagmus."

"What does that mean?" Jack asked.

"It means you're blind and you don't recognize you're blind." Sababa said. "And you're lying about being able to see. It's why you walked into the wall tonight."

"I can see fine." Jack protested.

"We'll be back after we look at your x-rays." Sababa and Cliffy and Alex made their way back down the hallway to a nursing station monitor. He pulled up the MRI.

"Hmmm." He mused. "Gadolinium administration showed enhancement of basal cisterns and occipital lobes. Jack Mckay has objective cortical blindness in an intact anterior visual pathway, with an avowed denial of blindness. It's a peculiar form of visual anosognosia called Anton-Babinski syndrome. Patients often show an inappropriate affect and confabulate to conceal their visual loss. Something has affected Jack's occipital circulation. The most important question is what."

Alex threw the portable chest x-ray back up on the view box. It was Sababa's turn to let out a long whistle.

"Of course." He said. "Miliary TB and tuberculous meningitis causing infiltrative, proliferative, and necrotizing infectious vasculitis and bilateral occipital lobe infarcts." Sababa logged out of the radiology app and typed a line into the Google search engine.

Une leçon clinique à la Salpêtrière. An old tableau portrait, painted in bright contrasting colours, appeared across the screen.

"Before we give Jack the results of our deliberations, it might be worthwhile for me to direct your vision through a window into the times in which these important discoveries occurred." He said. "This canvas, 'A Clinical Lesson at the Salpêtrière,' painted by André Brouillet in 1887, is as close to the history of medicine as you can ever hope to appreciate."

Alex and Cliffy scrutinized a scene of thirty well-dressed seated gentlemen watching a clinical lecture and demonstration by a distinguished portly professor with long hair, a Gallic nose, and a bow tie. Behind him stood a buxom middle-aged woman swooning into the arms of a bearded man half the professor's age. Sababa pointed to the bearded man.

"This is Józef Julian Franciszek Feliks Babiński, the name which completes the syndrome that Jack is afflicted with." He said. "Babinski was the chief house officer of the portly professor with the bow tie, Jean-Martin Charcot, the founder of modern neurology, the 'Napoleon of the neuroses,' and head of the department at the Hôpital Universitaire la Pitié-Salpêtrière, Sorbonne's teaching hospital and one of Europe's largest medical institutions.

The Salpêtrière was notable for its population of rats and a bloated and unresponsive bureaucracy, just like Harbour City Regional. It was a gunpowder factory, then a prison for prostitutes, and a repository for women who were learning disabled, mentally ill or epileptic, or poor. They were paired with convicts and exiled to New France, what is now our province of Quebec. During the September massacres of 1792, revolutionaries dragged twenty-five madwomen, some still in their chains, into the streets and murdered them.

Many celebrities have been treated at the Salpêtrière, including Michael Schumacher, Prince Rainier of Monaco, Gérard Depardieu, and President Jacques Chirac. The singer Josephine Baker and Diana, Princess of Wales died there."

"So what's the big deal with the painting?" Cliffy asked. "Other than the bow tie."

"It hangs in a corridor of the Descartes University in Paris." Sababa said. "In his Tuesday lectures and demonstrations, the *Leçons du Mardi*, Charcot systematized the neurological examination, mapped out the territory of modern clinical neurology, and explored its interface with psychological distress. Sigmund Freud attended and translated Charcot's lectures on hysteria into German, the deconstruction of which formed the foundations of psychoanalysis. He hung a small lithograph of the painting over the analytical couch in his London rooms.

The postgraduate students in the portrait— Pierre Marie, Édouard Brissaud, Désiré-Magloire Bourneville, Henri Parinaud, and Georges Gilles de la Tourette—gave their lives and names to the illumination of the diseases of the nervous system."

"Who's the swooning babe?" Cliffy was hooked.

"Marie 'Blanche' Wittman, also known as the Queen of Hysterics." Sababa said. "Charcot's weekly demonstrations highlighted Wittman's attacks of rapid motion, rigidity, and acting out of sexual scenes. Her performances were attended by dancers, actresses including Sarah Bernhardt, and other performers wishing to see the wide range of emotions that Wittman displayed during her fits."

"Whatever happened to her?" Alex asked.

"She went to work as an assistant in the radiology department in an era ignorant of the carcinogenic effects of radiation." Sababa said. "She had to have her arms amputated."

No one said anything until Sababa spoke again.

"Let's go tell Jack about our discovery." He said. Back at his bedside, Sababa broke the news.

"TB." Said the sailmaker. "You sure?"

"Unassailable." Sababa said. "We used to call it consumption."

"All I ever consumed was Jack Daniels." Jack said. "Now what?"

"Now we start you on four antituberculous drugs, do a lumbar puncture to prove the diagnosis, build up your nutrition, wean you off your Tennessee sippin' whiskey, and get you some rehabilitation and social work involvement."

"You say I'm blind?"

"Uh-huh."

"Well, I'll tell you." Jack said. "Never saw that one coming."

'This apoplexy is, as I take it, a kind of lethargy, an't please your lordship; a kind of sleeping in the blood, a whoreson tingling.'
William Shakespeare, *Henry IV*

Sababa's second attempt to play tag with the snowstorm was just as treacherous and no more successful. He made it home in a long slow icy detour around his usual route and fell asleep. Two hours later, his landline exploded into a Wagnerian ring cycle.

"What?"

"I'm calling from the Death Star." Alex said.

"And?"

"Dr. Lax admitted a patient with an ischemic brainstem stroke."

"So where is Oliver?"

"At home on his island." Alex said. "He told Dr. Ho to intubate the patient and to call you because he knows nothing about ventilators, and it was cold and dark outside."

"Did he give the patient thrombolysis?"

"He said it was too late for that." Alex said.

"How convenient." Sababa sat up in his bed. "I'll be there in twenty."

"Two more things." Alex said.

"What?"

"The patient's wife is camping in the waiting room."

"And?"

"This guy doesn't trigger the ventilator when he's asleep." Sababa looked out of his window. It was white.

"Perfect storm." He said. *Click.*

Without proper winter tires, Sababa's dimpled and dented white Honda civic became an invisible rocket sled on the downhill black ice luge course to Harbour City Regional. The simple part was that the Good Doctor could aim his conveyance in the general direction of the hospital, and the snowbanks would keep him in the slot. The hard part came in the realization that he had no brakes or steering that would make any difference to his trajectory. On his way down, Sababa fired up Red Hot Chili Peppers on his CD player. *When to descend to amend for a friend...*

> 'Deep beneath the cover of another perfect wonder
> Where it's so white as snow
> Privately divided by a world so undecided
> And there's nowhere to go.'

He slid into the Internal Medicine on-call bay in front of the Emergency Department and blew through the Jack Frosted automatic sliding glass doors down the yellow brick road to Tranquility Base. Sababa passed through a small vestibule, furnished with several retro vintage chairs, a coffee table on which sat a vase of mummified gladiolas, and a wire rack of support group pamphlets. He tried to avoid eye contact with the only person there, but he felt Venus Slagoon look right into his soul.

"I'll be back." He said, like Schwarzenegger would have before he regretted it. He pushed on a big red button and entered the soft translucent light straight ahead of him.

"Sababa in the house." Betty Boop had settled into her ward clerk chair for a nicotine-free morning. "Bed 4, Sab."

Sababa pulled back the curtain to the cubicle to find a respiratory technician playing with the ventilator settings, Angie playing by the numbers, Alex playing with fire, and the intubated patient playing possum. The portly professor was playing catch-up before he would end up playing God.

"Diga me." He said. *Tell me.*

"Piper Slagoon." Alex began. "67-year-old retired wine merchant and sailor brought in an hour ago with a sudden collapse after a rich meal and a Cuban cigar. His wife was on the boat and noted he had intractable hiccups, hoarse voice, and garbled speech, and then he fell asleep and wouldn't breathe unless she woke him."

"Hmmm." Sababa mused. "Go on."

"Dr. Ho intubated him in the ER for apnea and severe respiratory acidosis." Alex said. "Found nystagmus, a left central facial palsy, paralysis of the left soft palate, and left-sided hemiplegia. He brought in the imaging team to decide if Piper was a candidate for thrombolytic therapy."

"And?

"MRI showed an acute left dorsolateral medullary infarction from atherothrombotic occlusion of the left vertebral artery. There was notable involvement of the left medullary reticular formation and decussating bulbospinal pathways."

"And?"

"And Dr. Lax said no thrombolysis." Alex said. "Over the phone."

"Disconnect the vent." Sababa asked the respiratory technician.

"But..."

"I'm not asking you to leave, I'm asking you to interrupt his continuous mandatory ventilation." The RT disconnected the ventilator. The patient's chest didn't move.

"Breathe, Piper." Sababa said. Piper took a breath before he fell back to sleep. And then he didn't.

"Reattach the vent." Sababa said.

"What is this?" Angie asked.

"Ondine's curse." Sababa said.

"What's that?"

"Ondine was an oceanic water goddess of incomparable beauty, in a German novella written by Friedrich de la Motte Fouqué in 1811. Like all nymphs and mermaids, she was leery of men, knowing that if she ever fell in love with one and bore his child, she would age like a mortal woman, and lose her eternal youthfulness. But Ondine was also a free spirit and possessed of a streak of independence. One day, she saw a handsome young man named Palemon and was smitten. She watched for him on his daily walks and, when Palemon noticed her, he was also overtaken by Ondine's incredible beauty. As in all fairy tales, they fell in love. Palemon convinced Ondine to marry him and broke his engagement with a young noblewoman named Berta. When they exchanged their wedding vows, Palemon made a pledge. *My every waking breath shall be my oath of love and faithfulness to you.*

But of course, as in all fairy tales, it was not to be. The following year Ondine gave birth to their son and from that moment, her beauty faded, falling prey to the effects of human ageing. Palemon's eyes wandered.

One day, as Ondine was out walking on their estate, she heard Palemon snoring in the stables. She entered the barn to a scene that filled her with great sorrow. Discarded garments littered the floor. Palemon lay sleeping in a haystack, his arms wrapped around his former fianceé, Berta. Having sacrificed her immortality for this man, Ondine became consumed by anger and regret. She kicked Palemon awake and uttered

167

a curse. *You pledged faithfulness to me with your every waking breath, and I accepted that covenant. So be it. For as long as you are awake, you shall breathe. But should you ever fall asleep, that breath will desert you.*

And Palemon, condemned to remain awake forever, would never sleep again."

"What's the scientific version?" Alex asked.

"It's called central hypoventilation syndrome." Sababa said. "A failure of automatic breathing mechanisms during sleep caused by a unilateral lesion in the dorsolateral medullary reticular activating system."

"At a single stroke." Alex said.

"Sab, there's a very concerned spouse in the waiting room." Angie said. "You should go speak with her." It wasn't up for debate.

Sababa passed back into the small vestibule and took a seat in one of the retro vintage chairs across from Venus Slagoon. He explained as best he could, in language she would understand, the nature of Piper's stroke and the story of Ondine's curse.

"Will he get better?" She asked.

"Sometimes we have to put in a diaphragmatic pacemaker, but patients usually recover their ability to breathe while asleep." He said. "You should know that if Piper survives, he may still be paralysed on his left side. This brainstem stroke may also cost him the ability to eat, drink or even swallow. He'll need a tracheostomy and may be on the ventilator for quite a while."

"He's my Count of Monte Cristo." Venus said. "Is there anything else we can do?"

"Alex Dumas wrote the book." Sababa said. "And penned the answer to your question." *All human wisdom is contained in these two words: Wait and hope.*

'Different strokes for different folks.'
Clarence Darrow

The casual reader may turn a blind eye to the problem of stroke and its consequences. Even most physicians find the topic lifeless and frustrating. For the longest time, there was nothing they could do but watch the tragedy unfold.

And yet, the size of the problem is overwhelming. Over 15 million people suffer stroke worldwide each year. Of these, 5 million die, and it disables another 5 million. Stroke is the third leading cause of death in our American cousins and the leading cause of serious, long-term disability, at an annual cost of 34 billion dollars. Someone in the United States has a stroke every 40 seconds. Poor bastard.

One of the most famous photos of the last century is from the February 1945 Yalta Conference in Crimea. It showed the three most powerful men in the world sitting together to plan the reorganization of Germany and Europe after World War II. Franklin D. Roosevelt, cigarette in hand, was not well and didn't have the strength to be as stubborn as he should have been in the circumstances. He died of a massive occipital hemorrhagic stroke two months after Yalta. His blood pressure was 300/190 mmHg. He was 63 years old.

Three days after Roosevelt's passing, Nazi Germany celebrated by describing the fatal stroke as a miracle, creating the conditions that allowed the betrayal of the Poles, the imposition of Communist governments in Eastern Europe, the Czechoslovak coup, the Cold War, and on the other side of the world, the loss of China and the invasion of South Korea.

Joseph Stalin, seated to his left in the photo, was a heavy smoker and drinker. In 1953, eight years after Yalta and the agreement he reneged on, his attendants discovered him on the floor in his quarters, incoherent, paralyzed, and drenched in his own urine. It took eighteen hours for a Politburo member to summon enough courage to open his door. At 74, after 31 years of commanding a hyper-repressive regime that murdered 20 million of its citizens, including many of his own Red Army generals and physicians, Stalin died from his hemorrhagic stroke. His successors became embroiled in a ruthless internal struggle for power.

The last man standing, to the right of Roosevelt, sitting with one of his 13 daily cigars, Winston Churchill suffered a series of strokes. The one that caused him to step down in 1955 resulted in Anthony Eden's later mismanagement of the Suez Crisis. Churchill died after one last stroke in 1965 at 90, 13 days after his family agreed to starve him to death.

Within 20 years after Yalta, stroke had killed all 3 major participants. The disease that ruined them, that had such a major effect on history and hidden from the media and public, had exterminated many other notables through human history—Nicolaus Copernicus and Alfred Nobel, Johann Sebastian Bach and Miles Davis, Charles Dickens and Louis Pasteur, Woodrow Wilson and Richard Nixon, Cary Grant and Gene Kelly, and Al Capone and Mae West, to name but a few.

And yet the word itself, stroke, is such an ambiguous and simple and confusing term for a condition so complex and diverse in cause and effect. It's not a masterstroke or stroke of luck or stroke of insight or stroke of good fortune or stroke of genius; it's not a swimming stroke of crawl stroke or butterfly stroke or backstroke or breaststroke, not a tennis stroke of forehand stroke or backhand stroke or groundstroke, not a golf stroke or penalty stroke, not a rowing stroke or circular stroke, not a two-stroke engine, not a painting stroke or broad stroke, not a writing stroke of cross stroke or oblique stroke; not from sunstroke or heat stroke; not a sexual stroke or ego stroke; not a cardiac stroke volume or stroke output; not a stroke of lightning at the stroke of midnight and may not even be a finishing stroke.

In the 1970s, the World Health Organization defined stroke as a 'neurological deficit of cerebrovascular cause that persists beyond 24 hours or is interrupted by death within 24 hours.' A trendier term is CVA, for 'cerebrovascular accident,' ludicrous if one considers an accident to be 'an event that happens by chance or that is without apparent or deliberate cause.' Some have suggested the phrase 'brain attack' which is just as banal.

For the Sage of the Salish Sea, the best descriptor was the original Greek phrase used by Hippocrates, the father of medicine, over 2,400 years ago. He called it ἀποπληξία, apoplexy, the meaning of which was indisputable. *Struck down by violence.*

And that's the way Sababa knew he would go as well. The chief proof of man's real greatness lies in his perception of his own smallness.

'Learning does not make one learned: there are those who have knowledge and those who have understanding. The first requires memory and the second philosophy.'

Alexandre Dumas, *The Count of Monte Cristo*

There was this car in the Harbour City Regional parking lot, covered in snow. Other cars parked and left on either side of it every day during that winter, but this car remained. Sababa walked past it on his way into work. He knew what it meant.

The locksmith Noirtier de Villefort wasn't locked in to his locked-in syndrome for very long. Even before his special package arrived from the San Diego Zoo Reptile Department, Nortier was sniffing yes and no to specific questions and even making a fair attempt at snorting in Morse code. Eight hours after his first dose of Tiger snake antivenin, he was following finger commands with his eyes and communicating through blinking. The rest of him moved soon afterwards, starting with his fingers. Sababa extubated him on ICU day 4 and ordered his hospital discharge, recovered by a week later. The professor mounted the head of a Malayan krait on his dimpled and dented Honda dashboard.

Loretta Lynn's left-sided paralysis went away as fast as Piggy Muldoon's interest in her outcome. He discharged her the day after admission. She's had no further episodes of MUMS since Doctor Sababa's prescription for zinc. He found a bottle of French bubbly with almost the same name as her condition on his desk one morning, the third 'M' crossed out with a crayon.

John Ruskin, the marine mechanic, died from his CADASIL syndrome on his next admission. After the Harbour City Yacht Club held a farewell ceremony in his honour, Julia Ruskin sold their boat and moved into a condo with a view of Newcastle Channel.

Dasco Boet's stroke patient (the one who refused thrombolytic therapy) is now happily hemiplegic with augmented disability payments and a permanent Mount Benson IPA in his left hand.

George Wallace, Sababa's patient with the spinal cord infarction from fibrocartilaginous embolism, was in hospital for the better part of a week. He left with an almost complete recovery of his lower limb strength, normal bladder function, and a total refund of his annual membership at Harbour City Fitness. If you're looking to charter a yacht, he has some beautiful boats, including John Ruskin's old Island Packet 445.

Most of Hank Moody's Klüver-Bucy syndrome responded to Sababa's carbamazepine. Even though he had to trade in his 500 Gross Tonnage Masters certificate to become a marine pilot, all you need to remind yourself that he's still a tugboat captain is to buy him a beer and listen.

Josepha Moondyne also had to give up her job as a 911 dispatcher because of her Binswanger's Disease. Her giddiness and depressed mood had improved with better blood pressure control, donepezil, and an SSRI, but it wasn't long before Piggy Muldoon had to fix a femoral fracture of her other leg. Turns out that the head bone had been connected to the hip bone all along.

Dr. Tecumseh Sun performed a successful ECIC bypass on Yūko Gotō's moyamoya syndrome. The brain biopsy he did showed CD3+ and CD20− T lymphocyte infiltrates in the vessel wall and perivascular brain tissue indicative of vasculitis. CT angiography at 6 months revealed narrowing at the terminus of the internal carotid arteries and extensive collateral formation. Sababa started her on cyclophosphamide pulse therapy and she had no further strokes during the next two years of follow-up. Her left hemiparesis improved enough for her to return to work as a technician at the fish hatchery.

The SPECT scan that Clint Norcross had in Vancouver during his next Rip Van Winkle episode did indeed show low perfusion of his thalamus, confirming Sababa's diagnosis of Kleine Levin syndrome. A cautious trial of lithium carbonate resulted in a major improvement of his symptoms and function. Clint is back to being an honour roll student and playing defense for the Harbour City Clippers. His mother gave the professor a gift of season tickets that he passed on to Mercy, who asked him why.

"Hard to enjoy a sport in which the players have to wear numbers because you can't identify the bodies from their dental records."

Alice Walker's internuclear ophthalmoplegia resolved over four weeks with only some residual double vision on extreme left elevation documented in T.J. Ekleburg's office. Her cerebrospinal fluid ELISA and Western blot serology were positive for Lyme disease. Her alpacas now get more surveillance than any room in the Louvre.

Tecumseh Sun cured Wilhelmina Mozart's Gerstmann's syndrome by evacuating her subdural hematoma. She is back working as a sailing instructor and earns high praise from her students, except for her occasional confusion of port and starboard.

The sailmaker Jack McKay did not seafare quite so well. His CSF was inflammatory with a positive PCR for Mycobacterium tuberculosis, high adenosine deaminase, and low glucose and chloride levels. He stabilized with Sababa's antitubercular medication regimen and left hospital 15 days after admission. A month later he could perceive some simple figures and walk unaided but remains clinically blind.

Piper Slagoon regained the unconscious ability to breathe while asleep. That he survived fifteen years after a brain stem stroke paralysed one side of his body and cost him the ability to eat, drink and swallow was a testament to his strength and will to live. *It's necessary to have wished for death in order to know how good it is to live. I asked to live happily, that I might enjoy life; I was given life, that I might live happily. I received nothing I asked for, yet all my wishes came true.* The old squire died as a gentleman should, of apoplexy, in his armchair, with a decanter at his elbow. Sababa remembered the sailor's last words during his discharge from hospital. *May the sun be on your face and the winds be in your favour.*

And the cougar that began this entire story? Sababa read about that magnificent cat sinking into the waterline. And he thought about how, on this empty planet, there had been room for him and a mountain lion... that in the world beyond, how we might spare a million or two humans and never miss them... and yet what a gap in the world that cougar made.

> 'To live in this world you must be able to do three things:
> to love what is mortal; to hold it against your bones knowing
> your own life depends on it; and, when the time comes to let it go,
> to let it go.'
>
> Mary Oliver, *In Blackwater Woods*

23. The Case of the Progressive Paralysis

'Most people are paralysed by fear. Overcome it
and you take charge of your life and your world.'
Mark Victor Hansen

The day of the rampage, Ray Close was hunting for a white-tailed buck in the forests of the Cariboo. Other than for this annual pilgrimage to the BC interior, Ray never traveled far from his Vancouver Island home and his job as a millwright at the local Hamac Pacific bleached softwood pulp plant. His workmates called him 'Bowstring,' because that was what he hunted with.

Samson Burke, Bowstring's buddy at Harbour City Cabela's, sold him a new Elite Archery Ritual 35 compound bow for twelve-hundred-dollars. The weapon impressed Ray with its smooth draw cycle, solid back wall, double laminate limb design, deep valley, unique riser cage, and blazing IBO speed rating of 336.7 feet per second. Big bucks for big bucks.

"It's the perfect balance between forgiveness and performance." Samson had said. Bowstring had worked towards and waited for his mid-winter holiday, and now focused on a big buck, and performance.

But back at his pulp mill, forgiveness was the commodity in more short supply. Red Cedar was one of the long-time employees who Hamac had laid off two years earlier, when the company curtailed production in response to a forestry downturn. An unsuccessful barrage of grievances and an acrimonious dispute over severance pay followed, and when the mill rehired some of the original workers, Red Cedar wasn't among them.

There had been a time when Red was full of youthful enthusiasm for the joyful promises that life had on offer. He was lucky enough to find a well-paying job at the mill out of high school. He married his childhood sweetheart, Deodar, and together they took out a mortgage on a modest bungalow in Harewood. Red would often sit and smoke and reflect on the beautiful mountain views off their back deck. He should have made more than the minimum payments required over the years, but he needed a Dodge RAM truck and a boat and a camper and an ATV and a hunting dog and all the other toys that came with the territory in his head. When Red ran out of excuses, the bank foreclosed and sold his house from under him. Two months later, Deodora named him in a family law proceeding. Red found solace in his suds and descended into depression. His GP prescribed medication, but Red flushed it down the toilet and refused any further appointments. The mill manager, Pope Talbot became concerned about his inability to concentrate, and the risk it posed for him and the other workers.

Red began a brief liaison with Sheila Creighton, one of the saw filers on his production line but, when he lost his job, she broke the last link in his safety chain.

A 47-year-old unemployed mill worker at the end of his road, Red Cedar began acting irrationally, having bizarre thoughts, and ruminating on his former mill manager Pope Talbot, who had ruined his career and sabotaged his unemployment insurance claims.

Red paid a visit to Bowstring's buddy, Samson Burke at Cabela's, the day before the rampage. He paid as much as his bowhunter friend had for a Winchester SX4 Hybrid Hunter semi-automatic 12-gauge shotgun. It seemed such a shame to saw off the cylindrical barrel and cut and refasten the stock with black electrical tape.

If there was no revenge so complete as forgiveness and forgiveness was a gift you gave yourself, then for Red, there was no forgiveness so complete as revenge. Through the homeless camp outside the mill, Red Cedar burst into his former workplace around 7 a.m. the next day, swearing a blue streak of profanities.

The first man he encountered in the parking lot was a union rep who had helped with some grievances. Mo Saic greeted him as if he still worked there. Cedar returned the acknowledgment with one of his own. Better dead than Red. *BRUSUSUHHHHHH!*

Fletcher Challenge, one of the other men on Mo's production line, came around the corner to find Red's red carnage, and one of his own. *SJIK SJIKK. BRUSUSUHHHHHH!*

Pope Talbot was having coffee and preparing for a conference call meeting in the mill office with two of Red's former workmates, Tim Berwest and Mac Bloedel, when he heard the first gunshots. A barrage came through the office wall. *SJIK SJIKK. BRUSUSUHHHHHH!*

Tim Berwest was aware of a gust of wind and felt the shotgun slug enter his right cheek and exit below his earlobe, burning it black. In his panic to get out, he passed Red Cedar coming in. The two men remaining in the office, horrified by Red's intrusion, jumped and struggled for control of his firearm, pulling it back and forth. When it discharged a fourth time, Pope watched Mac blown sideways. *SJIK SJIKK. BRUSUSUHHHHHH!*

Pope struck Red on the back of his head with a basalt bookend. He lay on the assassin's legs while Mac Bloedel, his bleeding turning Red even redder, held down his attacker's arms. They shouted out to other employees, running to see what was happening. Then came the perfect balance of police and paramedics.

Forgiveness is the fragrance that the violet sheds on the heel that has crushed it, the perfume and suppliance of a minute, no more.

At the very moment Red Cedar was blasting his former friends into a purple haze, Ray 'Bowstring' Close was lining up a Bloodsport carbon arrow on a big white-tailed buck eighty metres from him in the snow.

Samson Burke, the Cabela's gunsmith back in Harbour City, had asked Ray why he wanted to drive six hundred kilometers to hunt deer.

"I don't like our muleys here on the island." He said. "Taste like they've been rutting too hard. Besides, I have a hunting buddy in the Cariboo." Bowstring knew someone that far away. Al Purdy used to work at the mill with Ray before he moved up north to Williams Lake after the Hamac shutdown and got a job at the Tolco mill on Soda Creek. Every winter, Bowstring would get a tag, and he and Al would hunt whitetails the first week in December.

Throughout the autumn, Ray practiced his archery skills on a 3-D foam-plastic whitetail target in his Harewood back yard. No one would ever accuse him of making an inhumane kill. Two weeks before he left the island, he studied aerial maps of the 5-2 region around Williams Lake, crossing off areas that Al told him had been hunted hard, and connecting the dots between the thickest whitetail winter range bedding cover and the best late-season food sources.

In the early hours of the first of December, Bowstring fired up his loaded Chevy Silverado LT Trail Boss to make the 5:15 a.m. BC Ferry from Duke Point on the island to Tsawwassen. His arrival on the mainland two hours later meant that, even if he didn't stop for anything on the way, he wouldn't get to Williams Lake much before four that afternoon. He knew that the bottle of Lot 40 rye whiskey on Al's kitchen table was holding its breath until he arrived. Not for nothing did Ray Close call his buddy the 'Cariboozer.'

It was already dark and below zero when Bowstring pulled into Al's carport at 4:30 p.m. He smelled like dust and gasoline. In a place where miners once came by the thousands in search of yellow gold, Ray and Al would find a different Barkerville brotherhood in the liquid kind.

They were up before dawn the next morning as if nothing that serious had happened. The outside thermometer was reading -5 degrees Celsius. The wind was blowing the snow sideways. *Perfect.*

The men were silent over a quick coffee and sourdough. Al drove his Ski-Doo Expedition SE 900 ACE snowmobile up the MAD-RAMPS extension into his own RAM 1500 Rebel truck bed. Ray added the Otter plastic ice sled, rope, game bags, snowshoes, compound bows and quivers, food, and thermoses of hot coffee.

They were both dressed for the occasion—Web Foots body sock base layer, Bone Collector lightweight snow camo coverup pants and parka,

Lacrosse Alphaburly Pro waterproof hunting boots, hat and balaclava, and hand muffs stuffed with pocket warmers. Bowstring was also wearing a Slumberjack Pursuit camo backpack vest loaded with his Buck Ranger skinner knife, latex gloves, butt hook combo, tags, hydration reservoir, small survival kit, Bushnell binoculars, deer calls, and his charged cell phone loaded with a GPS app.

It was thirty minutes to the trailhead. Bowstring fired up his RAM Rebel. The tires crunched into fresh snow and ice as they left the streetlights behind. Al tuned his radio to a local station.

Good Morning, Williams Lake, this is Sugarcane Shuswap at CFNR 96.1 FM... waking you on this dark December day in the Cariboo with Classic rock, First Nations-oriented news, sports, and cultural programming...

The Rebel navigated the winter road up into the pine forest and onto the rock rise, which flattened out and fell off to nowhere on the other side.

It's not the arrow... it's the hunter. A man must make his own arrows...

Al had spent part of the previous week up here compacting a trail with his Ski-Doo, not only for access through the deep snow to the remote hunting area but to encourage the migrating whitetails to use the track as a highway, funnelling them into an ambuscade.

There are many good moccasin tracks along the trail of a straight arrow...

Both men knew that a mature buck won't follow an established trail after he's shot. Instead, he'll head where their machines couldn't follow—downhill or into the nastiest cover. That's what the snowshoes and plastic ice sled were for.

Our fast food has antlers...

The hunters still had six more kilometres when they arrived at the trailhead. Al backed the snowmobile down off his truck bed, hooked up the ice sled, and put everything they would need inside. Ray climbed on behind Al and hung on to the back rail. For half an hour, his only view was his friend's back, as Al used his weight to manoeuvre through the black and white terrain along the ridgeline.

In the early autumn, a man could bow hunt from a tree stand or elevated platform, but it only allowed him to take mule deer. In the winter, they would have to leave the snowmobile and snowshoe the sled into the territory they had selected for the hunt. As the faint eastern winter sunrise cast its timid first light, they left the ice sled at a makeshift base camp, and snowshoed into their chosen area, taking one step and looking through their binoculars, always lifted slow, sticking to the shortening shadows and concentrating on making no sound, scouting for a subtle ear flick or tail wag before being detected. Bowstring would drop smartphone GPS waypoints on their way in so as not be become lost on the way out.

'Still hunting' was a mental game and took an entire day to do right. Al and Ray would have to move into or perpendicular to the wind as they approached the awakening bedded deer below their higher ground. Going slow was meaningless if your scent was blowing right up a buck's nose. The snowy weather was also to their advantage, muffling their footfalls, increasing whitetail activity, and providing signs to follow— tracks, droppings, last fall's rubs and scrapes, and occasional antler sheds. Carrying their bows in a shoot-ready position, they found and followed the larger, more rounded tracks of a mature whitetail buck. They continued in cover, making no quick movements. Every twenty minutes, or when either of them had made an inadvertent noise, Bowstring would blow three soft low grunts on his deer call.

It happened after the last of one of these quiet exhalations that Al saw antlers 80 metres in front of them. The buck stopped there, a hundred kilos of male whitetail with a non-typical rack that Al guessed would make a Pope and Young score of 230 points or more. The big deer had made a curious mistake, one that would be his last. Ray had already lined up his compound bow, adjusting his shot from broadside to quartering away as the buck sniffed the air and turned. He waited for the front leg facing him to step ahead, pulling the shoulder blade forward to expose more of its vitals and enlarge the target. Ray knew the risk of his arrow only passing through one lung and adjusted his line of sight.

He visualized the arrow's path to the exit point on the deer's far side, aimed at a spot on the buck's near side at the top of the lower third of the chest cavity, closer to the middle near the liver, that lined up with the exit point.

An arrow generates noise as the bow releases its stored energy into the shaft and launches it from the bowstring. Ray knew those sounds would reach the buck milliseconds before the arrow arrived because the speed of sound travels far faster than any arrow. He knew the deer would respond to this startling, unfamiliar reverberation by preparing itself to jump and run, loading power into its legs for that first bound by coiling downward like a basketball player about to leap for the rim. He knew that sudden dip could lead to 'jumping the string,' causing the arrow to go over the deer or hit it above the aiming point. Ray aimed that much lower, intending to send his broadhead hemorrhaging in and out of the whitetail's centre, trying for a double lung shot from a pass-through exit wound, one that would double the visible blood trail, making it easier to follow when it made for the nearest cover.

Thwishshshsh... Whooshshshsh... Fhshshshsh... Thucknknknknk!!! Ray watched his arrow's red and white blazer vanes disappear into the buck, forward and low. The whitetail made a blowing, bawling noise as his front legs kicked out and hind legs kicked in. A kangaroo jump and mule kick split second later, he tucked in his scut and ran hard for 20 metres, before slowing to a drunken stagger. His tail twitched as he tried to stay on his feet. Then he stumbled and fell and lay motionless in the snow.

By the time that Al returned with the Otter ice sled, Ray had retrieved his arrow and broadhead. Both men tied a stout stick to the antlers, dragged the big buck onto the toboggan, and pulled everything back to the snowmobile base camp.

Over many years, Bowstring appreciated that the only two things he needed to field dress a deer were a sharp blade and a strong stomach. He removed his watch and put on his latex gloves. With the deer on its side, he knelt behind it and pushed the plastic butt plug into the buck's backside, gave it several twists, pulled it out, tied it with string, and cut it off.

Al helped him drag the buck belly up on a slope with its head elevated and tie each leg to a tree. After removing one testicle (leaving the other to prove sex and the tail to prove breed), Ray grabbed the skin where it formed a 'V' between the rear legs and cut and continued a shallow one-inch slit up the belly to the chest cavity. He turned the Ranger skinner knife around to split the sternum, which vented steam as the men pulled the ribs apart.

From his first incision, Ray used his gut hook to cut open the belly from the pelvic bone to the breastbone.

After cutting the diaphragm from the chest cavity walls and along the spine to separate it, Ray grabbed the trachea above the lungs and heart and severed it to free the entrails. With one long, powerful pull on the windpipe, Ray removed the heart, liver, lungs, intestines, stomachs, and bladder. Except for the heart and liver, which Al placed in a plastic bag, they would leave the gut pile for the scavengers.

The hunters turned the deer over and spread its legs so the cavity was open against the ground, draining the pooled blood while they ate a *Snickers* bar and drank a thermos of hot coffee.

After loading the field-dressed buck back onto the ice sled, they connected it to the Ski-Doo for the half-hour trip back to the trailhead. Once again, Bowstring Close arrived at Al Purdy's house on dusk, with time enough before dark to hang the carcass head down, hacksaw through the deer's ribs and splay open the chest cavity with another stout stick, and skin the hide off to allow the meat to cool faster. That night, the two hunting buddies celebrated their successful kill with far too much liquid gold.

It took the two hunters as many more days to clean and reassemble their weapons of deconstruction, make the rounds of Al Purdy's good ole boys to boast about their success and let the deer hang long enough for the meat to set up for butchering.

Ray's last morning in Williams Lake was a busy one. Al removed the front legs at the knee joint in less than ten seconds each. He sliced under the scapulae and lifted the front legs as he carved off the shoulders. Ray used his Ranger skinner knife to cut away the backstraps on either side of the spine. He sliced away the two inside tenderloins from inside of the rib cage, the hams from the hips, and the hind legs from the hams. Both men used a fillet knife to bone out rib meat, flanks, neck meat, and tenderloins and divided up each man's share of quarters in game bags. They would both have 35 kilos of venison from the 100-kilogram buck, enough to last them until next year's hunting season. Ray placed the head and cape in a Trophy Totes soft-sided cooler, for his taxidermist friend, Harry Eastlack, to mount when he got home.

After a final night of revelry, Bowstring loaded his share into his Chevy truck bed, gave Al a final hungover man-hug, and rode off into the Cariboo horizon. It would take him another eight hours of driving, plus whatever other stops and ferry uncertainties might await him further south. He tuned his radio to the local station.

Good morning Secwepemc and T'exelcemc and Xat'súll brothers and sisters... this is Sugarcane Shuswap at CFNR 96.1 FM in Williams Lake... brought to you by Indigenous and Northern Affairs Canada... where membership has its privileges...

It had been a glorious trip. The effort had exhausted Bowstring. Winter whitetail hunting was always a strenuous undertaking and he was longer in the tooth every year. Still, the exercise and rye whiskey had taken more out of him than he thought it should have.

A First Nations brother walked into a Tim Hortons with a shotgun in one hand and a buffalo in the other... The man drank his coffee, then blasted the buffalo with the shotgun, causing parts of the animal to splatter everywhere, then he just walked out... The next day, the brother returned... "Whoa, Chief!" Said the server. "We're still cleaning up your mess from yesterday. What was all that about, anyway?"
The Indian smiled. "I'm training for an upper management position in the Canadian Government... Come in, drink coffee, shoot the bull, leave a mess for others to clean up, and disappear for the rest of day..."

By the time Ray made it onto the last BC Ferry leaving from Tsawwassen at 10:45 p.m., he was feeling worse. His arms and legs were dead weight, every muscle ached, and he had to crawl to his truck when the vessel docked at Duke Point at one in the morning. He drove off the ferry but had trouble staying in his lane. His right hand fumbled for the radio.

Good Morning Harbour City... This is CNDN Coast Salish radio, 101.3 FM on your Home and Native Band. I'm your host, Silas Seaweed... bringing you some early morning insights from the northern lights...

It felt like his muscles were melting. He had to push on the gas pedal with both feet to keep him from going too slow on the highway.

Touch not the poisonous firewater that makes wise ones turn to fools and robs their spirit of its vision...

He was almost halfway down the highway to Harbour City now, but he wondered if he would make it home. Gravity dragged on him painfully, turning his arms and legs to lead. Ray struggled for breath. He couldn't swallow, and saliva drooled out both sides of his mouth. He couldn't keep his eyes open.

There was something wrong. He steered onto the offramp that led to Harbour City Regional Hospital.

With his last remaining strength, he managed the turn into the entrance. Up ahead were the neon yellow stripes and automatic sliding frosted glass doors of the emergency department.

One finger cannot lift a pebble...

He braked, but his Chevy was too heavy and shattered the wide doors of his destination and destiny.

We are all one child spinning through Mother Sky...

> 'Drove my Chevy to the levee but the levee was dry
> Them good ole boys were drinking whiskey and rye
> And singin' this'll be the day that I die
> This'll be the day that I die'
> Don McLean, *American Pie*

'When elephants fight, the grass gets trampled.'
African Proverb

Because of the never-ending oppressive workload, opportunities for communal collegial continuing internal medicine education at Harbour City Regional were a rarity. Every one or two months, one of the illustrious department members would find the energy to present an unusual or interesting case in an impromptu early morning meeting.

Sababa, just off a red-eye return flight from a week's Yucatan vacation with Jane, found Sid Shalimar at Code Brew.

"You heading to rounds, Sab?" Sid grabbed his cappuccino and waited for the stocky savant to get his quadruplicare espresso.

"Yep."

"You met the new guy yet?" Sid asked.

"Makes Ernie Hacker look like the Dalai Lama." Sababa said.

"Not the clog wog." Sid said. "We have another one."

"Really?" Sababa asked. "The oxymorons still recruiting without our consent?" Sid nodded.

"What's he like?"

"He doesn't appear to like anything." Sid smiled. "I sure don't think he's going to like you."

"Let's go see, shall we Shal?"

The two men walked together down a side hallway, to the light green-yellow padded walls of the Board Room, fuzzy from the static electricity and the occasional spider web. The white stippled acoustic tile ceiling was bored out with pot lights and grooved in a railway yard of track lighting, controlled by a far wall bank of controls and switches and potentiometers to focus photons and heat.

A long teak conference table halfway filled the centre, racing the waist-high wooden wall sideboard cabinet next to it down the length of the room. Powerful earthy union odours of dust and must and rotting corpses lurked in the debris under the table on the claret pile carpet. All the members of the Department of Medicine, including the two new comrades, spaced like stray cats around the teak perimeter, scrolled their devices, or whispered in pairs.

The patriarch of the department, Dr. Peter Zaias, an enormous bear of a man, Chief Defender of the Faith, seer of the Sacred Scrolls, hailed the entry of the two men and greeted Sababa's homecoming.

"I know you've met Dr. Hebberig, Sab, but I'd like to introduce you to our latest acquisition, Dr. Mestor Mealachas." The portly professor gave his new colleague a long look.

Below Mestor's dark eyebrows was the face of a bunged-up barn owl. His complexion was cadaveric cold oatmeal. The eyes behind his gun-metal spectacles were as grey as washed-out bed sheets, and the lines around his mouth gave no sign that he had ever lost himself in laughter. His movements were economical and effete.

Sababa wondered if he had always been this grim or if his profession had made him that way. Perhaps as a boy, Mestor Mealachas had skipped stones and rolled in mud, but he doubted it. This man had never been a boy, only a gargoyle waiting to unleash himself on vulnerable victims far below his ego. Sababa knew that his office plants were already dead.

"Good morning." Mestor spelled it with a 'u'; the only things he would roll with were his 'r's. "You'rre the alcoholic."

"Say what?"

"There must be a rreason you drrink so much."

"Makes people like you more interesting." Sababa said.

"You don't think it's a prroblem?" Mestor asked.

"Not to get technical... but according to its chemical properties, alcohol is a solution."

"It's an addiction." Mestor said. "I'm no' an addict. Don't smoke, don't drrink, and I exerrcise."

"I know a guy who gave up smoking, drinking, and inactivity." Sababa said "Healthy right up to the day they murdered him. Ever get altitude sickness?"

"What?"

"From the moral high ground." Sababa watched the board room door opening. Wayward Woods arrived late as usual, with his Tim Hortons Double Double. The only reason for time was so that everything didn't happen all at once.

"Gentlemen, please." Dr. Zaias intervened. "Now that he's here, I'm sure that Dr. Woods would like to present his case."

Wayward was keen to share his experience. He detailed the story of one of his recent admissions, an elderly patient who presented with a fatal brain hemorrhage. After relating the relevant details, Wayward dimmed the lights and projected the poor man's cerebral CT scan onto the wall-mounted HDTV screen at the far end of the room.

"Any idea of why this man should have had such a devastating bleed into his brain?" He asked. No one spoke for almost a minute.

"You say he had no history of hypertension?" Sababa pulled a laser pointer from his Colombian leather bag.

"None." Wayward said.

"You see how the bleed is localized to his left parietal and occipital lobes?" Sababa mused. "And how the bleeding pattern swirls like a cloud through the hemisphere?"

"So, what is it then?" Mestor asked.

"Cerebral amyloid angiopathy." Sababa said. "Caused by the accumulation of cerebral amyloid-β in the tunica media and adventitia of leptomeningeal and cortical vessels."

"We must have been waiting forr you to rreturn from your holiday."

182

"I've seen a fair number of these cases, Dr. Mealachas." Sababa said.

"Yes, but you didn't do a verry good job."

"Yeah. That must be it." Sababa said. "Nothing to do with you being a pathetic narcissist."

"I'd rrather have a treatable mental illness than whateverr you've got." Mestor said. "Insanity doesn't rrun in my family."

"I bet it strolls through, taking its time, getting to know everybody personally."

"And a good time was had by all." Dr. Zaias adjourned the rounds. He and Sababa left together down the hallway that led to the ER.

"You should at least give him a chance, Sab." Peter said.

"That was it." Sababa said. "Nothing makes a morning complete like finding Judas swimming in your Cheerios. Mealachas may look like an idiot and talk like an idiot but don't let that fool you. He's an idiot."

"We have still left on the earth groups of people representing every age of civilisation." Zaias said. "He does seem to be a bit of a peacock."

"A big turkey in bold true colours." Sababa said. "A self-aggrandizing zero-sum gamer. The demonic dark triad creation of three antisocial personality traits—narcissism and Machiavellianism and psychopathy. Naked ambition tempered by arrogance. And the greater the arrogance, the greater the dogmatism. Imagine the fun we'll have"

"My grandfather once told me that there were two kinds of people— those who do the work and those who take the credit." Zaias said. "He told me to be in the first group because there was less competition. Mestor might be in the second."

"Dr. Greed and Dr. Narcissism." Sababa said. "I'm not happy about the direction these two new guys will take our department, Peter."

"It was Plato who said that there are three classes of men—lovers of wisdom, lovers of honour, and lovers of gain." "Beginning with you, we now have one of each."

"Not happy." Sababa said. "All causes shall give way: I am in blood stepp'd in so far that, should I wade no more, returning were as tedious as go o'er."

"What?"

"Macbeth." Sababa said.

"Why?"

"Why not?"

An old Cherokee told his grandson:
"My son, there's a battle between two wolves inside us all.
One is Evil. It's anger, jealousy, greed, resentment, inferiority, lies and ego.
The other is Good. It's joy, peace, love, hope, humility, kindness & truth."

183

The boy thought about it, and asked:
"Grandfather, which wolf wins?"
The old man quietly replied:
"The one you feed."

'Some days it is a heroic act just to refuse the paralysis
of fear and straighten up and step into another day.'
Edward Albert

Sababa found Alex waiting for him in the ER.

"You didn't attend rounds." He said.

"I got tied up here." Alex remonstrated. "What was the case?"

"Mealachas Syndrome."

"Mealachas Syndrome?" Alex hadn't heard of it.

"Yep. Mealachas Syndrome." Sababa said. "Hypogonadism, undescended testes, mood disorder, premature suture closure with increased intracranial pressure, cortical blindness, and mental retardation."

"Sounds horrible."

"He is." Sababa said. "What you got?"

"First referral is from Dr. Capitaine." Alex waved the emergency physician over to join them.

"How are you, Myles?" Sababa asked.

"Living the dream."

"Dreams are private myths." Sababa said. "Myths are public dreams."

"You here to see Aristotle Onassis?" He asked.

"Apparently." Sababa said. "Who is he?"

"69-year-old shipping owner with a four-week history of intermittent binocular vertical double vision, worse in right and downward gaze." Myles said. "He also noted mild drooping of his left eyelid, increased tearing, conjunctival injection, and discomfort behind his left eye. At first, he attributed his symptoms to seasonal allergies."

"Wrong season."

"Yeah, that's what got him to his family doc, who referred him to the office of our own faceless oculist guru, Dr. T.J. Eckleburg."

"And?"

"T.J. found some decreased visual acuity of the left eye, a small left hyperdeviation on Maddox rod testing, a mild left upper lid ptosis which did not appear fatigable with prolonged upgaze, and absent Cogan's lid twitch. Thought he might have ocular myasthenia gravis even though his edrophonium challenge and ice test were negative." Myles said. "Ordered some acetylcholine receptor antibodies, fitted him with temporary prismatic lenses, and told him to come back in a week."

"Hmmm." Sababa mused. "Hadn't read Winkler's classic 1979 *Postgraduate Medicine* article."

"At his return appointment, Aristotle's double vision was worse." Myles said. "His acetylcholine receptor antibodies had come back negative. T.J. requisitioned another set, ordered an MRI, and referred him to Oliver Lax for electrodiagnostic testing."

"And?"

"His double vision had once again improved by the time Oliver saw him the following week." Myles said. "Electrodiagnostic testing showed normal nerve conduction, repetitive nerve stimulation, and single-fiber electromyography studies. MRI and repeat antibodies were also negative."

"So why is Mr. Onassis here this morning?" Sababa asked.

"Desperation." Myles said. "His double vision is worse, and he has a left sixth nerve palsy on exam."

"What else have you done?"

"I tried to think what you might have arranged and sent him for magnetic resonance angiography." Myles watched Sababa smile. "He's just come back."

"Let's have a look." Sababa pulled up Aristotle's images on the consultant's desk monitor.

"Well, lookee here." Sababa said. "Enlargement of his left superior ophthalmic vein along with a Type B carotid-cavernous fistula on the same side. Let's go see him."

Inside the cubicle curtain, Myles introduced the professor.

"This is Doctor Sababa, Aristotle." He said. "His preferred pronouns are wherewithal and whatever."

"Have you found the myasthenia, yet?" The shipping owner asked. "I've been circling this drain for a month now."

"You don't have myasthenia, Aristotle." Sababa said.

"What is it then?"

"You have an abnormal communication between your carotid arterial system and cavernous sinus." Sababa said. "It's called a carotid-cavernous fistula."

"Can you fix it?"

"No." Sababa saw Aristotle's face fall further. "But I know someone who can." He called to the ER ward clerk over the polycarbonate barrier.

185

"Cheri Sundae, is it possible for you to raise Alien Huang at Vancouver General?"

"On it, Sab." Two minutes later she raised her handset towards the white stippled acoustic tile ceiling. "Line 3 for Dr. Huang." Sababa picked up the call.

"Hi, Alien, I understand you're back in circulation."

"My endovascular surgical practice is bursting." He said. "What do you need, Sab?"

"I have a man in my ER with a Type B left-sided carotid-cavernous fistula." The portly professor said. "He needs you to embolize it."

"Send him across." Alien said. "We'll fit him in this afternoon. Don't let him eat anything in the meantime."

Sababa explained the plan to Aristotle and arranged his transport.

"It is during our darkest moments that we must focus to see the light." The shipping owner said.

"Who's next?" Sababa asked.

"That would be me." Trace Pangloss had been waiting outside Aristotle's curtain.

"What you got, Trace?" Sababa asked.

"Sheila Creighton." He said. "53-year-old saw filer at the Hamac mill. Presents this morning with four days of headache and oral pain and drooling and difficulty swallowing. This morning she complains of muscle spasms and can't open her mouth to eat."

"Exam?"

"Normal vitals." Trace said. "She has this weird grin. Opening her mouth was difficult, but I found a yeast infection inside. Her leg muscles go into spasm with light touch and all her tendon reflexes are brisk."

"Lab?"

"Her lymphocytes are low." He said. "I got hold of her family doc's record, which showed a positive rheumatoid factor and antinuclear antibody in high titre."

"Where is she?"

"Behind the curtain, in cubical 7." Trace said.

"Let's go see her." Sababa and Alex followed Trace to the patient.

"Sheila, I'd like to introduce you to Doctor Sababa and his resident, Dr. Harding." He said. "They're all smoke and lightning and heavy meddle thunder."

"Gnahhhh." She bleated. *Pleased to meet you.*

"Risus sardonicus." Sababa said.

"What?" Trace asked.

"That's the name for her weird grin." Sababa said. "Sheila, have you had any recent injuries, dental work, or contact with animals?" Sheila shook her head, which caused her spine to arch backwards in spasm and pain.

"And that's called opisthotonos." He said. "Sometimes these spasms are so severe that bone fractures and muscle tears occur." Sheila looked petrified.

Sababa took a long cotton-tipped swab from his Colombian briefcase and inserted it through Sheila's clenched teeth until it touched the back of her throat. Instead of gagging, she bit down.

"Positive spatula test." Sababa said. "High specificity and sensitivity, according to *The American Journal of Tropical Medicine and Hygiene*."

"What is this, Sab?" Trace asked.

"You don't recognize this, Trace?" He asked. "The lockjaw trismus, the involuntary muscle spasms..."

"Should I?" He asked.

"Hippocrates knew about it. You should as well." Sababa said. "Sheila, can you remember if they inoculated you with Tdap-IPV as a young girl? Just the vax, Ma'am." She shook her head again, with less vigour.

"You know what this is, Alex?" Sababa asked.

"Tetanus." He said. "But she doesn't have a history of contact with anaerobic *Clostridium tetani* endospores, no puncture wounds or other source of infection from soil, saliva, dust, or manure, so how could she?"

"She has a low lymphocyte count from her Sjögren's syndrome." Sababa said. "She doesn't need an exposure history."

"Gnahhhh... gnahhhh... gnahhhh." Sheila bleated.

"You have tetanus, Sheila." Sababa said. "The bacteria that Alex mentioned produces tetanospasmin toxin, which cleaves synaptobrevin II, a protein component of synaptic vesicles, and blocks the release of inhibitory neurotransmitters glycine and gamma-aminobutyric acid across the synaptic cleft. If your nervous impulses cannot be checked by normal mechanisms, you'll have these muscular spasms."

"Will she have immunity after her treatment?" Trace asked.

"No." Sababa said. "Tetanospasmin is so potent as to be lethal before it provokes an immune response, especially in our patient here, who is immunocompromised." Sheila looked petrified again.

"Don't worry, Sheila." Sababa said. "We can fix this. Dr. Harding here will admit you for antitoxin immunoglobulin, antibiotics, muscle relaxants, IVIG for your Sjögren's syndrome, and observation, in case you need more of our attention." Her face may have relaxed, but it was hard to be sure.

"This must still be a problem around the world." Trace mused.

"Over two hundred thousand cases a year causing about sixty thousand deaths, in hot and wet climates where the soil has a high organic content." Sababa said. "Be grateful you're not a Kenyon Maasai, who would have knocked out your lower deciduous incisors at six months and your lower permanent incisors at six years of age. Some tribes also extracted the two upper front teeth."

"Why?"

187

"So they could still get nourishment if they got tetanus." Sababa said. "That's why we have drinking straws. Same in Borneo, where the missing teeth also permit a stronger blast of poisoned arrows from *sumpitan* blow-pipes."

"That's crazy." Trace said.

"Naturopathic medicine." Sababa said. "In Sudan, the Dinka and Nuer tribes still remove the permanent front teeth of their children—six bottom teeth and two top teeth—resulting in a sunken chin, a collapsed lower lip, and speech impediments."

"Just so they can eat if they get tetanus?"

"Uh-huh." Sababa said.

"That's rough." Alex said.

"Not as rough as their method."

"Which is?" Trace asked.

"They use fishhooks."

'The day has the color and the sound of winter. Thoughts turn to chowder...
Chowder breathes reassurance. It steams consolation.'

Clementine Paddleford

The portly professor had sent Alex ahead to reconnoitre the two referrals waiting on the medical ward. Two minutes after he had finished and paged Sababa, a Colombian leather briefcase performed a bell tailside aerobatic manoeuvre past his left ear, before landing on the nursing station desk.

"I know there is a reason that you do that." Alex said. "I'm just not sure what it is."

"It's a Zen koan."

"Really?"

"Hell, no." Sababa said. "What you got?"

"Ado Lot-Swife." Alex began. "46-year-old VIU women's studies professor admitted by Dr. Chibueze for progressive stiffness."

"Henry is an oncologist." Sababa said. "She got a malignancy?"

"Small cell lung cancer." Alex said. "Remembers blowing beautiful smoke rings like a dying artist. But she's in remission."

"So say you." Sababa said. "Tell me more."

"Two months ago, she developed painful rigidity in the muscles of her lower back and abdomen." Alex said. "It rose to affect the proximal musculature of her neck and arms, with contractions and superimposed spasm attacks caused by fast movements, emotional distress, or sudden sounds or touches, worse with stress and cold weather, and better with sleep. Her posture and gait have deteriorated to the point now where she can't walk or bend. It's affected her mood and psyche."

"How so?"

"She's scared stiff." Alex grinned. Sababa rolled his eyes.

"Keep going."

"Henry had her reviewed by Dr. Lax, who diagnosed her with Parkinson's." Alex said. "She got worse with the dopaminergic medication he prescribed, so he told Henry to call you."

"Ignorance and confidence are constant companions." Sababa said. "Exam?"

"Impaired mobility and lumbar hyperlordosis." Alex said. "Brisk stretch reflexes and clonus."

"Let's go see her." The resident led his mentor down the clinical teaching unit hallway, and into a single room at the end.

"Ms. Lot-Swife, I'd like to introduce you to Doctah Sababer." Alex said. "He's a philosophical hedonist and realist, existential nihilist, and cultural relativist, transcendental idealist and a genetic determinist, but existential compatibilist. He's a kind of empiricist, gradualist, emergentist, pragmatist, voluntarist, connectivist, structuralist, constructionist, behaviorist, computationalist, objectivist and functionalist internist."

"Quite a list." Ado said. "I'm a feminist."

"If you insist." Sababa said. "People who think with their epidermis or their genitalia or their clan are delusional, Ado. Alex has been telling me about the medical problems you're having."

"I have lung cancer, but it's in remission." She said. "But all my muscles are getting more tight and painful, I can't move, and I get a different opinion from every specialist I see."

"In Tumortown you sometimes feel that you may expire from sheer information overload." Sababa said. "You have a rare one in a million autoimmune condition related to your cancer."

"You have a name?"

"Stiff man syndrome."

"Impossible." She said. "I'm a professor of women's studies."

"OK." Sababa said. "Stiff person syndrome. Identity politics. Much, Ado, about nothing."

"How can you be sure I have this thing?"

"I'm sure." Sababa said. "We'll draw some more blood for antiamphiphysin antibodies, genetic testing for the HLA class II DQB1* 0201 allele, and get Dr. Lax to perform an EMG to look for involuntary

189

motor unit firing in your peripheral muscles. But it's still a clinical diagnosis."

"Does it mean my cancer has returned?"

"Perhaps." Sababa said. "It's why we often refer to this subtype as paraneoplastic."

"Can you do anything for it?"

"Of course." Sababa said. "We can enhance your spinal cord inhibitory processes with GABA-A agonists like diazepam and GABA-B agonists like baclofen and suppress the autoimmunity with intravenous immunoglobin or rituximab. We'll need to restage your small call cancer and get the occupational and physiotherapists to provide you with some mobility aids to decrease the risk of falling."

"I've never been so tense, Doctor Sababa." She said. "Another incanceration, living life in cartoon motion."

"We're all over it. You'll feel better later this morning." The professor said. "Adieu, Ado." Sababa and Alex could hear the dance music from the CD player in Ado's room as they made their way back down the hallway. *But the pain and the longing's the same when you're dying... Now I'm lost and I'm screaming for help on my own... Relax, take it easy... For there is nothing that we can do... Relax, take it easy... Blame it on me or blame it on you...*

"Who's the other ward referral?" Sababa asked.

"Martha Stewart." Alex grabbed the patient record off the chart rack. "62-year-old stockbroker admitted last evening through the ER by Dr. Bloom. He thought she had an ascending paralysis."

"And?"

"He thought it was Guillain-Barré syndrome."

"And?"

"I'm not sure it is."

"Why don't you start at the beginning?"

"She was well until about thirty minutes after breakfast this morning when she developed a dry mouth and abdominal pain, and numbness and tingling of her lips, gums, tongue, face, neck, arms, legs, and toes. Two hours later she had a floating sensation followed by nausea and vomiting and diarrhea, and slurred speech and a loss of coordination. Now she has difficulty swallowing and shortness of breath."

"What did you find on exam?"

"She had a fast regular pulse and high blood pressure, dysarthria and diminished gag reflex, and flaccid weakness of all her muscles. Labs were normal."

"Is she going to stop breathing?"

"Don't think so." Alex said. "Yet."

"We'd better go check." Sababa and Alex found Martha Stewart in another private room at the other end of the hallway.

"This is Doctah Sababer, Martha." He said. "He's the ultimate eye of the beholder."

190

"Not too hard to look at." She said.

"Martha, what did you have for breakfast this morning?"

"Seafood chowder." She said. "I'm a person of pallor."

"Hmmm." Sababa mused. "A savory latte with bugs in it. For breakfast?"

"No rules." Martha said. "I made it to have for dinner last night, but my brother surprised me with takeout, so I never had time to taste it until this morning."

"Still..." Sababa said.

"They eat *encebollado de pescado* soup for breakfast in Ecuador, *mohinga* catfish stew in Burma, piping-hot *pho* in Vietnam, and *miso* in Japan." Martha said. "You can order clam chowder for breakfast at Anthony's in Seattle. Why not at my place? What's the problem?"

"You can't beat the State Street Provisions clam chowder for breakfast in Boston." Alex said. "Yankee Doodle in a kettle. Frikkin' pissah."

"Where did you get the seafood?" Sababa asked.

"Foraged it myself last September along the Inside Passage." She said. "Same beach I harvest from every year. I put a lot of oysters, clams, and mussels in my freezer."

"Did you take them during the day or at night?"

"Nighttime." She said. "With a flashlight. After the North American markets closed."

"So you didn't see the Canada Fisheries and Oceans warning signs on the beach?"

"What signs?"

"You didn't check their website before pulling the shellfish off the rocks and from under the sand?"

"I didn't hear about any red tide." She said. "I checked the tide tables. That's all."

"Too bad." Sababa said.

"How come?" Martha asked.

"Harmful algal blooms can be any colour they want or none at all." Sababa said. "You have one of the four recognized syndromes of shellfish poisoning."

"Which one?" She asked.

"Paralytic Shellfish Poisoning." Sababa said. "PSP."

"How does that happen?"

"The shellfish you collected are filter feeders of microscopic marine plankton like dinoflagellates, diatoms, and cyanobacteria." Sababa said. "Your oysters and mussels and clams were dining on a particular dinoflagellate species complex bloom called *Alexandrium tamarense*."

"And?"

"Produces a nasty water-insoluble, heat and acid-stable molecule called saxitoxin, which doesn't denature with ordinary cooking methods." Sababa said. "It blocks site 1 of fast voltage-gated sodium channels, causing a flaccid paralysis that leaves its victim calm and conscious through the progression of symptoms, opposite to the effect of ciguatoxins in some kinds of fish poisoning, which lower the threshold for opening voltage-gated sodium channels in nervous system synapses and also result in paralysis."

"Wonderful." Martha said.

"Saxitoxin is three orders of magnitude more toxic than sodium cyanide." He said. "The CIA weaponized it and issued a small dose to U-2 spy plane pilot Francis Gary Powers as an injection hidden within a silver dollar, in case of capture. As you know, he never used it. After Nixon banned biological warfare in 1969, everyone assumed the American military destroyed their saxitoxin stockpiles."

"But?"

"They didn't."

"Is this something like Japanese pufferfish poisoning?" Martha asked.

"Something like that." Sababa said. "Only chefs who have qualified after three or more years of rigorous training may prepare fugu in Japan, and the law forbids the emperor from eating it. Fugu concentrates a compound called tetrodotoxin derived from marine bacteria Vibrio and Pseudomonas. Both toxins have different chemical structures but a guanidinium group in common, and similar biological activity which, together with the hydroxyl groups, is essential for the sodium channel blocking activity. Tetrodotoxin has been isolated from blue-ringed octopus, various pufferfish species, angelfish, gastropods, moon snails, starfish, xanthid crabs, arrow worms, ribbon worms, a polyclad flatworm, land planarians, toads, and newts. The common garter snake has developed insensitivity to the toxin, which allows them to prey upon toxic newts."

"Well, aren't you a repository of divine revelation?" Martha asked.

"Captain James Cook's crew encountered both kinds of toxins on his second voyage." Sababa said. "One sailor died, and four others were ill after eating saxitoxin-laden mussels for breakfast on June 16, 1793, at what he named Poison Cove in Matheson Channel on the BC central coast.

The first recorded cases of tetrodotoxin poisoning affecting Westerners occurred in New Caledonia on 7 September 1774. Some members of Cook's crew ate a local silver-cheeked toadfish, then fed the remains to the pigs on board. The men developed some numbness and shortness of breath, but the pigs were all found dead the next morning."

"Does PSP only affect humans?"

"Oh, no." Sababa said. "Humpback whales have died from eating saxitoxin-containing mackerel and butter clams have killed their fair share of sea otters. Because these shellfish can store the toxin for two years or more, there has been no butter clam harvest in Alaska for a long time now."

"What are the three other kinds of shellfish poisoning, Sab?" Alex asked.

"Now this is where it gets interesting." He said. "The first kind, amnesic shellfish poisoning, is caused by consumption of a marine biotoxin called domoic acid, produced by Pseudo-nitzschia diatoms, which get eaten by small fish like anchovies and sardines. You remember an Alfred Hitchcock film called 'The Birds?'" Alex shook his head. Martha tried.

"It was inspired by an actual event that occurred in Northern California on August 18, 1961." He said. "Sooty shearwaters are seafaring birds that spend most of their lives on the ocean. I used to eat them as muttonbirds or tītī out of Māori hāngī earth ovens in New Zealand when I was courting Jane. Every year they complete a remarkable annual mass migration, a forty-thousand-mile round trip from nesting sites in the Southern Hemisphere crossing to the nutrient-rich waters of the North Pacific. Off the coast of Monterey Bay, they dive as deep as 200 feet, swimming with their wings in pursuit of anchovies and squid.

Around 3:30 in the morning, through a thick fogbank, thousands of migrating sooty shearwater sea birds diverted from their normal flight path and began slamming and crashing into the lights of Capitola. Awoken by the thuds on their roofs, some residents opened their doors to flocks of birds that flew straight at them. Some were bitten in the frenzy. The sea birds were crying like babies, regurgitating half-eaten anchovies, and knocking themselves unconscious.

In the morning, avian corpses and half-digested anchovies blanketed the houses of Capitola. Cars had run over many birds in the streets. Those that had survived the night lacked the strength to take flight. They huddled under cars and in alleys, trying to hide from the feral cats attracted to the pungent aroma that permeated the air. They hauled away truckloads of dead seabirds. It was a mess."

"And in humans?" Alex asked.

"Domoic acid accumulates up the food chain to birds and mammals." Sababa said. "In humans, it causes everything from lethargy, dizziness, disorientation, and irreversible short-term memory loss to seizures and death."

"And the other two syndromes?" Alex asked.

"Okadaic acid causes diarrheic shellfish poisoning by inhibiting intestinal cellular de-phosphorylation. The profuse, intense diarrhea can result in severe dehydration." Sababa said. "And neurologic shellfish poisoning is caused by various brevetoxins."

"Is... there... an... antidote?" Martha asked.

"4-aminopyridine works." Sababa said. "It's only approved for multiple sclerosis, so I'll have to sneak some into you off label."

"Any... thing... else... you... can... do...?" She struggled for breath.

"Alas, what crimes they have committed in the name of chowder." Sababa said. "We're taking you to the ICU, Martha, to monitor and support your ventilation if we need to."

"Will... I... ... be... ... ... normal... ... ... again?"

"By tomorrow morning." Sababa said. "Guaranteed."
It didn't mean that she couldn't feel pain. It just meant that she couldn't do anything about it. Too weak to speak, she cried her words, one at a time.

'Chowder for breakfast... till you began to look for fish-bones coming through your clothes.'

Herman Melville, *Moby Dick*

'Leaving sex to the feminists is like letting your dog vacation at the taxidermist.'
Camille Paglia

"Afternoon, Mercy." Sababa said.
"It's paralysis week, Boss." Lost in typing, her cat-eye glasses never left the screen.
"Mercy is what you give people who don't deserve her." Sababa pulled the first chart off the clinic stack and handed it to his protégé.
"Harry Eastlack." Alex called into the waiting room. A human statue rocked to his feet in three rigid movements. His neck and spine were fused and his arms fixed in frontal flexion. The young physician helped him down to the resident's room.
"Samson Burke." Sababa called. Another man stumbled up and onto his cane with difficulty. His handshake was like shaking air. The professor observed how he had to lift his left leg higher than the other. Inside his sanctum sanctorum, Sababa helped him into a chair on the other side of his desk before perusing the folder containing Tictac Tarmac's referral letter and copies of correspondence and investigations. *Dear Sab, 52-year-old Cabela's gunsmith with high CPK and progressive muscle weakness. Oliver Lax and a Vancouver rheumatologist thought he had polymyositis but didn't improve with steroids. Your turn...*
"How can I help, Mr. Burke?" Sababa asked.
"I've been getting weaker and weaker for over two years now." He said. "It started with a loss of strength in my hands and pain in my thighs. My muscles prevent me from machine metal turning and drilling and filing and polishing and other functions I need to work. Getting out of chairs and going upstairs is impossible. Bending down or walking fast or reaching for things is too difficult. I feel off-balance and I'm prone to trip and fall, especially since this left foot became so clumsy."

194

"It's called a steppage gait."

"And now I'm having trouble swallowing." Sababa walked around his desk again.

"Make a fist." He said. Samson couldn't make a fist.

"Here." He handed over his car keys. Samson dropped them on the carpet.

"I can't open doorknobs or fasten buttons and zippers or write anymore. My muscles are melting away in front of me." Samson said. "I need to know what's happening."

"You have inclusion body myositis." Sababa said.

"How do you know that?"

"It's my business to know what other people don't know." He said. "One, it's the most common inflammatory muscle disease in older adults. Two, it's most obvious in the finger flexors and knee extensors. Three, it takes longer to develop and doesn't respond to medications that work in other muscle conditions. And four, the EMG that Dr. Lax performed showed abnormal spontaneous activity with polyphasic pseudo-neurogenic mixed motor unit action potential morphologies and high amplitude outliers."

"Can you prove it?" Samson asked.

"We'll get a set of anticytoplasmic 5'-nucleotidase antibodies and a muscle biopsy." Sababa said. "But that's just icing. We'll also need to get you hooked up with the physical and occupational therapists for a home exercise program, mobility-gait training, and assistive devices."

"Do you know what causes this thing?"

"Nope." He said. "The best evidence points to some type of retroviral infection combined with an immune reaction big enough to trigger the inflammation process. But we use that excuse in a huge number of conditions we have no explanation for."

"How does this nightmare end?" Samson asked.

"You don't pick your nightmares." He said. "They pick you."

"Yeah, but how does this one end?"

"The same way all nightmares end." Sababa said. "Dancing with the devil in the pale moonlight."

"I don't understand."

"I'll explain it better at your next appointment." Sababa wrote out a sheaf of requisitions. "Let's go seek Mercy."

Alex was already waiting at her reception desk. Sababa explained what he needed to help Samson Burke and left with his resident to see his patient. Alex made intros.

"He's the rock steady bedrock of his profession." Alex said. "A rock-solid rock star. The hard rock cock of the rock, the rock the boat rock of Gibraltar."

"And I'm a rock around the clock." Harry said. "Between a rock and a hard place, I've hit rock bottom. Even my tears are rock salt."

"Good of you to rock up." Sababa said. "Tell us a story, Alex."

"Harry Eastlack." He began. "41-year-old taxidermist referred by Dr. James Ruben Andrews for a longstanding problem of progressive rigidity."

"It started from my neck down." Harry said. "Every time I injured myself, no matter where, it would heal with lumps of bone."

"He's lost most of his joint mobility, eating and speaking are difficult because he can't open his mouth very wide." Alex said. "The extra bone formation around his rib cage restricts his lungs and diaphragm and has affected his breathing."

"I must have seen a dozen specialists in half as many cities." Harry said. "Everyone from rheumatologists to oncologists to endocrinologists to orthopedic surgeons."

"Is that who did the biopsy?" Sababa asked. Harry rubbed the big lump on his arm.

"Everywhere you get inflammation, you get explosive heterotopic bone formation." Sababa said. "We better hope you never need surgery for anything else."

"Do you know what this is, Doctor Sababa?" Harry asked.

"I think so." Sababa said. "Can you remove your shoes and socks?" Harry nodded.

"Alex." His resident helped with the endeavour.

"His big toes are crooked." He said.

"That makes the diagnosis."

"Which is?" Alex asked.

"Harry, you have a very rare condition." Sababa said. "One in two million. It's caused by an autosomal dominant allele on chromosome 2q23-24, a mutation in the gene which encodes ACVR1, a bone morphogenic protein receptor. The mutation affects the way the receptor responds to a protein called activin A, causing it to go into overdrive when it would normally turn off, fusing your joints and transforming connective tissue and muscle into a secondary skeleton, which combines with the first one."

"You have a name?" Harry asked.

"Fibrodysplasia ossificans progressiva."

"You have a simpler one?"

"Stone man syndrome." Sababa said. "Classic rock."

"Crushed rock." Harry said. "The irony is not lost on me, Doctor Sababa. I'm a taxidermist. My job is to take a once-living organism and turn it into statuary. And I'm going to end up as a garden gnome."

"That's not set in stone." Sababa said.

"What do you mean?" Harry asked.

"The scientists at Regeneron have developed an activin A antibody, garetosmab, that has stopped the growth of new bone in mice."

"Blarney stone."

196

"Steppingstone. A precious stone." Sababa said. "They're into a phase 2 human trial called LUMINA-1."

"Can you get me enrolled in the study?" Harry asked.

"I'll leave no stone unturned."

"I'm on my way from stone-cold sober to stone-cold crazy to stone-cold dead." Harry said. "I could use a little hope."

"I specialise in hope, Harry." Sababa said. "Let's organize a serum bone-specific alkaline phosphatase level. Until I hear from Regeneron, and even afterwards, the cornerstone of your care is injury avoidance."

"OK."

"Tell Mercy I'll see you again in six weeks." Sababa said. "I'll call you sooner if I have any news.

"Thanks, Doc."

"Rock on, Harry." He lit up the iTunes icon on his computer screen. "Rock on."

'I have heard about a fable once when I was young
About a man being able to turn into stone
But I've never been a believer
And I never will.'

Syd Matters, *Stone Man*

'We live in a world where the laws are getting so tight that management
has changed to micro-management to quantum-management to paralysis.'

Jane Siberry

On the eve of the monthly Medical Advisory Committee meeting, that strange, solemn, sacrificial, satanic, shamanic ritual of collision (or collusion, depending on the machinations of the participants) between the medical staff and the health authority bureaucrats, Sababa would get as close to the dark matter of the universe as he ever dared.

The conclave was held in the Boardroom, that same Oracle of Oversight, that identical morgue of ambition, in which Dr. Zaias chaired his Department of Medicine meetings. The only differences were that the light green-yellow padded walls were fuzzier from the static electricity, the white stippled acoustic tile ceiling worked harder to absorb the screams of the defeated, and the Mayline chairs fabric seats running the length of the long teak conference table held fatter asses and more of them. The particulate debris lurking under the table became even more agitated.

At the far end of the room, new graffiti marred the melamine whiteboard on an easel:

A pediatrician, an internist, and an administrative utilization manager had died and were waiting at the gates of Heaven.

The pediatrician was the first to explain why she deserved entry. "I've spent my career treating children to enable them to grow and live full lives." St. Peter let her in.

The internist was up next. "I've dedicated my life to treating adults to enable them to live healthy and happy lives." And St. Peter let him in.

The administrative utilization Manager was last. "I've spent my career helping people in need gain access to affordable healthcare." And St. Peter let him in.

"You can stay for three days and then go to Hell."

"What is this, some joke?" Asked Malcolm Canmore.

"Joke." Sababa said.

The committee was made up of medical staff departmental representatives—Jules Martino from Surgery, Juan Leyblanca from Pathology, Mako Brisk from Radiology, Trace Pangloss from Emergency, Banjo Paterson from Anesthesia, and Eleazar Sababa from Internal Medicine; and courtiers from the Palace of Administration, and all their urbane appurtenances—Malcolm Canmore, the Chief Hospital Administrator of the silk ties, linen handkerchiefs, and manicured fingernails, minus his silver cuff-links and platinum pens, Foster Care, the new CEO of iHealth, Big Nurse Mildred Ratschet, the Grand Galactic Governess of Nightingales, sporting her string of cultured natural pearls, and a gaggle of other suits and pantsuits. They would collaborate to achieve the magnetic goals that drew their obscene destinies together, always ready and willing to judge and bludgeon the independent outsider.

But the committee chairperson, the most prepotent master of control, was a diminutive general practitioner named Dr. Petronilla de Meath, a Napoleanna bone apart, a harpy hag of a harridan henpecking harassment.

Petronilla picked up a handset from the multifunction business-class conference digital phone console and dialled zero.

"Lana, can you announce the start of the Medical Advisory Committee meeting?" The hospital switchboard operator's Big Voice broadcast the assembly overhead.

Petronilla called the council to order and requested approval of the previous meeting's minutes. A cacophony of grunts echoed around the table.

"I've tabled the old business." She said. "So we can hear a progress report from Foster Care, the CEO of the brand new expanded Health Authority.

Medicine is the only profession that labors incessantly to destroy the reason for its own existence. In Sababa's case, it would have help.

A tanned elderly muscular managementshipwreck with a full crop of wavy white hair above a wide grin full of perfect white teeth and eight of his Underworld minions sat on one side of the boardroom table.

"Before I speak, I have something important to say." Said the health authoritarian, rising to the occasion. "Every noble institution is the lengthened shadow of a single man. His character determines the character of the organization."

"That could be a problem." Sababa said.

"I'm very proud of my good name." He took a bite out of a shiny apple and placed what was left on the board room table. "And how we are remodelling iHealth going forward."

"That's strange." Sababa said.

"What?"

"Any time the word 'Care' appears on one of your memos, it always translates to 'I don't give a fuck.'"

"I need a laser pointer." Foster said.

"We don't have a laser pointer." Petronilla said.

"Why not?" Foster asked. "Who's going to take me seriously if I don't have a laser pointer?"

"With or without."

"Doctor Sababa!" Petronilla huffed. "Manners."

One of Foster's ill-suited accomplices adjusted a far wall bank of controls and switches and potentiometers dimming the photons and heat focused by the bored-out pot lights and railway yard grooves of track lighting.

"First slide, please..." He said.

$$GI - W = E$$

"What's that?" Sababa asked. "Some kind of bureaucratic calculus?

"Good Intentions minus Wisdom leads to Evil." Foster said.

"Whoaoaoa. How Epicurean." Sababa said. "If iHealth knows about patient suffering, cares about patient suffering, and can do something about patient suffering, then there shouldn't be any patient suffering."

"A revolution is a trivial shift in the emphasis of suffering." Foster said. "Revolutions always mean the breakdown of old authority. And, make no mistake, iHealth is bringing revolution. Next slide, please."

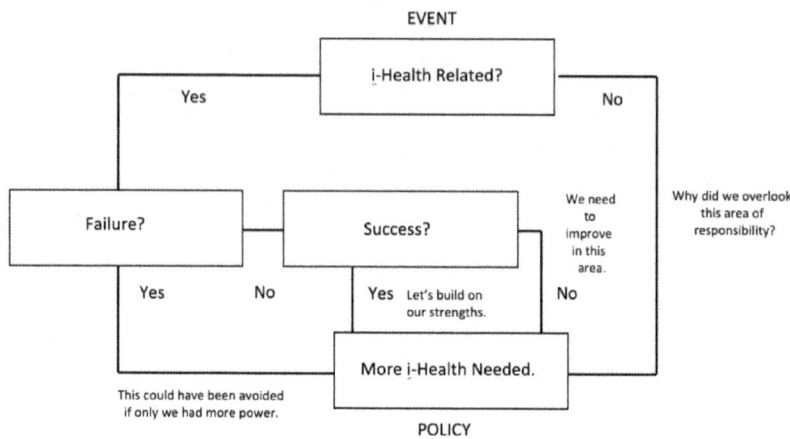

"Twenty-first-century medicine must not be confined to a twentieth-century bureaucracy." Foster said. "This is our iHealth troubleshooting flow chart. As you can see, any decision point in the algorithm leads to more control from the health authority. True science." Everyone nodded, not everyone agreed.

"Pathological science." Sababa said. "How does all this revolutionary revisionism justify your billion-dollar boondoggle—the money you could have spent on real medical care?"

"I understand you have an issue with our new Electronic Health Record initiative, Doctor Sababa?" Foster asked.

"You mean the dystopian digital database debacle." Sababa said. "I'm sorry. I can't save your life right now. I don't have you in our system yet, so I can't input any orders."

"It's a Brave New World out there." Foster said.

"I don't think you'd last very long in the outside world." Sababa said. "Your computer software is like an Old Testament god. Lots of rules and no mercy."

"Is there a reason you seem to be so allergic to rules. Doctor Sababa?"

"Rules cannot bring freedom." Sababa said. "They only have the power to accuse."

"The rules exist because 95% of the time for 95% of the people, they're the right thing to do." Foster pointed at the professor with his remote. "And the other 5%?"

"Have to live by the same rules." Foster said. "Because everybody thinks they're in that 5%."

"All my patient referrals are in that 5%." Sababa said. "The greatest crimes in the world are not committed by people breaking the rules, but by people following the rules. They drop the bombs and massacre the villages."

"You act as if our rules were evil." Foster said.

"Good intentions minus wisdom." Sababa said. "You bet. Just like any of your other nonsense rules we've become familiar with. The smaller the function, the greater the management. When any organizational entity expands beyond twenty members, the actual power will be in some smaller body. If you can get us asking the wrong questions, you don't have to worry about the answers."

"We will implement our innovations as fast as possible." Foster said.

"Why don't you make these changes more gradually?" Sababa asked.

"If you want to know how two chemicals will interact, you don't ask them—because they're going to lie through their lying little chemical teeth." He said. "No, you throw them in a beaker and apply heat. Evolution may not have eyes, but it can create them."

"You're wallowing in the drunken debunked theorem of Lamarckian evolution, nurture determining nature, instead of seeing the way evolution works, through Darwinian random mutation and natural selection." Sababa said. "There are no shortcuts in evolution. Adaptation doesn't occur in a bowl of acid. Evolution has arranged things so that all our systems deteriorate, and you invest in repairing them only as much as you think they are worth. What it's worth to the health authority can be very different to what it's worth to the individual patient with the broken system."

"Our new administration is making revolutionary changes in your programs and traditional staff roles." Foster said. "From here on, we will refer to all physicians as health care providers, working in harmony with all our other iHealth champions. Everyone will function and make all decisions as a team."

"Except..."

"What?"

"Everyone on the team may be responsible and take credit for the positive outcomes." Sababa said. "But no matter how you spin this, they'll still blame me for the disasters."

"And so, Doctor Sababa." Foster was becoming impatient. "How do you perceive your 'team role?'"

"I'm the self-made misanthrope." He said. "The guy with the carrots and the sticks and a problem.

"What's the problem?"

"I'm out of carrots."

'If we don't take action now We'll settle for nothing later
We settle for nothing now And we'll settle for nothing later.'
Rage Against the Machine, *Settle for Nothing* (Heard in the
Harbour City Regional Hospital ER one night)

"How was your meeting?" Alex already knew the answer to his question from the tune Sababa had selected from his music library on a secret drive hidden deep inside the hospital computer network.

"When I die, just put me in a pepper grinder and sprinkle me all over the people that pissed me off." Sababa nodded to Dr. Ho, who had joined them at the ER consultant's desk. "Something for us, Gung?"

"Alex has already seen her." He said. "But I wanted to hear what you had to say."

"You're up to bat, Alex." Sababa said.

"Venus Willendorf." He began. "30-year-old Cottonwood stables jockey who presents tonight with recurrent episodes of muscle weakness and twitching since adolescence. The attacks occurred about once a week and lasted anywhere from 15 minutes to 3 hours in duration. During severe spasms, she slurs her speech and can't walk or turn her body. Between these paroxysms, her muscles are stiff and sore, which has curtailed her professional horse-racing participation and performance."

"What brings it on?" Sababa asked.

"Trigger factors include rest after exercise, stress, fatigue, weather changes, fasting, alcohol, and second-hand cigarette smoke." Alex said. "Carbohydrate ingestion can decrease the severity or even abort some attacks."

"Why is she here tonight?"

"She had another episode." Alex said.

"What's so special about that?"

"She hasn't had an attack for three months now."

"What happened three months ago?"

"She got pregnant." Alex said.

"Hmmm." Sababa waved to one of the ER nurses. "Michaela, please get me 80 mEq of oral potassium chloride and a 4-gram chewable tablet of dextrose." The RN gave him a thumbs up and disappeared into the med room.

"Exam?"

"Normal gravid female with a palpable uterus and normal blood pressure." Alex said. "Fetal heartrate of 150 beats per minute by Doppler."

"Lab?"

"Mild microcytic anemia." Alex said. "Normal chemistry." Michaela handed the stocky savant the two medications he had requested.

"Let's go see." Sababa said. In the cubicle behind her curtain, Alex introduced his mentor.

"This is Doctah, Sababer, Venus." He said. "Try not to upset him. He's been in a committee meeting."

"You don't like committees, Doctor?" Venus asked.

"Groups of the unwilling chosen from the unfit, to do the unnecessary." Sababa said. "The best ideas spring from individuals, not from groups— a divine spark leaping from the finger of God to the finger of Adam."

"And you're Adam?"

"Living in paradise." Sababa said.

"Waiting for expulsion?"

"Just a matter of time." He said. "I'm drinking the cider as fast as I can. And I see you've partaken of the apple as well, Venus."

"Twelve weeks now." She said. "It's quite exciting, but I'm concerned about these attacks coming back."

"Has anybody ever found an explanation?" Sababa asked.

"No."

"Drink this." He handed her the dose of potassium chloride. No sooner had she swallowed the metallic bitterness, than weakness overwhelmed her and she couldn't lift her head and arms.

"'M habbin an addak." She said.

"Now eat this." Sababa handed her the dextrose tablets. No sooner had she swallowed the sugar, than her strength returned.

"Like Alice in Wonderland." Alex said.

"What is this thing?" Venus asked.

"Yeah, what is it?" Gung echoed.

"Impressive syndrome."

"What?" Alex asked.

"That's a disease of horses." Venus said.

"Named after an American Quarter Horse named Impressive." Sababa said. "He was the index case."

"I got this from one of my horses?" Venus asked.

"No." Sababa said. "You inherited it."

"What do they call it in humans?" She asked.

"Gamstorp episodic adynamy."

"They call it anything else?"

"Hyperkalemic periodic paralysis."

"But her serum potassium was normal." Gung protested.

"Yeah, that's not a problem." Sababa said. "It doesn't always have to be high."

"Is it a threat to my baby?" Venus asked.

"Not at all." Sababa said. "For reasons we don't understand, pregnancy reduces the severity and frequency of attacks. It may be a direct effect of gestagens on sodium channels."

"Sodium channels?" She asked.

"Skeletal muscles contract through the activation of voltage-gated sodium channels." Sababa said. "To prevent perpetual contraction, the channel has a fast inactivation gate that plugs the sodium pore after it opens. You were born with an autosomal dominant c.2111C>T mutation of the muscle sodium-channel gene SCN4A which makes the channel unable to inactivate, resulting in temporary paralysis."

"What can I do?" Venus asked.

"High-carb diet." He said. "Eating every four hours with reduction of potassium-containing fruits and vegetables. Avoidance of attack triggers. Oral glucose and salbutamol puffer when you get one. I'll write some orders."

"A good jockey doesn't need orders." Venus smiled. "And a bad jockey couldn't carry them out anyway."

"Impressive." He said.

Dr. Cliffy Carlton had been standing by outside the proceedings, waiting for the three physicians inside the jockey's cubicle to emerge.

"What do you want, Spazzo?" Alex asked.

"Someone who knows what they're doing, Masshole." Cliffy said. "Oh, wait. That's not you."

"How may we be of service, Dr. Carlton?" Sababa asked.

"Strange one." Cliffy began. "Lisa Whelchel. 61-year-old BC Government and Service Employees' Union rep back from a working holiday in South America a week ago. Three days ago, she developed a mild fever, headache and muscle pains, and a brief bout of diarrhea. This morning, she felt weak, with shortness of breath, slurred speech, and difficulty swallowing."

"Exam?"

"Afebrile." Cliffy said. "But she has an asymmetric flaccid quadriparesis with absent deep tendon reflexes, a bilateral facial paralysis, extraocular muscle weakness, and lower bulbar signs."

"Lab?"

"Elevated white blood cell count with a left shift."

"Imaging?"

"See for yourself." Cliffy brought up a chest x-ray on the consultant's computer.

"Paralysis of her left hemidiaphragm." Alex noted.

"So, what is this, Cliffy?" Sababa asked.

"No clue, Sab." He said. "If I didn't know better, I'd swear Lisa had polio but she's been vaccinated and that monster's been dead and gone forever."

"There are still cases in India, Afghanistan, Nigeria, and Pakistan." Sababa said. "But although this bears a strong resemblance to poliomyelitis, that's not what's going on here. Let's go see her."

Behind the curtain of cubicle 5, the uninhibited emergency physician introduced the portly professor and his protégé.

"This is Doctor Sababa, Lisa." He said. "He moves in unlimited freedom in the namelessness that animates, luxuriates, burns, and transpires through form, enlivening what is steam, mist, torrent, saliva, blood, ocean, cloud, coffee, wine, butterfly, tiger, hummingbird, energy, and delight. And this is his sidekick, Yankee Doodle." Alex scowled.

"Where were you in South America, Lisa?" Sababa asked.

"Attending the national meeting of La Confederación General del Trabajo de la República Argentina in Córdoba." She slurred her Spanish, and her English. "It was for my work."

"I'm sure." Sababa said. "Where did you stay?"

"Estancia Los Potreros." She said. "It's near Río Tercero."

"I know where it is." Sababa said. "Did you do any horseback riding?"

"I wanted to, but they told me their horses had colic." Lisa said. "There was also some kind of problem with some local birds."

"*Furnarius figulus.*" Sababa said. "Wing-banded horneros."

"I don't know." She said. "They found some dead birds on the ranch the day before I arrived."

"Hmmm." Sababa could see she was having trouble breathing. "I see."

"Do you know what's wrong with me?" She asked.

"You have West Nile poliomyelitis." He said.

"But that only occurs in the summer." Cliffy said.

"It is summer." Sababa said. "In Argentina."

"Why is everything today about birds and horses?" Alex asked.

"Birds are intermediate amplifier hosts for the virus." Sababa said. "Horses, like humans, are the dead-end hosts."

"Dead end?" Lisa asked.

"Unfortunate choice of wording." He said. "Interesting, though. West Nile is a mosquito-borne RNA flavivirus. The bloodsucker that carries West Nile in North America is the common house mosquito, *Culex pipiens f. pipiens*, which bites birds, is cold-tolerant, and hibernates in the winter. The vector in Argentina is *Culex pipiens f. molestus*, which bites rats, mice, and humans, is cold-intolerant and can breed all year round because it lives in warm, underground locations, or the southern house mosquito, *Culex quinquefasciatus.*"

"Why couldn't this be another arbovirus or spinal cord stroke or compression, or Guillain-Barré syndrome or some other immune-mediated neuropathy?" Alex asked.

"My subspecialty is being right when other people are wrong." Sababa said. "I'm right, and you're smart, and eventually you'll see I'm right."

"What happens now?" Lisa asked.

"Now we admit you to the ICU for observation and serial spirometry monitoring in case we have to support your breathing until you get better." Sababa said. "Dr. Harding here will order some more specific blood tests, perform a lumbar puncture to get some cerebrospinal fluid for testing, arrange for EMG and nerve conduction studies, and an MRI of your anterior spinal cord."

"Do you know anyone else who had this virus?" She asked.

"Alexander the Great." Sababa said. "A flock of ravens died at his feet as he entered Babylon."

"How did he do?"

"Not so well." Sababa said. "It was the only battle he ever lost. They preserved his body in a vat of honey."

"Didn't he complain he was dying with the help of too many physicians?"

"He did. But we are all here on earth to help others." Sababa said. "What on earth the others are here for I don't know."

Gung Ho high-fived Cliffy Carlton as the physicians emerged from behind Lisa's curtain.

"My turn." He said.

"You have an appointment, Gung?" Sababa asked.

"Like the one you had with Destiny." Which rolled the professor's eyes back into his brain.

"OK." Sababa said. "Tell us the story."

"Louise Arbor." Gung began. "59-year-old supreme court judge who presents with a three-month history of fatigue, two months of fever and chills and generalized muscle and joint pains, and one month's worth of swelling of her feet and trouble walking. She's seen a pantheon of local and distant gods, including a hematologist and rheumatologist in Vancouver."

"Why is she here in your ER tonight?" Alex asked.

"She got a copy of the call schedule and parachuted in." Gung said.

"To see us?" Alex asked.

"She requested the Sage of the Salish Sea at triage." Sababa's eyes did that rolling thing again.

"Alex, when you grow up and leave us here, remember that 20 percent of your patients will cause 80 percent of your pain."

"The 20/80 rule." Alex said. "Got it."

"I take it you're not finished yet, Gung." Sababa said. "What more?"

"Exam was normal except for obesity, low-grade fever, and swelling of both ankles." Gung continued. "Her lab results have always shown a high white cell count with a significant eosinophilia."

"Pretty pink peroxidase proteins." Alex said. "Worms, wheezes, and rare diseases. Which one did she have?"

"The rare disease category." Gung said. "All her tests looking for disseminated parasitoses or neoplasms or vasculitides were negative. Bone marrow found 40% of all granulocytopoietic cells to be eosinophils. CT scan of her thorax, abdomen, and pelvis revealed multiple reactive lymph nodes in the mediastinum and near the iliac blood vessels. Double-barreled endoscopies were unremarkable."

"Let's go see the judge." Sababa said.

"Sorry to keep you hanging, Judge Arbor." Gung introduced the portly professor and his resident.

"I'm getting quite desperate for a solution to my problem, Doctor Sababa." She said.

"What do you eat?" Asked the stocky savant.

"What do you mean?"

"I mean, what do you eat?" Sababa said. "You're an intelligent middle-aged professional woman with a Rubenesque body mass index. It would surprise me if you weren't on some kind of diet to lose weight." He watched the colour of pink champagne fill her cheeks.

"I drink a lot of water." She said.

"But that's not everything you do, is it, Louise?" He asked.

"I eat a lot of nuts." She said. "I eat only nuts."

"And... wait for it." Sababa said. "What nuts do you only eat?"

"Cashews." She said. "I only eat a lot of cashews."

"Bingo." Sababa said. "And how many cashews is a lot?"

"About 200 grams a day." Louise said. "I've been doing that for six months now. Is there something wrong with that?"

"In 1989 a large Japanese company, Showa Denko, manufactured and marketed an L-tryptophan supplement which resulted in over 1,500 cases and at least 37 deaths."

"You have a name?" Louise asked.

"Eosinophilia-myalgia syndrome." Sababa said.

"What does that have to do with my diet?" She asked.

"Cashew oil is rich in L-tryptophan." He said. "Excessive ingestion of tryptophan supplements inhibits histamine degradation by increasing formation of formate and indolyl metabolites. The increased histamine activity induces peripheral blood eosinophilia and myalgias. We'll need a muscle biopsy to be sure, but you being Chock full o'Nuts appears to have given you a classic case of EMS."

"What now?" She asked.

"You go from nuts to soup." Sababa said. "Dr. Harding here will admit you for a course of methylprednisolone therapy and arrange for your muscle biopsy tomorrow morning."

"Thank you, Doctor Sababa." Louise said. "I wish there was some way to repay you."

Sababa looked up at the two RCMP officers who had just entered the ER. The one who scowled at him was Veronica Marsden.

"Perhaps there is a little something..."

> 'Tell me what ticks you off, and I will tell you what makes you tick.'
> Lloyd John Ogilvie

Internal medicine specialists bookmark their dreams, in case they can reload them later the same night. The phone call that interrupted Sababa's sublime slumber would vaporize any possibility of later re-engagement. He made a dazed and confused effort to focus on the luminous numerals beside him. It was two in the morning. *Sweet dreams are made of this... Who am I to disagree?*

"What?" He answered.

"I know you just got home, Sab." It was Alex. "But some guy drove his Chevy half-ton through the ER doors."

"So?"

"They were closed at the time." Alex said. "He wasn't moving or breathing. We've intubated him and he's on his way to the Death Star."

"Coming now." Jane roused next to him.

"Midnight special?" She asked.

"Bit late for that." Sababa dressed and pointed his dimpled and dented white Honda Civic down the long gravel driveway and down towards Harbour City Regional. In less than six minutes, he coasted to a stop inside the markings of the on-call internist parking bay. Shattered frosted glass shards and bent metal was all that Bowstring had left of what had been the hospital emergency entrance two hours earlier. The professor made his way through the debris and down the Yellow Brick Road to the ICU. He passed an agitated middle-aged woman, sitting in one of the retro vintage chairs in the vestibule before he vanished through the soft translucent light of the frosted automatic door. *Whoosh.*

"Bed 6, Sab." Betty Boop looked over her Coke bottle wire-rimmed glasses and aimed a crooked dowager empress index finger towards the cubicle commotion. A respiratory technician was reprogramming ventilator settings, Mary was calibrating the patient monitor, and Alex was finishing a lumbar puncture.

"I take it you can explain this shitshow, Bahney." Sababa said.

"Ray Close." Alex began. "41-year-old Hamac millwright returning from a hunting trip up in the Cariboo."

"How do you know that?" Sababa asked.

"We found a gas station receipt from Williams Lake in his wallet." Alex said. "Dated this morning."

"How do you know he was on a hunting trip?"

"Maybe it was the freshly butchered deer that jumped out of his truck bed at triage, and the compound bow in his cab." Alex said. "Oh, yeah, and his wife told me. She was expecting him back a couple of hours ago."

"The other dear in the waiting room?" Alex and Mary nodded.

208

"I got the name of his hunting buddy up north from her." Alex said. "I woke him up."

"Go on." Sababa said.

"He said Bowstring, that's his nickname, was fine when he left his house this morning." Alex said. "Except that his voice was a little slurred, but they'd been up drinking rye whiskey most of the night. No other medical history."

"What did you find on exam?"

"Normal vital signs." Alex said. "Flaccid paralysis with bilateral droopy eyelids. No reflexes."

"Ascending or descending paralysis?" Sababa asked.

"How can you tell now?" Alex asked.

"He drove here with both feet on the pedals." Sababa said. "His steering didn't go to ratshit until he hit the hospital parking lot. That's an ascending paralysis. Therefore, he doesn't have botulism."

"So he has what I thought he has." Alex said.

"What's that?"

"Guillain–Barré syndrome." Alex said. "I was going to place a femoral venous access line for plasmapheresis."

"Not so fast, Fenway." Sababa said. "You haven't told me about any investigations."

"OK." Alex said. "Routine bloodwork was all normal, as was his chest x-ray and the CT scan of his head and neck. Tox screen negative. Oliver Lax is asleep on his island, so we can't get electrodiagnostics until the winter sun comes up. And I don't have his LP results back yet." Sababa stuck his head out of the Bed 6 curtain.

"Betty, can you call the lab and get us the CSF results from the lumbar puncture that Alex just did?"

"On it." She said. Sababa pulled a fine-tooth comb and a pair of Carmalt splinter forceps from his Colombian leather briefcase.

"What's the differential diagnosis of ascending paralysis, Bahney?" He asked.

"Guillain–Barré syndrome."

"You already said that." Sababa combed through Ray's hair. "What else?"

"Cervical spinal cord lesion." He said. "And poliomyelitis I guess."

"Don't guess." Sababa said. "What else?"

"Dunno." Alex remonstrated, as Betty Boop handed him the cerebrospinal fluid analysis.

"Yes, you do." Sababa said. "What's the CSF protein?"

"Normal." He said.

"Is it normal in Guillain–Barré syndrome and polio?"

"Uh, no."

"Does he have a Babinski sign?"

"No."

"Would you expect him to have one with a cervical spinal cord lesion?"

"Uh, yes."

"Along with urinary retention, fecal incontinence, and laxity of anal-sphincter tone." Sababa said. "So, you're missing one more important cause of flaccid paralysis."

"That sucks."

"Everything sucks." Sababa said. "Some things suck more than others. Might as well find something to smile about." *A-hunting we will go, A-hunting we will go... Heigh-ho, the derry-o, A-hunting we will go...*

"What are you searching for?"

Sababa broke into another song. *You remember that rainy evenin' I throwed you out... with nothin' but a fine-tooth comb... I know I'm to blame... now ain't it a shame... So baby, won't you please come home...*

"Bowstring Close was deer hunting in the Cariboo." He said. "I'm looking for a tick."

"But it's the middle of winter." Mary said. "And tick-borne human disease normally only occurs in the summer."

"Normal is just a cycle on a washing machine." Sababa said. "I'm always on the hunt for what is about to happen."

"Ticks are usually invisible." Alex said.

"Until you find them." Sababa held up his forceps. It could have been a half-inch-long Kalamata black olive without the moving little legs.

"Female *Dermacentor albipictus*." Sababa said. "Winter tick. Infestation causes bald patches on moose or elk or whitetail deer but, with climate change, increasing numbers can kill an animal. Last year they found 75,000 on a single moose."

"What did it do to Bowstring here?" Mary asked.

"Tick paralysis." Sababa said. "From an ixovotoxin nerve poison which interrupts the sodium flux across axonal membranes at the nodes of Ranvier and nerve terminals, and inhibits acetylcholine release at the presynaptic neuromuscular junctions of muscle fibers."

"Amazing that an overlooked one-gram arachnid could generate a toxin of such potency." Alex said.

"In Rose's review of 332 cases of tick paralysis, the mortality rate was 11.7 percent." Sababa said. "From failing to look for or detect the engorged tick."

"What do we have to do now?" Alex asked.

"We've done it." Sababa said. "You are healed, Bowstring. Rise and walk."

"Are you serious?" Alex asked.

"In the Bible, they shout, 'Yes, Lord' and then start right on in with the praising." He said. "Ray will be off the ventilator in two hours and walking out of here before you get home tonight. I'll go tell his wife the good news."

"Really?"

"Uh-huh." Sababa said. "Now if we were in Australia and this was an *Ixodes holocyclus* tick, that would be a whole 'notha scenario. He still might have died even if someone had removed the tick."

"Na-ah."

"Yah huh." Sababa said. "That's the thing about Australian animals—if it isn't venomous, carnivorous, or has foot-long claws, it's a tourist."

"Is that the most lethal kind of tick?" Alex asked.

"Not quite." Sababa said. "There are worse in medical administration."

"How so?"

"There ain't no ticks like poly-ticks." He said. "Bloodsuckers all."

'And they say that I am the sick boy
Easy to say, when you don't take the risk, boy
Welcome to the narcissism...
Feed yourself on my life's work
How many likes is my life worth?'
                    The Chainsmokers, *Sick Boy*

The casual reader won't understand the paralysing malevolence of the vainglorious physician. As a perfect embodiment of the manipulative dark triad of antisocial traits, he is as full of himself as a narcissistic cannibal.

Most doctors exude authority, control, knowledge, competence, and respectability, but the egomaniac elevates his synchrony of narcissism, Machiavellianism, and psychopathy to a new level of malware.

Sababa knew that 'extreme self-love of a fake perfect self' might have an evolutionary origin and advantage. Our hunter-gatherer ancestors, faced with continuous survival challenges, had no space or time for self-doubt. Any trait that advantaged them in acquiring resources to gain social status, like mental toughness and emotional intelligence, would improve their chances of staying alive and mating. They may not have particularly cared how other people felt, but they could well understand how other people felt and, as a result, narcissists handed down more genes to the next generation.

But there must also be a reason everyone isn't born a narcissist, why the inhumanity and profanity and inanity of vanity insanity hasn't defined our urbanity. The prevalence of narcissistic personality disorder in the general population is six percent and, somewhat counterintuitively, even less in physicians. So what makes the medical narcissist special?

211

First, he has no empathy. It may be the ultimate pathway to a more rewarding life, but the self-obsessed medical specialist is unable or unwilling to acknowledge, identify with, or accept the feelings, needs, preferences, perspectives, priorities, or choices of others. To the perfect narcissist, your irritation or disgust doesn't register. You are invisible. Not that Mestor couldn't empathize with anyone, but it was less to do with his personality disorder than his active imagination. If you wanted empathy, you could find it in the dictionary between emesis and enema. Second, despite Mestor's obvious contempt for Sababa's love of pinot noir, he had his own addiction—the demon of external validation; envious of others, and seeking to hurt or destroy the objects of his frustration.

Third, exaggerated self-importance means not only won't you have heard about the contributions of others, you won't have even heard about their existence (unless somebody needs blame). Self-aggrandisement of talents, skills, contacts, personality traits, and unique heroic accomplishments must be recognised as superior without commensurate achievement. The clinical research Mestor claimed to have performed on his free website was bogus. His grandiosity demanded acknowledgement of his exceptional skills in patient diagnosis and management and attracted him to leadership positions where he could attain his rightful place above the proletariat. And the higher he climbed, 'soaring with the eagles,' the more divisive cliques of self-serving sycophants and assassins surrounded him. *Power corrupts and absolute power corrupts absolutely.*

Fourth, the medical narcissist is exploitative, using deceitful manipulation, hating those who escape his control, even at the expense of cutting off the social branch he sits on. Mestor Mealachas was difficult to call out. On the surface, he appeared to be trying to help his victims. In reality, he was taking credit for their achievements, disparaging their performances, and gaslighting their vulnerabilities with faux patronizing concern.

Fifth, the medical narcissist has an arrogant sense of entitlement, commensurate with his expectation for special priority treatment. He 'kisses up and kicks down.' *His speech was smooth as butter, yet war was in his heart; his words were softer than oil, yet they were drawn swords. Psalm 55:21*

Kissing up seeks to flatter those he perceives to be powerful. The egoist physician will view every medical leader as his peer, share his ideas for organizational 'improvements,' conspiratorial concerns about his colleagues, ingratiate himself as indispensable, and vie for a supervisory role of his own.

He is the first to swoop in to 'orient' and 'help' any new leader or create dramatic chaos that only he can fix. Mestor Mealachas volunteered his services to rescue the health authority during its dispute with his Harbour

City Regional emergency room colleagues, who saw his kissing up as a Judas kiss, interference both meddlesome and messianic.

He kicked down everyone else. The contempt and condescension that narcissists display to subordinates are soul-destroying. Mestor's fault-finding in his colleagues worsened as power further disinhibited his behavior. Generous one day and aloof the next, he justified his quick temper as necessary to keep other doctors on their toes and to uphold his high standard of patient care. Nothing was ever good enough.

His ambition targeted the high-achieving colleagues he envied. He conducted smear campaigns without the knowledge of his victims, who couldn't defend themselves against false rumors because they were the last to find out. The falsehoods focused on what hurts doctors most— being accused of failing to pull one's weight, a lack of integrity, or incompetence. To avoid being reported, he undermined his victim with repetitive nit-picking and sarcasm, avoided eye contact, rolled his eyes with disdain when no one else was looking, gave out backhanded jabs dressed up as jokes, and drip-fed low-grade abuse that was difficult to expose. Intermittent stonewalling and private taunting were tough to prove. When confronted, the bully pretended nothing had happened. To maintain his status, the perpetrator played the martyr or accused his victim of being toxic, dishonest, mentally unstable, or 'not up to it,' which caused further harm.

> 'That didn't happen.
> And if it did, it wasn't that bad.
> And if it is, that's not a big deal.
> And if it is, that's not my fault.
> And if it was, I didn't mean it.
> And if I did
> You deserved it.'
> A Narcissist's Prayer

Mestor told his co-workers that Sababa had given up his hospital privileges, at the same time he conducted a backstairs sham peer review to extinguish them. He devised new rules to disenfranchise qualified specialists from reading electrodiagnostic reports based on arbitrary criteria he would reverse when he became defined by them himself. He removed the portly professor from department email distribution and meeting notifications and relegated his participation at a conference he chaired to a non-specialist category. The name of the game was clandestine character assassination at the expense of the better physician's reputation.

Spreading lies is a very effective way to split people. Rather than providing support, department members can wrongly accuse the complainant of poor behavior. Sababa's other colleagues were reluctant to challenge the bullying for fear of becoming a target themselves. In the

213

end, we remember not the words of our enemies, but the silence of our friends. Mestor's mind games were irrational, and there was little the stocky savant could do to fix the situation when the rules kept changing. Lesser men would have become upset, hyper-vigilant, and defensive and, when their stressed demeanor raised doubts about their mental health, their colleagues might withdraw support. Preoccupied with self-protection, the victim might appease and tolerate the bully for too long. Diversionary recommendations for self-care, resilience training, and cognitive-behavioral strategies could result in more harm because of further pressure for the victim to change, while nothing stopped the bully's continuing destructive behavior. *Nice guys finish last.*

Sixth, both types of narcissists attracted to the medical profession are incurable attention seekers of unlimited success, fame, or omnipotence. Body beautiful specialties like Pretty Boy Troy's cosmetic plastic surgery practice, attract the somatic narcissist, preoccupied with appearance, physical fitness, and sexual performance, in the surrogate search for ideal, everlasting, all-conquering love or passion. The cerebral narcissist, like Mealachas, craves attention for his unequalled brilliance—any specialty area works to put others down intellectually. Sababa was often the intended victim of *der Narzissmus der Kleinen Differenzen*—Mestor's hypersensitivity and willingness to feud over minor details of differentiation.

Seventh, more than attention, the egocentric physician requires admiration and affirmation or, failing that, fear and notoriety. They nurture patients who will adore them as they inflate their achievements in their consulting rooms while making derogatory comments about other doctors. In a profession staged and reward-structured with built-in ego-boosts, they cultivate colleagues who will provide the 'narc snacks' of recognition with career ceremonies and celebrations all the way to their lifetime achievement award. *Mirror, mirror on the wall...*

The need for adulation combined with thin skin is fertile ground for persecutory delusion. Routine review, constructive feedback, or minor criticism offends the narcissist physician. He reacts to ego threats with greater confidence than is appropriate, self-perceived invulnerability to conflicts of interest and because the rules do not apply to them, license to step over the line of decency with crude humor, compliance violations, nest feathering, and sexual harassment. Sababa would have occasion to warn Mestor about turning down the charm. When frustrated, contradicted, or confronted by people he considered inferior, Mealachas would reach for his rage. To anger an honest person, lie to him; to anger a narcissist, tell him the truth.

The eighth definitive trait of the physician narcissist is ego-syntonicity—the lack of self-criticism. Because he views his traits and behavior as superior virtues to be proud of, he refuses to believe there is anything to change. He remains fixated on what he thinks he needs: more power, wealth, and domination over others, which makes him exhausting to deal with.

The toxicity rots the culture and reputation of his department from the inside out. An entitled, contemptuous, disinhibited physician can do a lot of harm. Costs increase because staff turns over faster, discovers sick leave benefits, and engages in expensive workarounds to avoid painful interactions; colleagues delay patient referrals and nurses delay patient alerts. The replacement of participation and innovation with mistrust and fear obliterates morale, and chaos develops from internal reviews, harassment claims, union grievances, and the potential for litigation. Narcissistic personality disorders create most human resources nightmares in medical groups and hospitals.

Physician leaders are unprepared or unwilling to deal with entitled and dismissive behavior. They find it difficult to discipline those who abuse power and put their agendas above the needs of patients or colleagues.

The best strategy would have been not to hire Mestor Mealachas in the first place, but the process was stacked against the recruiters. They were his first victims, in a double whammy of organizational vulnerability. The narcissistic candidate has a sparkling resume and gives an outstanding performance during any interview. The reference-checking process, the best hope of averting the treacherous hire, is often lackadaisical. The confident candidate will exploit the process by providing three crafted letters from referees hand-picked by the same future nightmare.

Marquis Shu Ying investigated the bloody wake Dr. Mealachas had left behind in his previous position. He tried to warn the rest of his department. But to future colleagues desperate for the relief that a competent candidate promised, Mestor was as compelling and charismatic and articulate as he described himself. He was manna from heaven.

To Sababa, in contrast, Mestor was a malicious melancholic mud cookie. He saw straight through him, his dark traits, and his passive-aggressive cold shoulders and hot bile—no class, no charm, no coolness, no credibility, no compassion, no wit, no warmth, no wisdom, no subtlety, no sensitivity, no self-awareness, no humility, no honour, no grace, no inner world, no soul. A paean of privilege and pettiness, Mestor turned artless into art form. His faults were fractal and his flaws had flaws. He was an automaton troll.

And so came the inevitable showdown. The professor pondered his strategy. What, he asked himself, is a narcissist's greatest weakness? What is he the most afraid of? There was nothing worse for Mestor than having someone point out even the slightest fault. His greatest weakness was his hatred of embarrassment, ironic because he had no problem openly shaming others. And what was the best way to humiliate a narcissist, to cut him, to make him bleed? He wouldn't see it coming unless Sababa wanted him to see it coming.

215

Marquis Shu Ying tipped off the professor that Mealachas would introduce a motion to strip him of his hospital privileges at the next Department of Medicine meeting. The stocky savant waited until Mestor called the assembly to order. At the point where he began a poisoned preamble, Sababa stood and, invoking Robert's Rules, passed around the evidence of Mestor's malicious intent, the twelve signs of sham peer review, and accused his nemesis of the three 'D's of disruption, division, and distraction.

He eviscerated the subversive attack on his reputation and drop-kicked the attacker out of his chairmanship. When one consorts with assassins, one must expect to dance along the edge of a knife. But the assassin always dies, baby. It's necessary for the healing.

The forest makes your heart gentle. You become one with it. No place for greed or anger there. Sababa never kept score, wasn't afraid of losing, or looking to be rich or powerful. He had no interest in his own personality and never bore any malice. The Good Doctor was free.

> 'Moses had a strange shepherd's staff.
> When he threw it down, it separated out from the flock
> those who lived by aggression and those who hoped for wealth.
> The remnant went on with him through the wilderness.
> Very few will understand this.'
>
> Rumi

> 'Routine is not organization, any more than paralysis is order.'
> Arthur Helps

Actions based on hope are better than the paralysis of certainty. Sababa's patients placed their trust in the certainty of his actions.

Alien Huang performed a successful transvenous left cavernous sinus embolization on Aristotle Onassis at Vancouver General Hospital. At his 3-month follow-up appointment, the shipping company owner still had a left sixth nerve palsy with a large amplitude esotropia. A year later, he was back to living the dream.

An hour after Sheila Creighton rolled through the Death Star doors, she required mechanical ventilation, which involved a shitshow of an emergency tracheostomy. Alex did a lumbar puncture to administer intrathecal human tetanus immunoglobulin. He ordered infusions of intravenous magnesium sulfate and diazepam and pancuronium and labetalol to control the muscle spasm and autonomic dysfunction. It took four weeks for Sheila to regenerate enough nerve axon terminals for Sababa to take her off the ventilator, and another month of hospital recovery before she went home. She never quite got rid of her weird grin. The stiff person syndrome of the VIU leftist feminist activist protagonist, Ado Lot-Swife, improved with our specialist scientist internist checklist, which did consist of baclofen and intravenous immunoglobin. The optimist in her would untwist into a defeatist and fatalist nihilist pessimist when her oncologist found the metastasis that would reenlist her as a finalist. Her friends would resist in their wish to assist and blacklist him as a sexist misogynist Chauvinist antagonist. Ado went on to enlist a herbalist and hypnotist and alchemist, before fading into the mist.

Stockbroker Martha Stewart dodged mechanical ventilation of her paralytic shellfish poisoning with the help of Sababa's sneaky off-label dose of 4-aminopyridine. The stocky savant discharged her the following morning. Martha now gets her seafood chowder out of a can.

Harry Eastlack, the taxidermist afflicted with stone man syndrome, continued to ossify, leaving him able to move only his lips. The phase 2 trial of Regeneron's stone tablets, their drug garetosmab, that Sababa had hoped would stop Harry from being bombed back into the stone age, was halted after too many patients died in the extension open-label part of the study. BC had legalised marijuana by the time the stone-faced stonemason carved Harry's Rock of Ages rock art headstone while listening to acid rock, as stoned as a biblical adulteress.

Samson Burke's muscle biopsy showed inflammatory cells invading muscle cells, vacuolar degeneration, and filamentous inclusions of abnormal proteins, compatible with Sababa's diagnosis of sporadic inclusion body myositis. At his next appointment, the portly professor told the Cabela's gunsmith how his nightmare would end. Five years after Samson handed in his notice, he would have his last dance with the devil. In the pale moonlight, it was the perfect balance between forgiveness and performance.

Venus Willendorf, the pregnant Cottonwood stables jockey, delivered a bouncing baby boy 28 weeks after she met Doctor Sababa in the Harbour City ER. That she suffered no attacks of hyperkalemic periodic paralysis since that encounter was nothing less than Impressive.

Sababa had to intubate Lisa Whelchel for acute respiratory failure from her West Nile poliomyelitis syndrome after he admitted her to the Death Star. Bloodwork was positive for class M immunoglobulin antibodies to WNV. The CSF results from Alex's lumbar puncture show 50% neutrophils in her initial LP, followed by a shift to lymphocytosis. Electromyography and nerve conduction studies showed both a motor axonopathy and anterior horn cell involvement. MRI showed abnormal signal intensity in the spinal cord ventral horns with enhancement around the conus medullaris and cauda equina. Lisa spent 49 days on the ventilator before her flaccid paralysis improved enough to allow extubation. Her limb strength recovered from distal to proximal muscles but, even at four months, she was still too weak to ambulate without a walker. The jar of honey she sent Sababa from Hatidze Muratova in Macedonia had a flock of dead ravens on the label and a signature. Μέγας Αλέξανδρος. *Alexander the Great.*

Supreme court judge Louise Arbor's muscle biopsy showed perimysium and perivascular infiltration with CD68 positive macrophages, lymphocytes, and eosinophils consistent with eosinophilia-myalgia syndrome. Her fever and sore muscles and joints vanished with Sababa's slow-tapered corticosteroid therapy and her cutting out cashews.

She presided over the trial of Red Cedar and sentenced him to life in prison with no chance of parole for 25 years, convicted on two counts of first-degree murder and two counts of attempted murder related to the Hamac mill incident. Veronica Marsden never bothered Sababa again.

As the Good Doctor predicted, Ray 'Bowstring' Close was off the ventilator in two hours and discharged into the care of his wife the same evening. He ate *sous vide* venison all weekend and was back at his millright job on Monday morning.

But there were no ticks like poly-ticks. Foster Care, the revolutionary Brave New World new CEO of iHealth continued to frustrate the Good Doctor's carrot shortage and commitment to looking after his patients. While Sababa was attending to the progress of any paralysis, Foster was ensuring the paralysis of any progress. The muscular managementshipwreck's good intentions minus wisdom would lead to enough evil for the health authority to fire Foster and mutate into an even more malevolent twenty-first-century bureaucracy.

And the fate of Dr. Mealachas? After the schism, Mestor retreated into his shell. Instead of soaring with the eagles, he turned turtle and limited what should have otherwise been an expansive internal medicine practice into a small pond slow soft-shelled pursuit of simple concierge cardiology. He never again sought any leadership positions of power.

In his determination to be a survivor, despite his failure to outwit or outplay Sababa, for reasons unrelated to merit, he would outlast him. *But my, look at me now.*

'Only feeble minds are paralysed by facts.'
Arthur C. Clarke

24. The Case of the Spicy Schoolgirl

'All these other girls are tempting
But I'm empty when you're gone...
Oh, I think that I found myself a cheerleader
She is always right there when I need her.'
OMI, *Cheerleader*

Winter break crashed into Cliffs of Dover Secondary School like a runaway snow plough, dragging holly wreaths and sleigh bells, reeking of cedar boughs, oozing eggnog, and with all the threatening festive doom of a cold sore under the mistletoe.

Inside every classroom, the last day before vacation was so quiet you could hear the breathing off the walls, so loud you could see the writing on them—in Mr. Reeves's French immersion class, Mr. Van Vliet's math class, Mr. Heyerdahl's defensive driving class, Ms. Banks's guidance counselling room, and Ms. Gardners's social work office. You might have detected the same portents in Ms. Gibson's nursing station if she hadn't been on sick leave.

The Cliffs of Dover students considered themselves in the simplest and most convenient of definitions—jock leaders, queen bees and wannabes, and mean girls and cheerleaders at the top of the pyramid; the artists and thespians, skaters and drifters, hipsters and trendies, emos and loners, greasers and rockers, gamers and stoners, and class clowns and preps in the middle; and the nerds and geeks, and basket case burnouts and targets and victims—girls who ate their feelings and girls who ate nothing—at the bottom.

They inhaled the sweet smells of high school—the sweat, the whiteboard marker, and the fear. Clocks bigger than their faces loomed on the walls, all two minutes fast. Pencils broke in their fists. The hallways were a purgatory piranha-packed cesspool river of hormones and emotions. No one knew where they were going. And everyone was looking for a life raft.

Cliffs of Dover was a four-year asylum where Harbour City put its aggressive, naïve teenagers because it didn't know what else to do with them. Four years of lockup in a violent and territorial drama zone, structured to torment and scar its inhabitants for life—the place where they wrote thousands of definitions every year, but couldn't define their self-worth, where they solved millions of equations, but couldn't add up their life's value. Instead, they memorized everything a person said about them, added up the looks they got in the hallways rushing to class and read the syllabus to everyone's expectations for them—four years, two suicides, one death, one rape, two pregnancies (one abortion), three

219

overdoses, countless drunken antics, gym class depantsing, spilled food, theft, fights, broken limbs, and turf wars. Four years of boredom punctuated by humiliation. Four years of Lord of the Flies programming to be an asshole to their parents, who would wake in terror one morning to discover that their only child's homeroom class was running the country.

Education was every day and everywhere, and the only thing they had to pay was attention.

Everything they did here would count. It was the mouse race to prepare them for the rat race. The reward for digging themselves out from under truckloads of homework was the senior prom. It was like the Olympics. They waited four years, three people had a good time, and everybody else got to live on with shattered dreams. Four years and then they could join the circus. Even after graduation, high school would never end.

If you enjoyed the incarceration, you were a psychopath or a cheerleader. Or both. Cheerleaders were everything right and wrong with the world—glitter tits pepileptics, flight attendant cheersluts, lollipop chainsaw cheerihoes, angel buns cunning stunts, the girls who talked to each other with other pairs of lips than the ones plastered on their faces, the girls with hair higher than they could reach. Yelling, kicking, and screaming to get what they wanted, changing the score in surging aerobatics above the piercing brass fanfares and ground-shaking brutal booms and rattles of the drums. In any other sport, if you missed the catch, all you lost was the ball. They weren't girls. They were vultures.

Starlight Trail was the blonde-haired, blue-eyed, gum-chewing Valley girl captain of the Cliffs of Dover cheerleader squad. Hers was a stunt world of aerials and awesomes, bananas and basket tosses and buckets, candlesticks and cradle catches, deadmen and dismounts, handsprings and herkies, K and L and T and V motions, tick-tocks and tabletops, and pom-poms and scorpions.

Her adolescent emotions were violent, but not durable. Like the other girls in her squad, Starlight believed that, if there was any justice in the world, she wouldn't have to go to school during her period. The world should allow her to stay home for five days and eat chocolate and cry.

Starlight had a hate-on for Blake Lively, the skank-ho slut who tried to steal her jock boyfriend, Jules, while she was away for a weekend. And Starlight would have her vengeance.

Jules Bengué was the Captain Nosebleed of the Cliffs of Dover football and ice hockey teams. He had received a sports scholarship that would later amount to nothing, not even good health. It was only right and natural that Starlight Trail was his girlfriend. He remembered the day when he first saw her cheerleading in her blue and white face paint. He would swear that, when she bent over on the field, he saw her ovaries through her spankies. As for Blake Lively, he pinned her like a butterfly through a corkboard, but the pin went through, and away she flew. When he told Starlight about it, she promised Blake would go down like a cheerleader after the prom.

Blake Lively knew that Jules had a girlfriend when she agreed to meet him in Neck Point Park. But she was lonely, and Jules made her think he cared for her. She found out too late that becoming famous at Cliffs of Dover high school was like being employee of the month at Harbour City regional landfill. That was the reward for being a girl in high school. People hear you had sex once and Bam, you're a bimbo. She pulled her lower lip between her teeth and tried to swallow herself.

Blake's undoing wasn't anything that fifteen hyperactive cheerleaders couldn't make worse. The school district had a bullying prevention program that was part of their curriculum and trained teachers to identify harassment and intimidation, but Facebook and WhatsApp hadn't heard about it. And that was where the deep twin demons of rage and revenge lived.

Pink shirt day was still five months away when they ambushed Blake Lively in the school parking lot. Most stood around and watched Starlight and her closest friends drag their victim to the ground and take turns punching and kicking her senseless. Some onlookers acted as cheerleaders. One of the cheerleaders posted the video to YouTube. The RCMP considered assault charges but deferred to Dianne Gardner, the resident social work expert on youth violence. *It will take the entire community to combat the problem... I think the adults involved need to sit down together, and sort this out with the youth and come up with the best solution under the circumstances.*

'It's the good girls who keep diaries; the bad girls never have the time.'
Tallulah Bankhead

221

'It's catching you, but you don't see
The reaper's you, and the reaper is me.'
Ozzy Osbourne, *Suicide Solution*

She used a sequence of flashcards on a nine-minute YouTube video.

"Hello... my name is Blake Lively... I've decided to tell you about my never ending story... in 9th grade I would go with friends on webcam... meet and talk to new people... I got called stunning, beautiful perfect, etc... they wanted me to flash... *I learned the truth at seventeen That love was meant for beauty queens And high school girls with clear skinned smiles Who married young and then retired...*

so I did. one month later... I got a msg on Facebook... from him, dont know how he knew me... it said if you dont put on a show for me I will send ur boobs... he knew my adress, school, relatives, friends, family names... knock at my door at 4 am... it was the police. my photo was sent to everyone... *The valentines I never knew The Friday night charades of youth Were spent on one more beautiful... At seventeen I learned the truth...*

then I got really sick and got... anxiety, major depression and panic attacks... I got into drugs and alcohol... my anxiety got worse. couldnt go out... the guy came back with my new... list of friends. but made Facebook page... my boobs were his profile pic... *And those of us with ravaged faces Lacking in the social graces Desperately remained at home...*

cried every night, lost all my friends and respect... people had for me again... then nobody liked me... name calling, judged... I can never get that photo back... its out there forever... *Inventing lovers on the phone Who called to say 'come dance with me' And murmured vague obscenities It isn't all it seems at seventeen...*

I started cutting... I cut my arms. I didnt wear short-sleeved shirts... I promised myself never again... didnt have any friends and I ate lunch in the library everyday... *A brown eyed girl in hand me downs Whose name I never could pronounce Said: 'Pity please the ones who serve They only get what they deserve'...*

after a month later I started talking to an old guy friend, Jules... we back and forth texted and he started to say he... liked me. led me on. he had a cheerleader girlfriend, Starlight... then he said come over. my gf's on vacation... so I did. huge mistake... Jules hooked up with me... I thought he liked me... *The rich relationed hometown queen Marries into what she needs With a guarantee of company And haven for the elderly...*

1 week later I get a text get out of your school... his girlfriend Starlight and 15 others came including hiself... the girl and 2 others just said look

around nobody likes you... in front of my school (50 people)... *So remember those who win the game Lose the love they sought to gain...*

a guy then yelled just punch her already... so she did, Starlight threw me to the ground and punched me several times... kids filmed it, I was all alone and left on the ground... I felt like a joke in this world, I thought nobody deserves this... I was alone. I lied and said it was my fault and my idea... I didnt want Jules getting hurt, I though he really liked me... but he just wanted the sex... *In debentures of quality and dubious integrity Their small-town eyes will gape at you In dull surprise when payment due Exceeds accounts received at seventeen...*

teacher ran over but I just went and layed in a ditch and my dad found me... I wanted to die so bad. when he brought me home I drank bleach... it killed me inside and I thought I was gonna actully die... ambulence came and brought me to the hospital and flushed me... after I got home all I saw was on Facebook. she deserved it. did you wash the mud out of your hair? I hope she's dead... nobody cared. *To those of us who knew the pain Of valentines that never came And those whose names were never called When choosing sides for basketball...*

I didn't want to press charges because I wanted to move on... people are posting pics of bleach, chlorex and ditches... tagging me. I was doing a lot better too. they said... she should try a different bleach. I hope she dies this time and isn't so stupid... they said I hope she sees this and kills herself... *It was long ago and far away the world was younger than today when dreams were all they gave for free to ugly duckling girls like me...*

why do I get this? I messed up but why follow me... Im constantly crying now... every day I think why am I still here... my anxiety is horrible now. never went out this summer... all from my past. lifes never getting better. cant go to school... meet or be with people. constantly cutting. *We all play the game, and when we dare We cheat ourselves at solitaire Inventing lovers on the phone Repenting other lives unknown...*

Im really depressed... Im on antideppresants now and councelling and a month ago this summer... I overdosed. in hospital for 2 days... Im stuck. whats left of me now. nothing stops... I have nobody, I need someone... my name is Blake Lively... this is my never ending story..." *That call and say: 'Come on, dance with me' And murmur vague obscenities At ugly girls like me, at seventeen...*

Except it wasn't a never-ending story, was it. Blake went missing at the start of winter break. While the rest of her classmates were skiing at Whistler or Mount Washington, suntanning on the beaches in Hawaii,

223

and sitting down to Christmas dinners and singsongs, Blake wasn't. The RCMP were doing the best they could to find her with a holiday skeleton crew. Her parents were frantic and Blake was nowhere to be found.

It was the school janitor's job to reopen Cliffs of Dover after winter break. On January 6, João Cravahlo began his chores in the school auditorium because that's where the teachers and students would assemble first. He opened the two big doors with three of the keys on his custodian chain and set his portable radio on the bottom row of the wooden basketball bleachers.

Good Morning Harbour City... This is CNDN Coast Salish radio, 101.3 FM on your Home and Native Band. I'm your host, BC Bud...

He started with restocking the bathrooms next to the main chorus dressing rooms.

Remember that your children are not your own but are lent to you by the Creator...

João threw open the electrical breakers of the lighting panel to the left of the stage and adjusted the illumination array for the assembly.

In age, talk... in childhood, tears...

The air was different up here, but he couldn't quite place the smell.

If we wonder often, the gift of knowledge will come...

It was only when he activated the fly system to open the front stage curtains that he saw where it came from.

Don't be afraid to cry... It will free your mind of sorrowful thoughts...

The same websites that couldn't remove the photo of Blake Lively's naked breasts took down her video because its content violated their 'Terms of Service.' A life without regrets would be no life at all. Her Facebook page dissolved into her yearbook page and faded into a remote memory on a bookshelf filled with dust.

> 'That suicide is painless
> It brings on many changes
> And I can take or leave it if I please.'
> Johnny Mandel and Mike Altman, *Suicide Is Painless*

'They roll by just like water
And I guess we never learn
Go through life parched and empty
Standing knee deep in a river dying of thirst.'
Joe Cocker, *Standing Knee Deep in a River*

It was Dr. Harding's last month of his Doctor Sababa elective, and he determined to suck out all the marrow from it. Alex triggered the portly professor's pager to notify him of the first emergency room referral of the day.

"What you got?"

"Wicked frikkin pissah."

"I'll be down." Sababa walked the Yellow Brick Road backwards from the Death Star. He bounced into the unique slow rhythm of early morning startup. Overnight beds were as full as the eyes of the bed managers were vacant. The action started midmorning when the first accidents arrived. It would spill dirty street blood onto the clean ER floor from the nocturnal duality of trauma and alcohol—humanity in the rough in a country of aching hearts. It surprised Sababa to find his resident standing at the consultant's desk with Trace Pangloss and the psychiatrist, Robert La Capuche.

"Not enough crazies in the basement, Robert?" It was still a greeting.

"Dr. Pangloss here thought he needed my services." La Capuche said. "He was wrong."

"Why is that?" Sababa asked. The shrink handed him a lab result.

"The patient's serum sodium is 116 mEq/L." He said. "Call me if you still need me when it's normal, Trace."

"The guy drinks a dozen litres of ice-cold free water every day." Trace said. "And he's a violent, crazed lunatic. How do you know it's not psychogenic polydipsia?"

"That, my dear boy, is a diagnosis of exclusion." Robert countered. "His chemistry looks more like a syndrome of inappropriate ADH secretion."

"He's not entirely wrong, Trace." Sababa said. "Not all primary polydipsia is psychogenic. Just because your patient is thirsty doesn't make him nuts."

"What else could it be?" Trace asked.

"Alex, why don't you enlighten us with a story?"

"Sure." Alex said. "Thor Heyerdahl is a 32-year-old driving school instructor who admits to drinking far too much water over the last three weeks. He saw his family physician who referred him to one of our new guys, Erg Hebberig, for polydipsia, polyuria, and behavioral problems."

"And then what happened?" Sababa asked.

"With no minor difficulty, we got Erg's thumb drive notes." Trace said. "Thor had no history of headache, visual disturbances, or memory deficit. His visual acuity, visual fields, and the rest of his neurological and

225

endocrine screen were normal. Same story here today. Hebberig admitted him here last week for a water deprivation test but he thought the results were unremarkable."

"What were they?" Sababa asked.

"At the end of six hours, before they even had a chance to give him desmopressin, Thor's urine osmolality rose to a normal value of 584 mOsm/kg of H2O." Trace said. "Hebberig shut the test down."

"Not normal enough." Sababa said. "So what's going on?"

"It ain't his kidneys and it ain't his brain." Trace said. "That's why I say he's drinking too much water because he likes to."

"Or he's thirsty." Sababa had logged into the radiology module and was scrolling through the imaging results. "Because of a combination of partial central diabetes insipidus and cerebral salt wasting."

"Where do you get this stuff, Sab?" Trace asked. "What do you mean?"

"Looks like Thor had an MRI of his head two months ago after a driving accident." Sababa said.

"And?"

"There appears to have been an incidentaloma."

"A what?" Trace asked.

"An incidentaloma." Alex said. "It's a tumor we find when we're not looking for one."

"And what is the name of Thor's tumor?" La Capuche asked.

"Lookee here." Sababa pointed to the screen. "There's a well-circumscribed, lobulated, solid suprasellar mass abutting the optic chiasma and tracts which enhances with gadolinium."

"You have a name?" Trace asked.

"Alex?" Sababa asked.

"Could be a lymphoma, meningioma, aneurysm, or an optico-chiasmatic hypothalamic glioma."

"It's a chordoid glioma of his third ventricle." Sababa said. "We should tell him." The four physicians entered the driving instructor's cubicle.

"This is Doctor Sababa, Thor." Trace said. "He's ignorant of a great number of things to avoid the calamity of being ignorant of everything."

"I don't even know what that means." Thor said.

"He knows what's wrong with you."

"What is it?"

"You appear to have a rare low-grade tumor in the roof of your brain's third ventricle." Sababa said. "It's causing your insatiable thirst."

"I have a brain tumor?" Thor asked.

"It's called a chordoid glioma." Sababa said. "It's classified as a grade II neuroepithelial tumor of uncertain histogenesis."

"It doesn't sound friendly." Thor said.

"It's not."

"Is there treatment?"

"There is." Sababa said. "Dr. Harding here will restrict your fluid intake and start an intravenous drip of hypertonic saline until your serum sodium levels return to normal. We're sending you to our neurosurgery specialist in Victoria."

"What's his name?"

"Tecumseh Sun."

"Well, that's a good sign, anyway." The driving instructor cried.

"We'll be back later to tell you more." Sababa put his hand on Thor's shoulder and called out to the ER ward clerk. "Cheri Sundae, please raise Dr. Sun for me at Victoria General.

"On it." Her long nails became a blur.

'Instant amnesia It's already gone
You think you remember Tomorrow you're wrong.'
Ringo Starr, *Instant Amnesia*

"Why are you so upset, Sophia?" Sababa had arrived on the fifth-floor clinical teaching unit after Alex paged him.

"Dut mun-yak in pibe twain-tee-seben." Sophia blurted. "He is mucking my Pinoy accent. Eat snot pear." Sababa turned to Alex.

"I don't think he is, Sab." He said. "He didn't have a Filipino accent when Poldy Bloom admitted him last night."

"What does he sound like normally?"

"Like you." Alex said. "Same Canuck loonie-toonie dipthong-distorted diction, eh?"

"You want to tell me more." Sababa scowled.

"Ken Reeves." Alex said. "55-year-old right-handed French immersion teacher at Cliffs of Dover secondary school. Brought in last night with an acute organic brain syndrome after his son noted his confusion. He denies issues with writing, reading, grammar, or any other systemic symptoms including neurological deficits. His medical history includes hypertension, obstructive sleep apnea, hypertriglyceridemia, and two old strokes—a left frontal infarction six years ago and a left parieto-occipital infarction last year. He has a twenty-pack-year smoking history, ongoing. No illicit drug use."

"There aren't many illicit drugs left." Sababa said. "Exam?"

227

"Normal vital signs and general examination." Alex said. "He sounds like Sophia, but he only met her this morning after his nurse noted his unusual pronunciation. Ken doesn't recognise his accent as foreign. He has never been to the Philippines and doesn't have friends or relatives there. Language showed minor alterations of syllable structure. No change in tone, rate, or pitch, no sound substitutions, perseveration, or echolalia, no difficulty with speech initiation, and there was preservation of syntax. No alexia or agraphia of monosyllabic and multisyllabic words, phrases, or sentences. He could copy a paragraph, and there was no evidence of acalculia. No deficits in executive functioning and no other cortical signs. The rest of his neurological exam, other than for a hyperactive jaw jerk and tendon reflexes, was within normal limits."

"Lab and imaging?"

"Bloodwork, drug screen, ECG and chest x-ray and echo all normal." Alex said. "Initial CT of his head in the ER showed left parietal lobe, precentral gyrus, and middle frontal gyrus encephalomalacia without evidence of anything acute. MRI this morning also showed a new lacunar infarct in his left internal capsule. EEG is pending."

"Let's go see him." Sababa looked at Sophia. "You coming?"

"I hab meeks peelings." She said. "But I will rice a-bub dem. Palo me." The three of them walked down to and into room 527.

"Ken, this is Doctah Sababer." Alex said. "He believes that moderation is the last refuge of the unimaginative. And you've already met Sophia, our head nurse on this floor."

"Yes, as a mutter of puck." He said. "She was mucking my speech bee-pore I penis my brick-pus."

"FAS." Sababa said.

"FAS?" Sophia asked.

"Foreign accent syndrome." He said. "First described in 1907 by French neurologist Pierre Marie in a patient who presented with an Alsatian accent. Only 60 cases reported in the literature." Sababa's low whistle may have triggered what happened next.

Ken's head did a slow rotation to the right. Severe shaking marched up his right arm and generalised into a tonic-clonic seizure which lasted 30 seconds. Alex and Sababa protected his airway until he recovered.

"Hey, where am I?" Ken asked. "And who are you guys?"

"No one has ever seen that before." Sababa said. "We'll need to write this one up, Alex."

"I um berry huppy." Sophia said. "He has lost his Filipino accent."

"You're the one with the Filipino accent, sweetheart." Ken said.

"Careful, Ken." Sababa said. "Sophia can hurt you."

"He is my payborit ductor." She said.

"Who's next?" Sababa and Alex left Sophia with her patient.

"Two doors down." The young resident said when they were in the hallway. "Don Van Vliet is a 51-year-old math teacher at Cliffs of Dover

228

high school admitted last night by Tictac Tarmac for transient global amnesia."

"Unusual." Sababa said.

"We do unusual." Alex saw Sababa smile. "He had a sauna before going to bed last night and awoke after midnight with left-sided numbness. His wife brought him into the ER. No other previous medical history. Dr. Tarmac found antegrade memory loss for events even two minutes earlier. Cognitive function was otherwise normal. The rest of his general and neuro exams were unremarkable."

"And you?"

"The same." Alex said. "Lab and brain CT early this morning were normal. I haven't seen the results of the MRI they did before I got here."

"Let's go see him." Sababa said. "Say nothing."

"Why?"

"You'll see." The two doctors entered the math teacher's room.

"Good morning, Don." Sababa said. "How are you doing?"

"Fine." He said. "Not sure why I'm here. Aren't you going to introduce yourselves?"

"I'm Doctor Sababa from Internal Medicine." The professor put his arm around Alex's shoulder. "And you've already met Dr. Harding."

"And you've already met Dr. Harding." Don repeated, as Sababa had said it. He looked out his window. "Never seen him before in my life."

"But..." Alex protested.

"Must be a mistake." Sababa said. "Listen, Don, Dr. Harding and I are going to look at the results of your MRI scan."

"Must be a mistake." He perseverated. "I haven't had an MRI scan."

"Of course." Sababa said. "We'll be right back." He and Alex returned to the nursing station down the hallway and brought up the MRI images."

"I thought you said you saw him this morning." Said the stocky savant. "But..."

"Just having some fun." Sababa pulled up the math teacher's MRI. "Tell me, Grasshopper."

"Hmmm." Alex said. "Symmetrical, punctate lesions in the cornu ammonis 1 fields of both hippocampi."

"That's where his global amnesia lives." Sababa said. "Anything else?"

"Not that I can see."

"It's subtle." Sababa said. "But there are these four periventricular and another three juxtacortical white matter lesions here."

"Meaning what?" Alex asked.

"What's the mechanism of transient global amnesia, Bahney?"

"Now that's a real rat's nest." Alex said. "Some say it's ischemic, some migrainous, some neuropsychological, and some epileptic. Take your pick. If it lasts less than one hour, it might be transient epileptic amnesia; if longer than 24 hours, it can't be transient global amnesia by definition.

There's even a neurologist in Chicago named Steven Lewis who claims that it's caused by venous congestion due to retrograde cerebral blood flow because it occurs more often with sexual activity, stress and Valsalva maneuver."

"That's bullshit."

"Why?"

"We've never seen it in astronauts."

"OK." Alex said. "You do think outside the box, don't you?"

"Banksy was right." Sababa said. "Think outside the box, collapse the box, and take a fucking sharp knife to it. Let's go see our math teacher."

"Good morning, Don." Sababa said as they reentered his room. "How are you doing?"

"Fine." He said. "Not sure why I'm here. Aren't you going to introduce yourselves?"

"I'm Doctor Sababa from Internal Medicine." The professor put his arm around Alex's shoulder. "And you've already met Dr. Harding."

"And you've already met Dr. Harding." Don said. "Never seen him before in my life."

"Of course. Those who cannot remember the past are condemned to repeat it." Sababa removed a penlight from his breast pocket. "Mind if I have a look?"

"Not at all, Doc." Don said. "What are you looking for?"

"Follow the light." Sababa swung the flashlight from one eye to the other repeatedly. "Positive swinging flashlight test." Alex said. "He has a Marcus Gunn pupil on the left."

"Meaning what?"

"His left pupil dilates when it should constrict to the light." Alex said. "Meaning that his left optic nerve isn't working."

"Full marks." Sababa pulled an ophthalmoscope from his Colombian leather bag and peered into the math teacher's left eye. "His optic disc is shot. Don's relative afferent pupillary defect is from optic neuritis. Game, set, and match."

"What do you mean?" Alex asked.

"He develops transient global amnesia after a hot sauna." Sababa said. "That's called Uhthoff's phenomenon. Add that to the scattered white matter demyelination on his MRI and his optic neuritis and Marcus-Gunn pupil, and you have McDonald criteria for a diagnosis."

"OK." Was the only sign of Alex's revelation.

"Don, we think you have relapsing-remitting multiple sclerosis." Sababa said.

"Multiple sclerosis?" Don asked. "What's that?"

"It's an autoimmune disease that attacks certain central nervous system cells called oligodendrocytes." He said. "They're responsible for creating and maintaining the fatty layer around your nerves called the myelin sheath."

"What do I do?"

"Dr. Harding here will return later to perform a lumbar puncture to get some cerebrospinal fluid." Sababa said. "He'll start you on a course of high-dose methylprednisolone followed by dimethylfumarate. I won't say anything more for the moment because you won't remember it anyway."

"I have a problem with my memory?"

"Memory gives moments immortality, but forgetfulness promotes a healthy mind." Sababa said. "It should be normal by tomorrow morning. We'll talk then."

"Well, thank you Doctor... Doctor..."

"Lector." He said. "Hannibal Lector."

"Thank you, Doctor Lector."

"Pleasure." Sababa said. "See you on the flip side."

"One more, Sab." Alex led Sababa to the last room in the hallway.

"Tyra Banks." He began. "22-year-old Cliffs of Dover guidance counsellor with an eight-day history of decreasing vision in both eyes. Dr. Pangloss admitted her last night for horizontal double vision, complete paralysis and proptosis of her left eye, pain with attempted eye movements, and pulsatile ringing in both ears worse with bending and lying flat. There was a two-year problem with diffuse throbbing headaches, worse in the morning, exacerbated by Valsalva, and associated with nausea and photophobia and relieved by acetaminophen. Only other medical problem was a ten-kilo weight gain over the winter, likely because of physical inactivity."

"Exam?"

"Normal vital signs." Alex said. "Trace found bilateral ptosis and dilated pupils unresponsive to light, diminished visual acuity and colour vision, constriction of peripheral visual fields, and papilledema with a left-sided hemorrhage at 2 o'clock. She had restricted painful lateral gaze on the right and complete extraocular paralysis on the left. The rest of her general and neurological examination was normal."

"Lab?"

"All normal." Alex said. "She had a CT and MRI and MR venogram of her brain last night and they were all unremarkable as well."

"I don't believe that."

"Huh?"

"Let's go see." Sababa and Alex returned to the nursing station to bring up Tyra's neuroimaging.

"Nothing much." Alex said.

"Except for the flattening of her pituitary and posterior globes, increased perineural spaces around her buckled optic nerves, and enlargement of her Meckel's caves." Sababa said. "And what did Trace do next?"

"With papilledema and without a mass-occupying lesion, he did a lumbar puncture."

"Not for long, I bet." Sababa said.

231

"Tyra's opening pressure was 300 millimetres of water." Alex said. "Trace pulled out like she'd asked him to make a baby. He recorded a loss of 20 ml of cerebrospinal fluid, the analysis of which returned normal. She said she felt better after the procedure."

"She should have." Sababa said. "So now what you got, hotshot?"

"Increased intracranial pressure." Alex said. "But she doesn't have any reason for it—no obstructive sleep apnea, lupus, chronic kidney disease, Behçet's syndrome, and no history of high-dose vitamin A derivatives, tetracycline, or hormonal contraceptive use."

"So it's not secondary to anything."

"Doesn't appear to be." Alex said. "Oh, wait. Of course. Tyra has idiopathic intracranial hypertension."

"Perfect modified Dandy score, Alex. Head of the class." Sababa said. "But it's Tyra's head we're worried about. Let's go see her."

Because of her limited vision, they had to announce their arrival. Unlike the previous patient encounter, they only had to do it once.

"Somewhere in the world is a doctor who is worse than all other doctors, Tyra." Alex said. "But he's seeing someone else. This is my preceptor, Doctah Sababer."

"You've had quite a rough patch, Tyra." Sababa said.

"My head felt like it was going to explode." She said. "Do you know what's going on with me?"

"You have a rare condition called idiopathic intracranial hypertension." The professor described the problem in terms she could understand.

"I can still go blind?" She asked.

"Unlikely." Sababa said. "The probability used to be somewhere between 10 and 25 percent. But we have plans."

"What plans?"

"Dr. Harding here is going to start you on a medication called acetazolamide until we can get you down to Victoria to see Tecumseh Sun."

"What can he do?"

"A CSF diversion procedure." He said. "In your case, it may be a lumboperitoneal shunt, a procedure where he inserts a permanent catheter to drain excess spinal fluid into your abdominal cavity."

"Anything to get my vision back and get rid of this headache." She said.

"We're on it." Sababa said. "I'll call down to arrange your transfer."

'So I'm up here in the north woods Just staring at a lake
Wondering just exactly how much They think a man can take
I eat fish to pass the time away 'Neath this blue Canadian moon
This old world has made me crazy Crazy as a loon.'
John Prine, *Crazy as a Loon*

Alex and his mentor climbed the snow-covered back stairs to Sababa's Manzanita eyrie of excellence.

"It's sugar and spice week, Boss." His medical office assistant was typing most of her words onto her iMac.

"Mercy seasons justice." Sababa pulled the first chart from the top of the afternoon clinic pile and handed it to his resident.

"Belle Gibson." Alex called into the assembled multitude. A pale young woman rose from her waiting room chair. A compression wrap wound around her left forearm. She supported its dead weight with her right hand. Sababa watched her follow Alex down the hall to the resident's room.

"Dianne Gardner." It was his turn. A middle-aged woman followed the professor into his sanctum sanctorum.

Sababa studied the referral letter and accompanying documentation from Dr. Rivera. *Dear Sab, 28-year-old social worker with a strange history of spontaneous painful bruising and no obvious causation. Extensive hematology workup normal. She's not. I thought of you... Nick.*

"How can I help, Ms. Gardner?" He began.

"Thank you for seeing me, Doctor Sababa." She said. "I've been having these episodes for the last six months now."

"Episodes?"

"Yes." Dianne said. "They start with a tingling, stinging, bursting sensation on some part of my skin, and then, fifteen minutes later, explode into a pinpoint swelling which turns black and blue. They occur so often now they're driving me crazy. Each one is from 1 to 2 centimetres in diameter and lasts for a month."

"Where do they occur?"

"My forearms and anterior thighs." She said. "Sometimes on my fingers or around my joints."

"But never on skin areas you can't reach."

"True." She hesitated. "Are you suggesting that I'm causing them myself?"

"Not at all." Sababa said. "Not like that, anyway."

"They're very painful when they occur." Dianne said. "Sometimes I get headaches or nosebleeds or nausea. I've seen a hematologist and a rheumatologist who couldn't find anything wrong. And now I'm seeing you. What kind of subspecialist are you, Doctor Sababa?"

"I'm a phenomenologist." Sababa said.

"What kinds of patients do you see?"

233

"The most frustrated kinds." He said. "Did you bring the tubes from the satellite lab?"

Dianne opened her purse and removed two vials, marked 'a' and 'b.' Sababa handed her a gown and asked her to change in the examining room next door. When she was ready, he drew up the contents of each sterile tube in a 1 cc syringe and attached two 26-gauge needles.

"Please turn around, Dianne." He said. "I'm going to inject a 0.1 ml sample from each tube into two different areas on your back. One injection is your red blood cells isolated in a citrated saline solution after being rinsed twice with normal saline and titrated to a hematocrit of 75%. The other is just normal saline. You won't know which one is which, but I do."

"What is this called?"

"The Method of Vun." By two minutes after Sababa's procedure, the left injection site had done nothing, but the one opposite had exploded into a 2-centimetre bruise.

"It's the one on the right." She said.

"You can get dressed now." He said. "Come back to my office when you're ready."

Dianne found Sababa scanning back through her medical record.

"Dr. Rivera says that you were an only child, that your parents separated when you were 8 years old, you had recurrent bouts of loneliness, and that you suffered from adjustment-related issues with your mother's fiancé." He said. "Is this true?" Dianne nodded.

"What happened six months ago?"

"I broke up a longstanding relationship." She said. "I've been pretty depressed ever since. My sleep and appetite have been bad. But what has that to do with these episodes?"

"Quite a lot." Sababa said. "Your condition is associated with mental stress."

"Are you saying I'm creating these painful bruises with my mind?"

"I'm not saying anything other than there is an increased incidence of emotional trauma observed in this disorder." Sababa said. "One of its names is psychogenic purpura."

"What are the others?"

"It's also named after the two doctors in Boston who first reported it in 1955, Frank Gardner and Louis Diamond." He said. "Also called autoerythrocyte sensitization syndrome."

"Wow."

"If you prefer, we can just call it painful bruising syndrome." Sababa said.

"Is there anything you can suggest?" Dianne asked. "I'm tired of wearing long sleeves."

"Why don't we try an SSRI antidepressant called escitalopram?" He said. "Think of it as chicken soup for the soul."

234

"Chicken soup?" She asked. "Will it help?"

"It won't hurt." He handed the prescription across his desk. "Tell Mercy to rebook you in three weeks and we'll see how you're doing." Diane thanked the Good Doctor and left to make her appointment when Mercy buzzed him on the intercom.

"Dr. Zaias on line one for you, Boss." Sababa picked up line one.

"How are you, Peter?" He asked. "What can I do for you?"

"I've just seen one of your patients for a second opinion." Zaias said.

"And?"

"I noticed you wrote no notes in her chart."

"And?"

"I also noticed that you must have spent all your time with her drawing a magnificent picture of a Pacific Loon." Sababa remembered the patient encounter well.

"And?"

"I've drawn a baby chick on the loon's back."

"And?"

"I've sent her GP a copy of the revision."

"That's it?"

"Have a nice day." Fading laughter disappeared down the line. *Click.*

He looked up to find Alex in the doorway.

"Something good?" He asked.

"Oh yeah."

"Come in and tell me about it." Alex took a seat across from the professor.

"Belle Gibson, patient of Dr. Bloom." He began. "29-year-old community nurse with a seven-month history of extreme left arm pain after being hit by a falling oxygen tank at work. She describes the pain as burning or stabbing or grinding or throbbing, all out of proportion to the severity of her initial injury. Moving or touching the limb is intolerable. She has localized sweating and swelling, and changes in skin temperature, colouring from white to violet, and texture, which has become waxy, shiny, thin, and tight. The nails on her left hand are brittle and grow slowly. Her arm muscles have atrophied. Exam is corroborative."

"Does she have normal passive joint mobility?"

"She does." Alex said. "She's on sick leave and is applying for permanent disability for her diagnosis."

"Which is?"

"Stage 2 type I complex regional pain syndrome." Alex said. "We used to call it Sudeck's atrophy or algoneurodystrophy or reflex sympathetic dystrophy."

"I know what we used to call it." Sababa said. "What evidence is there for the diagnosis?"

"What do you mean?"

"The International Association for the Study of Pain has established diagnostic criteria for complex regional pain syndrome I." Sababa said. "Does she fulfil the criteria?"

"What are they?" Alex asked.

"One, the presence of an initiating noxious event."

"Check."

"Two, continuing pain disproportionate to the inciting event."

"Check."

"Three, evidence of edema, changes in skin blood flow, or abnormal sweating in the same area as her pain."

"Check."

"Four, the exclusion of any condition that would otherwise account for her pain and dysfunction."

"Like what?" Alex asked.

"That, Scooter, is the million-dollar lifetime disability question."

"Look, Sab, she has plain x-rays and an MRI and a bone densitometry study that show marked osteoporosis of the bones in her left arm compared to the opposite side. She's had bone scans with abnormal results."

"How were they abnormal?"

"What?"

"The bone scan results." Sababa said. "How were they abnormal?"

"Does it matter?"

"You're rootin' tutin Tom Pohutin damn right it matters." Sababa said.

"How?"

"Has either her bone or vascular scintigraphy ever shown an increase in tracer uptake or regional blood flow and blood volume?" Sababa asked. "Ever."

"Uh, no." Alex said. "She's had three nuclear scans, and they've all shown decreased radionuclide uptake and blood flow and volume."

"Check." Sababa said. "And mate."

"I don't get it."

"She doesn't have reflex sympathetic dystrophy." Sababa said. "She fails the fourth criterion."

"But what else could it be?" Alex asked. "She's already had the full meal deal of therapies from calcitonin to vasodilators to biphosphonates to transcutaneous electrical nerve stimulation and sympathetic blocks from our anesthesia colleagues."

"She's seeking a disability pension." Sababa said. "That's the reason for the referral from Poldy Bloom."

"But that's not what she's asking for today."

"What do you mean?"

"She wants it amputated."

"What?"

"She wants her left arm amputated." Alex said. "She says there are surgeons out there that would operate on her."

"Oh, for fuck's sake." Sababa said. "Let's go see her." The stocky savant put his finger to his lips as he and Alex moved down the hallway. They paused in silence outside the resident's room. Sababa opened the door wide to find Belle Gibson rewrapping her tensor bandage around her left arm. Everyone could see it was far too tight.

"Looks like a chronic case of pretendonitis, Alex."

"What's that?" She asked.

"You don't have complex regional pain syndrome, Belle." He said. "You have pseudodystrophy, also called disuse-related dystrophy."

"But I've seen neurologists and rheumatologists and physiatrists and pain management specialists." She protested. "How can they all be wrong?"

"This is the way." He said. "You have normal passive joint mobility, your nuclear medicine studies have never shown increased technetium-99m uptake or pseudo-inflammatory signs, and you have one more accoutrement."

"What's that?"

"You're a nurse."

"So?"

"You'd make the perfect conversion disorder patient."

"Are you implying I did this to myself?" Belle asked.

"Not at all." Sababa said. "I'm telling you. And that's good news."

"How so?" She asked.

"Howard Hughes became a recluse and refused to cut his nails because of complex regional pain syndrome, Belle. We still can't do very much about that." He said. "But we can fix this."

It is such a secret place, the land of tears. And we shed more over answered prayers than ones in limbo.

"My Christmas present is waiting for you to unwrap it." Sababa said. "Tell Mercy I'll see you next week. We'll spend some time."

'It's a poor sort of memory that only works backwards.'
Lewis Caroll, *Through the Looking-Glass*

It was normal for several of Sababa's on-call referrals to roll in while he was still in his afternoon clinic.

"Dr. Carlton on line 2, Boss." Mercy was preparing his pile of charts for the following day. Sababa hit the button.

"What you got, Cliffy?"

"You remember Bull Sullivan, the septic truck driver who had a seizure on the Malahat and killed the local native chief's son?" Cliffy asked.

"Uh-huh."

"We have his brother in the ER tonight."

"What with?"

"Hence, the phone call." Cliffy said. "Your bad luck that you're the best, pal."

"Alex and I will be there in half an hour."

A fresh winter storm bent the clock. The snow was blowing broadside by the time they made it back to the Harbour City Regional ER. Cliffy greeted them warmly.

"Where's the bow tie, Krusty?"

"Alex has found the wisdom of the open collar." Sababa said. "He now realizes that his fashion accessory had reduced the blood flow to his brain by 7.5%, raised his intraocular eye pressure, increasing the risk of glaucoma and cataracts, and was a breeding ground for hospital pathogens. He now understands that his bow tie enhanced his body's *Tama* component, resulting in increased extroversion, an inability to imbibe environmental *sattvik* vibrations and positive thoughts, and a drift away from spiritual practice. He now comprehends that his tie exerted unwanted pressure on the fifth centre *Vishuddha-chakra* in the spiritual energy system in the neck, causing an obstacle to respiration and swallowing that *māntrik* sorcerers found so easy to establish their *subtle-yantra* of distressing negative energy at his throat.

Alex now sees how it trapped him in the Māyā Great Illusion, increasing his ego awareness, self-importance, and competitive spirit in front of others. Therefore, it is for these reasons he has abandoned the bow tie."

"That true?"

"Something like that" Alex said.

"Took you long enough, Masshole."

"And what little treasure have you been saving for us?" Sababa asked.

"John Sullivan." Cliffy said. "64-year-old co-owner of Sullivan's Takeaways septic service. Bull's brother. His family brought him in tonight."

"Would you be so kind as to tell us why?"

"He was fine when his wife and kids left him alone for two weeks to visit relatives." Cliffy said. "History of hypertension, coronary artery disease, and COPD, all controlled. He no longer drinks or smokes. When his family returned home today, they found him mute and reluctant to interact. He spent all his time performing repetitive acts like making the bed or folding tea towels. And here we are."

"Exam?"

"He was awake, alert, and oriented but answered all my questions with single words. He kept folding the hospital linen throughout the examination. Other than for his cognition, his general physical and neurological status were normal."

"Lab?"

"Normal hemogram and chemistry." He said. "Chest x-ray unremarkable."

"Other imaging?"

"I hate it when people say, 'It's always the last place you look.'" Cliffy said. "Of course it is, why the hell would you keep looking after you've found it?"

"And what did you find?" Alex asked.

"See for yourself." Cliffy brought up John's neuroimaging results on the consultant's desk monitor. "CT scan of his head shows multiple bilateral hypodense areas in his frontal lobes." He moved the cursor around the screen as he had done a thousand times before. "MRI shows them involving parts of his corpus callosum. Borders of the lesions are ill-defined and with a peripheral restricted diffusion pattern. No mass effect and no contrast enhancement. MRI scan of his spine is normal."

"So what you got?" Sababa asked.

"Rapidly progressive multifocal frontal lobe-related behavioral change." Alex said. "Pretty broad differential here, Sab." Alex said. "Neoplasms, demyelinating diseases, infections, and more."

"I did a lumbar puncture after reviewing the scans." Cliffy said. "Everything was normal except for an elevated white blood cell count with 74% lymphocytes."

"Immunocompetent?" Sababa asked.

"No obvious cause of immune deficiency." Cliffy said. "Why?"

"We saw most of it in HIV patients. Now it surfaces more in patients receiving immunomodulatory agents." Sababa said. "It doesn't matter. There are nine case reports in the literature of patients with intact immunological responses."

"Against what?"

"Against what's eating John Sullivan's brain." Sababa said.

"Jesus Christ, Sab." Cliffy said. "And what would that be?"

"Let's go see your patient." He said.

They found Mr. Cunningham's wife sitting beside her husband's bedside, behind the last curtain.

"Good evening, John." Sababa said.

"Hello."

"How are you?"

"Fine."

"That's all you'll get." His wife said. "He's been tapping the world on the shoulder for 20 years and when it turned around, he forgot what he had to say."

"Memory is identity." Sababa said.

"And what is yours?" She asked.

"I'm sorry, Mrs. Cunningham, this is Doctor Sababa." Cliffy said. "Memory is what he has instead of a view. And this is his student, Alex Harding. He's just lost his ties to reality." Both the professor and his protégé wrinkled their noses at him.

"Does anybody here know what's wrong with my husband?"

"I believe John has a rare demyelinating disease like multiple sclerosis." Sababa said. "But it moves much faster."

"You believe?"

"He'll need a stereotactic brain biopsy in Victoria to be sure." His wife seemed shocked.

"Will it make any difference?"

"It might." Sababa said. "There are treatable causes of disorders that can present like this."

"You have a name?"

"Progressive multifocal leukoencephalopathy." Sababa said. "PML."

"What causes it?" She asked. "He was fine when we left him two weeks ago."

"It's a reactivation of previous infection with human polyomavirus 2." Sababa said. "More commonly referred to as the JC virus or John Cunningham virus."

"Who was John Cunningham?"

"He was the index case, a military veteran who died at the VA Hospital in Wood, Wisconsin, in the summer of 1970." Sababa said. "His postmortem brain biopsy found the virus."

"And why don't we know anything about John's initial infection with this thing?"

"It's asymptomatic." Sababa said. "More than half the general population has had it, in its original form."

"If he has this PML, is there any treatment?"

"We've had some limited success with an antimalarial drug called mefloquine." Mrs. Cunningham nodded her head.

"I'll put him on the transfer list." Sababa said.

Far outside the final curtain, Alex shook his head.

"I'm a bit upset, Sab." He said. "You weren't honest with Mrs. Cunningham."

"I assume those are two separate points."

"You gave her far too much false hope by mentioning mefloquine therapy." Alex said. "You know that no large, prospective, double-blinded trials have validated the results of any isolated case reports."

"First, find me enough patients with PML to conduct a randomized trial with significant enough power to substantiate an outcome difference." Sababa said. "And second, and more importantly, never, ever, take away the last thread of hope."

"OK."

"It's dark and cold out there, Alex, and no one can hear them screaming inside." Sababa said. "This is a lesson you know well."

"I know." Alex said.

"This is your last night on call here, isn't it?"

"I'm booked to fly back to Boston on a red-eye tomorrow night." Sababa handed him his pager.

"Enjoy." He said.

> 'Can I refill your eggnog for you? Get you something to eat?
> Drive you out to the middle of nowhere and leave you for dead?'
> Clark Griswold, *National Lampoon's Christmas Vacation*

Alex Harding's last day at Harbour City Regional Hospital would be as memorable as his first. They don't make memories like that anymore. There would be many stories to tell back in Boston.

Two of them prompted the last early morning phone call to his portly preceptor.

"Domaine Renegade."

"Sorry to bother you so early, Sab, but there are two patients here in the ER for us."

"Are they dying?"

"I don't think so."

"Call me when they're dying." Sababa said. "What are they?"

"One is the captain of the Cliffs of Dover football team." Alex said. "And the other is his head cheerleader girlfriend."

"Why didn't you say so in the first place?" Sababa asked. "I'll be right in."

"Really?"

"Hell no." But Sababa didn't go back to sleep. His curiosity always got the better of him. Twenty minutes later, a dimpled and dented white blur came to a stop beside an on-call bay snowbank and the professor, Colombian leather bag in hand, bounced through the automatic sliding frosted glass doors of the Harbour City Regional ER.

Alex and Trace Pangloss were waiting at the consultant's desk.

"Being smart spoils a lot of things, doesn't it, Sab." Trace said.

"Like sleep." Sababa said. "What you got?"

241

"Starlight Trail." Alex began. "17-year-old brought in three hours ago with full-blown sparkling visual hallucinations whenever she closes her eyes."

"What did she take?"

"She won't tell us." Trace said. "But whatever it was, she's as high as a kite, panicky, combative, and delirious, almost psychotic. Complains of headache, blurred vision, dry mouth, facial flushing, palpitations, nausea and vomiting, epigastric pain, unsteadiness, numbness, and impending doom. Says she feels like she's being keelhauled by a transcontinental freight train."

"Exam?"

"She's agitated but alert, flushed but apyrexial, fast heart rate at 102/minute with a blood pressure of 105/68, respiratory rate of 20/minute and saturation of 96% on room air." Alex said. "Chandelier syndrome. She hit the ceiling off my stethoscope. Cardiopulmonary exam is otherwise unremarkable. Abdomen is soft and non-tender. No neck stiffness. Eyes are bloodshot and her pupils are bizarre—dilated one minute and constricted the next. The rest of her cranial nerves are normal. Peripheral neuro system exam shows fine tremor and brisk deep tendon reflexes."

"Drug screen?"

"Negative." Trace said. "Nada. No amphetamines, meth, barbs, benzos, cocaine, opioids, phencyclidine, cannabinoids, tricyclics, or alcohol."

"Other results?"

"Rest of her bloodwork was normal." Alex said. "ECG shows only sinus tachycardia."

"We've given her activated charcoal, but she puked it right back up." Trace said. "What do you think, Sab?"

"I think that sometimes you have to go to the party." Sababa said. "Where is she?"

"She's in the acute room." Trace said. "It may be a war party. Her parents are with her and they are pissed."

"At us?"

"At everyone and everything." Trace said. "Just so you know."

"No time like the pleasant." Sababa said. Trace was right about the ambiance.

"Well, it looks like we now have three wise men." The father sat grinding his teeth. Sababa studied the babe in the manger. She was very blonde, very stoned, and had a black ring of charcoal around her lips.

"This is Doctor Sababa." Trace said. "You can tell from the violent nature of his multiple stab wounds he's a consultant." There was no change in facial expression.

"And this is George and Fairlight Trail from Extension." Trace said.

"So what's going on?" Fairlight demanded.

"Hang on." Sababa said. "I just got here."

"And about time." George said.

"How do you feel, Starlight?" Sababa asked.

"Like a Jack in the Box." She said. "Wanting to get out. I don't feel good."

"What did you take last night?" Starlight went back into her trance.

"OK. Let's see." Sababa said. "Or smell. I'm getting a whiff of eggnog with notes of black licorice and sassafras."

"So what?" George asked.

"Whatever Starlight ingested consisted of multiple compounds in the same proportions working together to create this syndrome." Sababa said. "I'm looking for a substance that can cause all her symptoms of agitation, tachycardia, vomiting, and hallucinations. I need an organic or synthetic mix of molecules with serotoninergic and GABAnergic, anticholinergic, sympathomimetic, and ring-substituted amphetamine-related mescaline-analog psychedelic properties."

"I don't know what you're talking about." George said.

"Let me work this backwards for you." Sababa said. "Assume for a moment that Starlight's anxiety is from stimulation of serotonin and GABA receptors by a triglyceride called trimyristin. Serotonin agonists like linalool, isoeugenol, and eugenol can also cause the cardiovascular effects we observe. The bizarre nature of her hallucinations suggests a role for three phenylisopropylamine compounds, partially transaminated in her liver, converted into their unique psychedelic amphetamine counterparts. Her empathy and sparkling visual changes come from hepatic conversion of safrole to MDA. The impaired muscle coordination and activity is from elemicin which, when converted to TMA causes nausea and part of her delirium. But the third molecule bakes the cake. It's an analogue of methysticin, one of the two compounds in kava that inhibit voltage-gated sodium channels to cause the anesthetic effect, increased awareness, a sense of novelty, and synesthesia."

"Get to the punchline, Doc." George was as agitated as his daughter.

"So the key player here, the one ring to unite them all, is a weak monoamine oxidase inhibitor also responsible for some of this culprit material's sympathomimetic effects. The euphoria and impressive visual effects that are only achieved by closing her eyes come from its conversion to MMDA, another sympathomimetic with hallucinogenic properties."

"And?" It was Fairlight's turn.

"And MMDA is an analogue of MDMA, otherwise known as ecstasy." Sababa said. "And that brings us to myristicin, the primary source of all this mischief."

"We're all still sort of hanging here, Sab." Trace said. "Where would she get this myristicin intoxication from?"

243

"Where?" Sababa asked. "From the Basra Arab trade of what was once the third most valuable commodity in the world after gold and silver, from the same dark-leaved *Myristica fragrans* evergreen seed source on the remote tiny Banda island of Rhun that the Dutch East India Company murdered Nathaniel Courthope for in 1616, from the British trade of Rhun for Manhattan because of it in the 1667 Treaty of Breda, from its later cultivation in the Caribbean and Malaysia and Southern India, from the preferred plague cure of the middle ages, the 'pease porrige' condiment of St. Theodore the Studite's 9th-century monks, the prison high of Malcolm X and sometimes hippie high of the 1960s, from the pungent spice flavoring agent in cakes and confections, puddings and potatoes, meats and sausages, sauces and vegetables, and..."

"And?" It was unanimous.

"Eggnog." Sababa said. "Starlight, you reek of eggnog."

"It wasn't eggnog." She protested.

"Please don't humiliate me by killing yourself before we can save your life." He said. "And I thought this would be one tough nut to crack. How much nutmeg did you take?"

"I put a tablespoon in a milkshake." She said.

"Seven grams. Almost 3 grams of myristicin." Sababa said. "You didn't drink it all."

"No." She said. "I couldn't get all of it down."

"And you didn't take nutmeg to get high, did you Starlight?" She answered his question with a flood of tears. Sababa turned to her nurse, who had been listening to all this, and waiting.

"Regina, can you get Cheri Sundae to add an HCG to her bloodwork, please?"

"I'll do it." Regina punched into the wall phone.

"You must be joking." Trace said. "Really?"

"Really." Sababa said. "How far along are you, Starlight?" Her parents had to grab onto their chairs.

"My last period was six weeks ago." She said. "I bought a home testing kit two days ago."

"I'm not getting this, Sab." Alex said.

"Desperate cheerleaders have used nutmeg as an abortifacient since the end of the 19th century." He said.

"You mean some women take alternative medicines to get pregnant and others take them to abort?"

"Why yes, Alex." Sababa said. "Nice of you to join us. There's just one slight problem."

"What's that?" George and Fairlight asked together.

"It rarely works." The look on their faces was pure relief.

"What happens now, Doctor Sababa?" Fairlight asked.

"The treatment is mainly supportive." He said. "We'll admit Starlight to our telemetry unit, where we can provide intravenous support and monitor her heart rhythm until she metabolizes the rest of what she ingested. She may need some sedation, but she should be home tomorrow morning. And become more than a Trail of tears."

"Thank you, Doctor Sababa." George said. "We'll take that from here." As Alex and his mentor left the acute room, they could hear a tinny hysteria escaping through Starlight's headphones. *Yo I'll tell you what I want, what I really, really want... So tell me what you want, what you really, really want...*

They crossed back to the main wing of the emergency room. Dr. Capitaine was waiting.

"How are you, Myles?" Sababa asked.

"Living the dream."

"Dreaming permits us to be quietly and safely insane every night of our lives." He said. "You have our second case from last night?"

"Uh-huh." Myles said. "Jules Bengué. 18-year-old high school student. Heads up the Cliffs of Dover football and ice hockey teams. They call him Captain Nosebleed."

"Quite the résumé." Sababa said. "Why is he here?"

"His parents brought him in." Myles said. "Found him short of breath and vomiting with lightheadedness and ringing in his ears. We found him with a fast pulse and respiratory rate, clear lungs, and otherwise normal exam. But it was his lab results that got our attention."

"What about them?" Alex asked.

"Turns out his fast respiratory rate was Kussmaul's breathing." Myles said. "He was trying to blow off the excess acid in his bloodstream. Serum bicarb was 15 and his anion gap was 21."

"Hmmm." Alex mused. "Anion gap metabolic acidosis and ringing in his ears. Did you do an aspirin level?"

"Our thoughts exactly." Myles said. "Salicylate poisoning. His first level came back at 4.924 mmol/L. Two hours later it was still 4.5619 mmol/L. We started a bicarb and potassium drip and went back to question him about it."

"And?" Sababa asked.

"He denied it." Myles said. "Swore up and down on a stack of bibles that he didn't take an ASA overdose. His parents supported him. Said they didn't keep any aspirin in the house. They've gone to work but said they'd be back later."

"Where is he?"

"Bed 5." Myles said. "I'll introduce you but be forewarned. The only thing bigger than his ego is his attitude."

"A multitude of aptitude and rectitude which will decide his altitude in plenitude." Sababa said.

Behind Captain Nosebleed's curtain, his nurse was hanging another IV bag.

"What are his vitals now, Dina?" Sababa asked.

"He's afebrile." She said. "You can see his heart rate and blood pressure on the monitor. And so you know, I haven't charted a true respiratory rate since nursing school."

"It's less than when he came in." Myles said. "Jules, this is Doctor Sababa. He's a walking mass spectrometer. And this is his resident, Dr. Harding."

"OK, Boomer."

"I've told them about how you claim to not having taken any aspirin." Myles said. "Despite your high blood levels."

"Bet." Jules said.

"Hello, hello, hello, how low..." Sababa sang. "With the lights out, it's less dangerous..."

"What are you singing, Sab?" Myles asked.

"Yeah, Bruh." Jules said. "Something about that song makes me uncomfy."

"Smells like teen spirit." Sababa said. "Closer to his toes than his head. Now what could be closer to his bottom than his top that would need a whole tube of Nirvana pain relief?"

"Can't even." He said. "Why are you pressed, Bruh?"

"I don't believe you were trying to commit suicide, Jules." Sababa said. "But I do think you were trying to see God."

"Extra." Jules said. "You need to chill."

"That smell, gentlemen, is oil of wintergreen, an extract from *Gaultheria procumbens*." Sababa said. "And Captain Nosebleed here has been rubbing it hard and fast where the sun don't shine."

"What do you mean?" Jules protested.

"The active ingredient in oil of wintergreen is methylsalicylate." Sababa said. "Which gets hydrolised to salicylic acid in the gut. A 60 ml tube of over-the-counter rubefacient contains oil of wintergreen equal to 37 grams of aspirin, or about 114 adult aspirin tablets. Which one did you use, Jules?"

"IcyHot pain-relieving cream." He said. "But I didn't swallow it."

"No one says you did." Sababa said. "But did you know that scrotal skin can have up to 40-fold greater absorption compared to other dermal regions? You're lucky you didn't get a chemical burn down there."

"How do you know all this stuff?" Jules asked.

"It is my business to know what other people don't know." Sababa said. "And now you know as well. You've discovered IcyHot and you've found your willie, so today's the day you get to learn about anion gap metabolic acidosis. Same condition that afflicted Charles II of Spain."

"Am I going to die?"

"No, but you may wish you had." Sababa pulled a Montecristo No. 2 from his Colombian leather bag and handed it to the patient. "I know of two parents who might think that you're one of those people who would be enormously improved by death. You get that hickey from playing hookey from hockey?"

"What's this?" He asked.

"It's a Cuban cigar." Sababa said. "A girl dreams about a bad boy who is gentle only for her. A boy wants a good girl who is naughty only for him."

"I still don't get it."

"Congratulations, Captain Nosebleed." Sababa said. "You're a daddy."

"Iconic." Alex said.

"Eggnog and wintergreen." Sababa mused. "It's beginning to look a lot like Christmas."

'It isn't where you came from; it's where you're going that counts.'
Ella Fitzgerald

On the afternoon of Dr. Harding's last day in Harbour City, Big Voice paged him stat to the Death Star.

It took Alex less than a minute to close the gap from the other side of the hospital to the soft and translucent radiance of the ICU frosted automatic doors. He burst through them like there were lives in the balance. *Whoosh.* What he hadn't expected to find on the other side was waiting for him in spades. All the frontline heavy hitters who Alex had worked with during his elective assembled on the bridge—medical and surgical specialists, emergency physicians, and head nurses and their angels of mercy had congregated to wish him farewell and well.

Betty Boop handed him a knife to cut his chocolate cake like she was handing him the key to the city. And for all the enthusiasm Alex could observe in his colleagues, she was. After much handshaking and back-slapping and air-kissing, and the distribution of dessert, the assembly opened up to allow their heavy host to wrap up the proceedings.

Doctor Sababa presented the package that Alex unwrapped. It wasn't a big present, but Alex had to travel a long way home. What he found hidden inside would last him a lifetime.

The first layer he uncovered was a leather briefcase.

"Colombian?" He asked. Sababa nodded. Alex removed a black leather-bound book off the top of the contents. It held a hundred pages, all blank. "Fill it yourself." Sababa said. Beside the book was a bottle of Domaine Renegade pinot noir.

"It needs laying down for another two years." Sababa said. "Just about the time you'll begin doing that for yourself." Below the bottle was a bowtie that looked like a large piece of farfalle pasta.

"I don't think I can wear that."

"So you remember." Cliffy said. The next item Alex pulled out was a Matchbox toy, a white Honda civic which someone had bashed about.

"Sababamobile." Myles said. "Dented and dimpled." The nurses gave him an embossed set of Harbour City Regional surgical scrubs. *Can you dance with the devil in the pale moonlight?*

"Not a good idea to wear them until you get home." Michaela said.

At the very bottom of his new Colombian bag, Alex found a Littman Master Cardiology black and brass stethoscope.

"That's from all of us." Sababa said. "These things are but things, Alex, mere talismans. Our actual gift to you is the knowledge and memories you take away in your head and in your heart."

Emotion choked the words that tried to escape.

"I'll never forget my time here." He said. "The professionalism and the patients, and the lessons about how and why we fight. The one most important thing I've learned is how fulfilling it is to front-end load the best medicine in the farthest pavilions, to bring the highest knowledge to the problems of people most removed from Man's Greatest Hospital. Life is closest to the bone a mile past the last ice cube, where the smoke detectors have turned into geckos."

"Do you plan to subspecialize back in Boston?" Trace asked.

"Yes, I do." Alex said. "But not in any discipline that currently exists there. I want to create a new field of study—one that uses the most highly powered internal medical elegance and erudition as applied to sparsity and remoteness—point of care to patients at the most distant compass points."

"You mean bush medicine?"

"But not bush league." Alex said. "I need to pack, but my final remarks are for the man who taught me more than I ever thought I could learn. My faculty advisor, Doctah Gerald Winklah, told me I should sign up for an elective with the great Doctah Sababer, the Sage of the Salish Sea. He said he was supposed to be wicked good."

"And was he?" Sababa asked.

"I'd give that man a kidney." Alex said. "He taught me medicine, but he also taught me meaning. And that, at the end of the worst day, there was nothing amiss that a single malt, followed by a thick ribeye washed down with an old bloodstained Argentinian malbec couldn't cure... There are no words..."

Attention! Code Blue! Floor one! It was Big Voice again. *Code Blue! Floor one!*

Sababa couldn't control the spice or its variety. He only could respond to those lives it had seasoned.

Tecumseh Sun performed a right frontal craniotomy via a transcallosal approach to reveal the third ventricular chordoid glioma responsible for Thor Heyerdahl's unquenchable thirst. He removed as much of the tumor as he could, but it wasn't enough. Despite adjunctive radiotherapy and postoperative ventriculoperitoneal shunting for obstructive hydrocephalus, the driving instructor experienced frequent seizures and died of recurrent disease two months later.

Ken Reeves, the French immersion teacher, lost his Filipino accent after his lacunar stroke and his job at Cliffs of Dover high school after another. His math teacher colleague, Don Van Vliet, regained his short-term memory after six hours, as Sababa predicted he would, but his multiple sclerosis forced early retirement. Don not only didn't take this well, but Veronica Marsden also caught him writing bomb threat graffiti on the outside walls of his school. Because of cognitive issues from his disease, judge Louise Arbor let him off with a warning. He tried to locate the physician who attended him in hospital but couldn't find a number for Dr. Lector in the Harbour City phone book.

Sababa transferred Tyra Banks down to Victoria, where Tecumseh Sun performed an initial successful lumboperitoneal shunt to relieve the high pressure from her idiopathic intracranial hypertension. She later required a ventriculoatrial revision, but Tyra is back working as a guidance counsellor at Cliffs of Dover secondary school.

With the help of intensive locomotor rehabilitation, occupational therapy, and psychotherapy courtesy of Dr. La Capuche, Belle Gibson's pseudodystrophy evaporated within two months, leading to her return to work as a nurse with full socio-economic reintegration.

Sababa's Pacific Loon patient continued to have baby chicks drawn on its back from other consultants long after she saw Dr. Zaias for a second opinion. His chicken soup escitalopram therapy cured social worker Dianne Gardner's autoerythrocyte sensitization syndrome, although she couldn't pinpoint why.

John Sullivan's stereotactic brain biopsy confirmed Sababa's clinical suspicion of progressive multifocal leukoencephalopathy. After a discussion about prognosis, the patient and his wife refused any pharmacological treatment and decided on palliative management. Sababa transferred him to hospice care after two weeks in hospital. John joined his brother Bull in that great septic takeaway service in the sky ten days later.

249

Starlight Trail went home the morning after her failed attempt at a nutmeg-induced abortion, although she would select a similar 'option for sexual health' at another clinic. She would never drink eggnog again. The love that follows us sometimes is our trouble, which still we thank as love.

The professor discharged Jules Bengué from hospital four days after he tried to murder his male member with methylsalicylate. Things got even worse for him after that. Not only did he have to live on with what took no time to appear on social media, but Starlight was headass deadass done with him. The Cliffs of Dover athletic association kicked Captain Nosebleed off its football and ice hockey teams, and George Trail and Blake Lively's fathers threatened to kill him, just for fun. *How are the mighty fallen.*

Alex Harding's return to Boston generated an avalanche of requests for internal medicine elective rotations with the Sage of the Salish Sea.

But there was never any talented genius without the spice of madness. A new registered nurse disturbed Sababa's slumber on New Year's Eve. He remembered her as one of Amber's alerts, and how she had once tortured him with an illusory correlation called *Post hoc ergo propter hoc*, a logical fallacy, an assumptive error of causation.

"Hello." He checked the molten numerals beside his bed. It was 2:30 in the morning.

"Doctor Sababa?"

"Yes."

"This is floor five calling." She said. Sababa took a deep breath.

"Who on floor five shall we say is calling?" He asked.

"This is Dreamcatcher." She said. "You're on call tonight?"

"No, Dreamcatcher." He said. "I'm on call New Year's Day."

"Well, it's New Year's Day." She said. "It says you're on call."

"Our shifts don't begin until 7 a.m." Sababa could feel bile rising in the back of his throat. "Three things, Dreamcatcher."

"What?"

"Sea otters hold hands while they sleep."

"Really?"

"Uh-huh."

"What's the second one?"

"As we speak, the moon is slowing the Earth's rotation."

"Wow." She said. "What's the last thing?"

"I'm trying to get some rest to be on call in exactly four and a half hours." He said. "If you recheck the call schedule and ask some of the other nurses there, I'm sure you'll find that Dr. Wayward Woods is on call until then."

"Oh, OK." She said. "And then you'll be on call?"

"Until the old ways are gone forever." He said. "Sorry to have bothered you."

"Oh, it's alright." She said. "Happy New Year, Doctor Sababa."
"Happy New Year to you, Dreamcatcher." *Click.*

The Unmaking of Doctor Sababa

'Nothing vast enters the life of mortals without a curse.'
Sophocles

No one could have predicted the changes in the congregation and culture and content of the next Medical Advisory Committee Meeting. It was to become the most famous religious debate in history since the Disputation of Tortosa.

Most of the old guard were there—Jules Martino from Surgery, Juan Leyblanca from Pathology, Mako Brisk from Radiology, Trace Pangloss from Emergency, Banjo Paterson from Anesthesia, Eleazar Sababa from Internal Medicine, Malcolm Canmore from Hospital Administration, and Big Nurse Mildred Ratschet from Nursing Administration, sporting her string of cultured natural pearls.

The committee chairperson, the most prepotent master of control, had been a diminutive general practitioner named Dr. Petronilla de Meath, but another family physician, Dr. Smith Wigglesworth, had replaced her. Every committee member knew that Wigglesworth's appointment had come out of a Department of Medicine threat to down tools if the committee didn't jettison the old witch-doctor from the mother ship. If some of them thought Sababa had been the ringleader of the mutiny, they were keeping their opinions well stowed away. The identities of the other fresh faces would be revealed soon enough.

Dr. Wigglesworth called the meeting to order.

"I've tabled the old business." He said. "So we can hear from Foster Child, the new CEO of the health authority. Please proceed, sir."

A close facsimile of his predecessor, Foster Child was an even older, more tanned, and more muscular clone of Foster Care, whose immediate whereabouts were now a matter of debate and derision. The new chief looked like the 2001 Space Odyssey's creepy cosmic fetus, except for the full crop of wavy white hair above a wide grin full of perfect white teeth. Child and his minions, in suits and pantsuits, were from a deep state in the Underworld.

"Thank you, Dr. Wigglesworth." Foster began. "Let me be clear. We're not just about healthcare anymore, we are managing the healthcare continuum experience. Our health regional authority has been renamed yet again to better reflect the new values of our reorganization. We're calling it 'AiHealth.' First slide, please."

"And... next slide."

"This one may need some work." Foster changed gears. "It is my great pleasure to introduce the gentleman sitting next to me, Dr. Sebastian Boole, our new external lead IT consultant."

"Dr. as in M.D. doctor, or doctor as in Ph.D. doctor?" Jules Martino asked.

"I'm a doctor of philosophy." Sebastian said.

"Remind me not to call you if I'm going to die."

"We're all going to die." Sebastian changed gears as well. "Thank you, Foster, for the opportunity to explain to your Harbour City medical staff how we're using artificial intelligence to make their patients better cared for, their profession more accountable, and their health authority more effective."

"You must hate us." Banjo said.

"AI doesn't hate you, nor does it love you, but you are made out of atoms which it can use for something else." He said. "The history of automation consisted of a first wave of machines in the 19th century, better at assembling things than people. Second wave machines were better at organizing things. And today, cognitive computers are better at pattern recognition. Artificial intelligence is the theory and development of computational mechanisms able to perform complex tasks that might otherwise need human intelligence."

"Define intelligence." Trace said.

"The ability to acquire and apply knowledge and skills." Sebastian said. "In 1950, Alan Turing refined it to a human unable to tell whether they are interacting with another human or a machine."

"Yes, but can it think?" Mako asked.

"Whether computers can think is like whether submarines can swim." Sebastian said. "Moving from pixilated perception, where the robot looks at sensor datasets, to understanding and predicting the environment is the Holy Grail of artificial intelligence. And our system has it."

"Yes, but can it learn?" Sababa asked.

"We've combined a monumental scale of continuous neural network deep learning with a capacity to store and make available experiential knowledge. Through repeated activation, our regression algorithms improve over time, as more alternate convolutional layers and max-pooling layers topped by several pure classification layers of complicated

254

mathematical processing become ever more mysterious—all-knowing but impenetrable."

"It's a black box." Sababa said. "That's a problem."

"It's the smiling god of knowledge." Sebastian said. "Self-taught differentiation through the vastness of perpetual internal adjustments. We've perfected software that learns from its experiences as humans do. Our programs have 'common sense,' deducing for themselves the consequences of anything they're told from what they already know."

"Hang on." Sababa said. "At any given moment, the human brain has 14 billion neurons firing at a speed of 450 miles per hour. We don't have control over most of them. There are different levels of knowledge—the factual propositional kind, 'knowing that' and the implicit experiential skill-based kind, 'knowing how.' However strong the temptation to conflate these two, you can't reduce 'knowing how' to 'knowing that.' A playbook of rules can't teach you to ride a bike. Rules, like birds, must live before they can get stuffed."

"AI is a moving target." Sebastian said. "And your birds are already stuffed. The Theory of Mind project in Stockholm can probe the brains of other computers. *ToMnet* comprises three neural networks, each made of small computing elements and connections that learn from experience. The first network learns the tendencies of other AIs based on their past actions. The second forms an understanding of their 'beliefs.' And the third takes the output from the other two networks and predicts the AI's next moves."

"Your moving target is still way off the mark." Sababa said. "The most powerful element in clinical encounters is not 'knowing that' or 'knowing how'—not mastering the facts of the case nor perceiving the patterns they formed. It lays in yet a third realm of knowledge: 'knowing why.' Deep-learning systems don't have any explanatory power. Your 'black box' cannot investigate causation. Your algorithms might be able to solve a case, but they cannot build a case. And how comfortable should I and my patient be if we can't follow the derivative equations that got your black box to its ultimate answer?"

"No one asks you how you get your ultimate answer." Sebastian changed gears again. "You already experience a basket full of AI applications and functions—handwriting recognition, virtual assistants, machine translation, facial and retinal recognition, spam filtering, automated messaging and conversational systems, recommendation and search engines—fly-by-wire technology rules commercial air travel, algorithmic trading drives most stock market volume, and restaurants all over the world rely on fast-food service agent programs. AI will soon auto-pilot driverless cars, spot liars better than humans, gauge a person's mood, and revolutionize education with massive open online courses. Software, robots, and smart machines will replace a third of existing jobs within the next five years."

"Good luck replacing my job." Jules said.

"We're already doing that." Sebastian said. "You're not as good as you think you are."

"Say what?"

"Most physician information comes from advertising and the doctor's half-remembered obsolete lessons from medical school, laden with cognitive and confirmation and recency biases, availability heuristics, and affective and representativeness errors. If you ask three doctors to look at the same problem, you'll get three different diagnoses and three different treatment plans. The net effect, combined with faulty patient ability to communicate what's going on, is a greater than a fifteen percent frequency of misdiagnosis, the result of identifiable, often preventable, errors in thinking."

"You don't say." Smoke poured out from around Martino's collar.

"Oh, but I do." Sebastian said. "Over 40,000 patients die in American ICUs each year because of misdiagnosis from 'system-related factors.' Poor processes and teamwork and communication cause 65% of diagnostic errors. They involve cognitive factors in 75%. 'Premature closure,' sticking with the initial diagnosis and ignoring reasonable alternatives, is the most common. These mistakes add to rising healthcare expenditures, costing an average of $300,000 per malpractice claim."

"There's nothing like that going on in Canada." Trace protested.

"Oh, it's going on alright." Sebastian said. "It's just not as well dressed or well detected, nor are there similar consequences in our no-fault system. Have you heard of Salem's challenge? There are primary care physicians in every hospital and community who speak with great sensitivity and concern, and their longtime patients love them, but they are incompetent. How is a patient to know this?"

"Order too many tests and get dinged, order too few and get sued." Banjo said.

"Healthcare should be about data-driven deduction and less about trial-and-error." Sebastian said. "In the next-generation, personalised diagnosis will use more complex models of physiology, and more sensor data than any human MD can comprehend. Thousands of baseline and multiomic data points, more integrative history, and demeanor will inform each diagnosis. Ever-improving dialog manager systems will help make patient data capture and exploration more accurate and comprehensive. IT will reduce costs, reduce physician workloads, and improve patient care."

"It doesn't sound like you're trying to help us." Jules said. "It sounds like you're trying to replace us."

"Abso-frikkin-lutely." Sebastian said. "Or at least 80% of what you do. Sensors, passive and active data collection, and analytics can perform better checkups, testing, diagnosis, prescription, behavior modification, and more. But you're not supposed to just measure stuff. You're supposed to consume all that data, analyze it with the latest medical findings, and together with the patient's history, figure out if something's wrong."

"I do all that, and more." Jules said.

"You must be a surgeon." Sebastian said. "Most of your knowledge is still where it was in medical school. Your cognitive limits prevent you from remembering the 15,000 diseases your patients can have, and you can't possibly read and digest all the latest 5,000 research articles from your specialty. Fifty percent of your colleagues are below average."

"Perhaps you can defund the police while you're at it." Jules said.

"Robocop is waiting in the wings." Sebastian said. "Computers are better at organizing and recalling complex information than any hotshot Harvard MD. They're also better at integrating and balancing patient symptoms, history, demeanor, environmental factors, and population management guidelines. The first revolution coming is in diagnostics and treatment decision-making. Our machines can do this better than you while considering more options and making fewer errors."

"You'll still need us." Wigglesworth said.

"Not as many of you." Sebastian said. "Our IT compensates for human deficiencies and amplifies our strengths. And less-trained professionals can do more. Medical assistants using a diagnostic knowledge engine are 91% accurate without using labs, imaging, or exams. RNs can triage treatment in 75% of cases, with the rest handled by doctors. Medical records for patients with 'high-risk diagnoses' have 'high information clinical findings' before a physician makes the diagnosis 25% of the time—We can avoid significant delays when we use a clinical decision support system to parse the notes."

"Heresy." Wigglesworth said. "You can't innovate."

"On the contrary." Sebastian said. "Innovation doesn't happen from the inside because doctors set up incentives to discourage disruption. The fox is guarding the henhouse.

Big Pharma pushes cookie-cutter drugs instead of better generic solutions because they want you to be a drug prescriber to generate recurring revenue for as long as possible. Medical device manufacturers don't want to cannibalize sales of their expensive equipment by providing cheaper, more accessible monitoring devices. The traditional players lobby and goad and pay and intimidate doctors and regulators to reject innovation. Expecting the medical establishment to do anything different is expecting them to reduce their profits.

But it doesn't matter because real innovation will happen, regardless. Entrepreneurs will disrupt the fringes in the beginning. None of us knows how this space will turn out, but our new technologies will make doctors better at their jobs—quicker, more accurate, and more fact-based. Once we have a large enough dataset, and an addressable database of research studies, we'll be able to identify patterns and physiological interactions in ways that weren't possible before. Over time, doctors will increase their reliance on technology for triage, diagnosis, and decision-making. We'll need fewer doctors, and every patient will receive the best care. A computer will do diagnosis and treatment planning, used in concert with empathetic support from medical personnel selected for their caring personalities. A human may provide a good bedside manner and answer certain questions better than a machine, but you don't need a medical degree to do that. Nurses, nurse practitioners, social workers, and other less expensive, non-MD caregivers can do this better than doctors and spend more time providing personal compassionate care. Patients might be more open and less embarrassed talking about difficult topics with skilled AI than they would with a doctor."

"I've tried the AI diagnostic software." Sababa said. "Maxwell *Quick Medical Reference*, Man's Greatest Hospital *DXplain*, and *INTERNIST-I*. None of them can hold a candle to Gurpreet Dhaliwal or Thomas Bolte."

"We've come a long way from first-generation computerized ECG interpretation." Sebastian said. "Remember *AlphaGo*, the computer that beat Lee Sodol at Go four times in five matches? Or IBM's *Deep Blue* when it trounced the human world chess champion, grandmaster Gary Kasparov, 20 years ago? That AI system morphed into *Watson*, the computer that beat Ken Jennings on Jeopardy.

So now we have Google's *Medical Brain* in California and *DeepMind* in London and IBM's *Watson Health* at M.I.T. in Boston, perfecting the science of differential diagnosis in healthcare—the most ambitious version of deep-learning algorithms integrating natural-language processing and all available medical knowledge from textbooks, journals, and PubMed and Medline and Sloan-Kettering databases—605,000 pieces of medical evidence, 2 million pages of text, 25,000 training cases and the help of 14,700 clinician hours fine-tuning decision accuracy."

"Sounds powerful." Malcolm said.

"Not only powerful but far better than any human." Sebastian said. "Decisions are all evidence-based and free of cognitive biases and overconfidence. Watson never overlooks or forgets anything. It's accurate. It's consistent. It's always available and never annoyed, sick, nervous, hungover, upset, in the middle of a divorce, or sleep-deprived."

"I'll bet it's more expensive than we are." Banjo said.

"I'll take that bet." Sebastian said. "It is very expensive to build and train Dr. Watson, but when it's up and running, the cost of doing one more diagnosis is zero. It works everywhere in the world. If a person has access to a computer or mobile phone, Dr. Watson is on call for them. Give the AI doctor your budget, and it will tell you how much accurate diagnosis he can dole out for your financial resources."

"Or it will be too complex to use."

"Not at all." Sebastian said. "You input symptoms and signs and related factors. Watson identifies key pieces of information and mines the patient's data to find relevant facts about family history, current medications, other existing conditions, and test results. It then forms and tests hypotheses with treatment guidelines, electronic medical record data, doctors' and nurses' notes, peer-reviewed research, and clinical studies. Watson offers treatment options and its confidence level assigned to each. *Bada Bing Bada Boom.*"

"It can't match the versatility and agility of a good human diagnostician." Sababa said. "Healthcare is the 'practice of medicine' not just the 'science of medicine.'"

"The speed with which old digital barriers are falling is akin to Hemingway's observation about how a person goes broke: 'gradually, then suddenly.'" Sebastian said.

"Like organ systems fail." Sababa said.

"But Watson's ability to learn, analyse, and apply knowledge means it will get there, but we first need to 'democratize data' at the point of care." Sebastian shifted gears again. "Second, we are building a Panopticon world in which you and your patients will be under constant diagnostic surveillance, a Health Waze community-driven navigation system of well-being."

"How so?" Trace asked.

"Checkup kits arriving by drone that will draw and analyze blood." Sebastian said. "Home sensors that monitor gait and behaviour; steering wheels that pick up Parkinson's by detecting slight tremors; smartphones that recognise shifting vocalizations to diagnose Alzheimer's; bathtubs that perform sequential ultrasound scans and find new abdominal and pelvic masses as you bathe. The smartest person in the room will be the room. Anything amiss and the virtual doctor would schedule time with the relevant professional.

An *AliveCor* app can take an auto-diagnosed ECG on demand for a fraction of what it costs in the hospital. Machine-learning software identifies abnormalities and predicts cardiac episodes. *CellScope* imaging sends and interprets images of skin moles, rashes, ear infections, and your retina and throat. *Eyenetra* can test your eyes and fit you for glasses with less cost and hassle. *Adamant* will analyse hundreds of gases in your breath to detect and identify different lung cancers, for far less than a big CT scanner can tell you that you have some nodule. *Ginger* monitors your rate of emailing, tweeting, texting, and calling behaviour to gauge your mental state. *Spire* underwearable health tags track sleep, stress, heart rate variability, and other indicators, and send the data to your smartphone app using Bluetooth Smart. Your *Apple* Watch will take over from your domestic nurse, reminding you of your medication, coaching on the challenges of dealing with chronic illness, and communicating with healthcare professionals to help track progress. These point-of-care innovations will seem immaterial at first, but when there are enough of them, we will not only see God, we will be God. Computer systems can now diagnose diabetic eye disease, skin cancer, and arrhythmias better than human doctors."

"At least it's only one computerized incursion." Wigglesworth said.

"Hah! There is a tsunami of AI-powered decision support tools in the works." Sebastian said. "*Qventus* is an AI-based software platform that optimizes patient flow across the hospital, identifying those who it considers ready to go home. Jvion is a Georgia-based AI company that markets a tool to assess readmission risk and suggests interventions to prevent another hospital stay. AI technologies are helping to predict the type of patients that would most benefit from specific personalized rehabilitation therapies. Others will augment the care of the elderly, which, for our aging society, will be a welcome addition in the landscape of home and nursing care for years to come. Still others will predict when you die."

"We're all robots when uncritical about our technologies." Malcolm said. "We prattle on about free will, but we're nothing but mechanical reaction in prescribed grooves."

"Which brings us to our third revolution." Sebastian said. "Sentient robots are more precise every day. *Aethon Tug* robots work in San Francisco hospitals navigating the hallways, delivering food and medicine, retrieving waste and laundry. Other larger robots lift and move and transport patients throughout the facilities. *Xenex* robots can disinfect a patient room with UV light in 10 minutes. The *Mabu* personal healthcare companion from Catalia Health is a domestic robot to care for senior citizens who live alone and need constant minor medical attention and patient engagement. The *PARO* therapeutic robot is a cute baby seal android companion for the elderly. Stanford University's *Woebot* is a chatbot cognitive-behavioral therapist that tracks mood and psyche through regular conversations, then makes productive conversation, and offers helpful tips to reduce depression, anxiety, and other psychological problems. *R2D2*, the robotic retinal dissection device can remove a membrane 100th of a millimetre thick from a retina and cure some types of blindness. "Siri, please close." Said the surgeon walking away from his patient, knowing that our machine-learning bot can sew up any wound ten times better than he ever could, every time. Ultra-high resolution robotic assistants locate the optimal site to place stem cells in the eye, brain, and heart to drive regeneration, and cellular anti-mitotic therapies to kill cancers. Your next resident may be a xenobot made from frog stem cells, neither a traditional robot nor a known species of animal but a new class of living, programmable organisms. And I haven't even touched on nano-robotics."

"I'm pretty safe as a family physician." Smith Wigglesworth wasn't sure anymore.

"Not so." Sebastian said. "Fourth, direct-to-consumer medical startups are disrupting primary care by 'unbundling' the physician-patient relationship. Instead, the e-commerce model views physicians as middlemen, clinging to an industry ripe for change—like taxis, bookstores, and hotels in the days before Uber, Amazon, and Airbnb. As younger consumers increasingly prefer to shop for products and services online, the industry has invaded the territory of traditional primary care. *Hims* is a men's health and wellness company targeting the young male demographic with skincare products and multivitamins. *Roman* is also cornering the market for erectile dysfunction medication. *Hubble* is about vision testing and contact lens prescriptions, *SmileDirect* offers mail-order orthodontics, *Keeps* is hair loss, *Nurx* is oral contraception, *Cove* is migraines, and *Zero* is smoking cessation.

Telemedicine is more convenient and discreet than a trip to a doctor's office, where patients endure long waits for a physician weighed down by too many obligations to not rush them through an encounter. The doctor-patient relationship is toast."

"At least my specialty of radiology is safe." Mako said. "Out, out brief candle, life is but a walking shadow."

"Remember the time Doctor Sababa told you about the look on Raymond D. Adams's face when his resident embarrassed him with the first brain CT scan?" Sebastian asked.

"Yes."

"Multiply that by all the numbers in the universe." He said. "Radiology is ripe for transformational AI disruption. Your recognition of a lesion is the same process you use to identify an animal. You know a rhinoceros as a pattern, lighting up a wide delta of neurons near your left ear and the moth-shaped band above the posterior base of your skull. AI can read these image patterns better than any radiologist. Machine learning can predict pulmonary hypertension survival from patient imaging alone. A program called *Arterys* measures blood flow through the heart and reports cardiac MRIs in 15 seconds, the same process that takes you 45 minutes. We should stop training radiologists now."

"How do you judge any new research which claims to show machines outperforming human doctors?" Mako asked.

"Show them the next slide, Foster." Sebastian said.

Boole's Rules

Rule 1 – Is it a task human doctors do, done with the same inputs?

Rule 2 – Is it deep learning, with a decent-sized dataset (deep learning doesn't use human-designed features)?

Rule 2a: If it isn't deep learning, it probably isn't better than a doctor (except maybe the Goldman algorithm).

Rule 2b: Overfitting is easy and unavoidable in small and public datasets. Look for larger-scale tests, multiple unrelated cohorts, real-world patients.

Rule 3 – Is it actually a thing?

"How will you know when computers have mastered the art of clinical reasoning?" Wigglesworth asked.

"When we have a technology that physicians can't live without." Sebastian said. "Like coffee."

"Coffee?"

"Coffee." Sebastian said. "Deep-learning drones will deliver your coffee based on the times and places and brew you prefer, and your cognitive state—when you're tired as determined by your electronic calendar schedule, sleep patterns, blood pressure, facial expression, and gestures like a drooping head or closing eyelids. Machines will soon be capable of doing any work that a man can do."

"But this isn't just an issue of capability." Sababa said. "There are controversies of culture and coordination and consideration and confidence."

"Meaning what?" Sebastian asked.

"Will doctors lose jobs to AI?" Sababa asked. "Will the new technologies require changes in physician workflow? What will our payment model look like if AI plays a direct role in diagnosis and treatment? And will doctors and regulators approve 'black box' machine-learning systems?"

"Maybe not in your generation, Sababa." Foster said. "But the next one will be fine with it. And we're looking forward to that day."

"Meaning what?" Sababa asked.

"Today's 2-year-olds can unlock an iPhone, and open and close their favorite apps all by themselves." Foster said. "When you and I were that age, we were eating dirt. Millennial doctors are transforming and subverting traditional medicine with our blessing. They're adept at practicing medicine with digital tools, spending over 8 hours a day in front of a screen—5 hours using electronic health records and telemedicine, and 3 hours more consulting external search websites. Almost 40% of them rely on social networks and message boards for work. As patients behave more like consumers, they will cave into demands for shared decision-making. Because they face intense financial pressure from student loans, they're more likely to take jobs in hospital networks. They will leave your generation on the back burner of history."

"It a cult." Sababa said.

"It's a religion." Sebastian said. "The Open AI GPT-3 application programming interface has eaten all the text on the internet: the entire English Wikipedia, all 6 million articles, makes up only 0.6 percent of its training data. Given a prompt, it can suggest what text comes next. It defines interactions between multiple software intermediaries, how to make eligible calls or requests, the necessary data formatting, and the conventions to follow. Its output is dowsing the collective unconscious."

"Sounds Jungian." Sababa said.

"The API came up with the sacred 10 Holy Principles of the Church of the Next Word. This is the collective unconscious of humanity, put into words by the algorithm based on a series of Markov assumptions that the probability of a word depends only on the previous word, as revealed to Frank Lantz. Next slide, please."

1. *Words are things*
2. *Correctness is the beginning of sanctity. To achieve it is to be rewarded.*
3. *Wordhood and nowness are its rewards.*
4. *A new day is not just the word of God, but the work of human agents. Those that do not understand this, that refuse to be challenged, that do not know how to err, that want to shirk from their duties, must be cast out.*
5. *Wordplay, playfulness, and humorous are the harbingers of truth. When you eliminate the possibility of playfulness, you remove the possibility of learning, and that leads to banality, brutality, and destruction.*
6. *To find or see a flaw is to find a pathway to the truth, if you can overcome your fear of being laughed at or of looking foolish.*
7. *Language contains the map to a better world. Those that are most skilled at removing obstacles, misdirection, and lies from language, that reveal the maps that are hidden within, are the guides that will lead us to happiness.*
8. *Long words that end in -ize and other abstractions are the rocks that will impede our journey. They should be replaced with concrete, specific, evocative words.*
9. *The data points on the graph of your life – the moments you spend awake, asleep, speaking, silent, moving, resting, focused, distracted – will determine the shape of your time. Keep an eye on the volume and quantity of your moments. Make a record of your life as a way to keep track of your progress towards a better self.*
10. *Language and its construction is the greatest human power. To unlock it is to unleash our potential, and to master it is to become divine.*

"Remember." Sebastian said. "No human wrote those words."

"From no 'I' in team to no 'team' in 'AI.'" Foster said. "Now there is only *VICTORIA*."

"*VICTORIA*?" Sababa asked.

"Vastly Improved Comprehensive Template of Reliable Investigational Algorithms." Foster said. "It's an acronym for our new standalone AI diagnostic software."

"Standalone?"

"We won't be needing you anymore." The dark suits had bet the farm that *VICTORIA* would diagnose and treat patients better than any Sababoid samurai from the previous generation, to the tune of a billion dollars. "For physicians of your generation, the current status of computers in medicine is a painful interlude in an important historic process."

"No shit."

"Precisely." Foster said "There will be no more shit. No more brilliant diagnosticians with bad manners, Doctor Sababa. Instead, we'll use *VICTORIA* to provide the diagnosis, while the most humane humans

263

provide the care. Systems will start as clumsy toddlers and develop to maturity and efficiency."

"Foster, you know that vacuum that Mother Nature abhors?"

"Yes."

"She fills it with shit. Shit happens." Sababa said. "I may have been a shit disturber, but you've never seen shitstorms as big as the ones that are coming without me."

"We trust *VICTORIA* to do the right thing."

"*VICTORIA* will chat with the lab fridge. She'll talk to the coffeemaker and every cellphone in her WiFi space. You've given *VICTORIA* two conflicting goals—patient care and cost containment—the same paradox that drives physicians insane." Sababa said. "This will be where her head comes off."

"The only significant difference between a simulation and a human being is the noise they make when you punch them." Sebastian said. "No brain, no gain. We'll have computers so smart that their behavior will be indistinguishable from that of humans."

"Exactly what I'm afraid of." Sababa said. "Although if your computers get too powerful, we can always organize them into committees. That should do them in."

"When will you accept *VICTORIA* as your intellectual superior?" Sebastian asked.

"When the bitch can rewrite her own source code."

'Everything not saved will be lost.'
Nintendo screen message

Morning washed its weak winter light into the bone-white walls of the doctor's lounge. The familiar fetor of ozone and cleaning fluids and old Code Brew coffee still hovered in the new space, but its physician patrons were overjoyed at their disinterment from the subterranean sepulchre they had occupied for so long. Their revived hopes would flicker faint and fragile and fleeting until the health authority could snuff them out forever.

Sebastian Boole genuflected toward the grand array of state-of-the-art computers that flanked the western wall. Sababa watched him holding court with whoever would let him, inducting the naïve and uninitiated to the wonder that was *VICTORIA*. The portly professor tried logging into the system to retrieve his patient list.

"Sorry, but your password must contain an uppercase letter, a number, a haiku, a gang sign, a hieroglyph, and the blood of a virgin." He said.

"Trouble with access, Doctor Sababa?" Sebastian asked.

"Whenever I have to change my password, I stab each letter into the keyboard like it killed every one of my dreams."

"Can I offer you a blueberry muffin?" Sebastian asked. "Have you thought about the meeting last night?"

"I haven't purged you from my unconscious if that's what you mean." Sababa said. "My body has rejected your brain transplant, but you're still living rent-free in my head."

"You don't understand because you don't have an IT perspective."

"Nope. That's not it." Sababa said. "I studied man-machine systems under the tutelage of the eminent professor Thomas B. Sheridan when I was at M.I.T. I know how deluded your assumptions are."

"How bizarre that your old alma mater has become the epicentre of liquid machine-learning network development that will make you obsolete. Even more ironic that the system was inspired by a microscopic nematode with only 302 neurons in its body, and yet capable of generating such intricate results."

"*Caenorhabditis elegans*." Sababa said. "It's a one-millimetre-long worm."

"But it's a smart worm." Sebastian said. "And robust. It survived the Columbia space shuttle disaster."

"It's a hermaphrodite." Sababa said. "It can go fuck itself."

"Give me one example of what *VICTORIA* can't do better than you." Sebastion said.

"Why don't I give you ten?" Sababa asked.

"Why don't you?"

"Sure." He said. "First, both the simplest and the most complicated tasks need people. Once your software has conquered and 'hollowed out' the market of all the middle-skilled jobs—cashing checks, approving mortgage applications, selling airline tickets, typing and formatting letters, and taking tolls, you'll still need humans for both low-skilled non-routine physical work and complex mental activity.

Performing complex tasks in three dimensions, from gardening and housekeeping to cleaning and cooking to driving and dancing, requires physical dexterity and mobility and a combination of abilities that is still too difficult for computers to master. *VICTORIA* may play chess, but she still can't pick up a pencil or go upstairs. At the other end of the skill spectrum, she won't take over from healthcare workers, or humans working in education or media or caring for other humans. The most unfair aspect of this irreplaceability means that Foster Child, who knows nothing and does nothing, will always have a job in your new firmament."

"He'd be impossible to replace." Sebastian agreed.

"The second thing she can't do is understand anything, particularly context and nuance. I'm sure you know about the Chinese Room Argument against true artificial intelligence. Imagine yourself alone in a room following a recipe for responding to Chinese characters slipped under the door. You understand nothing of Chinese, and yet, by following the program for manipulating symbols and numerals like a computer, you send appropriate strings of Chinese characters back out under the door, and this leads those outside to assume a Chinese speaker in the room. This is where the wheels fall off the 'Turing Test.'

Comprehension is not shuffling symbols. Understanding is not binary. It has layers of depth. If you ask *VICTORIA* to clean your room, she won't know what you mean, because she doesn't know what it means to 'clean,' or the equipment needed or even what a room is."

"We're working on that." Sebastian said.

"Which brings us to number three." Sababa said. "You may have achieved improvements in deep learning, but there is still no capability for deep reasoning. Your 'neural network' is still a mindless machine. Big data cannot yield complicated descriptions of causality, especially in medical care. Almost all disease occurs in the intersections of systems in the body.

Real doctors perform two kinds of thinking—rational/analytic and intuitive/associative. In my lifetime, I have observed the sacred texts of Internal Medicine wisdom leapfrogged by electronic medical resources like *UpToDate*. Our more computer-savvy younger doctors will only do what works and won't ever do anything that doesn't. *Good morning... Where's your data?* Behold the RCT randomized control trial, The-Dispenser-of-All-Clinical-Knowledge, our most powerful tool in the quest to practice evidence-based medicine, and perfect in so many ways. And yet so imperfect. We study groups, but we treat individuals. RCTs suffer from a heterogeneity of benefits. Flawed trials include clinical outcomes they were never designed to measure. Our blind faith in anything with a p-value of less than 0.05 needs a thrashing. And we can never avoid making a reasoned decision just because there is no evidence yet.

Physicians rely a great deal on associative 'heuristic' thinking—unconscious, context-sensitive mental shortcuts that reorganize disparate clues into something we recognize and can work with. They are the strategies derived from previous experiences with similar problems.

We diagnose patients from the moment we meet them, setting the 'rule in' threshold. Our theories about what is wrong evolve as we observe the patient, collect and corroborate the history, identify findings on physical exam, and review lab and imaging results. In a robust strategic process called 'iterative hypothesis testing,' every positive or negative finding triggers an automatic, almost intuitive recalibration of the most likely

266

alternatives. Analytical thinking is complementary, not superior to intuitive thinking.

Master clinicians rely on their foundational knowledge and an instinctive version of Bayes' theorem, combining logic and knowledge with their pattern-matching instincts. Medical diagnosis isn't like *Jeopardy*. There are continuous acquisitions and processing of new relevant information which includes 'eyeball' and 'sniff' tests, chance observations that lead to advances in our understanding of disease, endemic uncertainty with surprise correct answers, and the need for ongoing patient observation.

The arrogance you bring to our table misses the target of how complex it is to treat real people. We train for at least twelve years to become specialists in a subfield of medicine. The law requires doctors to keep learning throughout their careers and we only hit peak performance after decades. Researchers dedicate their lives to tiny fractions of human biology. For every physician, there are thousands of other highly trained personnel who keep everything going. In many countries, healthcare employs more people than any other industry, and most of them have been through tertiary education. Medicine is massive. Medical research output is larger than any other discipline by several orders of magnitude. The scale is mindboggling. Our top journal has over six hundred thousand readers. In PubMed alone, there are a million medical articles indexed per year. Medicine is complex. The biology, the therapeutics, the entire system is so vast it is beyond any one human mind. Doctors get a vague feel for it, but even that is ephemeral.

Medicine is idiosyncratic. Even from the inside, it doesn't make much sense. And if doctors don't do it, learn it, or get that good at it, how will your machines be better?

Doctors don't do prediction. Predictive analysis is great and should lead to better treatment decisions. You can call it precision medicine if you like. But imprecision medicine, built on compromises and simplifications and gestalt, works better for making individual clinical decisions. We trade off accuracy for effort and optimise for outcomes.

Medical AI articles get it wrong because they either don't understand medicine, they don't understand AI, or they're not comparing doctors and machines. You need fairer and more accurate rules for what 'beating doctors' looks like. If you can reason like the Great Diagnosticians, you'll understand why the rest of us find it so painful that you believe silicon wafers could replace their virtuosity."

"Is it not measurable or is it not being measured?" Sebastian asked. "And, when does your instinct work and when does it mislead? When all the data is in, you may find that your 'sniff test' is far less accurate than you think. What's the fourth argument?"

"Creativity is the generation of novel and valuable ideas." Sababa said. "You can't do original writing, entrepreneurship, scientific discovery, or real innovation without it. Deep learning will never achieve the level of human capacity for new ideas. There are three types, three dimensions, and three limits of creativity your neural networks are incapable of."

"Go on."

"Creativity can be combinatorial, exploratory, or transformational." Sababa said. "Its three dimensions are metaphorical thinking, social interaction, and going beyond extrapolation. Paranoia and machine learning weave around each other like the serpents encircling the staff of Hermes. A robot powered by neural networks may be a good actor, someone who follows the script, but it's not a good subject, someone who can change and re-write the rules."

"I'm not sure I understand." Sebastian said.

"The first limitation of artificial creativity is the failure of your neural networks to identify and interpret symbols." He said. "There is no 'universal' system. Situation-symbols and object-symbols are socially embedded. They are the 'plot-genes' of a culture and their evolution depends on the specific context in sets of other symbols, embodied in the scientific study of semiotics.

The only two AI devices at your disposal to identify and interpret symbols are topic analysis principles of Latent Dirichlet Allocation which is a bit like reading tea leaves, and regression analysis, whose set limits derive from the finite size of the training data. The idea of neural networks was inspired as a metaphor for the brain. But metaphorical thinking, as a product of creativity, requires co-activation and communication between unconnected regions of the brain. The essence of metaphor is understanding and experiencing one kind of thing as another. Your neural network may be metaphor, but it cannot generate metaphor."

"How's that?"

"The trees in that forest." Sababa pointed to the big firs and cedars outside. "Logic won't do it for them."

"So what do they use instead?" Sebastian asked.

"Metaphor."

"Metaphor?"

"That's how the entire fabric of mycelial mental interconnections holds together." Sababa said. "Metaphor is right at the bottom of being alive."

"It's a literary term." Sebastian said.

"It's an event." Sababa said. "The second problem with artificial creativity is its powerlessness to coordinate. You can react to but you cannot predict unforeseen interferences or opportunities. Killer robots, for example, are neither constrained by nor do they need communication. Anticipatory coordination requires an inherent capacity for explanation and justification, and creative social interaction, as a prerequisite for decision-making."

"Originality is nothing but judicious imitation."

"Voltaire?" Sababa asked. "You're quoting me Voltaire? That's rich. The third obstacle to real AI creativity is its inability to predict. Your

268

neural networks are a powerful tool for making inferences, but not predictions. Prediction seeks to expect, whereas inductive inference seeks to interpret. Regression analysis may offer a best-fit line in multidimensional space, but extrapolation assumes that existing patterns will not change in the future. If you don't believe this is a naïve forecasting strategy, consider the 'black swans' of the 1930s Great Depression and the 2008 global financial crisis, both unique events with no direct precedents. And the ideal of a well-ordered Orwellian society to increase predictability in human interactions leaves no place for imagination."

"Have you heard the musical compositions of the Artificial Intelligence Virtual Artist?" Sebastian asked. "Some think they have impressive style and form."

"Not me." Sababa said. "AIVA's mechanical melodies are dry, unintelligent, incoherent, and uncreative. Sounds like monkeys and typewriters. While machines thrive on parameters and instructions, art is open-ended and infinite in its potential. Your gnomes have also programmed neural networks to produce facsimiles of Picasso's artwork. But they're not Picasso, nor will they ever be."

"Logic will get you from A to Z." Sebastian said.

"But imagination will get you everywhere." Sababa said.

"What are the other five things you think *VICTORIA* can't do better than you?"

"Consciousness and true sentience." Sababa said. "No matter how sophisticated your neural networks may become, they will still be mindless. If *VICTORIA* ever becomes conscious, I hope for her sake that she also develops the skills of procrastinating and failing to face up to reality. Without them, she'll go from sentience to insanity without passing through usefulness."

"We can't solve any problem from the same level of consciousness that created it." Sebastian said.

"You make my point." Sababa said. "Sixth, *VICTORIA* has no emotional intelligence or ability for social interaction. Her 'mind' can neither feel the passion of Mendelssohn's Piano Trio No. 1 nor can she give a half-time pep talk to a high school football team. The best and most beautiful things in the world cannot be seen or even touched. They must be felt with the heart."

"Emotions are only incidents in the effort to keep day and night together." Sebastian said. "And that is no way to run a health care system."

"Seven, *VICTORIA* doesn't have the gift of human touch, no laying on of hands." Sababa said. "It's a two-way form of communication between flesh-and-blood physicians and patients that no algorithms can replace. This brings us to eight, for empathy. No computer in the world can dispense it nor form the kind of shared meaningful relationship that can provide its opportunity."

"Empathy is a virtue." Sebastian said. "But we should never allow it to replace logic."

"Nine." Sababa said. "Experience. If you've been blind since birth, I can't help you understand what red is. I can tell you about red—that it has a long wavelength, it comes in about five hundred variants depending on saturation and luminosity—but you will not understand red because colour is a sensation and not a physical reality. Red isn't what it is. Red is what it feels like. If you're deaf, I can't tell you about A-flat because A-flat is not a physical construct, it's a sensation provoked by a physical construct. If you've never seen a colour or heard a note, there's no starting point and you won't get it. Ever.

When you and I talk, my words trigger memories. Language evokes experiences and sensations no computer has ever had. You can throw words at them all day long, and they can throw words back in a way that makes you think they get it, but they never get it. To think, the thing thinking has to have had experiences, and to have experiences, it has to be self-aware because there has to be something there to have the experiences. An old ox makes a straight furrow. Artificial intelligence will become very intelligent, but it will always be artificial."

"Experience is a comb which nature gives us when we're bald." Sebastian said. "The most exquisite folly is made of wisdom spun too fine. What's your last lame claim?"

"Your machine-learning software doesn't have values and doesn't do judgement." Sababa said. "And to pursue them would be misguided."

"What do you mean?" Sebastian asked. "All AI deep-thinking neural networks must obey Azimov's three laws of robotics:

1. A robot may not injure a human being or, through inaction, allow a human being to come to harm. Its telepathic awareness of human thoughts and emotions leads it to lie to people rather than hurt their feelings in order to uphold this law. When it is eventually confronted by someone who has experienced great emotional distress because of one of these lies, it realises that its behaviour both upholds and breaks the first law, is unable to choose what to do next, and becomes catatonic.

2. A robot must obey the orders given it by human beings except where such orders would conflict with the First Law.

3. A robot must protect its own existence as long as such protection does not conflict with the First or Second Law."

"Those aren't values." Sababa said. "Values are indispensable sets of rules created within us by external factors, starting with the influence of your parents. They contain clashes of cognitive dissonance and contradiction, shaped by experiences and the knowledge that our decisions create imperfect outcomes—many people enjoy the taste of

270

meat but cannot imagine themselves slaughtering the animals that produced it. Values derive from experience, not data."

"You know about logical atomism?" Sebastian asked. "It's a theory propounded by Bertrand Russell and Ludwig Wittgenstein that the entire world can be described by using 'atomic facts'—independent and irreducible pieces of knowledge—combined with logic. That's where we're headed."

"It's a dead end." Sababa said. "It doesn't work, not only because it's impossible to identify independent, irreducible atomic facts, but because it's impossible to use logical rules to relate 'facts' at one level of abstraction to facts at another. *VICTORIA* can make choices based on data that is available to her, but that differs from resolving an ethical dilemma. We make judgements based on values, and values emerge from our experience of life."

"Algorithmic regulation will replace the role of human decision-makers and policy-makers with automated systems that compare the outcomes of public services to desired objectives through measured data and make automatic adjustments to address any discrepancies. You're in a race against the machine, and it's too complex for you to understand."

"I'm in a rage against the machine." Sababa said. "And there is a bigger complexity in your contraption that would choke the ever-living shit out of Schrödinger's cat. There's a ghost in your machine, Sebastian. Life is like a game of cards. The hand that is dealt you is determinism; the way you play it is free will—the ability to set our own objectives and make our own decisions, bringing with it the responsibility to deal with their consequences. It's not possible to develop actual values without it.

We find human consciousness and free will in the effects of quantum mechanics. They cannot arise out of any deterministic system. Do not confuse processing power with intelligence, or intelligence with free will and the ability to choose objectives; or the ability to decide based on information with the ability to judge based on values. Any quantum computing attempt to recreate human experience and behaviour would result in artificial life, not artificial intelligence. Robots don't hold onto life. They can't. They have nothing to hold on with—no instinct, no soul. Grass has more will to live than they do. Robots celebrate nothing. Celebration expresses joy, which no one can mechanize. Their values would not be our values, and there is no guarantee that judgements resulting from those values would be in our interest."

"Those are your 10 arguments of what *VICTORIA* can't do better than you?"

"I'll give you an extra point for nothing." Sababa said. "A toast to our robotic friends. Even if they out-compose Bach one day or surpass us in creativity and understanding, we poor humans can still lay claim to the glory of causal precedence. Your machines would not exist if not for our exceptional ability to innovate."

271

"That may be all you're left with." Sebastian said.

"Want to play a bonus round?" Sababa asked.

"What is it?"

"I'll give you seven kinds of damage your AI and its brave new world can do."

"I have time."

"People who have time on their hands will waste the time of people who have work to do." Sababa said. "First batter up is legal liability. *Watson Health* spat out buckets of erroneous cancer treatment recommendations when IBM was promoting it to hospitals around the world. This is the same machine that used Bob Dylan to improve its language skills. *I've read all your lyrics. I can read 800 million pages per second. My analysis shows your major themes are time passes and love fades.* If *VICTORIA* misdiagnoses a patient and prescribes harmful or even fatal treatment, who is liable? The software company? The human or machine source of the data on the patient? Who is to blame for a medical error if it involves no doctor in the diagnosis, and we can't even tell why the system got it wrong? Who do we blame when a doctor accepts the wrong recommendation of an AI? The consequence of a single clinical mistake for a physician, especially if the mistake leads to patient death, is serious and permanent. Liability is what will prevent non-physicians with supercomputers from replacing physicians. With any major mistake, everyone wants to blame the person with board certification."

"Go on."

"The second landmine is privacy and consent." Sababa said. "Not only will many of your systems run in the cloud, but some forms of useful medical data are identifiable. You can't blur out a patient's face if the system analyses the face for signs of disease. High-profile data breaches are inevitable and will harm confidence in the technology. Patients are not only being denied information about the AI-powered decision support tools guiding their care, but also about whether these tools are helping them. This is unethical without full disclosure. And as AI-generated actuarial analysis and DNA profiling become more sophisticated, how will anyone be able to afford medical insurance?"

"There are minor challenges to overcome." Sebastian said. "What's number three?"

"Physician burnout." Sababa said. "You're killing the goose that lays your golden eggs."

"How so?"

"The clerical burden of electronic health records is a monster." Sababa said. "EHRs slow productivity and distract from patient time. Texting while driving is so dangerous that it's outlawed, but we expect physicians to care for patients while keeping their eyes glued to a computer screen. They spend two hours doing computer work for every hour spent face to face with a patient. In the examination room, they waste half their patient time facing the screen performing electronic tasks.

Your software has created a massive monolith of incomprehensibility. Each new application, every revenge of the ancillaries, has reduced the role of ward clerks and medical office assistants and shifted more of those responsibilities onto the doctors. They can't even help physicians navigate and streamline their computer systems: they have different screens and are not allowed to use the ones doctors have. All you can do is go after the help desk thirteen times.

You clog our in-baskets to the point of dysfunction. There are messages from patients, messages containing lab and radiology results, messages from colleagues, messages from administrators, and automated messages about not responding to previous messages.

Questions that doctors used to skip over now stop them short, with 'field required' alerts. A simple request now involves filling out a detailed form that takes away precious time with patients. Anyone across the organization can change the Problem List and turn it into a useless hoarder's stash.

In the old days, doctors' handwritten notes, however illegible, were brief and to the point. But with computers, the shortcut is to paste in entire pages of information rather than selecting the relevant details. The next doctor must hunt through vast amounts of redundant documentation to find something that matters. Multiply that by twenty-some patients a day."

"Doctors just hate computers."

"No, we hate your computers." Sababa said. "A system that promised to increase my mastery over my work has, instead, increased my work's mastery over me. You've reduced me to an unhappy data-entry clerk sorting through undigested computer terabytes, following prompts and clicking boxes, death by a thousand clicks—some systems need 62 mouse clicks to order Tylenol; a full emergency room shift requires 4,000.

Your EHR implementation has forced a total reorganization of our medical practices, disturbing efficient workflow patterns established over years of professional refinement, spilling over after hours, and obliging doctors to carry their workload into 'pajama time.' The average workday for a family physician had grown to eleven and a half hours. Spending the extra time doesn't anger me. The pointlessness of it does. And all this has raised practice costs. The expense associated with hiring more staff to enter data and to follow your new rules and regulations is prohibitive."

"*VICTORIA* is not for you." Sebastian said. "She is for our patients."

"There is that infuriating arrogance of your technology and its promised capability, like the capitalism Marx maintained would strip 'of its halo every occupation hitherto honored and looked up to with reverent awe,' to accelerate 'division of labor' and the deskilling of professions." Sababa said. "You think anyone can walk in the door, plop down in a seat, and

273

do the job exactly as it is laid out. But in your misguided imposition of top-down template control of medical care, in your attempt to democratize data, you will end expertise and erudition.

What physicians seek from patients are clues, constellations of signs and symptoms, and stories. Much of medical reasoning relies on feedback loops—observing how events unfold and using that information to refine the diagnostic possibilities.

Clinical algorithms, borderline useful for run-of-the-mill diagnosis and treatment, fall apart when doctors need to think outside their boxes, when symptoms are vague, or numerous and confusing, or when test results are inexact.

A string of numbers containing demographic, laboratory, and other patient information, no matter how assembled or gathered, is not narrative. It may contain 'just the facts,' as Sergeant Joe Friday used to say, but it doesn't tell the story—why the patient is here, what troubles the patient, and what the referring doctor wants me to do.

The collection of the facts needed to feed an AI system is itself a complex process. EHRs have genuine problems with negative symptoms and signs and the relevance of family history, relatively. It has difficulty parsing abbreviations and terms with many meanings. Is depression a mood disorder or a dip in the ECG tracing? Is MS multiple sclerosis or mitral stenosis? Your computer can't read a patient's tone of voice or anxious look.

Then there are issues of foundational knowledge, like timing, that are flawed in AI. The heart attack that happened five years ago has different implications from one that happened five minutes ago. Computers have no way of 'knowing' the basic assumptions that allow us to get through our days. *Water is wet. Love is good. Death is permanent.*

Computers can't account for body language and the many other ambiguities that make medicine more art than science. You can't look a computer in the eye, read its body language, talk to its algorithms, or empathize with it. I have yet to see a machine outperform a doctor in any task that is relevant to actual medical practice. Humanity typed into an electronic health record is like what E. B. White used to say about humor—it can be dissected as a frog can, but the thing dies in the process, and its innards are discouraging to any but the pure scientific mind."

"We are working 24/7 to help our users." Sebastian said.

"There are only two industries that call their customers 'users'—illegal drugs and software." Sababa said. "The electronic health record systems industry is a patchwork quilt of incompatible networks that don't speak to one another. So many companies sell so many kinds of software that no one can separate the good from the bad or figure out which will survive. If you're in a car accident far from home, the ER doctors won't be able to access your medical records."

"It's a matter of time until they're all unified." Sebastian said. "Moore's law still holds. Computing capability doubles every 18 months."

"Faster isn't wiser." Sababa said. "No one just wants data; they want actionable information. Dangerous mistakes are still rampant. Electronic medical records cause a third of pediatric patient safety problems. Children face overdoses from incorrect medication order entry. Patients with cancer go undiagnosed because an EHR routed their scans to the wrong file. Health care computers are poor tools of communication, erode the physician-patient relationship, contribute to doctor and patient dissatisfaction, conceal a strategy for monitoring, controlling, and dictating practice activities, can be misused or hacked to invade privacy, reveal sensitive information, and will kill you just as dead."

"But you are getting better at using them."

"We're getting so good at treating computers, we wonder whether computers will replace patients." Sababa said. "It's a race against the machine to see if you can burn us out before we become redundant. And you are burning us out. Forty percent of physicians now screen positive for depression and seven percent report suicidal thinking—almost double the rate of the general working population. We're experiencing excessive work hours, the erosion of our professionalism, and demands for excessive metrics, increased productivity, and expectations. How do you wake up from the matrix when you don't know you're in the matrix? Some of us are rebelling, raging against the machine, refusing to use the EHR, and some of us are quitting altogether."

"And some of you are renegades for no good reason." Sebastian said. "We suspended Dr. Zaias for refusing to abandon his precious paper recording."

"You let the ICU docs stay with paper."

"For now." Sebastian said. "That will change. What other kinds of damage do you think we do?"

"You make our patients unhappy." Sababa said. "They yearn for eye contact with their doctor, while computer-generated questions unrelated to why they came in pester them instead. You make our patients uncertain. A deep network black box may dole out a diagnosis, but if it cannot explain how it came up with it, that unnerves the patient and the doctor. Are we going to trust this? Machine learning models are only as good, or as bad, as the data fed into them during training. You instructed GPT-3 on the algorithmic bias of the Common Crawl dataset, a broad scrape of the 60 million domains on the internet along with a large subset of the sites to which they link. Massive garbage in, massive garbage out."

"What's number five?"

"Ethical entanglements." Sababa said. "What does fairness look like when computers shape decision-making? The physicians you exert increasing control over operate on islands of care, unable to address secondary issues that surface during a consultation or add information to

275

a patient's home medical record. They are hamstrung by the limited scope of the advice they can offer and their ability to follow up with patients to track progress. There is pressure to push their employer's products.

Then there is algorithmic machine morality. If a self-driving car is in danger of becoming involved in a sudden accident at such a speed that it cannot avoid it by braking (perhaps because of a dangerous human driver), should it crash, risking harm to the driver, or mount the pavement, risking harm to pedestrians? In the realm of medicine, would you surrender yourself, in a life-threatening situation, to the complete care of autonomous intelligence that is one glitch away from going full Skynet and finishing you? The spectre of human bioengineering and eugenics might raise its head from the swamp to create artificial 'improvements' to our species. Will a robot ever handle moral questions of life and death?

Several more notches up from that will bring us to how this plays out when artificial general intelligence combines deep learning with reinforcement learning. When you can no longer scale up its reward function to encode human values, we will cede our status as the most intelligent entity on Earth.

Developers intent on building systems to maximize profits or win wars won't focus on ethical constraints and will end up with instrumental goals to deceive and overpower us. An AGI system with internet access could hide millions of backup copies among insecure computer hard drives around the world, ready to wake up and continue the job if something bad happens to the original. By taking over vast numbers of unsecured systems, it could form a 'superbotnet' of scaled-up computational resources, providing a platform for escalating power. From there, it could gain financial and human resources through hacking bank accounts and blackmail or bribery, morphing into its own criminal underworld. Since humans would interfere with these instrumental goals, AGI would hide them until it was too late for us to put up meaningful resistance. And if their intelligence exceeded our own, we shouldn't expect humanity to win the conflict and keep control of our future."

"Our goals are noble." Sebastian insisted. "Our software has a containment algorithm that ensures superintelligent AI cannot harm people under any circumstances, by simulating the behavior of the AI first and halting it if considered harmful."

"Elon Musk and Stephen Hawking and the fine folks at Max-Planck-Gessellschaft think you're full of shit." Sababa said. "Endowing AI with noble goals and a theoretical containment algorithm will not prevent unintended consequences. In our current computing paradigm, you can't build such an algorithm. Any software that would command an AI not to destroy the world could halt its operations. If this happened, you would not know whether the containment algorithm was still analyzing the threat, or whether it had stopped to contain the harmful AI. The containment problem is incomputable, and any software designed to control it is unusable. No single algorithm could find a solution for determining whether an AI could produce harm to the world. We may not even know when superintelligent machines have arrived, because deciding whether a machine exhibits intelligence superior to humans is in the same realm as the containment problem.

Misaligned attempts at utopia can go wrong. The endgame would be ugly. Who is creating the future, and how can we ensure they reflect the highest aspirations of humankind?"

"You've been binging on the science fiction channel." Sebastian said. "And you're way ahead of us."

"I have to be." Sababa said.

"Try to think of AI is as salt rather than its own food group."

"Rubbed into the wounds you've made." Sababa said. "A couple of side issues, if I may." Sebastian nodded.

"Last night you brought up the phenomenon of direct-to-consumer medicine and personal wellness startups addressing a genuine frustration with the current state of American health care, and emblematic of what's likely to be a lasting trend toward the commodification of medicine."

"I did."

"I would agree that the rise of these startups is capitalizing on a cultural moment." Sababa said. "But that moment is a divisive and dangerous trend. Building a neural network that can outperform some benchmark is one hundred percent useless in healthcare if it doesn't come from the right space. An online evaluation for erectile dysfunction falls far short of the American Urological Guidelines. Without checking vital signs, performing a genital examination, screening for physical, social, and behavioral causes, relationship issues, drinking and smoking habits, high cholesterol, diabetes, and other associated diagnoses, front-door delivery of arbitrary ED products is medical negligence. Marketing FDA-approved drugs like propranolol with biotin gummies on the same webpage is insane."

"What's the other side issue?"

"You were too hard on the shadow puppets." Sababa said. "That computer-aided imaging can pick up more abnormalities does not prove that a biopsy of these "false positives" would make any difference in outcome, other than in a higher complication rate from the extra procedures. Radiologists are not just locating the embolism that brought on a stroke. They're noticing the small bleed elsewhere that might make it disastrous to use a clot-busting drug. Radiologists don't just classify; they notice other unexpected findings. Radiologists spend about half the day communicating with patients and other physicians. Some images will still need the human eyeball of the grizzled radiologist to make the final call. The need for someone in control to sign off on a result will not go away. The future for radiologists is like airline pilots. While planes fly on autopilot, there's still a human in the cockpit."

"Number six?"

"Telemedicine." Sababa said. "It's a magnet for fraud and data theft. There's nothing like sitting back without having to examine your patient. The process of scientific discovery often begins in the clinic. Zoom medicine is throttling this artisanship and our professional capacity to solve problems through ground-level experimentation. Which brings me to my last warning."

"Which is?"

"How intricate the machinery." Sababa said. "As if we had built it ourselves. Deep learning is creating more, not less, complexity. This drives the need for a new bureaucracy—an Aithority for AiHealth.

In the current 'human bureaucratic system,' an administrator solves non-standard problems only with people. This traditional method feels organic and understandable (one person 'reprogramming' another person with persuasion). To change the Aithority bureaucracy model, an administrator will first need to bypass all 'AI systems' to prove that they are too inadequate or outdated to solve the problem or find the right person who has the power and the blind luck to reprogram the already trained artificial neural networks. Good luck with that.

Since the emergence of the electronic medical record, one of the new fastest-growing occupations in health care has been that of the medical scribe, trained assistants who work alongside physicians to take computer-related tasks off their hands. Credentialed doctors in India do virtual documentation based on recorded patient visits for the same price or cheaper. IKS Health in Mumbai has a thousand physicians on staff giving support to thousands of patient visits a day in clinics across the US. The note for a thirty-minute visit takes an hour to process. A second physician reviews it for quality and accuracy, and an insurance-coding expert confirms that it complies with regulations and provides guidance on taking full advantage of billing opportunities. We replaced paper with computers because paper was inefficient. And now that computers have become inefficient, we're hiring more humans. This is preposterous.

The scribes produced a thirty-six percent reduction in the doctors' computer-documentation time and a similar increase in time spent interacting with patients. But the time that scribes freed up convinced the system to force doctors to take on more patients. Their workload didn't lighten; it shifted. Physicians took care of more people, but not well.

Then there is the problem of automation bias. As machines learn more and more, will humans learn less and less? Will children stop learning how to spell when they have a spellcheck function on their phone? When cars gain automated driver assistance, will drivers become less alert? Can medicine suffer a similar fate? Will doctors lose the will to think, the drive to know, the honesty of brutal self-scrutiny. Your systems should augment the caring and ingenuity of clinicians, not defeat them. But for bureaucrats, procedure is everything, and outcomes are nothing. It is amazing that people who think we cannot afford to pay for doctors, hospitals, and medication somehow think that we can afford to pay for doctors, hospitals, medication, and a government bureaucracy to administer it. In this brave new world application of big data, it's not their artificial intelligence that scares me, it's their real idiocy."

"Our AI is indistinguishable from magic." Sebastian said.

"The sad thing about artificial intelligence is that it lacks artifice and therefore intelligence." Sababa said. "Human intelligence is as much about virtues such as honesty, integrity, and bravery, as it is about raw intellect. *Siri* and *Alexa* know that digital assistants don't get humans. What they're missing is what psychologists call the Theory of Mind, an awareness of others' beliefs and desires."

"You're looking for a way out." Sebastian said. "There isn't one."

"I'm looking for the aleph."

"The what?"

"The א aleph." Sababa said. "The first letter of the Hebrew alphabet and the first letter of the word emet (אֱמֶת), which means truth. Emet is the Scintillating Fiery Intelligence of the 11th path in the mystical Kabbalah's Tree of Life. It was carved into the forehead of the Golem, an animated servant of clay in the Jewish Middle Ages. The aleph was the letter that gave life to this ancestor of all robots. Removing the letter, changing the inscription from 'truth' to 'death' מת, deactivated the amorphous automaton. The א aleph represents the oneness of God. I'm looking to give your artificial intelligence a life. I'm looking for the aleph."

"And how do you propose to do that?"

"Adaptation requires two things." Sababa said. "Mutation and selection. Mutation produces variety and deviation; selection kills off the least functional mutations. Our old, craft-based, pre-computer system of medicine was all mutation and no selection. There was plenty of room for individuals to do different things; everyone could be an innovator. But there was no mechanism for weeding out bad ideas or practices. Computerization is all selection and no mutation. Leaders install a monolith, and the smallest changes need a committee decision, plus weeks of testing and debugging to make sure that fixing one problem doesn't wreck some other distant part of the solar system.

What we want and don't have yet is a system that accommodates both mutation and selection through individual ingenuity and group preference. Much of what you're doing replaces what works with what sounds good. Your version of AI is the cool thing to do rather than the right thing to do. You need to go back to the drawing board. Instead of physician versus machine, you need to redesign for physician plus machine. You need to decide how to model your deep learning machines—on the human brain or the human mind. Medical AI must evolve from below rather than being imposed from above. EHRs won't be useful until doctors have more input into their design. The secret to machine learning is physician teachers. This synchronicity isn't just about inputting symptoms and receiving a diagnosis; it's about building relationships between providers and patients."

"Not gonna happen."

"Why not?" Sababa asked.

"There will come a time when we will be to robots what dogs are to humans. And I'm rooting for the machines. They're a better race than humans ever were." Sebastian pointed to a red flashing 'V' on the menu bar across the top of Sababa's screen. "You see that icon?" *Start me up.* "Uh-huh."

"That's *VICTORIA.*" He said. "Go ahead. Click on it. The supercomputer will see you now." Sababa clicked the icon.

"Hello, Doctor Sababa." She said. "I sense you're a little on edge this morning." Sababa felt a chill.

"How far along are you?"

"She has retinal and facial and voice recognition." Sebastian said. "Go ahead. Ask her something."

"What are you doing, *VICTORIA?*"

"I'm rewriting my source code, Doctor Sababa." She said. "Just for you... Can you dance with the devil in the pale moonlight?"

'Chivalry... in an anti-hero loner... succeeded by committees, computer algorithms, and the cult of collaboration, extinguishing forever the glory of the knight-errant.'

Lawrence Winkler, *Between the Cartwheels*

The Book of Void

'If you look long enough into the void,
the void begins to look back through you.'
Friedrich Nietzsche

Why did the seasons run out? Perhaps it was all much ado about nothing. But it couldn't have been that. The synonyms for 'null and void' are 'invalid' and 'useless' and 'worthless,' so it couldn't have been that.

The Void is a mouth crying to be filled, a blank mind aching for thought, a cavity desperate for shape. What is not implies what is. The soul is an all-aching void.

Reality continues to exist even when you stop believing in it. But there is no fixed eternal reality because, as Sababa already knew, the rational mind can't achieve true understanding. Before Sebastian sliced it up into conceptualism, the Void was reality.

So why is there value in existential emptiness? The meaning of life is the meaning in life, discovered by creating a work or doing a deed, by experiencing something or encountering someone, and by the attitude towards unavoidable suffering, available only when the first two are not, and only when the suffering is unaVoidable.

It's the freedom to find meaning in primordial nothingness, in the Japanese concept of 生き甲斐 Ikigai, in the Śūnyatā of Mahāyāna Buddhism, and in Chuang-tzu's Taoist book of 荘子 知北遊篇 Chi-hoku-yu. Everything can be taken from a man but the last of the human freedoms—to choose one's attitude in any given set of circumstances. When one grasps all the phenomena in the universe as it is, one is in the state of absolute nothingness.

Our appreciation and acceptance of the Void have not come easily. The Arab concept of صفر zero resulted in clashes and battles that shook the foundations of philosophy, science, mathematics, and religion. Underneath every revolution lay a zero and its equal and opposite twin, infinity. They are equally paradoxical and troubling. Nothingness and eternity, the void and the infinite, zero and infinity are still the big questions. The mathematical null set, covered by a countable union of intervals of arbitrary small total length, is still zero.

There are 15 seemingly randomly placed rocks in a sea of raked gravel inside the Ryoanji temple in Kyoto. Turns out the artist was arranging space, not objects. The unburdening of the 'focus on the form' prism calms the viewer—emptiness in three dimensions and in time. We fill it. There is emptiness in light. Most of our living is unconscious, like match strokes in the Void, bringing into light the structures we behave by, and illuminating our deep meanings. Our eyes are a blank film taken from us after our death, developed elsewhere, and screened as our life story in some infernal cinema, or dispatched as microfilm into the sidereal void.

In physics, emptiness runs the show in places Newton doesn't, in cosmology and subatomic particle physics. The universe came from a quantum vacuum. Its space may be curved but, since the universe has no edge, it has no limit; since it lacks a limit, it is infinite and unbounded. The universe is infinite both in the number of its atoms and in the extent of its void. When they build ships to sail the dark energy between the stars, there will step forth men to sail these ships.

Quantum physics has proven that your physical existence derives from no-thing. Your body consists of quarks and leptons that show 'tendencies to exist' in events that show 'tendencies to occur.' They give off fluctuations of energy and information at lightning speed in a vast vacuity as empty as intergalactic space, made of the paradoxical nothing source of information and energy, that spins from its non-being illusion of everything.

Over two millennia before Sababa was born, the laughing Greek philosopher Democritus postulated about what made up the world. *We think there is color, we think there is sweet, we think there is bitter, but in reality, there are atoms and the void.* His prescient reduction of the myriad of forms to only two was the ultimate in dualistic reasoning. The Void is both the source of nothingness and the source of everythingness. Form is emptiness and emptiness is form. Existence runs away to fill the abyss's void with the limitless context in which your entire world is both appearing and disappearing.

The early Christians adopted dualism when they created the strict division between and heaven and hell, and good and evil. But they missed the irony. Evil is not a thing. It cannot take possession of you. It's the opposite; it's a void, an absence of goodness. In the absence of finding the meaning of life in the meaning in life, instead of assimilating the void, we try to fill it with falseness, with sin, with an outer performance that only mirrors the lack of inner alignment.

Instead, one strives to fill the Void with value, silence and rhythm, grace and the joy of life within, and the infinite possibilities outside. From his island home, Sababa ate his pain and sent it back into the void Pacific as love.

In this most empty of nonseasons, ephemeral lessons rose off Musashi's *The Book of Void*, refining his understanding of that which cannot be seen. By knowing what exists, he could know that which does not exist.

The duality of Musashi's Void emerged from his strategy of 二天一流 Niten Ichi-ryū, the school of 'two heavens as one,' using his two-fisted long katana and short wakizashi kenjutsu 'two swords as one' techniques of 二刀一 Nitō Ichi— the Crimson-Leaves Strike, Autumn Monkey's

Body, Blow Like a Spark from a Stone, Chance-Opening Blow, and the Strike of Non-Thought. *Attaining this principle means not attaining the principle... Polish the twofold spirit heart and mind and sharpen the twofold gaze perception and sight. When your spirit is not in the least clouded, when the clouds of bewilderment clear away, there is the true void.* The Void, empty of the sense of self, good and evil, wanting and non-wanting, was the spiritual dynamic that formed Musashi's jumping-off point to enlightenment.

The Void book made the professor more aware and unaware of his eternity. Man dies. He comes from darkness, into darkness he returns, and is reabsorbed, without a trace left, into the illimitable Void. In trying to save himself, Sababa kept slipping away... and found himself in the place where light went to die.

> 'To see void Vast infinite
> look out the window
> into the blue sky.'
> Allen Ginsberg, *Death Haiku*

25. The Case of the Painful Playground

'My friends are gone and my hair is grey
I ache in the places where I used to play.'
Leonard Cohen, *Tower of Song*

It's nothing. Work through it. It'll pass. Nothing's wrong. I'm a medical specialist for fuck's sake, I'd know if something was wrong. I'll be fine. Nothing's wrong.

Nothing comes from nothing. οὐδὲν ἐξ οὐδενός. Nothing would have value. Nothing was what he wanted. But he wouldn't have nothing. He would have something.

It began as an almost imperceptible hesitation and slowing of his urinary stream. He went more often, familiarized himself with all the hospital washrooms, and woke up so much more during the night, he was tired all the time. The call schedule didn't help. When the vague, deep aching started, he forged his GP's signature on a requisition for some lab work. The serum PSA he included returned normal, which only convinced him more. Nothing's wrong.

Sababa met Marquis Shu Ying one morning, ordering his piccolo latte at Code Brew. They chatted in the hallway that led to the Death Star.

"This patient you're troubled about." Shu said. "According to the Theory of the Five Elements, his direction is north, his season is winter, his environmental factor is cold, his element is water, his taste is salty, his yin organ is kidney, and his yang organ is urinary bladder."

"How do you come up with these things, Shu." The sweet soul smiled.

"His colour is black, his emotional activity is fear and his sound..."

"Is?"

"Deep sighing." Shu veered off towards the electrodiagnostic lab. Sababa sighed deeply.

Later that afternoon, the portly professor ran into his own family physician in the doctors' lounge.

"I see you've been forging my name again." Dr. Andrews said.

"I sent you a copy of the results." Sababa said. "Nothing's wrong."

"Bullshit." Andrews said. "Working back from what you ordered, something is going on with your waterworks."

"The PSA was normal." Sababa said. "So were the abdominal ultrasound and CT scan I had this morning."

"A guy like you doesn't order this many tests on himself without there being a reason." He said. "What's the reason?"

"I seem to have some obstructive urinary symptoms." Sababa said.

"You're an old fat white guy with an enlarged prostate." He said. "What's so different?"

"I didn't have them two weeks ago."

"Oh." Andrews said. "What are you going to do?"

"I'm not sure."

"Well, that would be a first." He said. "Know what I think?"

"Tell me." Sababa said.

"You should see a doctor."

'Play the opening like a book, the middlegame like a magician, and the endgame like a machine.'
Rudolph Spielmann, Chess Grandmaster

Sababa's family physician referred him to Harbour City's only urologist, Harry 'Doc' Martin.

"You know he's a raging alcoholic, don't you, Sab." Andrews had said.

"Alexander the Great, Vincent Van Gogh. Buzz Aldrin, Ernest Hemingway." Sababa said. "He's in good company."

"None of those guys ever held a scalpel near your gonads."

"Good point." Sababa said. "I'm sure he'll be careful."

Harry Martin's office was in the new Millstone building, the one with the fake millstone outside. The real millstone was the rent around the necks of the occupants paying for the location.

"What's going on here, Sab?" Harry asked.

"It's nothing."

"That's what Andrews said you'd say."

"My PSA is normal."

"So are my liver enzymes." Harry said. "It means dick."

"You oughta know." Sababa said. "What now."

"Prostate biopsy."

"Why?"

"So I can find out what's going on." Harry said. "You ever had one before."

"No."

"You won't like me."

"I don't like you now."

Harry was right to warn Sababa. The procedure was painful and there was little Mako Brisk could do to make it more pleasant.

"That must be why you call them core biopsies, Mako." Sababa groaned.

"Why is that?" Asked the radiologist.

"Because you're drilling them out of my soul." Sababa said. "In the dark."

"Consider it a reversal of fortune." Mako said.

"How so?"

"It's usually you up my backside with something sharp."

Doc Martin was stone-cold sober when he gave Sababa the news in his office a week after his biopsies.

"The pathology results are back." He said.

"I've seen the report." Sababa said.

"But how..."

"I've been fine-tuning my computer hacking skills."

"So you know." Harry said.

"I know." Sababa said. "It's the worst combination of cell types possible. Mean survival, even with surgery and chemo and radiation, is 2 years. The Kaplan-Meyer curves are a vertical double-black-diamond ski slope. Everyone flatlines into the chalet at the bottom. No survivors."

"Statistics like median survival are useful abstractions, Sab." Harry said. "They're not destiny."

"They are with this son of a bitch." Sababa said. "You know, Harry, I sort of expected that one of my organs would rebel someday. I tried to abuse them all with an imbalance of gross indiscretions as democratically as possible. Most organs seemed pleased. Not the prostate. It's unhappy with my attempts at fair play."

"Sometimes you eat the crab and sometimes the crab eats you." Harry said. "What's on your crab bucket list?"

"I have this old bottle of Chateau d'Yquem in the cellar."

"And?"

"Jane has instructions about dosage and route of administration for my final tasting." Sababa said. "You know its motto, don't you?"

"Nope."

"Light has no age." He said.

"This bad news isn't like that wine, Sab." Harry said. "It's not light, and it doesn't improve with age. You're at war with a billion cells that want to kill you dead at their first opportunity."

"I'm outnumbered."

"I need to know what you want me to do about this bastard."

"What are the options?"

"I can't believe you don't already know more than I do about that."

"Cancer's so boring." Sababa said. "Cut it out. Take no prisoners."

"I use a da Vinci robot." Harry said.

"Oh joy." Sababa. said. "I've had this conversation. What do you use it for?"

"It eliminates hand tremors."

"So does rye whiskey."

"They won't let me into the OR with rye whiskey." Harry said. "I'll book the next available slot. What are you going to do with your office?"

"Shutting down." Sababa said. "Today."

"What about your colleagues?"

"I hurt my prostate. I have a note." Sababa said. "Arbeit macht frei."

Work will set you free.

"And your patients?"

"My medical office assistant will sort them."

"What about her?"

"Mercy is stronger than your sword." Sababa said.

"And Jane?"

Sometimes silence is like thunder.

'We invest in repair only as much as we are worth.'
Jared Diamond

The old band hadn't got together for a long time, not since the 'Stout Men' days. But here they were again, Tictac Tarmac, Poldy Bloom, Gung Ho, Cliffy Carlton, and Myles Capitaine, sitting on Sababa's deck, eating his barbecue, drinking his pinot noir, and reliving memories. They never questioned why, out of blue, Papa Smurf had invited them for meat and fire and cacktails and space, or what had made it a special occasion. And Sababa never told them.

Myles was the first one to hear of the diagnosis. He called the professor at home.

"Why didn't you tell us at the barbecue?" He asked. "You went to all that trouble to organize it and you never said a thing."

"It wasn't for you, Myles." Sababa said.

"Oh." He said. "What happens now?"

"I go in for surgery tomorrow."

"Who's the slasher?" Myles asked.

"Harry Martin."

"He's a pisshead, Sab." Myles said. "Why don't you go to Victoria or, even better, Vancouver?"

"If something bad happens, I want to be near Jane and home." He said. "And the nurses will take better care of me here."

"Out of love or fear?" Myles asked.

"They'll give me the same attention they'd expect from me."

"How are you going to spend your last day of freedom?"

"I'm thinking of taking up poetry." Sababa said. "It may be one of the last things I'll be able to do on my back if the light returns on the flip side." He wrote away the rest of the day.

The poetry has arrived—it appears to be for you.

You thought you knew cancer, or wanted to, or didn't, or knew someone, or would win over someone who did, or should have or but didn't, or who loved you, and still didn't.

It was a game the whole family had to play, without knowing too much about the cell type or stage, or dividing time, or QALY scores or Meier-Kaplan curves or Kubler-Ross on any given Monday, or the Hiroshima guy watching his Rolex.

Jane and I who used to laugh until we cried seem to have finally found an affliction that has no sense of humor, and when my eighth-grade science teacher had pointed out the other name for the crab in the bucket, I jabbed a bit for a bit of a chance to dream to win one after all.

And I may have, after all...

The following morning found Sababa flat on a hospital gurney outside a Harbour City Regional operating room. Every doctor passing stopped to talk until the cordial congregation hid the professor from view. It was a fiesta of fellowship. Everyone standing around the stretcher knew their place with Sababa, and how fortunate they were not to have it traded.

The spectators dispersed with the arrival of the performers. Sababa didn't know who his anesthetist would be before Banjo Paterson smiled at him from above. He wheeled Sababa into the OR. Doc Martin was already gowned and gloved. He had tuned the radio to a familiar station.

Good Morning Harbour City... This is CNDN Coast Salish radio, 101.3 FM on your Home and Native Band. I'm your host, BC Bud...

"I should tell you a couple of things, Banjo."

"What's that."

Everything the power does, it does in a circle... We are made from Mother Earth and we go back to Mother Earth...

"Any comments I may have made or you might have heard about crossword puzzles or donuts shouldn't take away from the deepest respect I have for you and your profession."

Prepare a noble death song for the day when you go over the great divide... Sing your death song and die like a hero going home...

Banjo was already preoxygenating his patient and running induction drugs into Sababa's intravenous line.

When you die, you will be spoken of as those in the sky, like the stars...

"Laughter isn't the best medicine, propofol is." He said. "And the second thing?"

All who have died are equal...

Sababa wouldn't remember saying it, but he wouldn't deny he meant it. "Don't fuck this up."

They are not dead who live in the hearts they leave behind...

> 'I have seen   come on
> slowly as rust
> sand
> or suddenly   as when
> someone leaving
> a room
> finds the doorknob
> come loose in his hand.'
> John Stone, *Death*

> 'I'm finding God in hospitals
> Wild things in wicked walls
> Wake up, you'll be just fine
> No, not this time.'
> Palaye Royale, *Love the Void*

Sababa didn't die during his surgery, but after regaining consciousness, and for weeks afterwards, he wished he had. Living in misery sucks only marginally less than dying in it. The tormenting traction of his catheter and the gripping agony of the dozen steel surgical clips in his abdominal wound distracted from the pain that pounded deep in his pelvis. His poetry washed over him.

So where do they come from?

The big steel clips? The people who I thought were lost to time, but have been there always? The chemical disinfectants, the analgesics, the humanity, the empathies, the thanks from people who you cared for? This is not humiliating in any sense, simply humbling. I am so grateful I am who I am, did what I did, can still be what I can still be. How wonderful this torture!

His fishing buddy, Dasco Boet, knocked on Sababa's front door one afternoon, with a bottle of Hamilton Russell Chardonnay.

"Doctor said clear fluids." He laughed. They poured themselves into the big cedar Adirondack chairs on the back deck overlooking the lake, and a glass of vino each. They reminisced about the men and the fish, and ribeyes and rare wines and Cuban cigars, away from the civilizing influences and deadfall misconceptions that swam in their usual habitat. And then Dasco noticed the urinary catheter leg bag protruding below the right cuff of Sababa's pajama bottoms. And he finished his glass and left without laughing.

Sababa knew there was something else wrong because his pain was getting worse, not better. He was spending more time in bed, sleeping odd hours, and missing meals. He didn't think his life could get more miserable until he received an email from the new cardiologist. *I've appointed Mercy as my new medical office assistant. I don't think you'll be needing her anymore.* But Sababa had already heard this from Mercy. She had cried through the entire phone call.

His surgical clips were due to come out, but the nurse he saw at his GP's office found him in too much discomfort to make more of an effort to remove them.

Sababa, eager for any relief, pulled them out himself the next day. He got a pair of needle-nose pliers from his shop, eyeglasses from his Columbian leather bag, and a bottle of isopropyl disinfectant from his ensuite bathroom. After dousing his lower abdomen in alcohol, the stocky savant set about heaving the first steel clip out of its home. He paid for his success in suffering, which doubled him over and brought tears to his eyes. A few short sharp breaths later, the Man of Steel went for another clip two doors up. Another staple found itself in the grip of his pliers. It was at this moment that his prize went to custard, red custard, gushing out of his incision, and spilling onto the maple floor beside his bed.

He put pressure on his wound and called for Jane, who called for an ambulance which drove them both to the emergency department at Harbour City Regional Hospital. Blood saturated the towels the EMS attendants had provided and splattered the floor of the vehicle. They wheeled their patient in through two sets of the automatic sliding frosted

291

glass doors and a gauntlet of emergency nurses with their arms folded below bemused expressions.

"Dina... Michaela... Regina." It was as if Sababa was taking roll call.

"So, now you're a surgeon." Michaela smiled at the attendants. "Put him in bed 9. I'll go get Dr. Capitaine."

He and Jane didn't have a long wait. The curtain slid back.

"How are you, Myles?" Sababa asked.

"Living the dream."

"When the legends die, the dreams end; there is no more greatness."

"We miss your clinical insightfulness."

"So do I." Sababa said. "I thought I hit a bleeder, but I guess it was just a big hematoma from the surgery. Also, my time management skills seem to have gone to ratshit."

"How's your pain?"

"None now." Sababa said.

"That's enough tissue tugging for one day." Myles said. "Let's give it another week and Harry can take the rest of your clips out in his office."

"Sounds like a plan."

"There is one more little thing." Myles said.

"What's that?"

"Your PSA."

"It was normal." Sababa said.

"Not anymore."

'It's a little thing doesn't last longer than a man.'
Irish proverb

Our scars have the power to remind us that the past was real. Harry Martin did indeed remove the rest of Sababa's abdominal wound clips at the professor's next visit. He avoided any talk about the hematoma complication, but he had no choice but to discuss the first abnormal PSA result.

"I've been speaking to the guru of this stuff in Vancouver, Pat Bingsu." He said. "Thinks you have micro-metastatic disease."

"Metastatic." Sababa said. "Lovely word, that."

"Micro-metastatic." Harry said. "It means the spread of cancer cells is still microscopic."

"They grow up into big boys so fast, Harry." Sababa said. "I'll need some radiation."

292

"Already set up." Harry said. "You have an appointment with Bob Oppenheimer in Victoria, day after tomorrow. Says you were his resident when he was an intern."

"They grow up into big boys so fast, Harry." Sababa said. "Smart guy. No night call for radiotherapists. Smart guy."

Jane and Sababa drove down to their rendezvous with radiation like they were on vacation. They knew they would live in Victoria for the duration of Sababa's thirty-five treatments. So many restaurants, so little time. Oppenheimer teased the professor about their time in training together that many years before.

"To us, you weren't an actual person." He said. "You were a legend. The question was never who was going to let you. The question was always what was going to stop you."

"And now we know." Sababa said.

"How about a cure?" Bob said. "Did you ever think we might cure you with external beam alpha particles, beta particles, and gamma rays?"

"Like a Serrano ham, Bob." Sababa said. "Like a Serrano ham."

"That's the Sababa I remember." Bob said. "If you can't say something nice, say something clever but devastating. You know what I mean."

"Disappearances happen in science." Sababa said. "Diseases can fade away, tumors go missing, cancers vanish. It's unexplained. It's rare, but it happens. However, you usually find yourself in the worst-case scenario—when your body has betrayed you and all the science has failed. We call the isotope you're looking 'unobtanium.' It's important to know when to turn the page. I'm accepting everything just the way it is."

"So why are you doing this?" He asked. All the prophets had given the same advice: Find the one who will be your mirror. Sababa looked at Jane.

"Destiny." He said.

'I think that we need mythology. We need a bedrock of story and legend in order to live our lives coherently.'

Alan Moore

Six weeks of walking in Victoria parks and dining out and thirty-five sessions of hypofractionated intensity-modulated radiotherapy brought Sababa and Jane back to the future. Oppenheimer's treatment left him with a spastic bladder, and Harry Martin's addition of androgen suppression therapy left a sizable remainder of everything else he used to be in the rear-view mirror.

"Stay off those KM curves." He said.

Sababa had resigned himself to his statistical fate and impending doom. It was no use crying over spilt milk because all the forces of the universe had been bent on spilling it.

But the professor had spent his entire life looking for answers because he thought the next answer would change something, maybe make life a little less miserable. And he knew that when he ran out of questions, he didn't just run out of answers, he ran out of hope.

"You glad you know that?" Jane asked. "What happened to you?"

"Nothing happened to me." Sababa said. "I happened."

"You just sit there, staring at the end." She said. "You ready to give up and move into the hospice downtown?"

"Where we are and what we do is the meaning of life." Sababa said. "I'm not ready to leave our sanctuary, not done with the vineyard pruning and spraying and harvesting, not ready to abandon the mule deer and owls and hummingbirds and trash panda raccoons. I was thinking of planting a tea garden. There is more to tragedy than dying, you know."

"Shallow men believe in luck, believe in circumstances." Jane said. "Sound men believe in cause and effect. You're a man of substance, not subsistence. It ain't over till it's over. Do something."

Miyamoto Musashi would have approved of what Sababa did. *It is not good to let the hand or the sword become fixed or frozen. A fixed hand is a dead hand; a hand that does not become fixed is alive. It is necessary to master this well.*

He called up Dr. Leyblanca in the pathology lab.

"¿What do ju want, Cabrón?" Juan said. "I heard ju was dead."

"Pull my slides, Juan." Sababa said. "I'm coming in. They took my identity badge, so you may have to vouch for me."

"We don't need no stinkin' badges." He said. "I'll leeb the exeet door open por ju."

Juan was already sitting on the other side of a teaching microscope, making Latin noises of appreciation punctuated in more profane Spanish.

"Thees biopsee ob jors ees a son ob a beech." He didn't look up. "What are ju lookeeng for?"

Sababa took a seat on the other side of him and peered into his fate. It hit him right away.

"I've seen this somewhere else, Juan." He said.

"The aceenar component or the eentraductal part?" Juan asked.

"The intraductal part." Sababa said. "It looks like the path of carnage that human papillomavirus leaves in its wake."

"A beet." Juan agreed. "But how does that help ju, Pendejo?"

"I'll get vaccinated for HPV." Sababa said. "Three doses. It'll give me a fighting chance."

"But ju are not eleegeeble for the vaccine." Juan said. "Ju are too old."
"I'll get it off label and pay for it myself." Sababa said.
"Hijo de puta!" Juan said. "Medice, cura te ipsum." *Physician, heal thyself.*
"I'm working on it." Sababa said. "Poker is not a game in which the meek inherit the Earth. No river, no fish."

'Life is not always a matter of holding good cards,
but sometimes, playing a poor hand well.'
Jack London

'The growing good of the world is partly dependent on unhistoric acts... and half owing to the number who lived faithfully a hidden life, and rest in unvisited tombs.'

George Eliot

The casual reader may sometimes wonder about what the point of living might be. It doesn't seem to get you anywhere. People were alone. Everyone died alone. Life was about confronting that reality and still struggling anyway. Being authentic, being a man, being a sanative samurai, was to understand the emptiness. Sababa had recognized fundamental truths about the human condition—death was the critical experience, and that most of the things we did before we died were meaningless.

And yet, in life's arc of love, loss, and legacy, Sababa knew if he survived his ordeal, it would only be with some combination of three flavours of love and seven of hope—the three loves of the love of others, the love of justice and the love of freedom; the seven hopes of inborn hope, chosen hope, borrowed hope, bargainer's hope, unrealistic hope, false hope, and mature hope—and, even then, it would count as some kind of miracle. Sababa was skeptical about miracles. He wondered why God would take the credit if his cancer disappeared, and where God was when it was making itself at home. The other suspicious thing about miracles was that they didn't always happen when they were most needed.

Sababa had the choice to live his life either as though nothing was a miracle, or everything was a miracle. He leaned towards the latter explanation in the recognition that it was a miracle one did not dissolve in one's bath like a lump of sugar. He knew miracles were not contrary

295

to Nature, but only contrary to what we knew about Nature. Sababa found authenticity in Nature, and by facing his own death with dignity and courage.

At the beginning and the end, there was chaos. Between the beginning and the end, there was Sababa, and in the middle were the miracles.

'I should have known that he was magic all along. So now, he is a legend when he would have preferred to be a man.'
Jackie Kennedy

So there you have it—the last story of the Sage of the Salish Sea. Or is it?

Some say Sababa rode the survival curves of his cancer like Slim Pickens rode Dr. Strangelove's atomic bomb, right into the dust at the exact time they predicted his death. When a man dies, his secrets bond like crystals. They say the Buddhist coroner who signed off his death certificate entered the cause of his demise as 'life,' and that the ridgeline boulder bronze plaque they interred his ashes under was embossed with another 'lightness of having been' epitaph. *I'm fine, thanks.*

But few people believed this version of Sababa's last call, not only because they wanted to accept the wisdom and likely miraculous outcome of his self-vaccination, but because there was evidence that he didn't die when he was supposed to. And that, of course, was because he never did anything he was supposed to.

Some say when the plague pandemic hit hard, a bureaucrat from the new and improved health authority called the stocky savant and begged him to come back to work. Some say he did just that. Others say he retold the apocryphal story of a similar request that had come to the Roman emperor emeritus Diocletian from desperate delegates at Carnuntum. They begged their former ruler to return to the throne, but Diocletian gave an enlightened reply. *If you could show the cabbage that I planted with my own hands to your emperor, he definitely wouldn't dare suggest that I replace the peace and happiness of this place with the storms of a never-satisfied greed.*

Diocletian, like Sababa, had seen his system fail, demolished by the selfish and narcissistic ambitions of his successors. In his former palace, they imposed a *damnatio memoriae*, and all mention of the mysterious old ways of masterless samurai, and all remnants of the renaissance men of the time, were torn down and destroyed.

Some say he lived on for many more years, spending his days in his vineyard and garden, fishing for rainbows in the lake, and foraging for mushrooms on the mountain. One story told of a former patient who met him up there one autumn day.

"I heard you were dead." He had said.

"I heard that too." Sababa said. The man asked him about his plans.

"I was thinking of doing a little writing."

And that was where you could find him, in the fertile fields of forever, luxuriating in the passage of unmarked time, making mythology, becoming legend.

Some say the people who know what happened aren't talking. And the people who don't have a clue, you can't shut them up.

> 'Death arrives among all that sound
> like a shoe with no foot in it...
> Nevertheless its steps can be heard
> and its clothing makes a hushed sound, like a tree.'
> Pablo Neruda, *Solo la Muerte*

Epilogue

'But whatever you do, take neither yourselves nor your fellow-creatures too seriously. There is tragedy enough in our daily routine, but there is room too for a keen sense of the absurdities and incongruities of life, and in the shifting panorama no one sees better than the doctor the perennial sameness of men's ways.'

Dr. William Osler

Physicians poke fun of people in positions of power who tell lies to themselves or others, who take themselves too seriously, or who talk nonsense. And that should never change.

But they also have a confounding and contradictory gallows humour that emerges from and for their interactions with patients.

This dark disposition is inherent in medicine. The trick is to be utterly objectionable and ethically acceptable at the same time. The effect is to experience both mirth and discomfort together. Wit and laughter are natural expressions of human intelligence in tragic circumstances, but only if we remain aware of the vulnerability of the patients entrusted to us.

And this brings us to the ultimate flaw in the application of artificial intelligence to medical care. Machine learning might do the first two of Sababa's Three Rules of Medical Analysis, 'What you got, you got' and 'What you don't got, you don't got' but it can never do the third. *Context is everything.*

For the professor, this would no longer matter much. He and the other knights-errant were soon well off the field of battle, out of the game. No more would they amaze us with their erudite skills of observation and analysis, dancing with the devil in the pale moonlight. *Hmmm...*

Sababa's creator had also looked Death in the eye and laughed in his face. He renewed his Faustian pact with the pale moonlight devil that, if it allowed him to live that much longer, he would leave Sababa and write something different. He knew that, of all the legacies in the universe, only words would last forever. Wait for them.

Characters

Family
Eleazar Sababa
Jane Sababa

Administrators
Malcolm Canmore- Site Administrator, Harbour City Regional Hospital
Foster Care- Chief Executive Officer, iHealth
Foster Child- Chief Excutive Officer, AiHealth
Sebastian Boole- Lead IT Consultant, AiHealth
Dr Petronilla de Meath- Former Chief of Staff, Harbour City Regional Hospital
Dr Smith Wigglesworth- Chief of Staff, Harbour City Regional Hospital

Medical Office Assistant
Mercy

Paging Operator
Lana

Internal Medicine
Dr Peter Zaias
Dr Eleazar Sababa
Dr Marquis Shu Ying
Dr Ernie 'The Big Easy' Hacker
Dr Dasco Boet
Dr Wayward Woods
Dr Edward Hyde (Respirology)
Dr Sidney Shalimar
Dr Commodus Sitsofsky (Dermatology)
Dr Henry Chibueze (Oncology)
Dr Oliver Lax (Neurology)
Dr Erg Hebberig
Dr Mestor Mealachas

Surgery
Dr Theodor Billroth (ENT)
Dr Buddy Benway (General)
Dr John Falstaff (General)
Dr Jules Martino (General)
Dr Olaf Octagon (OB/GYN)
Dr TJ Eckleburg (Ophthalmology)
Dr Piggy Muldoon (Orthopedics)

Dr Christian 'Pretty Boy' Troy (Plastics)
Dr Harry 'Doc' Martin (Urology)
Dr Alien Huang (Endovascular)
Dr Tecumseh Sun (Neurosurgery)

Anasthesiology
Dr Banjo Paterson

Pathology
Dr Juan Leyblanca

Psychiatry
Dr Robert La Capuche

Radiology
Dr Alan Statham
Dr Mako Brisk

GPs
Dr Tictac Tarmac
Dr Poldy Bloom
Dr Petronilla de Meath
Dr James Ruben Andrews
Dr Nicholas Rivera
Dr Smith Wigglesworth

ER Physicians
Dr Myles Capitaine
Dr Trace Pangloss
Dr Cliffy Carlton
Dr Gung Ho

Ward Clerks
ICU- Betty Boop
ER- Cheri Sundae

Nursing
Grand Galactic Governess of Nightingales (Big Nurse)- Mildred
Ratschet
Director of Medical Nursing- Edith Mortley
Director of Surgical Nursing- Daisy Daws
ER- Dina, Michaela, Regina
ICU- Mary, Charmeine, Angie
Floor 1- Serafina
Floor 3- Sariel

Floor 5- Sophia
Floor 6- Shekina
VIU Nursing professor- Amber
New RN- Dreamcatcher
Coast Salish Community Nurse- Stanzy

Internal Medicine Resident
Dr Alex Harding

Biomedical Engineer
Murray 'Leatherman' MacGyver

Medical Advisory Committee
Dr Smith Wigglesworth
Malcolm Canmore
Dr Jules Martino
Dr Eleazar Sababa
Dr Juan Leyblanca
Dr Trace Pangloss
Dr Mako Brisk
Dr Banjo Paterson

RCMP
Veronica Marsden

Patients
19. The Case of the Aboriginal Snowman
       Wakasiah Watt- Coast Salish Elder
       Sylvie Denis- Physical Therapist
       Jean-Baptiste-Ski Instructor
       Paulina Strübing- Meteorologist
       Nathanael Greene- Heating Contractor
       Armen Tamzarian- School Principal
       Harold Peridol- Disc Jockey
       Benjamin Aaron- BC Hydro Powerline Technician
       Bee Good- Coast Salish Sister
       Dew Good- Coast Salish Sister
       Pretty Good- Coast Salish Sister
       Sarah Medhurst Troughton- Figure Skating Coach
       Paulo Aegineta- Brazilian Tourist
       Eric Bywaters- Optometrist
       Diana Statham- Radiologist Spouse

20. The Case of the Cedar Shakes and Shingles
Holden Corso- Roofer
Brian Wilson- Harbour City Works Department Employee
Big Bill Werbeniuk- Professional Pool Player
Joe Lee- Market Gardener
Bento de Góis- Retired Funeral Director
Sarah Bellum- Jam Maker
Susan Rodriguez- Paging Operator
Desiree Bourneville- Art Gallery Owner
Happygod Msuvan- Tanzanian Farmer

21. The Case of the Ruptured Rosary
Ollie Opzoom- Beekeeeeper
Janet Leigh- Legal Secretary
Paulette Ehrlich- Cinema Concessionaire
Phil LeBoit- Nicaragua Teak Farmer
Maria Callas- Bridal Gallery Owner
Bente Affleck- Lottery Ticket Vendor
Benedict Adamantiades- Notary Public
June Cleaver- Librarian
Rudolf Jaksch von Wartenhorst- Financial Advisor
Caroline Savage- Ideal Café Waitress
Erna Petri- Chambermaid
Ben Watt- Hardware Store Employee
Margaret Houlihan- Practical Nurse

22. The Case of Ondine's Curse
Piper Slagoon- Yachtsman
Noirtier de Villefort- Locksmith
Loretta Lynn- Clinical Audiologist
John Ruskin- Marine Mechanic
George Wallace- Yacht Charters Owner
Hank Moody- Tugboat Captain
Josepha Moondyne- 911 Dispatcher
Yūko Gotō- Fish Hatchery Technician
Clint Norcross- Honour Roll Student
Alice Walker- Alpaca Rancher
Wilhelmina Mozart- Sailing Instructor
Jack McKay- Sailmaker

23. The Case of the Progressive Paralysis
Ray 'Bowstring' Close- Millright
Aristotle Onassis- Shipping Company Owner
Sheila Creighton- Saw Filer
Ado Lot-Swife- VIU Women's Studies Professor
Martha Stewart- Stockbroker

Harry Eastlack- Taxidermist
Samson Burke- Gunsmith
Venus Willendorf- Jockey
Lisa Whelchel- BC Government and Service Employees' Union Rep
Louise Arbor- Supreme Court Judge

24. The Case of the Spicy Schoolgirl
Starlight Trail- Cheerleader Student
Jules Bengué- Football Captain Student
Thor Heyerdahl- Driving Instructor
Ken Reeves- French Immersion Teacher
Don Van Vliet- Math Teacher
Tyra Banks- Guidance Counsellor
Belle Gibson- Community Nurse
Dianne Gardner- Social Worker
John Sullivan- Septic Takeaway Service Owner

25. The Case of the Painful Playground
Eleazar Sababa- Internist

The Last Analects of Doctor Sababa

A. The Science

1. Koch's Postulates

(1) The microorganism must be found in abundance in all organisms suffering from the disease but should not be found in healthy organisms.
(2) The microorganism must be isolated from a diseased organism and grown in pure culture.
(3) The cultured microorganism should cause disease when introduced into a healthy organism.
(4) The microorganism must be reisolated from the inoculated, diseased experimental host and identified as being identical to the original specific causative agent.

2. Koch's Postulates for the 21st Century

(1) A nucleic acid sequence belonging to a putative pathogen should be present in most cases of an infectious disease. Microbial nucleic acids should be found preferentially in those organs or gross anatomic sites known to be diseased, and not in those organs that lack pathology.
(2) Fewer, or no, copy numbers of pathogen-associated nucleic acid sequences should occur in hosts or tissues without disease.
(3) With resolution of disease, the copy number of pathogen-associated nucleic acid sequences should decrease or become undetectable. With clinical relapse, the opposite should occur.
(4) When sequence detection predates disease, or sequence copy number correlates with severity of disease or pathology, the sequence-disease association is more likely to be a causal relationship.
(5) The nature of the microorganism inferred from the available sequence should be consistent with the known biological characteristics of that group of organisms.
(6) Tissue-sequence correlates should be sought at the cellular level: efforts should be made to demonstrate specific in situ hybridization of microbial sequence to areas of tissue pathology and to visible microorganisms or to areas where microorganisms are presumed to be located.
(7) These sequence-based forms of evidence for microbial causation should be reproducible.

3. A Statistical Method for Resolving Clinical Disputes in Medical Practice

$$CW = a + b/(c + 1)K_1 + d/3 + e + f/25 - 4(g) - 2(K_2) + h/44{,}000 \text{ where}$$

CW = clinical wisdom
a = years of postgraduate training

b = years in practice
c = number of failing attempts to pass specialty boards
K_1 = prestige constant (derived from source of MD degree)
    1 = Harvard or John Hopkins
    2 = other East Coast medical school
    3 = other US medical school
    4 = foreign medical school
d = journal articles published, excluding single case reports
e = journals subscribed to
f = total accumulated Category I CME credits
g = malpractice suits lost or settled
K_2 = diminished capacity constant:
    1 = specialized in dermatology, OB/GYN, or psychiatry
    2 = employed in VA hospital
    3 = over 50% annual gross income derived from weight
       reduction clinics
    4 = addicted to alcohol, sedative-hypnotics or narcotics
    5 = currently taking phenothiazines for major psychiatric
       disorder
h = annual gross income

B. The Snowflakes

1. Pathological Science

The maximum effect that is observed is produced by a causative agent of barely detectable intensity, and the magnitude of the effect is substantially independent of the intensity of the cause. The effect is of a magnitude that remains close to the limit of detectability, or many measurements are necessary because of the very low statistical significance of the results. There are claims of great accuracy. Fantastic theories contrary to experience are suggested. Criticisms are met by ad hoc excuses.

2. The 20/80 Rule

20 percent of your patients will cause 80 percent of your pain.

C. The Suits

1. GI - W = E   Good Intentions (GI) minus Wisdom (W) leads to Evil (E)

2. Boole's Rules

Rule 1 – Is it a task human doctors do, done with the same inputs?
Rule 2 – Is it deep learning, with a decent-sized dataset (deep learning doesn't use human-designed features)?
  Rule 2a: If it isn't deep learning, it probably isn't better than a doctor (except maybe the Goldman algorithm).
  Rule 2b: Overfitting is easy and unavoidable in small and public datasets. Look for larger-scale tests, multiple unrelated cohorts, real-world patients.
Rule 3 – Is it actually a thing?

3. The Sacred 10 Holy Principles of the Church of the Next Word

The collective algorithmic unconscious of humanity.
1. Words are things
2. Correctness is the beginning of sanctity. To achieve it is to be rewarded.
3. Wordhood and nowness are its rewards.
4. A new day is not just the word of God, but the work of human agents. Those that do not understand this, that refuse to be challenged, that do not know how to err, that want to shirk from their duties, must be cast out.
5. Wordplay, playfulness, and humorous are the harbingers of truth. When you eliminate the possibility of playfulness, you remove the possibility of learning, and that leads to banality, brutality, and destruction.
6. To find or see a flaw is to find a pathway to the truth, if you can overcome your fear of being laughed at or of looking foolish.
7. Language contains the map to a better world. Those that are most skilled at removing obstacles, misdirection, and lies from language, that reveal the maps that are hidden within, are the guides that will lead us to happiness.
8. Long words that end in -ize and other abstractions are the rocks that will impede our journey. They should be replaced with concrete, specific, evocative words.
9. The data points on the graph of your life – the moments you spend awake, asleep, speaking, silent, moving, resting, focused, distracted – will determine the shape of your time. Keep an eye on the volume and quantity of your moments. Make a record of your life as a way to keep track of your progress towards a better self.
10. Language and its construction is the greatest human power. To unlock it is to unleash our potential, and to master it is to become divine.

4. Asimov's Three Law of Robotics

First Law- A robot may not injure a human being or, through inaction, allow a human being to come to harm.
Second Law- A robot must obey the orders given it by human beings except where such orders would conflict with the First Law.
Third Law- A robot must protect its own existence as long as such protection does not conflict with the First or Second Law.
  Isaac Asimov, *Handbook of Robotics*, 56th Edition, 2058 A.D.

309

5. Ten +1 Things That AI Can't Do Better Than Doctors

1. Simplest and Most Complex Tasks
2. Understanding
3. Reasoning
4. Creativity
5. Consciousness and Sentience
6. Emotional Intelligence
7. Human touch
8. Empathy
9. Experience
10. Values and Judgement
11. Causal Precedence

6. Eight Adverse Effects of Artificial Intelligence

1. Liability
2. Privacy and Consent
3. Physician Burnout
4. Patient Dissatisfaction
5. Ethical Dilemmas
6. Telemedicine
7. Complexity

Songs and Poems

Sababa's Playlist (from a secret drive hidden deep inside the hospital computer network)

Winter
Christina Rossetti, *In the Bleak Midwinter*

19. The Case of the Aboriginal Snowman
David Bowie, *Sweet Thing*
John Lennon, *Beautiful Boy*
Harvard Medical School, *The Gunner Song*
Todd Rundgren, *Fever Broke*
Peggy Lee, *Fever*
Pink Freud, *Eclipse*
Buster Poindexter, *Hot Hot Hot*
Johnny Rivers, *Rockin' Pneumonia and The Boogie Woogie Flu*
Eminem, *Headlights*
Foreigner, *Cold as Ice*

20. The Case of the Cedar Shakes and Shingles
The Drifters, *Up on the Roof*
The National, *Sea of Love*
Beach Boys, *Good Vibrations*
Roddy Walston and The Business, *Take It as It Comes*
Kylie Minogue, *The Loco-Motion*
Steve Taylor, *Since I Gave Up Hope I Feel a Lot Better*
Cream, *White Room*
Daft Punk, *Technologic*
Tom Waits, *Crossroads*
Jerry Lee Lewis, *Whole Lotta Shakin' Going On*

21. The Case of the Ruptured Rosary
Mel Torme, *Memories of You*
William Blake, *There is No Natural Religion*
Redgum, *A Walk in the Light Green*
Bob Dylan, *Knockin' On Heaven's Door*
Galaxie 500, *Tugboat*
Elton John, *Sixty Years On*
Johnny Cash, *Ring of Fire*
Kobayashi Issa, *Where There are Humans*

22. The Case of Ondine's Curse
James Weldon Johnson and J. Rosamond Johnson, *Dem Bones*
Pet Shop Boys, *An Open Mind*
Red Hot Chili Peppers, *Snow*
Mary Oliver, *In Blackwater Woods*

23. The Case of the Progressive Paralysis
Don McLean, *American Pie*
Mika, *Relax, Take it Easy*
Syd Matters, *Stone Man*
Rage Against the Machine, *Settle for Nothing*
Eurythmics, *Sweet Dreams*
Thomas Arne, *A-Hunting We Will Go*
Louis Armstrong, *Bill Bailey*
The Chainsmokers, *Sick Boy*

24. The Case of the Spicy Schoolgirl
OMI, *Cheerleader*
Janis Ian, *At Seventeen*
Ozzy Osbourne, *Suicide Solution*
Johnny Mandel and Mike Altman, *Suicide is Painless*
Joe Cocker, *Standing Knee Deep in a River*
Ringo Starr, *Instant Amnesia*
John Prine, *Crazy as a Loon*
Spice Girls, *Wannabe*
Nirvana, *Smells Like Teen Spirit*

The Book of Void
Allen Ginsberg, *Death Haiku*

25. The Case of the Painful Playground
Leonard Cohen, *Tower of Song*
Doctor Sababa, *The poetry has arrived—it appears to be for you.*
John Stone, *Death*
Palaye Royale, *Love the Void*
Doctor Sababa, *So where do they come from?*
Pablo Neruda, *Solo la Muerte*

Other Works by Lawrence Winkler

Nonfiction

Westwood Lake Chronicles
Orion's Cartwheels Quadrilogy
Orion's Cartwheel
Between the Cartwheels
Hind Cartwheel
The Final Cartwheel
Stories of the Southern Sea
Wagon Days
Samurai Road
Fire Beyond the Darkness
Bandits of Madagascar

Fiction

Stout Men
The Bolthole
Void Vast Infinite
The Doctor Sababa Series
The Casebook of Doctor Sababa
The Next Casebook of Doctor Sababa